LONE COWBOY

MY LIFE STORY

BY

WILL JAMES

ILLUSTRATED BY THE AUTHOR

CHARLES SCRIBNER'S SONS

NEW YORK ·

1930

Will James

Pryor, Montana
1930

Dear Folks—

Here's a long story for you with no names in it to speak of—. So, you wont be bothered by the names of the creeks and cow camps you might never heard of — And of riders you wouldn't know— But if you have been in the cow country and are acquainted with the lay of it you'll have a lot of fun recognizing the spots where I drifted thru — If you don't know the cow country I think you'll like to come out and get lost in it for a spell— You'll know it by the time you ride with me thru these pages — The whole West— from the Far North to the South——

There's more than plain riding and covering territory in this story — There's the sunshine, rains, blizzards and crosses of life on the range, — from the times I first remember— my raising amongst cowboys and trappers — my teachings from them, the open country and animals — More teachings after I'd growed up while always sitting on a horse sowing my wild oats - reaping 'em — cutting my wisdom teeth on sharp edges of experience, and then finally lining it to ride for High Points——

Here's a gentle horse for you—
Climb on and follow me.

WILL JAMES·

ILLUSTRATIONS

LONE COWBOY

CHAPTER ONE

IT was one June day in 1892 when a long-reach wagon pulled by four tired horses came to a stop amongst the elders and quakers bordering a little creek which run into the Judith Basin in Montana. The young woman who had been driving the team climbed down off the wagon seat and throwed the lines to one side. The horses would stand, they'd be glad to.

On the same trail the wagon had took, and a quarter of a mile back, rode a long lean cowboy. He was hazing upwards of ten head of saddle horses with him. As he seen the wagon stop he left them to graze and he loped up to where the woman was busy unhooking the team.

"Now, Bonnie," he says, as he slid off his horse, "don't you go to bothering with that." He smiled at her. "I'll show you what *you* can do."

He climbed up in the wagon, yanked out a heavy tar-

1

paulin-covered roll of bedding and slid it to the ground. He jumped down after it, unrolled the bed, throwed back the dusty tarpaulin, and pointing to the bedding he says:

"This is what you can do, Bonnie. Stretch out on that and rest up while I unhook the team."

"But I ought to start setting up camp, Bill."

Bill frowned, and smiled, "You do as I tell you, Bonnie," and to end the subject he added on as he turned to look at the loose saddle horses, "Them ponies sure don't seem to have no grudge against that tall green grass do they?"

The team was unhooked, grained and turned loose. The tent was set up and a comfortable camp was made. All the while Bonnie was made to stay where she was and look on.

"We ought to make the town to-morrow or early next day, Bonnie," says Bill.

But it was many days before the town was reached, and, that night, without the help of a doctor, the woman went thru the sufferings of childbirth. . . . I had come into the world.

No tag was needed around my neck where I came into the world at, for I don't think there was another child to within thirty miles of there. I was born close to the sod, and if I could of seen far enough I could of glimpsed ponies thru the flap of the tent on my first day while listening to the bellering of cattle and the ringing of my dad's spurs.

My dad was a Texan, born and raised in West Texas. My mother was from Southern California. Both was of the Scotch-Irish nation, with some Spanish blood on my mother's side. I was about a year old when I lost my mother, and, by the time I was four, my dad went and joined her acrost that Range Beyond.

I remember the time of my dad's death, but to go back

on my earlier childhood I have to use the tally of what an old timer told me, the Old-timer who adopted and raised me. He seemed to know my dad mighty well.

According to what he told me, My dad had come up trail from Texas with many herds of the southern cattle during the "eighties." He'd delivered some herds as far north as Canada. After the last drive, he'd come to figger that for a cow country the North was sure enough all of that. It was colder up there but the grass was sure a plenty, so was the water, and there was no droughts, like there was in the South, no tick fever and it sure was the place to mature beef.

So, early one spring he sells out what holdings he has in Texas, hooks up four horses to a wagon, has my mother take the lines, and he himself brings up the rear with ten head of picked saddle horses. (The Old-timer often said that the brands on some of them horses was sort of hard to read.)

It was my dad's and mother's first intentions to keep going till they reached some place in Alberta, Canada, and start over again in the cow business up there. Then I comes along and stops the outfit in Montana. If I'd been born a month later I'd been a Canadian, and four months sooner would of made me a Texan.

But anyway, whatever I would of been, I was sure good in holding up the outfit. . . . It didn't move for many days, but soon as was possible, my dad, after hunting up a pasture for his saddle horses, hooked up the team again and, slow and easy, took us to town. (I don't know which town it was). After a spell there, we drifted on north some more just for a short ways and my dad found a cow outfit to work for where me and my mother had a good roof over our heads. He'd given up the idea of going any further north for the time being, and when fall begin to set in he decided to winter where he was. In Montana.

It was along the next spring when my mother took down with some sort of cold which, to-day, I guess is called the flu, and soon after that my dad found himself with no one but just me.

The Old-timer told me that my dad liked to lost his mind when my mother went and that her death come near being his own too. He'd got wild and reckless and I was all that kept him from doing things that would sure enough have killed him. He'd went back to riding the "rough string" (spoiled horses) and taking on bronks, something my mother had made him promise never to do again. A Montana rough string is sure not at all mild but he more than welcomed the fighting they done. Fast action and danger made him forget the hurt he packed in his heart.

And fast action and danger is what he went after. With them big rough horses he'd go and pile his rope on everything that was wild and needed roping, and lots of big stuff that didn't need roping. The time and the place he done that never mattered to him, and many a cowboy held his breath at watching the "fool things" he'd do.

He tore the riggin' out of his saddle twice that year and, by the end of the summer, the saddle horn had been jerked off too, but he never bothered having it replaced. He fixed his own riggin', tied his rope thru the fork, and went on roping off of the rough ponies just the same.

"And" as the Old-timer said, "the rough string sure had the rough took off of 'em that year."

I didn't get to see much of my dad that summer, only for a day or so about once or twice a month. He had left me in care of a couple who was running a small outfit on the outskirt of the range he rode on. They had no children and they was mighty glad to have me. Once in a while the Old-timer, who later gave me this story of my childhood, used to

Fast action and danger made him forget the hurt he packed in his heart.

come and see me and rest his horses while visiting. Sometimes he'd bring me a chipmunk, in a cage which he'd made, or a squirrel. He always kept me supplied with horned toads, young woodchucks, young beavers, and even young porcupine. The very young porcupine has no quills but they don't stay that way long, and soon as the quills begin to show, they somehow or other disappeared. Most of the young animals I had made good pets and a few of them stayed around the ranch even after they was full grown.

My dad took on a contract breaking horses. He stayed at a ranch, but being there was no one there to take care of me he left me where I was. Once a week or so he'd ride over on some big snorting bronk and stay over night.

But the horse breaking contract didn't pan out so good. He'd been pretty well bruised up in being so wild the summer before and then one day, about Christmas time, a stump-headed bronk bucks off the side of a mountain with him, turns over, and leaves him lay in a willow thicket at the bottom. One of the boys finds him there just by pure luck, brings him in and takes him to a hospital in a buckboard. He layed there between sheets till away into the next summer, and when he come out he couldn't afford to be wild at all for the rest of that summer. He was with me most of the time then and I must of got to know him again.

That summer was my first time on a horse, for soon as my dad could ride a gentle horse he'd hoist me up on top with him. I'd set on the bastos behind the cantle and hang on to his cartridge belt and the Old-timer told me that we used to go on powerful long rides that way and run in stock to boot.

I didn't feel so good when my dad left me again that fall. He'd gone to finish up his contract breaking them bronks. He turned them over as broke the next spring and then went to work on the round-up. He didn't call for the rough string that year and he'd lost a considerable of his wildness. Maybe his heart had healed some and maybe not, for he'd got awful quiet as he worked and none of the boys could ever get more than a grunt out of him.

I pegged along sort of lonesome that summer and the next winter on account he couldn't come and see me very often and, to make things worse, the Old-timer had left for the far North into Canada, where he'd set his trap line. I liked the folks I was with a whole lot, they was mighty good to me, but I liked my dad first and the Old-timer second. I wasn't getting much riding while my dad was gone, and I wasn't getting so many pets as when the Old-timer was around. But the folks tried to make up for that as best they could. A wooden horse on rockers was made for me. That's one of the first things I remember. The body was hewed out of a cottonwood log and painted gray and there was a real horsemane and tail on him. I had a lot of fun saddling and unsaddling him with an old sawbuck pack saddle tree. Then Mommy, as I called the lady there, was a great hand at calling me in often and handing me things to eat which I had a weakness for.

I had some more fun down by the corrals and stables too, had a piece of light rope and I'd try to rope chickens. Then I'd go to the pig pen, and calf pen, and play horse by the mangers in the stable. I'd put a halter around my neck, stick some hay in my mouth, then nicker and stamp my feet. I'd snort too and pull back like a bronk.

But with all of that to play at I was lonesome. I was often calling for someone, and I'd set down for long spells and just stargaze. It was during them lonesome spells that I would often pick up things and want to make marks, tracing something in the dirt with a stick, or, with a hunk of charcoal I'd pick up from the last fire at the branding pen, I'd go and mark up the rough boards of the bunk-house porch. . . . That winter, while the cold winds blowed outside and the snow piled up and I couldn't go out, is when I first got acquainted with a pencil and some blank paper, and I spent many hours a day making funny marks which, to anybody else, didn't mean nothing but to me meant a lot. To me they was all pictures of animals, mostly horses. My dad would say they was sure fine and once in a while he'd criticize and pass such remarks as "The hind legs on that horse are a little too straight, son" or "you forgot the dew-claws on that steer."

When spring come, my dad rode up again and I can remember how glad I was when I seen the white tarpaulin of his bed hitched on to the horse he was leading. That meant he'd be with me more than a day or so, and sure enough, he was with me about a month.

I think the greatest surprise and pleasure of my life was when he took his roll of bedding off the pack horse, after he rode in that evening, for under the bed was a little bitty saddle that looked just like a full size one, and just my fit. My dad lifted me up on it and he says, "This is your outfit, son, this horse and this saddle." I was so tickled that I just hollered and throwed both my feet up on the pony's withers.

The horse, as I remember, was a little long-maned black. I don't think he weighed over six hundred. He was round as a butter ball, and gentle as a gentle kitten, but the saddle is what interested me the most. I'd already seen lots of horses, but a saddle like the one I had, all for my own self, struck me as a gift that even Santa Claus couldn't compete with in handing out. There was even a brand-new rope on it. I know that that night was sure long for me and I was sure watching for daybreak so I could get out and try my horse and rigging. They had a hard time getting me in to eat the next morning.

Dad and me took many a good ride together that month. I was with him steady, all excepting when he'd be gone for an all-day ride, then I'd hit out by myself. The little black horse had to be shod and fed lots of grain so he could stand up under the work I was giving him, and come a time when they had to hand me a fresh horse while the black recuperated.

I was sure a happy kid, and, to make things even better, here drifts in the Old-timer one day. He'd long ago sold his furs from the winter's trapping and come South again. But I wasn't looking for no more pets just then, I was very busy with my horse, my saddle and my rope, and with my dad's and the Old-timer's company to fill in I sure had my hands full. There was one month when I hardly touched a pencil or try to make marks on anything. I sure wasn't lonesome no more.

If my mother had been along then and all of us settled on our own place, as had been my folks' first intentions, I guess I'd been the happiest kid in the world, for, even tho I didn't remember her, I think I missed her just the same, specially when my dad was gone. I missed someone besides him and I didn't know who. . . .

My dad had given up the idea of going to Canada to start for himself again, for, as he told the Old-timer, he couldn't think of settling anywhere or building any home, with Bonnie *gone*. His intentions was to keep on riding for the outfits around here and there, keep a saving his wages, and some day, when I got big enough, to start me out in life with a good spread of my own.

But that never came true, and when he left me after that great month we had together, a month which I'll always remember and be thankful of living thru, I never seen him no more.

He'd gone to join the round-up wagon again. Some time later a big herd of cattle was gathered, many thousands of head, which was being run thru corrals and chutes at some

"He was in the fight."

home-ranch. They was being separated and vented. Some outfit had changed hands or bought up more cattle.

By the chute of them corrals is where my dad drawed his last breath. The only way he had against his way of cashing in, as he said before he died, is that he was afoot and not at all being wild. His idea of going to the Other Range was while setting on top of a hard bucking, roman-nosed bronk, his rope tied hard and fast and a big steer in the loop.

As it was, he was peacefully prodding cattle thru the chutes to the squeezer when his time come. There was quite a herd of cattle in that same corral where he was working, and amongst that herd was a big "staggy" steer that'd just broke a horn. The blood from that broken horn was running down that steer's face to his nose and he was on the fight, not with his own breed, but with anything strange, like a human.

He seen my dad a standing there, and my dad, being busy, wasn't paying no attention. He'd just stooped down for the prodding stick he'd dropped when the big steer caught him broadside with his one good horn, hoisted him in the air, took him on a ways and then flung him against the chute. The horn had pierced him thru the stomach like as if it had been done with a knife, only worse.

The cowboys rushed to him, straightened him from the crumpled position he was in, and, so they told the Old-timer, they seen at a glance that nothing could be done. But, they said there was a smile on my dad's face when, after a while, he opened his eyes, and the first words he'd said was, "Well, boys, I'm due to join her soon now" . . . Then, after a while, he'd added on, "The only thing I regret is to leave little Billy behind. . . . Tell old trapper Jean that all my gatherings are his and to see that my boy is well took care of. I leave him to him."

He'd talked on for a little while and within an hour from the time the steer had picked him up he'd closed his eyes and went on the Long Sleep.

CHAPTER TWO

NO one told me of my dad's going, not for many many months. All I was told is that he'd took a herd acrost the border and that no one knowed when he'd be back. The thought was that maybe the news of his death wouldn't hit me so hard if I sort of got used to being without him for a long spell, but I was suspicious of something because, as I wondered, why didn't he come to see me before leaving on that long trip? He always had before.

I kept a asking every once in a while as to when my dad would be back, and I'd always get the same answer, "I don't know, Billy, but he ought to be back most any week now." But, regardless of them same answers, I kept on asking till finally, near a year later, the Old-timer had to let me know.

I can't begin to tell just how I took the news. I took 'em pretty tough I know. I couldn't play at anything and many a time I'd hit out back of the corrals where nobody could see me, lay flat on the ground and have a cry.

But I couldn't fool the folks on my crying much, they could tell by my eyes just what I'd been doing. Mommy would give me some pie or something or. make my favorite candy, but I wasn't caring for none of them good things just then.

Then one evening during late spring the Old-timer gets me up on his knee and tells me that we'd be hitting out with a pack outfit early in the morning and drift on and on and see all kinds of new country and lots of things I'd never seen before. That interested me some but not in any way like it should of.

But the Old-timer was wise, he knowed that new country

with all the new sights would sure be good medecine for me. The next morning I kissed Mommy good-bye, shook hands with Lem, her husband, got on my horse and started out alongside of the Old-timer. It made me feel bad some more to leave the folks, but the trail ahead promised a lot and it wasn't long when, for the time being, I'd forgot both Mommy and Lem. I've never seen them again or since and I wouldn't know now of the place where they lived. Some day I want to try and find 'em.

(What goes on in my *starting* out with Bopy might sound a little like from imagination, folks might wonder how a kid of four or five years would remember of happenings being on any certain day and up to the minute,—I dont disagree on that and some of the things I tell of might of happened six months before or after. I'm only trying to make a fitting story of what did happen and I'm going by what I can remember, some of which is mighty clear, along with what Bopy kept a repeating to me.)

We camped out that night and the interest I took in being in the way while I was really trying to help was a good starter towards making me forget. We picketed the ponies, that is, I picketed my own anyway, even if the Old-timer did have to look over the knots I'd tied. My next way to help was to stack on a lot of pine limbs on the fire that had been started and burned down to a fine bed of coals. The result was the Old-timer had to wait till the fresh supply burned down before he'd begin to use his skillet. I'd also made the coffee boil over.

That supper of fried beef and fried potatoes, biscuits and coffee, sure tasted good, even if there was no butter, and I must of took on quite a bait there that first night because there was nothing around to remind me of my dad. We was in a good camp, and the Old-timer was with me.

After supper was over and the tins washed and put away

The trail ahead promised a lot.

by the "paniers" (pack bags) we both reared back against the bed-roll and watched the fire. I felt pretty big, for a five-year-old.

Pretty soon the Old-timer begin to talk. He said something about us going to the other side of yonder mountain. He pointed it out to me. It looked very far away and the setting sun was coloring the peaks of it. We was just going to drift around and around, he said, and not camp no place long. That sure suited me fine.

The Old-timer went on talking and then I got the drift that him and me was going to be pardners, pardners for good, and that made me feel still bigger. He told me of what my dad had said before he died and I knowed then why he took me away. This wasn't going to be no little camping trip, and I was glad, for I liked to roam and, next to my dad, there was no one I'd rather roamed with than the Old-timer.

Jean Beaupré was his name, or one of his names, as I found out years later. My dad called him Trapper Jean, and that's what he was, a trapper during winters and he'd make a stab at prospecting during summers. He was a French Canadian from away up in the far Northwest Country, and of the breed that was first in all countries. . . . Right to-day you can see traces of that same breed all thru the West, from Alaska to Mexico, and they was here even before the eighteenth century came in. They was roaming trappers and traders, could talk sign language with all Indian nations and manage somehow to get along with 'em. There's many creeks, mountains and rivers that they named, and long before Lewis and Clark came West.

The Old-timer, Jean Beaupré's dad was of the Northwest, the same as him. He could talk many Indian languages and sign talk all mixed with French. French was his main language and he could talk very little *anglais*. I remember it used to be pretty hard for my dad to understand him sometimes, and as I'd hear Trapper Jean talk I'd got to natural like picking up many of his French words, specially when he spoke to me alone.

Him and my dad used to have many a long talk, most always when they was away from the house at the ranch, and as I got big enough to understand, I could see where they'd been great friends. One had either done the other a powerful favor at one time or one knowed something the other knowed which nobody else knowed of. Anyway I do know that, soon as my dad went, there was no more holt for him in that country. He'd appropriated me and left soon as I was big enough to travel. There was no kin between him and my dad but the way he took care of me and watched over me, even before I could remember, showed a kinship that blood relations often fail at showing. Ten thousand dollars worth of black-fox hides wasn't worth anything as compared to one of my eyelashes.

I know that on my account, on mine and my dad's, he stayed in Montana two winters where the fur trapping didn't begin to compare with that in the far North, which was his regular trapping territory. He'd wanted to be with us, and, being my mother was gone, to sort of watch over me while my dad was away. I remember him as early as I did my dad. He was on the job when I started to walk and when I started to talk. I called him "Bopy" from the start. That was as close as I could get to pronouncing Beaupré, and being the folks at the ranch always called him Beaupré, that was the first name I heard which I could call him by.

So, in this story of me, while I was with him, I'll keep on calling that old-time trapper, Bopy. For that's what I called him always.

I don't know how I slept that first night out, most likely I was spooked up some. I think I was awake at daybreak and looking towards that tall mountain to the west. I must of wondered what it looked like on the other side, because that was natural with me and I've been wondering what it looks like on the other side of every mountain and hill ever since. Maybe being born on the trail sort of marked me that way.

I was up and dressing soon as Bopy woke up (dressing was just slipping on my pants and shoes) and then I moseyed around camp. I throwed some sticks on the coals where we had our fire the night before and I hinted strong for some matches but I didn't have no luck in getting them, so the next best thing to do was to go down the creek and wash before I was told to, and while I might not be watched. I didn't take no soap with me and I was careful not to get no water on my wrists and my ears, specially my neck. That water was cold.

I was glad to get breakfast over and see the outfit packed so we could start out. I had my horse up to camp a long time before Bopy did and I tried to saddle him but everytime I'd slip the saddle up on his back the saddle blanket would slip off, or, being the little saddle, even tho light, was still too heavy for me I couldn't lift it very well and I'd shove the blanket off. The horse was too high for me, too. I tried to get him next to a rock for me to stand on and saddle him from there, but the minute I raised the saddle he'd move. Finally Bopy had to come and saddle him for me.

It took us a couple of days to get up in a pass of the tall mountain. There was a lot of snow up there, and from that pass we could see at least fifty miles both ways, to some more mountains. Bopy stopped there a while. I looked all around and got to feeling littler and littler. Finally I said, "Gosh-amighty, Bopy, if the world is as big on the other side of them mountains as what I can see of it on this side, it sure is a powerful big world."

We skirted down off the bare pass and got down to timber
line where we rode thru a lot of twisted trees which reminded
me of deformed fingers or horns all pointing one way. Then
we got down to straighter timber and finally thru some thick
forest of big tall straight trees. I sure liked them. We seen
two deer and one big porcupine while coming thru the timber
and I looked for Bopy to reach for his rifle and draw down
on 'em, but he didn't and both him and me watched the deer
as long as we could. I'd seen quite a few dead deer brought
in at the ranch but these was the first live ones I'd ever seen
and they sure struck me as being mighty well worth watching.

The afternoon was pretty well along when we came to a
little meadow surrounded by quakers and pine. The grass
was tall there and a little stream run thru. It was sure a
great spot and we unpacked. That is, Bopy did, and we
camped there. The mesquitoes got pretty thick towards the
evening and we built a good wood fire—I helped at that—
then pulled some swamp grass and put it on top to make a
smudge. The smoke from that smudge sure done a fine job
of ridding the horses from them mesquitoes and they grazed
at peace right where the smoke was the thickest. We took
on some of that smoke ourselves so we wouldn't have to fight
our heads so much. But the mesquitoes didn't seem to bother
Bopy hardly at all and if one did try to pierce his hide he'd
never slap it, he'd just brush it off, like it was a pet. He
used to tell me that if you kill one the others get peeved and
pick it out on you.

We went further on down country the next day and by
noon we came to a deserted dugout cabin. A corral was close
to it, a good creek, lots of grass and timber, and we made
camp there, not in the cabin because a pack rat had appropriated that and built a big nest in the center of it and it

would of been a lot of work cleaning out. Besides, we liked
it better outside. . . . I've camped outside many a cabin in
the years that came later, cabins that was well fit to use. I'd
pass by better places to camp in so as I could be near one
but I would never get inside unless it stormed, because I felt
mighty close-in and short of air sleeping in a house after
being so used to sleeping where the breeze went thru my
foretop. The only reason I had for liking to camp near a
house is that it gave me a sort of silent company.

We camped by the dugout for a few days. It was fine
there because no mesquitoes was around. Bopy wasted a lot
of time by the fire and cooking different things in them
few days, things he thought I'd like and which I was used to
getting at the ranch. Along about meal time he'd once in a
while go to the creek which was right close, haul out a few
trout and, soon as he could, lay 'em in a hot skillet which
was half full of bacon grease, sizzling hot and waiting on
the coals.

While I wasn't watching Bopy cooking, or getting in the
way with my trying to help, I'd go over to the dugout and
watch for the pack rat. But I could never see him, so one
time I took a stick and begin scattering the big pile of bark
and chips and small sticks which his home was made of. Bopy
caught me at that and stopped me, asking how would I like
to be left out in the cold snow and without a home when
winter come?

That night the pack rat visited our camp, chewed two
latigoes off one of the pack saddles to small pieces and put
them on top of his pile. The pack rat is also called a trade
rat, and for every piece of the latigo he took away he
brought back a chip or a small stick. There was quite a
bunch of them around the pack saddle.

When Bopy seen what the pack rat had done the next

morning he picked up a long stick and headed for the dug-out. "Now," I thought to myself, "I'm going to see that pack rat." But I spoiled it all by following him too close. Bopy turned around and, seeing me, went back to cooking the breakfast. The lesson he'd given me the day before about leaving that pack rat in the cold and so on must of come back to him and he didn't want to spoil my impression of that.

The few days at that camp done a heap to make me forget of my dad's death, for, with the cooking outside, fire build-ing, watching the ponies and many other things a kid of my age can find to stick his nose into, I had my hands full. Then I had my horse, my saddle and my rope, and once in a while Bopy would cover up the camp, see that the leading pony was picketed to stay and hit out afoot with a prospector's pick in one hand and a rifle in the other. He'd be going out making his regular dab at prospecting and go hunting some promising looking ledges and leads. He'd hoist me up on my little black horse and have me follow him. He'd go up some wash most always, looking for some ledge that stuck up, and when he seen some perticular place he wanted to investigate that was too rough or steep for a horse to climb, he'd take me off my horse and tie the reins high up to a limb so I couldn't reach and untie 'em. Then he'd tell me to stick close to my horse. That I always did, for a horse was more to me than a friend, he also meant safety. Once on his back you can get away from danger and you're not just a hop-ping slow crethure on two legs. I couldn't understand that then but I sure enough felt it. That must of been something I inherited from my dad, and even tho I couldn't as yet climb my horse without help, I never strayed away so far so I couldn't always see him. Bopy knowed that.

Bopy was sometimes gone as long as two or three hours. He'd get interested in some ledge and forget time, but I

never worried any or got lonesome that I remember of. A
new spot or country always interested me and I'd prowl
around looking for holes to dig into, wondering what was
in 'em, picking up pretty rocks like Bopy did and stacking
them up so we could take 'em to camp like he did the ones
he'd find. I could never understand why he would never take
mine.

I'd watch the squirrels, birds and rabbits. They'd let me
get pretty close and there was lots of 'em around. When I
got tired of fooling, I'd go by my horse and sometimes go
to sleep.

My horse was a lot of company to me. I used to like to fool
around his legs and his chest, that was as high as I could
reach, and feel the muscles under the smooth hide. I guess
that's where I received my first lessons in the anatomy of
a horse and the reason why I draw horses without ever once
sketching one from life.

It was while fooling around my pony's legs one day that
I discovered one way of doing a thing which for a long time
I'd been trying to do. I had a hold of him by the tail and,
while playing, I jumped up and with the help of that tail I
managed to get both feet on his hocks. The pony, being very
gentle, stood for that and there I was, high enough so I
could look over his rump. By letting one hand go of my holt
I could reach the skirting of my saddle. If I could only reach
one of them saddle strings I could pull myself up over the
horse's rump, on his back and finally into that saddle.

The thought of being able to do that sure made me act
and do some tall thinking. I jumped down, and after figgering out a way, I got me a piece of limb, reached the saddle
strings with it and layed 'em out straight on top of the
pony's rump and where I could reach 'em. Then I got a holt
of his tail again, jumped on his hocks, reached for the sad-

dle strings and the rest was easy. I was setting in my saddle mighty proud when Bopy came back from his prospecting that time. He was as surprised as I was proud, and he
never helped me on my horse no more from that day on.

Then I got a holt of his tail again, jumped on his hocks, reached for the saddle
strings, and the rest was easy.

And from that day on, Bopy had to change his tactics in
tying my horse when he left me alone. He had to use a long
rope and climb a tree and tie it high enough so that by
making my horse move ahead and standing up in the saddle
I couldn't reach and untie the knot. He didn't trust me to
ride alone in that country like at the ranch. This one was
strange to me and the timber being pretty thick would of
made it easy for me to get lost.

But I used to ramble around some, out of his sight, on the
way back to camp. Him being afoot made him too slow for

me and I'd run ahead a bit. Sometimes when he would stop to look at something I'd manage to get away good, but before I'd get too far I'd always hear a shot from his old muzzle loader and that would sure be bound to fetch me back on a high lope to see what he'd killed. Lots of times he didn't kill anything, he'd just shoot to get me back and he'd say that he missed. I never caught on to that because whenever I was with him and he shot, something went down and I liked to go get it. It'd be a snowshoe rabbit or grouse and always small game, he had no use for big game during summers because it'd only spoil before we could get a quarter et up. And so, along with a few of the best samples of the ore which he'd knocked off the ledges that day and which he'd pile up with other samples already gathered at the camp, we'd also have meat to put in the pot for the next day or cut up and fry for that night.

In the forenoons, after a day's prospecting and collecting of ore samples, is when Bopy would go to work assaying. He'd take his pan to the creek, pound his rocks to a powder, put the powder in the pan and, with fresh supplies of water added on, he'd work the pan in a slow circling motion, letting out a little amount of the crushed rock which had been pounded to dirt with every one of them motions. If there was any particle of gold or heavy mineral in the ore it would stay in the bottom.

He would take a lot of time doing that, and once in a while I'd hear remarks from him as to how he thought he'd "struck it," but later on, when he'd get a chance to send a sample of the same supposed-to-be-rich ore to a town assayer, he'd always get reports that would make him leave that prospect without a monument, unclaimed.

I used to like to watch him pan out his ore, wondering what he would find at the bottom, but, after a few pannings

and grunts that told of no findings, I'd mosey away and to
looking for other things that would be of interest to me.
Sometimes I wouldn't find anything right quick and then
was the times I'd begin to think of my dad again and feel
sort of alone. I'd go to stargazing and making marks in the
ground that tears kept me from seeing.

It was at them alone-feeling spells that I'd sometimes
rummage thru the paniers of the pack outfit a hoping I
would find something blank to draw on, for it was then I
hankered to draw most, and even tho the drawing was
mighty poor it suited me all right. It relieved me of things
that was in me which words couldn't put out and I was
always at peace when I was drawing.

But the old paniers, as often as I looked thru 'em while
we was camped at the dugout, never produced one scrap of
paper of any kind, not any even as big as my thumb nail.
Bopy caught me searching around thru them one day and
asked me what I was looking for, and I told him. . . .

We moved camp the next day early, and we didn't poke
along as we usually did. It was just after noon when we
come to a fence and further down, about half a mile, I could
see houses and corrals. Bopy stopped in the thick of a patch
of timber, tied up the two pack horses and told me to stay
right there with 'em, that he'd be gone just a little while, and
then he rode away on a high lope towards the gate that
opened the fence into the ranch.

When he came back it was on a high lope too and he had a
smile on his face that was a yard wide. He didn't explain
anything to me what he'd went to the ranch for. Instead he
reached for a little canvas bag that was tied on one of the
packs and pulled out half a dozen long strips of "jerky"
(dried meat). He handed me a couple and we went to chewing. That was our dinner for that day and we et as we rode.

Bopy took the lead, and with me following behind the pack horses, we headed on up towards the foothills along the same range of mountains, but straight away from where we'd left that morning. It was near dark that evening when we found another good place to stop and camp at. I took care of my horse and picketed him in a good grassy spot, but I don't think I helped much after that. I think I went to sleep on the bed-roll, for I remember I used to do that often after a long ride like we had that day. In the meantime Bopy would go on setting up camp and cook supper and when all was ready and hot he'd wake me up. I'd be hungry as a wolf. It'd take me just a few minutes to eat and then the bed was unrolled and I'd be dead to the world in one other minute.

I'll always remember that one morning when I woke up and, moseying around as usual, went to where my saddle was laying. On top of it was a big thick tablet of writing paper, the first I'd seen that wasn't lined or was so white. Alongside of it was two pencils. They was also the longest I'd ever seen.

It was hard to get me to breakfast that morning and I didn't take the time to eat much of it when I got there. I was still chewing on my last bite when I went to my pencils and tablet again and I was so anxious, as the Old-timer told me, that I couldn't draw half as good as I did while at the ranch. I was just like a feller wanting to talk too fast and trying to put ten words in the time of one.

But I wasn't wasting any paper, that was more than precious to me, and if I did make wild drawings I sure used up all the space on one side of each sheet and the same on the other. I was just beginning to cool down good that morning when Bopy comes along, peeks over my shoulder and tells me how he thinks he's going to be very busy to-day and that I'd better stay in camp and watch things. That watching part was just to give me some responsibility so I would stick close, but he knowed daggone well that that tablet alone would hold me there till dark. He pointed to the fire and showed me the hole where the little dutch oven was that held the noon meal. It was a stew which he'd started the night before, and the little oven was surrounded with low coals to keep it good and warm. All I'd have to do would be to scrape the ashes off the lid, lift it off and help myself. There was cold biscuits and a creekful of cold water to go along with that.

After all the instructions was handed out, Bopy picked up his prospector's pick, his rifle and some jerky, and away he went hunting up more ledges that hinted to precious metals.

I know I was glad he left because it's at such a time, when I have something in my chest, whether it's good or bad, that I want to be all alone with what I put down on the paper or board in front of me. Someone around about then, whether that someone talks or keeps quiet, is just like a stranger butting in when you're talking confidential to an understanding friend.

I layed flat on my belly and, propped on my elbows, hat away back on my head, I drawed till the sun, beating down on my backbone, made me hunt a tree for shade. With my back against the tree and using my knees for a table, I drawed some more. I was good in that position for a long time, specially right then because I was stumped. A horse's leg was bothering me and no matter how often I erased that leg it wouldn't fit the horse I had drawed. Finally I erased the whole horse and kept the leg and made another horse that would fit it. It worked out all right.

I do that often right to-day, but what I can't understand is why, while I was trying to draw that horse under the tree and working so hard to get it right, I never thought of looking at the four horses that was grazing to within fifty yards of me and study from them for help to get that leg right.

The sun went past high center and I was still drawing, and time was near middle afternoon when an empty feeling

I layed flat on my belly and, propped on my elbows, I drawed till the sun, beating down on my backbone, made me hunt a tree for shade.

in the pit of my stomach reminded me that there was other things besides drawing which needed attention. When I finally put my tablet and pencil down and looked towards the spot where the oven was buried, my appetite hit me full force and I hightailed to that spot. My breakfast had been kind of light.

I managed to get some ashes into the stew as I lifted the lid, but I made out a good meal just the same, and I went to drawing some more that afternoon and up till the time when Bopy came back to camp with his usual pickings of ore samples, and a young sage chicken. I was glad to see him come because my hankering for drawing, or markings which went with my feelings, had been satisfied a considerable and now I was ready for talk. I did talk and jabbered all thru supper time till we crawled in between the soogans (bedding, quilts) for that night's rest.

I went right into drawing again the next morning, but I waited till after breakfast and then I drawed only for a couple of hours. I begin to find lots of faults with the drawings I'd done the day before, and which I thought had been so fine then, and the ones I drawed the second day struck me as worse. So, for the time being, I put my tablet and pencils carefully away between the under soogans of the bed and went to the creek to watch and talk to Bopy while he panned out his would-be pay dirt.

My drawing from then on was kind of in spells like. As before, I went along with Bopy again on prospecting trips and seldom would my tablet and pencils hold me in camp. By this time, with the tablet, Bopy, my horse and outfit, the country around and all that was new and strange, I was having my hands full taking everything in that interested me, and I was beginning to forget my lonesomeness for what all is natural but which I'd never knowed, the love of a mother and the steady companionship of a father.

CHAPTER THREE

BOPY and me covered many a mile that summer and we set up many a camp in many a different place, sometimes high up, other times in the foothills, and then again in the brakes and badlands, wherever the ledges and country showed "signs." The Old-timer had accumulated quite a pile of "sample rock" by then and, far as I can remember, none of 'em tallied up so high. One of the pack ponies was under at least fifty pounds of them samples when fall come in, and when the reports came back from the assayer's office old Bopy begin to look for a camp again and where the fur trapping was good.

The camp, I wish I could find it again, was one of Bopy's own, one of the many he'd built hisself. It was late in the fall when we came to it. The grass had turned to a yellow-brown and frost was beginning to color up the quakers and cotton-woods. We turned the ponies loose in a fenced pasture. The grass was tall and thick there, there was no more hobbling nor picketing, and we didn't leave the skillets nor bedding outside because heavy rains mixed with flurries of snow made things damp and cold. Besides, we'd struck a home camp and where we was to hole-up for the winter.

Inside of the camp, a dirt-roofed, one-roomed log cabin, and under a wide long bunk, was about a hundred traps and of all sizes from the small one-spring muskrat trap up to the cayote and wolf trap, and to the fifty-pound lock bear trap. But after looking around some, them traps didn't interest me none much. They was just like so much steel and nothing more as compared to what I'd spotted in one corner of the cabin. There, and all stacked up, was a pile of magazines, newspapers and books. The pile was higher than me, but it sure wasn't long before I made camp right there in that corner and took the top off that pile till it was reduced, or scattered, to my size.

I don't know how old them magazines and papers was and I didn't care because I couldn't read anyway, but I do know they was a heap older than me. They'd been gathered and stacked there for many years. The pictures is what took my eye. They was pictures of all things I'd never seen and which was as strange to me as anything strange could be. I remember seeing pictures of people dressed in clothes of the kind I'd never seen before, whiskers cut sort of queer, pretty women with lots of hair, and ponies without tails nor manes.

Bopy spent many a long evening explaining all which stumped me in them pictures and I know that after he got thru, which was never, I still didn't understand, for I'd never seen what them pictures pictured.

I went thru that stack of printed work mighty quick. It was my first acquaintance with such and I found a heap from that first acquaintance which wouldn't allow me to linger with one so I could get to the other. When I went thru that stack the second time I was a little slower and more watchful, the third time was still more slow, and then I

settled down to really seeing what was between the leaves
of what I picked up.

I didn't get to do no drawing for quite a spell along about
then, and after I had looked at all the pictures over and over
again about sixteen times I begin to wonder what all them
funny marks was that was under them, the writing, that's
what Bopy said it was, but I didn't know what he meant.
and, as he told me, he couldn't understand nor explain it.
Bopy couldn't read English and very little French.

The trees went bare of leaves, snows came and covered up
the grass, a dry-log shelter was built for the ponies and hay
was stacked up alongside. Bopy drug out his traps, seen
that the chains, pins and anchors would hold, and scattered
'em out on the trail of drifting herds and beaver-damned
streams. I didn't see none of the goings-on much, my nose
was buried in things printed and only once in a while, when
my bones would ache from laying or setting on the floor and
when I couldn't see no more, would I get out and look at the
great world which was all around me that *couldn't* be
printed.

It was about when I was getting my fill of printed work
and when I was starting to drawing again, (it was getting
sort of raw and cold to be out, unless you had to) when
something happened which held up my growth a considerable.

Some animal was robbing Bopy's traps, killing and eating most all that'd been caught in 'em, and Bopy set out
to catch that animal.

According to most trappers, a trap is not so good till
there's some rusted blood from a few victims on it. That
goes well for some furs, but not so well for the furs that
bring the big price, because many animals are wise to traps
and where the scent of blood means just that, a trap. So,

Bopy, instead of taking out a blood-stained trap, begin to wash out three or four that wouldn't give no scent.

He'd mixed up something made out of cottonwood ashes which turned out as ninety-nine percent lye and one percent something else. The mixture would of made boughten lye seem mighty weak and when he got thru there was, as well as I know, no scent as to any trap.

But Bopy had overlooked something. That was me. He'd left that strong mixture in a lid of some can on the floor and while I was rummaging around with the printed work or drawing, I happened to see that lid there on the floor.

He was gone for just one minute, I think, maybe just to hang out a trap, but in that time, I took a holt of that lid. What was inside of it looked to me like sirup, that's what I thought it was, and I drank it down.

It all went down smooth enough but it wasn't but a short spell afterwards, maybe a few seconds, when an awful pain hit my middle. Bopy came in, looked at me and then looked at the lid. He told me afterwards that he was a heap scareder than I was when he realized what had happened. I was plenty scared enough myself, and the pain from drinking that lye, two long swallows, made me do nothing but groan and holler and wish I was amongst the departed.

But Bopy, as always, was on the job again. With his skinning knife he tore the top off a can of condensed milk and poured the whole contents down my throat. I well remember the biting of that lye but I also remember the soothing of that milk. It stayed down me about one minute and then it came up and out in big curdled hunks. A doctor said afterwards that that was all which could have saved me.

That winter was a painful one. I layed and groaned and I wasn't caring for my tablet of white paper, my pony, saddle or rope, nor for any of the printed works that was again stacked up in the corner. My stomach was burnt out and I couldn't hold nothing down and I couldn't be fed only with "gruyo" (mush) on account that my mouth and throat was seared up with scabs from the burns of the lye. A little spoonful of gruyo at the time, at one corner of my mouth, was all I could take.

Bopy didn't get many furs that winter. He never left me alone for more than two hours at the time and always he'd rush back like as if the house was afire. I'd either be asleep or having a tummyache and many a time he came in and found me laying on the floor over a big stick of wood. Them sticks of wood was the only relief I could get from them awful pains in my stomach. They seemed to stop circulation or something somehow and in some way so I could rest. The sticks I picked on was never less than four inches thru, and the rougher they was the better I liked 'em, because to me the outside pain was a big contester against what all I felt inside. C631763 CO. SCHOOLS

Bopy found me asleep many a time that way and on many a stick I couldn't lift but which I could roll or drag away from the side of the fireplace. I remember hunting them up like as if my life depended on 'em, and I wouldn't be at peace till I could lay over one good rough one.

I remember how old Bopy, watching me, would sometimes roll up something soft, like a soogan, and tell me to lay on that, and I remember how I turned down his well meant favors and tell him to please leave me be. I wanted the stick.

I must of been a lot of worry to Bopy during the next few months that followed because I was a pretty sick kid and I was hard to get along with. Maybe sometimes Bopy wished he'd left me at the ranch, but I don't hardly think so. His actions sure never showed that, and he always done what-

ever he could for me whether I was sick or well, and always
with a smile showing thru his whiskers. He'd watch over me
like any good mother would, and with the same care and,
thinking back, I know by the way he acted that I was a
responsibility to him which he was mighty glad to have. I
was so dependant on him, someone for him to worry about
and come back to camp for, and that way I think I filled up
a mighty wide and empty gap in his life.

As far as I know, Bopy had never married, and he never
talked to me of women. His life was the lone wolf's and with
his drifting on and on always, making camp wherever night
found him, it sure wasn't the kind of life that goes well in
double harness.

I was a big interruption in his life, but I wasn't an interruption for long, only for a couple of years. After that I
was good dependable company and he was still free to roam
as he wished. That winter I was so sick from drinking the
lye was about the only time I really tied Bopy down. I took
near all his time and disturbed many of his sleeps, but he
never showed he begrudged that any, and he'd always be
trying to think up of something to entertain me by and make
me forget the pains I always felt.

"Comment est tu, Billee?" (how are you) he would always
ask as he'd come in from his trap line. He'd bring in the
fresh-skinned hides to stretch, close the door as quick as he
could, stir up the fire and see that I was warm, and then he'd
go to talking, telling me of some of his experiences of that
day with the animals he'd caught. Bopy never was much on
talking but he sure did talk a lot to me that winter, and
many a time he talked on while I'd be sound asleep.

By that time he'd got so he talked to me most always in
French. Only once in a while would he bring in a few words
of English, just when I couldn't understand the French.

But his English was near as hard for me to understand as his French. I'd got to know that last pretty well by then, so, being it was about fifty-fifty on the two languages, Bopy finally dropped the English entirely and went on to speak to me in the tongue he knowed best.

It was along towards spring when the pains begin to ease up inside of me and it got so I only felt 'em for an hour or so and right after I'd et. I'd hunt me up a stick then again for a spell and lay on it till the pain was gone. The pains would leave me wore out, and when I'd got relief from them I'd usually go to sleep.

Them two swallows of lye sure had made a slim kid out of me. That fall, just before taking them, I was a big knock-kneed fat kid and as round as a butter ball, but I sure wasn't that way when the following spring come. I wasn't much more than a skeleton and the effects of that poison stayed with me till I was near full grown. But I think that, with the bad of that happening, there was some good too, for I never caught none of the diseases and sicknesses that kids seem to get. During the World War, and in one tent I was in at the cantonment, there was three boys died of the "flu." There had only been five of us in that one tent.

But I guess I suffered enough from the poison that one winter to deserve being immune of some sicknesses. It was well along springtime before I begin to take much interest in anything again. Gradually I'd get a little deeper in the stack of magazines in the corner and stay longer, then I started using my tablet and pencils some more.

It was about then, when I begin to perk up some, that Bopy took it onto himself to try and teach me what all them funny marks meant on the magazine sheets. He had lots of time on his hands then because the trapping season was well past. He'd shipped his furs by another trapper who had

stopped by on the way to town, received his check, had a
freighter bring a load of grub, and now, outside of hunting
for a little fresh meat when he felt like it, there was nothing
to do but wait till the ridges got bare of snow and the ledges
showed again.

Being Bopy couldn't read English, I think them first few
lessons in grammar was near as hard for him to teach as
they was for me to learn. He knowed the letters by name in
French and that was all. From them letters picked here and
there on the page, we'd build up a French word and started
to work that way. I printed all the letters the same as they
was in whatever magazine we'd work from. One day we'd
work on letters and the next day on numbers and Bopy seen
to it, once he got me started, that I done at least an hour's
studying every day.

That was the start of my schooling from the only teacher
I ever had. I took to grammar natural-like and I got so that
it was very seldom I misspelt a word, I was more apt to do
that on common words, as I still do.

My schooling was limited to grammar and arithmetic
only. That was all Bopy could begin to handle, but he
stayed with me pretty steady on them two subjects. Then
one evening that spring he rides back to camp from the post
office with a big package of books, French thin-leafed books
full of small writing. There sure was a lot of reading in
them. He'd also brought me a couple more tablets and some
pencils. I was all set.

I didn't do much riding that spring, it hurt me to set on
a horse and cramps would double me up till I'd have to get
off. So, when I wasn't moseying around outside or laying
down on a stick of wood in the sun, I'd be with my books,
tablets and magazines, drawing and reading. I often wished
I could of read what was in them American magazines.

It was late that summer before I could set on my horse and be comfortable again. By that time I'd got along pretty well with my education and I could make out and write quite a few fair-sized words, but that all was left aside when I got to riding again. I'd been too sick to miss my horse and outfit that winter and spring, and it wasn't till I got in my little saddle on the little black's back and uncoiling my rope once more, that I lost interest in all books and reading and writing, even drawing.

It sure tickled old Bopy to see me on my horse again, and he used to grin and tell me I looked a heap better in the saddle now that I wasn't so fat. After he seen that I was sure enough all right again and, outside of short spells of cramps once in a while, was fit to travel, he gets the pack saddles down off the pegs one day, loads up the paniers and, with two pack horses, as the summer before, one for the chuck and one for the bed, we straddle our saddle horses and hit out for another long trip along the foothills of other ranges. I took just one tablet with me and one pencil.

But I didn't do much drawing nor writing on that trip. I was hankering more to be on my horse and seeing new country. We made a circle of quite a few hundred miles, crossed many a mountain and valley and camped by many a stream. All excepting a couple of times, I went wherever Bopy went that summer, even when the horses had to be left behind.

It was at one of them times when I was alone that, moseying along and going around the point of a rock, I came acrost my first bear. I'd strayed from my horse a little further than usual that time, and there he was in a clump of cherry bushes, a big black hunk of fur. I don't remember if I was scared or not, most likely I was not because Bopy never told me of any danger in any animal and I'd never as yet read any stories about 'em. But, whether I was scared or not, I remember the bear was. I'd been watching him quite a while before he spotted me, and when he did he reared up, fell all over himself, and lit a running, woof-woofing and a snorting at every jump till he went out of sight. To me he looked like a pretty big bear, but Bopy had seen him too and he said he was only about half grown.

It seems like happenings go pretty well in numbers when they start because, on my way back to my horse, I hears a buzzing sound and there to within a few feet of me is a rattlesnake all coiled up. That's what Bopy said it was after I'd described it to him, and he warned me never to go near one of them. I'd seen lots of snakes before at the ranch but this one was the biggest I'd ever seen and I'd never heard one buzz before.

I started looking for a stick, to try and kill it with, I guess, but before I found one the snake had crawled into a hole. I could see its head in there and long red tongue a working. I tried to dig it out with my stick but the hole was too deep. That's what I was working at when Bopy came back to me that day.

There was lots of game in the country we was in that summer. We seen deer pretty near every day, and elk, and once we run acrost four grizzlies in one bunch. Bopy killed the biggest one—a bear hide is always worth something—and we had bear hump and other good parts of bear meat for a few days then. Bopy never killed an elk or a deer till cold freezing weather set in. It would keep then, and in the summers we always made out on small game, and once in a while a hunk of beef, if we was near some ranch where we could get it. I always liked beef best of all meats, and I still do.

We stayed out that fall till the snows begin to come to stay. There was quite a few cold rains and light snowstorms

Going around the point of a rock, I came acrost my first bear.

before that, and some mornings we'd wake up to find an extra blanket on our bed. That blanket was of snow. Sometimes we'd find a deserted cabin to hole-up in during them first storms, but not always when we wanted 'em. The sky was pretty black, a high wind was blowing, and snow was beginning to fly past us as again we got sight of the cabin where we'd passed the last winter, me with a rough stick for steady company.

I don't remember if I was glad to see the place and get under shelter again. I know I sure liked to be out and just be a drifting around like we had been, and, even tho I had to put on cold wet socks many a morning, wet shoes and damp pants, and eat my breakfast while slushy snow fell by my ears into my tin plate, I never hankered for the cosy warm inside of a cabin. The pitch-wood camp fire was plenty good enough, and the hot coffee, and a few grins and good words from old Bopy made me feel warm inside, and big.

But, as Bopy said, we sure reached our home camp just in time that fall. A heavy blizzard swooped down over the country which lasted three or four days. When it cleared up it turned mighty cold and there was two feet of snow on the ground. Me and Bopy stuck mighty close to the cabin during that storm and all was hunkydory. We had lots of good wood and grub, the ponies was under shelter, and there was plenty of hay to feed 'em with.

While the storm howled on outside, Bopy drug out his traps from under the bunk again and begin sorting 'em. Me, I went back to my corner and renewed my acquaintance with the printed stuff. I looked all the pictures over good first and that made me want to draw. I stayed at that for quite a spell, and then I tried to read some more of them French books.

With all of that I was kept pretty busy. I hardly heard

Bopy moving around and going in and out, and we didn't get to say much to one another till meal times.

But when the skies cleared, even tho it was mighty cold, I went out with Bopy again and watched him set out his trap line. He set out a bigger circle that winter and put out more traps, and instead of walking his trap line as he did the year before, he went a horseback. That made it fine for me and I went out with him about every other time or, as Bopy thought, whenever the weather wasn't too rough. His trap line took in about twenty miles.

In the evenings, when Bopy wasn't busy stretching or scraping the fat off his skins, he'd hand me more schooling and I got to know every letter and number that winter, and how they worked when a few are put together. By spring I could write and spell and pronounce many words out of the French books which neither Bopy nor me could tell the meaning of.

The winter went on mighty peaceful and without any events out of the ordinary happening, not excepting maybe one, one that was a great surprise and pleasure to me. A rider had come by our camp and left a package and when he'd rode on, I was right on the job watching Bopy open that package. A cardboard box was unwrapped. He handed it to me and said, as he'd said more times afterwards:

"C'est pour toi, Billee. Bonne et heureuse nouvelle année." (It's for you, Billy, Good and happy New Year.)

I don't think I hardly heard him as I took the cover off that box and looked inside. There, all shining, was the copper toes of a little pair of boots. Part of the top was red and a star was designed in the center of that.

That was my first New Year's present from Bopy, and whenever he was where he could get me a present he'd always pick on New Year's day to give it to me, for according to his bringing up, that was the big day for cheer and to celebrate and give presents on. Christmas was a day for quiet and peace. All he'd do on Christmas day was to spread out the best meal he could and he was sure a bear at doing that. He'd start on it the day before.

There, all shining, was the copper toes of a little pair of boots.

If Bopy believed in any religion, he never showed it. He never spoke to me on that subject and I've never seen him kneel nor pray. But, regardless of that, I've had a hint many a time while I lived with him that he had a great lot of religion, only his wasn't of the kind where you kneel and pray and donate, while asking for favors. His was silent and came thru his being and senses at what he seen and felt, and from his heart.

Bopy done good at his trapping that winter. He didn't have to bother with me as he did the winter before and, as

I've already said, his trap line covered more territory and he'd put out more traps. Then I was with him a big part of the time and when I did stay in camp for the whole day alone, he never worried about me. He knowed I wouldn't play with matches and fire. I had plenty of training with that on our trips, and he knowed I was well cured of drinking or eating anything unless I knowed mighty sure what it was. I'd had one good lesson on that, too, which I still felt the effects of once in a while.

The worst I'd do in tinkering around was to try and mix up something special good to eat, like I'd watch Bopy do, and then burn it, or I'd go out and feed the horses too much hay. Then I'd play at setting traps and forget to bring 'em back where I found 'em. The only trap I could spring was the muskrat trap and I didn't spring that one very often, not after I'd got my fingers caught a few times and pinched good.

Bopy, coming back in the evening and, seeing by different signs what I'd been doing, would never say anything. But the next day he'd tell me to saddle up and come along with him, he'd decided that would do me good.

And it would do me good. For the next day or so I'd go back to my drawing and trying to read, and I wouldn't go to tinkering around much.

The winter went on with things going along that way. Bopy had shipped his usual collection of the "sample rock" which he'd gathered the summer before to the assayer, got the report as to their value, throwed the report into the fireplace and had kept right on trapping.

The pelts had accumulated, made up good-sized bales and was shipped. Bopy got his check, had a load of grub freighted in, and there was nothing to do again till spring broke up for sure, and snow drifts melted off the ledges and leads. (The fur trapping season ends with February. After that month, even tho there's still a lot of severe weather to come, the hair begins to slip and pelts don't bring no price much.) During that time—from the end of the trapping season till warm weather, which is at least two months—was when I received serious schooling, long spells of it and most every day, and often I'd look out and wish the snow would hurry up and go and the sun would get hot. I always hated to study.

I was a sure enough tickled kid when finally Bopy put my books back in the corner one day and called it enough. The country was turning green, the trees was budding and I followed Bopy out to get the pack outfit ready.

CHAPTER FOUR

WE went in a different country again that summer, always in a different country. We crossed many ranges of high mountains, fenced-in places in the valleys and passed by where I could often see ranch houses in the distance. We went on and on and seldom stopped to camp for a whole day. Finally, after many days we run out of mountains and from the high pass of the last one I looked down to see wide open country with no more mountains in sight bordering it, nothing but little knolls and low ridges cut up by dry looking washes. I was surprised to see no trees in that country, none excepting one narrow crooked line of 'em away off and where a river run. There was a lot of sage brush everywhere, white sage, black sage, rabbit brush and buck brush, besides many other kinds of brushes. Some of them was good feed for stock, and there was also quite a lot of grass in between, covering the land. The whole landscape was dotted with scattered bunches of cattle and horses. Once in a while Bopy would point out a band of antelope to me, and going thru that country we met a rider most every day.

Meeting a rider that way was quite a happening for me. It gave me a chance to show off my copper-toed boots, and while the rider and Bopy talked, I'd do all I could to see that them boots of mine was noticed. The only handicap I had was that there was no silver-mounted spurs on 'em. But, to me, the red top with the star in the center and the copper toes sort of made up for the lack of spurs.

We came to a wide river, crossed it on a ferry and I was glad to get on the other side and get off on solid land again, that water spooked me up. I'd never seen so much all at once and so muddy. A couple of days later we came to a low range of hills. They was covered with juniper and pinôn with quakers and willows in the gullies. There was a lot of prospect holes in that country, some regular tunnels deep in the side of the hill. And then shafts just as deep that went straight down.

Bopy would never pass up none of them "diggings" without investigating. He'd study the formations, the lay of the country around, and pound out a few choice rocks. Sometimes, if there was water near, he'd camp by one of them holes for a day or two, just a studying out where the mistake might of been that the vein was lost and the digging abandoned. But with all his investigating, I don't remember ever seeing Bopy do any "mucking" (digging). He wanted to make his find without too much effort and I think now that his prospecting was more as a side interest to go with his roaming, something to help lead him on. Bopy never showed that he cared for riches.

Sometimes, following a trail from some of the bigger diggings, we'd find a shack or cabin or dugout. They was made out of everything that could be got the handiest, rough lumber, timber, rocks or mud. Some of 'em had windows made out of bottles stacked in the opening and chinked in between with mud. A few places, at first glance, looked as tho the owner had just left that morning and would be back that evening. The bunk would be there with bedding still on it. There'd be wood by the stove, skillets and pots behind it, overalls hanging on the wall, shoes and miner's tools in a corner. On a home-made table would be salt and sugar in cans, pepper and a punched can of milk. The shelves above it would still be holding the tin plates and cups, seasonings, rice and raisins and, below, flour and potatoes.

If there was no calendar on the wall, nor no writing left, it was hard to tell right quick how long the owner had been gone. Flour and potatoes, if that was left in a sack, gave the best signs. Mice went to work scattering the flour, and time went to work on shrinking the potatoes till they was about the size of, and looked like, dried prunes.

Piled up newspapers could sometimes tell to within a couple of months, and once in a while some prospector would leave a dated note in a can with wordings that averaged something like this, "Whoever wants my diggings is welcome to them. I've put all the money I had in these here grounds and got nothing out." Sometimes it would be signed, but whoever left the note had gone to be grubstaked and hunted for new signs in new territories, for, once a prospector always a prospector.

It used to be a lot of fun for me to explore some of the deserted cabins. After I'd get thru exploring, I'd go to playing it was my cabin and I was the prospector, and if there was any magazines scattered around anywheres or anything with pictures, well then, I didn't care if Bopy didn't move on for a spell.

I was playing prospector one time and gone up a dry wash behind the deserted cabin. I had one of them little prospector's picks with me that I'd found, and I was going to locate me some promising sample rock to crush and pan out, like Bopy did. It was while going up the dry wash that I run acrost a funny looking skull, and up a ways further some slim bones. All the skulls I'd seen before was big and long and most of 'em showed where horns had been on 'em at one time. This one was round and small and had a hole right in the center.

Wondering what it was I brought it back with me and asked Bopy that evening. It was the skull of a white man he said as he looked it over, most likely some "claim jumper." The hole in the center had been made by a bullet and, taking Bopy to the place where I found the skull, he thought the dead man had been buried there, but the rains and melting snows had washed out the remains to bleach in the sun.

One day in our ramblings thru that country we run acrost a whole town, the first town I'd ever seen, and it was deserted. . . . But I got a big thrill looking thru it. I'd never seen such big houses as was there, two and three floors high, and whole rows of 'em with no space between. . . . Some was made out of brick and stone, with big high steel shutters on the windows, and steel doors. I wondered what was inside of them.

In the houses I could get into I found enough things new and of interest to keep me exploring forever, I thought. There was fancy chairs and bedsteads, bureaus and dressers with some clothes still in 'em, pictures on the wall, and everything that's in any home where folks live steady, from the top story down to the cellar.

In some places there was pianos and pump organs. Bopy made me acquainted with them music boxes and for a while I had a lot of fun making noise. But I never was cut out to handle music so, after a while, I went on exploring some more. I was looking for the big houses now, with the fancy front porch, because them always had good pictures on the walls inside, and the part of town where the shacks was didn't interest me no more.

We picketed or hobbled our ponies on the streets in that town. The grass had growed tall there and many a blade and bunch of it edged thru the cracks of the board sidewalk.

I'd got to know the town pretty well in a short while and I'd
picked up quite a few things and stacked 'em at camp so
I could take 'em along when we moved. But soon as Bopy
found that out he made me take 'em all back and put 'em

They wasn't even mates.

exactly where I'd found 'em. He said something about good
men never taking things that don't belong to them. And so,
as much as I hated to, I took everything back, all but two
old rusty spurs which I'd found while I was rummaging
around the livery stable. They wasn't even mates but the
way I begged Bopy to let me keep them I guess he thought
they was sure worth everything to me. I finally got his con-
sent.

I was sorry to see Bopy start packing up the next morning and getting ready to move on. I hadn't seen *all* of the town yet. But, as Bopy said, the minerals and prospects had been mined and prospected to death right there. The country had petered out and the town was dead.

Out of town a ways we passed the dumps. There was steel rails on 'em, and ore trains leading out of the main shafts over which was long corrugated buildings, full of machinery, where the ore was ground and the minerals separated from the rock. As I remember it now, the town and the mills looked like they had died over night and the folks left the next morning, leaving everything behind and like as if they'd be back any minute to resume work and stir up the home fires.

I wanted to stop and investigate the mills, but Bopy rode on and the only consolation I had in leaving so soon was the spurs on my heels which I kept a looking at often, and the hopes from Bopy's words which gave me to understand that we might run acrost another town like that again soon.

But I looked over many a ridge many a day after we left, always expecting and hoping to run acrost another town like that down in some opening below, but I'd always be disappointed after topping every ridge. I didn't get to see no other such town that summer, nor for many years afterwards.

We roamed around all thru them juniper hills that summer, run acrost many a prospect hole and many an abandoned shack and we run acrost prospectors too. Some of 'em would be driving a burro or mule team and a few was in their own camps and working out a claim. Bopy would sometimes camp over night by one of them old "sourdough's" (bachelor) shacks and spend the evening a talking on the different prospects they'd missed finding, in what countries and so on.

They'd talk ore and formation till I couldn't see straight, and anyway I was having a hard time to understand because my French was sure getting mixed up with my American by then, and finally I'd go to sleep.

Some of them prospectors we stopped to talk to had at one time and another struck it rich sure enough. There was one we met who said he was worth a half a million at one time. That's what he'd sold his "holdings" to a company for, and it was still paying millions, to the company. With that half million this prospector went out and had a good time, paid out his share to keep the bright lights bright, and then settled down to business with what he had left.

He had enough left to build two big hotels over two saloons in two towns. He made more money, but before he got thru, them hotels cost him a heap and, when both towns went "bust," he just had enough left to get himself a burro team and rig and fill the rig with grub and powder.

He made two more stakes after that but just a few thousands each time, and the times was so far between that he had all his money on the bar and in the ground, before he struck his third find. Now he was working from what was left of that and, as he said, it was getting low.

Fall was creeping in on us when we struck some little higher mountains. Snow was up on the peaks of 'em and Bopy begin to look for a place where there'd be a solid roof over our heads for the winter, and solid walls around us. One day we drifts in to what looked to me like a town, only there was no tall buildings. They was all low, dirt-roofed log houses, long and rambling. There was many corrals, round ones, square ones, and all shapes, long strings of stables, sheds, shelters, and there was many hundred head of cattle and horses in some of the corrals.

It was just getting dark when Bopy pulled up in front

of one of the long log houses. A cowboy came out and said, "Get down stranger and put your ponies away. You can leave your bed right here." Bopy didn't say a word and done as the cowboy told him to. Our ponies was fed hay that night.

I don't know how big my eyes was but I know they was sure full size when we got back and went in the door of the long log house. It was the first real bunk house I'd ever seen and I remember every detail of it well even now. I'm going to write it down before time makes me forget.

All around the house, which was at least sixty feet long and thirty wide, was a double deck of bunks and built to the wall. There must of been at least thirty of 'em. On most of the bunks was a tarpaulin covered bed. The lower bunks was first choice. At the ends of them bunks hung broken bridles that had been brought in to be fixed, rawhide braidings that was unfinished, and chaps and spurs.

At both ends of the house was a long box stove that could easy take a three-foot log. Between them stoves was three tables and over each one was a big hanging kerosene lamp. . . . It sure was what I call a bunk house.

But the lay of the bunk house wasn't what interested me most as I first walked in there with Bopy. It was the boys. There was about ten cowboys there a warming up by the stove. They'd just come in from a cold day's ride and talking of that day's work and what had to be done to-morrow. They edged to one side as we came in, to give us room by the stove. But as both stoves was going there was lots of room.

Now more cowboys kept a coming in every few minutes, one or two at a time and all passing a joking remark as they came in. When the bell rang and all trailed out towards the chuck house I know I counted about twenty riders.

Me and Bopy had bumped into the main camp and headquarters of a big cow outfit. And big it was, sure enough.
I remember Bopy telling me later that there was on an average of eighty cowboys working the year around on that
"spread." Each rider had from eight to twelve horses in his

I know I counted about twenty riders.

string. That meant the company had to furnish about eight
hundred head of saddle horses, and there'd have to be at
least three thousand head of "stock" horses (brood mares
and colts), in order to furnish and raise enough saddle horses
to keep the cowboys mounted.

The outfit ranged upwards of a hundred thousand head
of cattle, and, figgering that each critter takes from ten to
twenty acres to range on, and near twice that for horses, that
outfit did take a certain amount of territory.

I wish I could remember some of the talk and stories that
went around that evening when all gathered in the bunk

house again after the meal. All of them boys are old men now and many of 'em must have gone Yonder.

Bopy left me the next morning to go to another house. There was a big porch on that house and curtains in the windows. It must of been where the superintendent or range boss lived. Anyway, I went to moseying around the corrals and stables and when I come to one of the corrals where a lot of the boys was working, I camped right there and looked thru the bars and forgot time. They was separating horses and running the ones they wanted, or didn't want, into another corral. Some of 'em had to be roped and drug out.

In another corral they was separating cattle by the help of a chute. I stopped there for a while and then went on to another corral where two riders was busy taking the rough off spooky bronks (taming unbroke horses). There I stayed and stayed. I stayed till four or five bronks was topped off in their first saddling, and when the boys begin to talk to me thru the bars, and grinned, and finally hoisted me inside the corral, I could never begin to think of leaving. Maybe Bopy was looking for me but I never thought of that, for this I was seeing sure beat any thrill or fun I ever had while exploring the deserted town. And I didn't know but what we'd just had breakfast when the dinner bell rang.

Only about half of the boys was at the table that noon. The others was out on the range doing their work and wouldn't be back till night. Bopy was there at the table and grinned at me when I came in with the two "bronk stompers" (bronco busters) I'd been with all forenoon. He hadn't been looking for me none at all. He knowed where I was all the while and during that time he sure hadn't been idle. For, out by the commissary, was a wagon loaded with a winter's supply of grub, a hundred traps and many sacks of grain. That's what Bopy had been up to that morning when he left me. He'd been up to see one of the main heads of the outfit, inquired as to how trapping was in the neighboring country and the answer had been that it was good, too good. Too many varmints, like big cayotes, which was part gray wolf, was killing many young calves every spring and the result was that Bopy was offered all the grub and traps and everything he needed, and wages to boot, if he would only take one of the cow camps on that company's range and do his best to catch all the varmints that he could.

Both Bopy and the boss was glad to shake hands on that and the next morning early we pulled out with quite an outfit of our own. One of the ranch hands came along to drive the team and bring it back and me and Bopy rode behind the wagon, bringing up the pack horses.

I hated to leave that ranch a heap worse than I did the deserted town, but after I was made to understand that we would ride back again some time and stay a few days, that eased my feelings some and I begin to look forward as to what kind of a camp it was we was going to.

We got there late that night and by that I figger we must of went quite a ways from the ranch because we had traveled right along. When we got to the cow camp I didn't care to investigate and see what kind of a place it was much, not right then. I went to sleep till Bopy called me to eat. It seemed that right after I got thru eating it was morning again.

The cow camp, as I investigated it that morning, turned out to be quite a place. There was a well chinked, two-roomed log house that Bopy was busy throwing bucket after bucket of water into and sweeping out afterwards. He swept the water and dirt out that way quite a few times and after he got thru the floor must of been clean. The camp hadn't been used for a couple of winters.

I moseyed on down to the corrals. There was lots of them, all made of junipers and stood up in the ground right close together. There was enough corrals to hold a couple of thousand head of stock. There was chutes too, and bronk pens with snubbing posts, and a slaughter pen with a hoisting wheel. I had a lot of fun in them corrals and running thru them chutes. I'd play wild horse by the hour, put a rope around my shoulders—I knowed better than putting it around my neck—and after fastening the rope to the snubbing post and giving myself plenty of slack, I'd run as fast as I could till the rope jerked me to a stop. Then, like I'd seen the bronks do at the ranch, I'd turn and snort and paw the air or throw myself.

Other times I'd go thru the long narrow chutes where many a thousand head of wild longhorn cattle had been run thru and separated or branded. I'd kick at the sides of the chute, and try my best to look wall-eyed wild. Sometimes I'd even add on a tail which I'd cut off a dry cowhide on the corral fence, and fasten that to my middle with a string so as it'd hang good. Then I sure would get wild. I'd watch my shadow all I could and glance around for something to hook. I'd run thru the chutes and "squeezers" and being so wild I'd near knock a hip down doing it.

I think I had a natural interest in watching animals, what they done, and how they might of felt. Cattle interested me the least. I liked to see a big herd and watch the cowboys work, brand and round 'em up when I was a kid, and even try to help when I had the chance, but, to me, cattle was just beef, an animal to raise and ship to market and set up on the table in a big platter a smoking hot. With a horse it's very different, he was a pardner to work with, and I think I felt that from the first. I got to feeling for the horse and never thought about the cow, only when playing wild in the corral, and then I'd always be mean and try and hook something.

What I mean by feeling for the horse brings up one play I used to pull every once in a while. I'd pick out a time when it was raining or the wind blowed good and bringing on the snow. Then I'd get a horse tail I'd found somewhere and fasten it behind me, take a rope and with one end tied around my neck and the other end to the hitching rack which was by the house, I'd stand there and stomp, like I'd seen many a horse do. I'd turn my tail to the wind and storm and shake my head once in a while when the snow or rain got in my ears. I'd get a lot out of seeing the horse tail blow between my legs. It was just like it did with real horses I thought, and I'd stand there, on one leg and then the other, till sometimes I'd be soaking wet or near froze, or till Bopy would catch me at it.

I sure got back to playing cowboy again that winter. The visit at the ranch had stirred up what was in my blood which I'd inherited from the generations before me. My rope begin to get a lot of use and got stretched many a time. While riding my little black, I'd run by a post or a brush and throw my loop at it. Sometimes I'd catch what I throwed at and sometimes what I'd catch would be pretty solid and, my rope being tied hard and fast to the saddle horn like my dad used to do, I'd get quite a jerk when me and my pony hit the end. I'd come near falling off many a time.

The ponies sure had a dandy place that winter, a long log stable and plenty warm, and there was a stack of good hay by it that would winter ten head of stock thru any long winter. Then we had grain too, and Bopy had to lock that up so I wouldn't founder any of the horses by giving them too much at once. The western range horse never has to be coaxed to eat his grain. He lives natural, is seldom ever sick and his appetite is always with him no matter how fat he might be. Once he's tamed and gets acquainted with grain, he'll sure be always on the lookout for it and get mighty restless when he sees a sack or a can of it coming his way.

Our horses was always fat, even when after a long summer trip. Bopy sure seen to that, and if they showed signs of getting leg-weary he'd always stop at some good grazing place a few days and let 'em rest up.

It was thru that winter, with everything all set to the good, that I begin getting a little flesh back on my bones too, and, outside of feeling a little sick at the stomach once in a while at meal time, I'd pretty well got over the effects of drinking the lye.

What helped make the winter good was that once in a while, near every week, a cowboy or two would drop in, put his horse in the stable and stay over night. The talks that went around then between the three or four of us interested me a heap more than any talk I'd ever heard while the subject was on prospecting. Quartz-talk never did interest me.

With the visits of the cowboys, the fun I had at playing cowboy and once in a while going with Bopy on his trap line, then my drawing, reading and writing and all, I don't remember of one lonesome minute. Bopy had been thoughtful enough to include a big stack of magazines in with the load of grub and grain.

Bopy had a good winter too. He had over a hundred big cayote pelts to show for his work, not counting a few badger and bobcat pelts. I think the report from the assayer's office on the rock he'd gathered the summer before had been the same because Bopy had kept right on trapping. New Year had come, and I remember what a thrill I got when Bopy unwrapped a big package and produced me a present. It was a little papier mache dappled-gray horse on a little board and wheels.

I don't know how many different kinds of bridles and riggings I made and fastened on that horse. I played like he was a pretty bad horse and I'd always hobble him before saddling or tying the pack on him and I'd put a blindfold on him. When the snow begin to melt and patches of bare ground showed once more, I'd got me a lot of willow sticks, cut 'em to right lengths on the chopping block by the wood pile, and built me some corrals, just high enough to what I figgered would hold my horse in. Then I built some sheds, and after I'd get thru "taking the rough" off the little gray and giving him his every-day first saddling, I'd tie him up under the shed and leave him there.

One morning I went out to give the little gray his every-day work-out as usual, when I got quite a jar and surprise. There'd been a heavy rain the night before, and the roof of the shed being considerable leaky, had let in most of the rain that'd fell on it. Consequences was, the gray papier mache horse was a pretty sorry looking sight.

The rain had soaked the glue. His mane and tail had fell off and the outside layer of him, which I called his hide, had peeled and curled and it was just like a fresh-skinned hide. When I pulled him out from under the shed his four feet came out of the little board, and there I was, with not much horse left.

That was quite a jar to me at first, but I found that there was some good even in that sad happening. I found that that little gray horse-hide sure looked good a hanging over my little corral fence, just like the cowhides that'd been throwed over the big corral to dry. Then again the horse looked better with his four feet on the ground instead of on that little board with wheels, and even tho his body didn't look so good no more, I managed to fix him up so he looked pretty near like a horse again. I put his eyes back in, and pinned his

mane on and fixed his tail so it'd stay, and went on to try
and break him to saddle the same as before, till a late spring
snowstorm came along and then he was hopeless. He'd fell
all apart.

But my teaching time had come along about then. Bopy
was giving me more lessons in reading, writing and arithmetic, and, with other things down by the corrals, I didn't miss
the papier mache horse much. Then there was my drawing,
which wasn't neglected either. I never did neglect that for
very long, and during the long winter evenings or when it
was storming too hard to be out, I spent many an hour making things on my tablet with my pencil. Most of my drawings was of horses, about four out of every five. I'd draw
them running, standing, and bucking, and from all angles,
most of the time with a cowboy a setting on top of 'em and
with a rope in his hand, then maybe a few cattle somewhere
around. From the start, I always liked to draw something
with a little story in it. It always made it more interesting
for me to draw while trying to put that story over.

When I drawed a horse I'd a lot of times stick in a bear or
a wolf for him to spook up at or run away from. I knowed
even then that horses didn't like them animals. Or I'd have
horses or cattle drifting with the storm and maybe a rider
alongside, like I'd once in a while seen that winter.

I kept most of the drawings which I thought was good at
the time I made 'em. They'd be shabby at the edges and
wrinkled from being packed, and sometimes I'd sure surprise myself at seeing the improvement I'd made from the
earlier to the later ones. I'd laugh at the old ones and show
'em to Bopy, who agreed with me that the new ones was
better. Then I'd tear up the most of the old ones.

My edducation, my drawing, my roping and riding had
improved a considerable by the time the range was bare of

snow and grass was tall enough to keep our horses in shape while traveling. Then, as usual, Bopy took down the paniers, tied on the pack and away we went. As Bopy promised me, we went to the ranch first and stayed there a few days. The boss was more than pleased with the catch Bopy had made during the winter and he seen to it himself that the paniers was filled with all we would ever need for a long trip, and then some. It's a wonder the pack horse stood up under the load for the first two weeks.

Them few days at the big ranch was more than enjoyed by me. I'd be handed a gentle little horse every day, always a new one, and it was hard for any of the cowboys to leave me behind on any short ride. I think I had just as much fun with them as they did with me, and that's sure saying a lot. If, while bringing in some cattle or horses, an animal broke out, I was always hollered at to "head 'er off, cowboy" and most of the time I could do that, when they wasn't too wild. I'd work with the boys at the chutes and in the corrals and I don't know how much in the way I was. None ever said, and I'd often hear one tell Bopy how I was sure making quite a hand of myself. Wether that was true or not, I'd feel mighty pleased and proud.

There's no use saying that I hated to leave that ranch. I hated to more than I can tell, and maybe I showed it so that the foreman thought something ought to be done about it. He grabbed me by the back of the neck, took me to the corrals with him, waved his hand towards the many saddle horses that was in one of the pens and told me to take my pick. There was some fine horses in there and I wish I had the chance to take my pick out of such a bunch again. But that time I pointed out a little gray horse, he reminded me some of the toy horse I had that winter. The foreman looked where I was pointing, then laughed and shook his head, remarking that I was pretty poor at picking out a good horse. Then he took down his rope, made a loop, and dabbed it onto a fat little sorrel with white mane and tail. I hadn't seen him amongst all them other horses and he was sure a surprise and picture to look at as he was led out to me. He was even prettier than my little black and, as I found out afterwards, just as quick and fast and gentle. I was sure well mounted from that day on.

My interest in running my fingers thru the white mane of that little sorrel horse, done a lot to keep me from looking back as we left the ranch, and after we got out a few days I settled right down to looking ahead again and wondering what was on the other side of every ridge and mountain. We passed many ranches, but from a distance, and none looked near as big as the spread we started out from. I think I kind of snickered as I sized 'em up 'cause, to me, they was pretty small potatoes as compared to the big ranch where we wintered. And, right then, I felt like I belonged to that outfit.

It was many years later, and while drifting thru, that I came back to the same outfit. That is, I think it was the same. It had the same lay and all, but there wasn't one of the boys or foremans I recognized and none remembered Bopy and the little boy that had been with him, me.

Me and Bopy had drifted on north that summer. The reason I know it was north is because the sun was always at my right as we started out in the morning. Then again, as I remember now, the mountains got to be more often and bigger, taller timber, more grass and water, and less sage. We must of been following along the Rockies.

When fall set in that year we had passed many tall ranges and we was again on flat and rolling country. We must have went east of the Rockies some but we didn't get very far away from them because, with the morning sun, I could also always see them to my left.

Along with his ore picking, Bopy also found himself talking "cow language" quite a bit that summer on the way north because there wasn't a cow camp nowheres which we spotted that I would allow him to pass without a beller from me. I always wanted to get to that camp and mix in.

That's why, maybe, Bopy picked on another cow camp to trap from that winter. I wasn't interested no more in bear, beaver nor cayote, nor any animal that's trapped. I wanted to see a cowboy stretch his rope on a range-steer or watch him take the rough off a bronk. Bopy got the same proposition as he had the winter before, from another big cow outfit. Grub and traps was furnished us again, only it was better for me that winter, because we was in a cow camp that was *being used*. Three riders was there all the time and, like a kid, I kind of forgot Bopy and took to the cowboys more, . . . they was faster.

CHAPTER FIVE

MY eighth winter passed like one great happy day. There was no nights in it for it seemed like I'd no more than close my eyes after each day's hard play, when I'd hear the coffee grinder and look up to see Bopy turning the crank. Bopy was always the first one up. The cowboys and me could take on more sleep than he could, but after the old coffee grinder was heard we all would jump out, wash and pitch in to spread out the first meal of the day.

Many a kick I got in the rear for being in the way that winter. Not only while in the house, but I'd get 'em when I was down at the corrals too. But with every one of them kicks there'd be a laugh mingling with the ring of the spur rowel, and some remark like "drag yourself out, Pistol. . . ." Lots of times I'd get a kick when I wasn't at all in the way. My hair would be pulled and I'd be drug around the corrals by the seat of my pants. I'd get peeved sometimes and tackle one of them wiry bowlegs, but that was just the same as bumping up against a pine tree. Once in a while one of the cowboys would *let* me throw him but he wouldn't be down for long, because I'd be scattering corral dirt all over him.

I had a lot of fun that winter and I was treated rough. I was dared to ride big husky calves and colts and there wasn't a day passed when I wasn't bucked off at least once. If I piled off too often I'd get another kick and the cowboys would talk amongst themselves, loud enough so I could hear, and say, "We'd better kill him, he'll never be a cowboy."

I used to take that to heart and the result would be, when I'd make a better ride that "they had hopes for me and maybe I would be a cowboy yet." That sure used to please me.

What used to give the cowboys a lot of pleasure is that I was so sensitive to what they said. They took a lot of delight in stirring me up and get after me if I didn't do a thing just right, and they'd have a lot of fun in seeing me get peeved and trying to do better. I got no compliments from them but when one or two of 'em was alongside of me and throwed a paw on my shoulder, that meant a heap more than all the words in the world.

From what I've seen of how most kids are treated since, I guess many folks would of thought, seeing how the cowboys handled me, that I was being framed to a fast death, but that sure wasn't it. Them boys knowed what they was doing. They didn't see nothing soft about me and they noticed that if I did buck off I wouldn't get hurt easy, and there was no whining. Instead I asked as to where my critter went and I'd climb on some more. If my elbows or shins or nose was skinned I'd pass that off and say it was "nothing." Not that I wanted to play tough but I knowed then that no cowboy, that is one, ever whined.

The boys noticed how sensitive I was as to that and, if I

lost some skin on the side of the corral somehow they'd say, "poor little boy." That would make me peeved and then I'd catch 'em grinning at one another.

I remember many times how old Bopy used to ride in from his traps and see me with all my clothes about tore off. He'd try to head the boys off in being so wild-like with me, and tell me to come along with him for a spell. But the boys would just laugh a bit and I wouldn't go along, and when I'd hear them telling Bopy not to worry, that I was getting to be a sure enough cowboy and all, why old Bopy would just grin too and hit for the house.

Bopy knowed the cowboy breed. He knowed that any one of them would of broke their necks rather than have me bruise a little toe. They was rough maybe, but they savvied as to how rough they could be, and when I picked on a tough calf or pony there was no time when they wasn't worried as to how I'd come thru. They had a pride in me to see me come thru, the same as Bopy had a pride in me in seeing me do whatever I did, and they wouldn't allowed to be disappointed. I don't think I disappointed 'em.

Little boys are mighty scarce in trappers' and cowboys' lives. They might of treated me a little rough at times, but to them I was just like a gift from Above. . . . I can understand that now myself because I've touched some little paws and cheeks of little fellers. I've watched 'em get peeved when my punch was a little too stiff and they reminded me of myself when I was drug around some.

Me and Bopy and the cowboys was all a big family. We all picked on one another and when spring come I couldn't understand why we all shouldn't go together, to wherever we was going. The boys sort of grinned at that, but at the same time, and with their grins, I'm pretty sure of some quivers running along the frost-bitten cheeks of them cowboys as

Bopy and me lined out early that spring. I don't remember of being very happy either.

But, as a kid does, I soon forgot things and it wasn't but a few days later when with new country every day, I kept a looking ahead as usual, a wondering what next would come up. But, right to this day I sure remember them boys. I forgot their names and the name of the outfit they was riding for, but I sure have a memory picture of them.

Bopy and me kept a drifting on north that summer. The morning sun kept a hitting us on the right and come a time when there was no more tall mountains on our left for the morning sun to reflect on. We'd left 'em away off to one side. We was headed north and east, mostly north.

One day, in our drifting, Bopy stops the outfit by an iron post a standing all by itself on a ridge. He steps off the wagon and I steps off my horse and we gather by that post. It was the dividing mark between U. S. A. and Canada. Bopy points to the south from that post and waves an arm and says, "C'est ton pays, mon enfant" (that's your country, my child). Then he waved to the north and said as to how that was *his*. But as I understood him say then, he wasn't so free in that country and that I'd have to be careful not to mention the name of Jean Beaupré from now on. I didn't savvy what he meant but I understood. (Savvying means more than understanding.) Anyway there was no danger of me mentioning the name of Jean Beaupré, because I could hardly ever remember that name and I never called him by any other than Bopy.

As I found out later, and from Bopy himself, the reason he was so careful of the name Beaupré not being scattered from that iron post on north, he was wanted up there for some things he'd done years before, some mixups he'd got into. He didn't come out and tell me of any killings, but whatever it was he was wanted for, sure must of been serious because the authorities sure wouldn't been still looking for him if them mixups had just been plain fights.

He said the happenings had been along with the time when he first met my dad, when my dad had come North with one of the herds, and quite a few years before I was born. Bopy only hinted, but I got the drift that my dad had been in them mixups too, whatever they was, and that it was thru them that the two got so thick, for some things one might have done for the other when things got hot.

My dad's name had been cleared but Bopy's had been marked down and he'd been hunted. But knowing Bopy as I did, the squareness and principles of him, I know that whatever he done which might of been against the law, sure was something he couldn't help doing, or where he figured he was in the right. Bopy's laws was like his religion, they was of his own making.

But, as Bopy used to tell me, whether you make your own laws, or follow them that's on the books, nobody can't tell when you get mixed up in the thick of trouble sometimes and have sudden happenings make you a hunted outlaw.

If Bopy was afraid of being caught for what he'd done he never showed it much. Of course he sure didn't advertise himself, he was careful and done all he could to be seen as little as possible. Like for instance, when we run out of grub and we seen a town in the distance he'd always wait till dark before going in that town to get a supply. Then again he'd dodge all ranches, also duck out of sight of every rider he seen, if he had the chance. But there was times when he couldn't duck without throwing suspicion, then he'd ride up bold, say Howdy and go on. He'd look back often and for a long ways after passing a rider, specially if that rider was a "Mountie."

He used to tell me that about the only thing he could be recognized by was his talk, his mixture of French and English. As for his looks, he'd disguised that. It sure was a good disguise too, and I'll never forget it. All he had to do after he crossed the border was to shave off that mop of red-brown whiskers of his. That seemed to change him from head to foot and even his talk seemed to sound different. I used to stare at him like he was a plum stranger and sometimes I'd laugh. He'd laugh too at the look I'd have on my face.

He'd tell me that it always pays to keep a good disguise in mind in case a feller got in trouble, and another thing, to take on a new name with every new country while drifting around, whether you get in trouble or not, because then, if you do get in trouble more than once, it would be hard to trace you back and connect you with the other. Besides, he'd say, while you're drifting around and not doing no perticular good to your right name there's no use packing it. Save it till the time comes when you're settled and when you can make it sound like something besides just a name.

That advice was pounded into me pretty strong and, believing as I did in all that Bopy said, I followed that advice for many years after I lost him, or till I thought there was no more use of me doing that. I was glad I changed my name a few times, but sometimes that got sort of confusing. I'd be riding for some strange outfit and somebody would holler at me by the new name I'd just given and I wouldn't even turn my head or answer. I wasn't used to the new name yet and I'd forget. Some thought I was deaf, others got suspicious, and then I'd often answer when somebody else's name was called which wasn't supposed to be mine at all. That didn't look right either.

Quite a few times, when I'd be signing a bill of sale or something, I come near writing another name than the one

I'd just given. That wouldn't of looked so good for me if I had, and it would of been hard to explain that mistake.

So, with all of that, and soon as I thought I would behave myself, I begin to use one name for good. I hadn't settled down as yet and I didn't see where that name would shine so much, but I was getting tired of jumping up and answering to the name of Bill while I'd be using some other name.

I used to wonder why would Bopy take the chance of going into a country where he was wanted and liable to get caught when he could just as well stayed south of the line where he was a lot safer, and one day he told me. It was that the trapping was so much better to the north, and besides, the strip where he was taking any chance of being caught much was only a few hundred miles wide. Once he got into the north woods and in his trapping territory, he felt safe again.

"And there's not much danger now," he'd say. "Them trubbles he come long tam ago."

Bopy didn't get to do no prospecting on his way north that summer. It wasn't a country of minerals, and no ledges nor diggings showed anywhere. For the most part, all excepting where creeks and rivers had washed a way thru, the country was as level as a floor. Long miles of grassy prairie with nothing ever in sight but bunches of cattle and horses grazing along. There was lots of antelope and we'd see bunches of 'em every day.

I liked that country. I liked the stretches there and the quiet. Not that I could appreciate that then but I know now that's why I liked it. Timber and mountain country always made me feel sort of closed in some, and even tho the high rough peaks are mighty pretty and great, I liked the far away stretches of the prairie more. The sameness didn't bother me none because I liked it for what it was and I didn't want no change. To me there's no place like open prairie to see a sunset or sunrise from. The grass would turn to all shades, the prairie birds would be a humming all around and the nicker of a horse or the beller of a cow could be heard for miles.

It was while crossing them prairies that I seen my first train. We was a couple of miles from it as it went by. When I looked at it wondering, Bopy told me that it was a string of long wagons with iron wheels that rode on steel rail, that them wagons was all pulled by one big black steel horse which went as fast as any of our horses could go and keep that gait up for days and nights. He said people rode behind that steel horse and in them wagons when they wanted to go a long long ways away.

I sat on my horse and watched the train disappear over the sky line and till I could see no more of it but the smoke. Then I remarked, "It went over the hill." But there was no hill, Bopy told me, it was as level where the train was as where we was, only that the earth was round, like a big ball, and that the train was just going around it. It took a long time for Bopy to explain to me how it was that the train wouldn't be falling off the earth when it got further on and started going down the side of the big ball.

We moseyed along pretty slow thru that prairie country, and whenever we come to some good creek or river we'd camp for days at the time. We didn't see but very few people, the few we seen was mostly riders, bull-whackers and freighters. When we got further north and where the timber started again, we begin to see ox trains off and on, strings of ten and fifteen oxen, each one hooked single to a cart filled with supplies for out-of-the-way settlements. Some of them supplies was hauled acrost country for hundreds of miles and each ox train would have a couple of men who

We begin to see ox trains off and on.

herded the oxen in file along the trail. Some freighters had
bull teams, three or four teams to two or three wagons fastened together. Bull and ox teams averaged from fifteen to
twenty miles a day. Then there was long strings of horse
teams too and when the skinner and bull-whacker happened
to camp close by one another there was many discussions as
to which teams was the best. The bull-whacker had no use
for horses and the skinner had no use for bulls, but both
kinds of teams sure had their merits. The horse teams could
make more mileage in a day, but when it come to a bad place
acrost some creek the bull team was more sure of pulling
acrost. In boggy places I've often seen two bulls outpull four
good horses.

We'd drifted on north, covered quite a scope of country
and it was middle summer when we got into rolling timber
land. Then it begin to get rocky and rough and a poor country for horses. It got worse and worse, more swamps and
underbrush and rocks, and Bopy would often get off his
horse and walk. As for me, I'd stay on my horse till I'd *just
have* to get off. I didn't remember seeing the cowboys get off
their horses for any kind of country, and felt like it was
sure a disgrace for me to get off too, because I thought that
if there ever was a cowboy I sure enough was one. I'd even
laugh at Bopy for walking sometimes. Bopy would just
shake his head and grin back.

One day we run into a well used road cutting acrost the
forest and we begin to pass teams and wagons going and
coming. We made camp by a little lake that night and the
next morning Bopy shaved again. Then he put on a clean
shirt and clean pants, and he told me to change my outfit
too. It was noon that day when, in a big clearing, we run
into a town of log and frame houses. The sight of that town
was sure some surprise to me and I was more than tickled

when Bopy headed on right for the centre of it. I set my horse tight and wished for about a dozen eyes so I could take on the sights. It was the first town I'd seen that had people in it.

As I remember the town now it must of been about three hundred size and there might of been about fifty people in sight all along the wide street, but it looked to me then like there was thousands. We passed a few store windows and that sure got my eye, but what got my eye the most was when I spotted two little boys about my size and a playing at the back end of a wagon.

I'd never figgered there was little people like me, all I'd ever seen was big people like my dad, Bopy and the cowboys. The boys jabbered at me as I rode by, and stared too, but they wasn't staring at me, they was staring at my horse and outfit. They'd never seen such an outfit before.

This town and country was away to the north of the range land. Cattle was few there and what few there was was close to the town and kept under fence and put in some stable in the winter. It wasn't a cow country, too cold and too much snow and timber. No cowboys ever came there and nobody ever hardly rode. When they did, it was on some work-horse and bareback.

That's how come the kids was so curious about mine and Bopy's outfit, but I don't think they was near as curious about our outfits as I was about them. They came along and followed us. Pretty soon they run acrost some other kids, and then one little one that was dressed just like I remembered Mommy dressing. Of the half dozen kids that gathered, that one with the ˜kirts drawed most of my attention. It was the first girl I'd ever seen.

They all trailed along with us till we got to the other end of town. We found a small livery stable there and Bopy begin to unpack and put the outfit away. Bopy and the stable man knowed one another, and while the unpacking and taking care of the horses was going on I edged out to the stable door and looked for kids. They was standing out a ways all in a bunch and jabbering for all they was worth. When they seen me in the door the jabbering stopped and they was sure sizing me up.

I was keeping my eye on that little one with the dress and the long black hair. I'd liked to knowed more about them little people and specially that one, but, so far, I hadn't had the chance to ask Bopy. Finally the biggest one of the bunch started edging towards me. The others followed along, and when they got close enough they all begin to show their teeth in grins. Then the biggest one spoke, but I could hardly understand him, and when I spoke back he could hardly understand me.

Well, the first crack was made anyway and most likely we'd sure been understanding one another before long only Bopy came out of the stable and I had to leave them to follow him along. Bopy told me afterwards that them kids spoke more Indian than they did French.

There was lots of Indians north of there. They'd trap and hunt and fish for a living, and most of 'em stayed around the big lakes. About everybody in the town spoke mixed French and Indian. And the biggest part of 'em was traders, trappers and freighters.

Bopy and me went around town to a trader's post. It was the first store I'd ever been into, and while Bopy went to buying supplies, I was sure busy looking around at all the strange things. While I was looking around somebody handed me a long striped stick and I didn't know what to do with it. I looked at the stick, then at the person who handed it to me, and when that person seen that I didn't know what it was, I was told to lick it. I did, and with that sweet tasting stick and my interest for all that was around, I don't think I could of had more use for my senses. I seen some more little people too and I let one suck on my stick for a spell.

Bopy and me stayed in town that night. We stayed in a real hotel, it was a two floor building and made of logs. It struck me mighty stuffy in there after being so used of sleeping outside, and I didn't sleep well. Besides I wanted to be out and looking around, I wanted to see some more of the little people.

We was out early the next morning and after breakfast at a regular table, we hit out for the stable. The street was deserted and I didn't get to see no more little folks. We got to the stable and there I received a shock. All our pack outfit, grub and all, was in a wagon, all but the pack saddles, and I looked out to see our horses in a pasture, then Bopy tells me the news.

He told me that from now on I'm not a cowboy no more, that I was to ride in a wagon drove by a freighter and that all our horses would be left behind for the winter. Bopy tried to grin and say that in a joking way but it sure didn't go well with me. I sure hated to leave my outfit. Poor Bopy done his best to explain why that had to be. He said that the snow would be too deep for horses where we was going, that no horse could live there thru the winter. The stable man would take good care of 'em and we would have them again soon as spring come.

I couldn't even take my rope along, for, as Bopy said, every ounce of weight will sure count when we get to where the team and wagon can go no further. We'd still have to go a couple of hundred miles after that. I also had to take off the boots which Bopy had got me that spring and put on a heavy pair of laced shoes. I sure felt disgraced for good then, for here I was, just like anybody else and not a cowboy no more.

What got to worry me a whole lot, being I wouldn't be riding that whole winter, is that I'd get knockkneed again like I was when I was smaller. I had a little tin-type picture with me which was taken while I was about four and when I was with Mommy and Lem at the ranch. I was round and fat in that picture and my knocknees wouldn't at all let me touch my ankles together. Now I was tall and slim and there was a nice bow started in my legs. I kept a standing up often that winter and putting my ankles together to see if the bow was coming out.

As we started out of town I hid down in the bottom of the wagon so none of the kids would see me in such a disgraceful way and I didn't come up for air till we was well out. When I'd see anybody coming along the road I'd duck some more. But I didn't have to keep that up for long, the next day after we left town we didn't see another soul. We traveled many many days after that, following a rough road that wound around thru solid forest. We crossed swamps where the road had been bedded over with a thick layer of branches and limbs, and went over some parts where, on account of steep drops off rocky points, it took us half a day to make half a mile.

The country was pretty, the trees had been touched by the first frosts and they was all colors, but I didn't like it nowheres like the range land we'd left to the south. This was no cow country, poor place to be a horseback in, there was no ranches and no riders, and a man had to turn pack horse.

We got to the end of the wagon road. There was no going any further from there, not with a wagon, rocky rough country and brush and timber had been making going mighty hard on the last few days, and now we'd come to where only such as what a mountain goat would call home-like.

We unloaded the wagon, stacked up our gathering and the next morning the freighter pulled out. I was glad to see that wagon go, it always struck me as awkward and even being afoot was better than having to ride in it. I could at least play horse when I was afoot, anyway, and rein myself around and shy at things, and from there on I had plenty of chance to play horse, pack horse.

Bopy made two packs, one for him and one for me. Mine sure looked small as compared to his, and I tried to add on more but Bopy wouldn't let me, he said it'd be plenty heavy enough by the time sundown come.

We only could take about half of our stuff, the other half was rolled up in heavy canvas and hauled up a tree. Then we slipped on our packs and started. Both our packs was tied in a long narrow bundle which stuck up above our heads, and it was held on by a wide leather strip which rested on the forehead. The weight was on the neck and between the shoulders.

I don't know how much I packed on the first trip, I don't think any more than fifteen pounds, and I found that Bopy had been right when he said it'd get plenty heavy enough by sundown. Far as that goes, it got heavy enough by noon, and when we finally made camp that evening and I took the pack off, I felt like my head would shoot up and leave my shoulders, from the sudden relief of the load.

I think that with my feelings for the horse, and playing I was one of them under a pack, had a lot to do with me bearing up on that first trip. I played pack horse with the same feeling as I had when I used to tie myself to a post and turn tail to the storm like I'd seen saddle horses do, and when I got tired following Bopy, I imagined I was one of our own pack horses that used to keep going when they was tired too. But I wasn't shying at things when Bopy decided to make camp that evening.

Bopy would look back at me often to see how I was making out and I'd grin at him. I think I surprised him on that first trip because he told me after we was camped that I didn't have to take that pack all the way. I could of left it and picked it up on the next trip but he'd wanted to see how far I'd carry it. We'd covered close to fifteen miles of mighty rough country that day.

I sure had some stiff neck the next morning, and not only the neck but my whole spine plum down to my tail bone, not mentioning my legs and shoulders. I found that out sudden when Bopy called me to breakfast. I'd jerked my head up at his call and that's one time I sure answered him back with a squawk. My muscles felt like they'd been jabbed thru with thorns.

Bopy sort of grinned at me and I tried to grin back, but I couldn't do that just then. It took me a few minutes to crawl out of the blankets and I was sure careful not to turn my head in any way. But after I washed a bit and got something warm under my belt I felt a little better, and I finally returned the grin Bopy had given me when I first woke up. I thought it was funny to have a stiff neck but it didn't strike me so funny to have them other parts of me stiff too.

Bopy thought some of leaving me in camp that day and go back after the rest of the stuff alone, but he knowed he couldn't make the trip in one day. So, after talking things over with me, if I wanted to go with him and so on, it was decided that I would go. There was one cheerful thing about going back, I wouldn't have nothing to pack.

We left late that morning, after I got some of the stiffness out of me, and we traveled slow and easy. When we got to the other camp the stiffness was pretty well out of my body, but my neck kept a reminding me that it sure wasn't to be used like it was on a pivot.

I took on a light pack the next morning, don't think it weighed over five pounds, and Bopy eased the band on my forehead. I sure flinched under that weight and I wasn't thinking of the pack horse I imagined I was at first. But, as Bopy thought, that little weight was just the thing to take some of the stiffness out of my neck. And sure enough, it was about gone by noon, . . . and stiff again the next morning.

But we had all our belongings together again now and there wouldn't be no more packing for a spell. We was along a river and we was to travel on that. Bopy hunted up some big dry timbers, cut 'em to good lengths, drug 'em to the shore and laced 'em together there. He made a higher place of light poles for where our grub and blankets was to go and by noon that day we hit out on the water.

The whole proceedings interested me a whole lot, but I didn't like that idea of traveling on water so well. Water always did spook me up. Sometimes we'd come to narrow places where the water took on a lot of speed and riding was rough. Bopy sure had to be on the job with his pole at them places.

I was glad when we pulled ashore for the noon bait, and glad when we did it again that night. I was sort of getting used to the water by the next day, but the day after that it got pretty rough, specially towards evening. We was getting near a big fall, I could hear the waters tumbling from where we was camped that night.

On account of that fall, we left the raft and begin hoofing it with our packs again. We hoofed it for two days, and I done a little better that time. Anyway I was getting used to feeling stiff. We made a half circle out of the rough country along the river and when we came back to it far below the falls, we found the water sort of quiet again. Bopy built another raft and I didn't mind riding on it so much now, just to sort of recuperate. The country on both sides of the river was mighty rocky and rough, and it sure would of made tough traveling for us.

We stayed on the river for quite a few days that time, and till the country on both sides opened up some and got less rough. Then, when the river made a sudden turn, Bopy steered ashore and there we left the raft and the river for good. We hoofed it some more.

CHAPTER SIX

THERE was many long *stiff-neck* days for me after we left the river, and every day I'd slip under my pack again to work out the stiffness I'd got the day before. Finally whether my neck got too stiff or numb to feel, I got so I could turn my head in the mornings without getting hardly any of the stinging pains, and there wouldn't be no stiffness in my body at all. I was just begnnning to get real good when we come to the end of our trail.

I don't know how far north we traveled from the river, we must of went a hundred and fifty miles. The first day after leaving the river Bopy located a place where he usually cached his stuff when coming into that country. It was a place that looked like a big coop, made of very heavy timber wedged together, and strong enough so that even the strongest bear couldn't claw it down in trying to get what was inside. We made two trips from the river to that cache. Bopy put away half of the stuff in there, closed the place tight and, slipping on our packs, we hoofed some more to the north, always north.

After we left the cache the country begin to change some.
It got less rocky and once in a while we'd see little clearings,
and lakes half hid by tall coarse grass and reeds growing all
around the edge. It was at one of them lakes that I seen my
first moose, a big bull. He just stood there, head up, and
stared at us for a spell, then he turned slow and begin stepping high for the timber. It wasn't till he got in there that
he took on any speed, and the way we could tell of that was
by the crashing in the timber. We seen a few bears once in
a while too. Bopy said he'd get some of them later, when he
got rid of his packing.

There was a lot of country we passed where I figgered a
horse could be used easy enough. There'd be long stretches
where the timber wasn't so thick and when I'd see some opening, I'd imagine I was riding one of my ponies acrost there
and heading off something. About then I'd stumble on a
snag and I'd come to life. Or we'd be crossing a muskeg
where only a few inches of sod kept us from bogging down
out of sight. The whole surface would shake for many yards
around us, and with every step we took.

Bopy would remark that it sure wouldn't do to try to ride
a horse acrost such places. I'd come back at him with saying
that a feller could ride *around* them places. That would sure
make you go out of the way often, he would say, and anyway, it would be impossible to get a horse up in this country.
How about the rivers, and the rafts, and the rocky brushy
country between here and the settlement? Then what would
I do with a horse when the snow got eight feet deep, as it
would soon be, and nothing to feed him? He would bring on
many more points to show me how a horse was plum out of
the picture here, but that was most all wasted talk because
I'd hardly listen to it. I missed my horses.

I know that's the one reason why I sort of took a dislike

to that country from the first, there was no horses, nothing but wild animals that had to be shot or caught in a trap and skinned. Everybody walked, nobody was bow-legged, and, if anybody was bow-legged, they wasn't bow-legged right, like a rider would be. They all looked flat-footed and awkard to me.

But, with my dislike of that country, I don't think I made things so that Bopy felt bad about taking me to the North. I'd bust out once in a while and say what I thought, but that wouldn't last long, and it wouldn't happen often, and after I'd get that off my chest I'd be all right again for a long spell.

I was glad when we finally reached the main camp of Bopy's trap line that fall. There was the place that marked the end of our hoofing and packing things. But the main camp was a kind of sorry looking sight when we got there. Bopy hadn't been to it for quite a few winters and, during that spell, time and deep snows had sure layed a heavy hand on it. The roof had caved in, filling the place pretty well up with dirt and raising the dickens with the shelves and everything in general. The door was down, and there was nothing in the window to keep the breezes and snows from blowing in.

But, as Bopy said, he'd sort of expected that, and that is why he'd come North earlier that year, to fix up the place and be all set again before the furs got good enough to start putting out his traps.

The work of straightening up the camp and making it fit to live in again was sort of interesting to me and I done all I could to help. If I did miss going down to the corrals and playing horse as I did at the cow camps to the south, it wasn't for long. Bopy would watch me and soon give me something to do, something that was most always to my liking.

While scraping out the dirt that'd fell in with the roof, and getting out the timbers from under it, Bopy found an extra rifle of his. It was one he had there for use in case anything happened to the one he always carried. The rifle being wrapped in canvas was still in good shape, and after oiling it good, Bopy started to show me how to handle one of them things.

It was one of them muzzle loaders and about a foot taller than me. Bopy took a lot of pains in showing me how to load it. First a little powder was poured down the barrel from the powder horn—Bopy made sure I understood that there should be very little powder, too much would knock me over and maybe hurt me, he said. After the powder a little piece of paper was tamped in with the long stick that was carried under the barrel, then about a dozen bird-shot was poured in, another wad of paper, and the whole thing tamped again. The only thing to do after that was to pull back the hammer and slip a little copper cap on that little thing that stuck up under it. Bopy told me it was best not to put the cap on till I was ready to shoot.

With a lot of instructions and advice and repeatings on all about a gun and the dangerous end of it, I was finally tried out many times, and at last I was told to go ahead and bring home the bacon. "Mais n'oublis pas ce que je t'ai dit" ("but don't forget what I told you"), Bopy said, as a last word.

I remember I was pretty excited when I seen the first thing to shoot at. It was a duck. It was still early enough in the fall for a few to be that far north. I missed that first one, I couldn't hold that long rifle barrel steady enough and there was no tree near the pond for me to rest it on. The next time or so I had better luck, there was the crotch of a tree for me to use and I got my duck, but I near toppled

over backwards as I did. I had put in too much powder in
reloading. I was more careful from then on.

I had a lot of fun with that rifle, even if I didn't see so
much that was worth shooting at. The small animals of that
country was most all the kind that stayed near streams, and
they'd duck under water soon as they heard a leaf rustle or
a twig crack. I don't remember of getting anything but a
glimpse of some of 'em. About all I could get to shoot at was
big white rabbits and ducks and things like that. I seen bear
twice, but Bopy had warned me never to shoot big animals,
to save them for him because I might spoil the fur and so
on. Anyway he had a lot of reasons to give so I wouldn't
ever try to get the big ones. His main reason, as I found out
afterwards, was that as long as I didn't bother the big animals, they wouldn't bother me. He knowed of what might
happen if I stirred up a big healthy bear or moose with a
load of my little bird-shot, and he wanted to make sure I
wouldn't rile 'em up that way.

Bopy had took me around the first time he let me have the
rifle and showed me the line of my reservation, places I
wasn't to pass when I was alone. Back of the cabin was a
rocky ridge, that was the west line. At the point of that
ridge and for the south line was a lake. A creek run into the
lake from the north and that made the east line. There was
no plain north line, so Bopy took his axe and made one by
falling trees along there. My territory was about half a mile
each way.

I don't think Bopy ever worried about me while I was in
there. He knowed that when the man scent was well scattered along in that little territory few animals would ever
come near, and I was doing a good job at scattering that.
I was all over that place hunting and playing, and got so
I knowed every tree and rock in there. I'd go along the creek

and watch the fish, then to the little lake and pole away on
the raft Bopy had made me. I was always toting my long
rifle. . . . If I'd been like most kids and had read the story
of Daniel Boone or of the other pioneer scouts, I might of

On the raft Bopy had made me.

had more fun then. But I don't know, I kind of think Bopy
was just as much of a hero to me as Boone or any other
could be to any kids, because I used to play I was him lots
of times. I'd try to imitate his knowing-how of all things.

That's why maybe my reservation got to feeling a little
small. I'd keep looking on the outside of it and want to explore, and being I was warned never to stray away from my
line, it looked all the more interesting out there. I think I'd
been apt to sneak out now and again if Bopy hadn't threat-
ened with one thing. He'd said that if he ever caught me

outside of my line we wouldn't go back South when spring come and I would never see my horses again.

That was plenty to hold me and make me lose a lot of interest of the outside country. And most likely I'd never forgot that warning or tried to get out if I hadn't shot at a rabbit one day. The rabbit was across the creek and my shot just crippled him. Being all excited, I crossed the creek and followed him a trying to reload at the same time. I followed him for quite a ways and finally I found him, all stretched out and dead.

In following the rabbit I hadn't took no notice of the direction I went, and when I picked him up and turned to come back I natural-like thought I was headed back the same way I came. It wasn't till I'd went a long ways that I realized I was lost. I stopped and looked all around me, but the timber was so thick I couldn't see very far and there was no hill in sight that I could get up onto so I could see further. I walked on faster in the direction I thought was right, but that didn't seem to get me nowhere only into more and more timber. Then as it got dark I begin to get scared, not of the dark nor of being lost because, after all, I was only in a strange country and it was only night coming on. I was well used to that. What really scared me was that Bopy would hunt for me and find out that I'd crossed the line of my territory. *Then I wouldn't get to see my horses no more.*

The thought of that started me to running. My heart was beating fit to bust, I sure didn't want to lose my horses. I was running as fast as I could and still packing the long rifle and rabbit when I was stopped in my tracks sudden. I thought I'd heard a shot. I stood still for a few minutes waiting to hear another. I knowed that if Bopy had missed me he'd send out a couple at least, and I was just giving him time to reload. I was hoping I wouldn't hear no second shot and that the first one was only my imagination because I didn't want Bopy to know that I'd run out, as the punishment for that sure had me worried.

But the first shot hadn't been imagination, because soon I heard another which was plain enough. The jig was up. I'd been discovered running out of my territory, and I sure felt bad. There was only one thing to do now and that was to answer the second shot. I blazed away up in the air, reloaded and started towards where the sound of the second shot had come. It had come from my right and I'd been going south when I should of went west.

I didn't have much heart in going back to camp. Getting lost didn't mean nothing to me but my horses meant everything. I didn't realize then what a fix I'd been in if I hadn't heard them shots, because I was sure lost and I was passing the place at a distance where I'd miss it altogether. It was a bad country to be lost in, specially at that time of the year when heavy snows was due to come most any time. I had on light clothes, no matches and, outside of scattered trapper and Indian camps, the nearest shelter was at least three hundred miles.

It was pitch dark when I come acrost the creek that run by our camp. I followed it up a ways and then I could see the light of a fire thru the trees. Bopy was gone when I got to the fire by the cabin. He was out somewhere looking for me. I heard another shot. I answered, and some time later he showed up.

I didn't feel very proud of myself just that minute and I didn't know what reception I'd get, but I looked up at him and tried to grin as he came in the firelight. Bopy didn't grin and his eyes was bigger than I'd ever seen 'em. He looked at me, my clothes all wet from crossing the creek, then at my rifle against the wall and noticed the rabbit hanging on a peg alongside. To him, that all must of been plain reading and he knowed my story as well as if I had told him.

He didn't say a word to me. Maybe he was afraid of what he'd say once he got started. Instead he left me with a feeling that I didn't do right and went to cook up the evening meal. The feeling stayed with me pretty well till he called me to eat, and I must of showed some of how sorry I was because as Bopy handed me my plate he put his arm around my shoulder and patted me. That made me feel more sorry than ever because I got the hint even then how much I must of worried him.

It took quite a few days before I got up enough nerve to ask him if, after what I done, we would go back South when spring come and see my horses again. In that time not a word was said about me jumping the reservation and I got to worrying, worrying that it was all settled and understood now, and we never would go back South. Finally I asked Bopy if we would. He looked at me very serious-like and for a long time, then he said, "I don't know, Billee. It all depends on how good you can be to make up for what you've done."

That didn't encourage me very much but it gave me some hope, something better than the feeling I had that all was settled and that we would never go back. . . . I sure done my best to *make up* from then on, and the bounderies which Bopy had pointed out to me to stay inside of might just as well been high stone walls. I wouldn't gone acrost that for a thousand rabbits.

The cabin was all fixed and in good shape again. The walls and the whole inside had been cleaned up, the dirt floor well tamped, new heavy ridge logs and pole rafters was hoisted up for the roof, willows and dry grass on top of that

and then a heavy layer of dirt. Bopy said that *that* roof
would never cave in. The logs was chinked and pointed up
with fresh mud and grass mixed, the door was put back in
place on wooden hinges, and the window was fixed again.
For glass, Bopy used a heavy piece of paper which he'd
brought for that purpose. He'd greased it and stretched it
with four sticks that was wedged at each corner. There was
a shutter of split and hewed timber on the outside which
was closed when it stormed. The big fireplace was fixed up
too and got in good working shape. Then there was a lean-
to with an inside door and where dry wood was kept to feed
up that fireplace. Enough wood could be stored away in
there for a week. In that lean-to had been some tanned moose
and caribou hides, a couple of them was spread on the floor,
and, after our bedding was on the bunk, the grub on the
shelves all made of hewed timber, and the new table on all
fours and the fire going in the fireplace, that was, to my way
of thinking, all a feller could want in the way of a home.
. . . It sure was all right.

But we didn't get to enjoy the comforts of that home for
a spell, for the work on it was no more than done when Bopy
said that on the next morning we'd be hitting out for the
cache near the river and get the rest of our stuff. I sort of
welcomed them news because I was all rested up and it'd be
fun to get out of my reservation when I had a right to.

We traveled light on the way to the cache, all Bopy took
was two blankets, a cooked rabbit and duck, salt and tea,
half a dozen pan-size bannocks and a can to heat things up
in. Bopy figgered on getting our meat as we went. We had
no trouble at that because game was more than plenty there,
and fish too. At night we'd both roll up in one blanket apiece
and near the fire. If it got too cold and we had to turn over
too often, so as to heat both sides, we'd just get up and hit out

on our way till we was warmed up again or till we got tired. On account of keeping warm we traveled more at night than we did in daytime, because with the heat of the sun and a fire to boot, we could keep comfortable and sleep a lot better during the day than we could at night. Night traveling was no harder than day traveling, we could see plenty good enough, but I often wondered how Bopy could find his way so well thru hundreds of miles of that country and without ever wandering. To me it looked all alike and there was very few tall landmarks a feller could go by. That was a mystery to me, specially at night. He never even seemed to look where he was going. He didn't use a compass, and, far as I know, I hardly think he ever seen one.

I don't think I took my shoes off during that whole trip, and as far as my other clothes was concerned, such as my coat, my cap and all, they stayed on steady, like my hide. When I was still and sleeping I'd just add on a blanket.

The trip down to the cache and back took us about two weeks, or maybe more. I was pretty well hardened in by the time we got down to the cache, and I took on a pretty good sized pack on the way back. My neck and shoulders stood up good under it too, after the first few days, so good that I asked Bopy for more weight. We was about half way back to our camp when a snowstorm struck us. There was a good stiff wind with it which we had to face, but being we was in the timber most of the time, we got away from the worst of it. But the snow kept a piling up, and from the time the storm struck us we sure didn't linger much. We'd keep on going till we couldn't go no more, then we'd roll up in our blankets and fall asleep. But we slept no longer than we had to because the snow was getting deeper and deeper and we had no snowshoes with us.

We'd sleep and rest for only a couple of hours at the time,

then throw some meat on the coals, boil up some tea, take down all we could and go on some more.

I think Bopy was just as tired as I was when we finally got to the door of our cabin, and I know I sure was tired. Of course he had to pack near ten times the weight I did, and he sure didn't hold back on covering ground during that trip, not on account of me because I came right along. I was pretty well hardened in, long-legged and nine years old going on ten, and I think a kid of that age is hard to leave behind.

But I remember I was mighty glad to get sight of the cabin. It sure felt good to get inside, stomp off the snow and take off the packs, and, after a match was touched to the dry wood that had been already stacked up in the fireplace and the flames shot up, I don't think any castle could of furnished half the meaning to the word *home* that that little cabin could. . . . Bopy thawed the icicles off his new crop of whiskers, then looked at me and grinned. I grinned back. *We savvied.*

The storm kept on for a few more days. In that time, Bopy and me rested up and done nothing much but cook things. On the last day of the storm Bopy went out on his snowshoes. He was gone about two hours and came back with a yearling moose. The next day he made me a pair of snowshoes. They was long and narrow and my interest for some time to come was in learning how to manipulate them things. I took many a fall but I finally got the hang of 'em and I'd get quite a lot of fun at looking back at the tracks I made.

That winter struck me as very different than any winter I'd passed before. I missed daylight thru a glass window, but any window wasn't of no advantage there much because, being so far North, the daylight hours was very few during winter. Of course, the "Northern Lights" made things pretty bright during the night, specially with the snow, but not bright enough so as to make windows of much use in lighting up the inside of the cabin.

Them short days and light nights was one of the things which made that winter sort of strange for me. The shimmering of the "Northern Lights" or the reflections of what some called "The Midnight Sun" always had me guessing, it was something I'd never seen in the country to the South. Then there was the "Sundogs" which was on both sides of the sun in day-time, and, with all them strange lights a shining on a frozen world of deep snow, it didn't make me feel like I was any too much at home.

The only place where I felt at home was inside the cabin. That cabin compared pretty well with the others I'd wintered into, and I really appreciated it more than the others because the country around it didn't strike me so well and I stayed inside most of the time.

When I did go out, it would always have to be on snowshoes. Bopy didn't have to warn me no more to stay inside my reservation, because the snow would be from four to eight feet deep and being that hunting was an old game to me now, I soon lost interest in hoofing it thru timber and more timber and packing a long rifle. I missed a bare knoll and open country. I wanted to see distances and get away from that closed-in feeling. What I missed most was going down to some corral and stables. I missed my horses, touching of their hides and saddling one up and going some place with bridle reins in one hand and a rope in the other, instead of packing a rifle and sticking my feet in snowshoes in the place of stirrups.

So that's why I didn't stay out so much that winter, I'd get homesick. And that's why I stuck pretty well by the cabin, I felt all right there.

I think I drawed more horses during the few winters I was in that Northern country than I ever did before or since. It seemed like drawing 'em brought 'em nearer to me. If I drawed a rump or a back or a neck of a horse it was near like as if I touched them parts, and that had a whole lot to do in keeping me contented. If I drawed a man on horseback throwing a rope, or doing anything, I'd imagine myself in that picture and doing whatever was put down there. I drawed lots of saddles too, and boots and spurs. I'd often draw cattle and, far as that goes, most everything that went with the life of the range rider. Once in a while I'd draw a bear or a wolf or deer and other wild animals, but them I couldn't feel at the tips of my fingers like I did my horses, and I had no special hankering to draw the rump of a bear like I did that of a good pony.

Bopy had managed to bring up a few tablets for me and some pencils, and them was as important to me as all the grub in the house. They fed one part of me while grub fed another. He'd also brought one of them French books. I read that over and over again and the more I read it the more new things I'd find there that I'd never seemed to notice before, specially when Bopy read with me. But Bopy couldn't be much help to me no more and I asked him the meaning of many words which he couldn't give no answer to. Sometimes I'd find out the meaning by reading ahead and back of the word, and when I'd tell Bopy he'd laugh. Old Bopy had come to the end of his string as far as teaching me anything on reading and writing was concerned.

Bopy wasn't with me much that winter, another thing that made that winter different than the others before. He'd be gone three days at the time while covering his trap line. He had two camps on that trap line, each camp was only a shelter of logs with a place in one corner where a fire could be built. The smoke got out between the upper logs. There was a bunk built in each camp. While following his trap line, Bopy would manage to take care of his traps, reset 'em when they needed to be, skin the animal he'd caught while he was on the trail and while they was still warm, and make one of the camps for every night. He'd spend two nights and three days on his trap line, and two nights and one day with me, and that was done as regular as the days came. Few storms ever kept him from making the round because, as he'd say, when an animal is in a trap too long it'll die and freeze, and that makes it tough skinning, and many get away.

I hardly ever went out with Bopy on his trap line, only when I'd begin to get real restless and then one of them trips would do me for quite a spell. That would satisfy me and I'd go back to my drawing, reading and writing. For a lamp I had a canful of tallow and a string of twisted cloth swimming in it. It throwed a pretty good light if I kept the can filled to the top. Sometimes, if it got real cold, I'd stretch out on a hide in front of the fireplace and work there, with my drawing and so on. And when Bopy was gone, there'd be the cooking too. Bopy would most always leave some stew or something already cooked and which would last me for a day or so, but I was getting to be quite a cook by then and I used to mix up what I thought was some great baits. The only drawback was that I had to be mighty saving with everything excepting meat. Flour and things like that, that was heavy to pack, was scarce and not to play with. I was told I could use a certain amount a day and no more. Then there was dried fruit, and dried potatoes which was good medicine against scurvy. Bopy told me how scurvy killed many Indians and some white folks most every winter and how sometimes one little potato could of saved 'em. So I was pretty careful with them dried potatoes, and one a day is all I'd cook. I liked to watch 'em swell up when I'd put 'em in boiling water.

Everything was cooked in a pan, nothing was ever baked as there was no way to do that, and I got to missing the good sourdough bread that Bopy used to make, huckydummy and such like. I missed the coffee too. Coffee was too heavy to pack and, as Bopy said, one pound of it didn't go one quarter as far as one pound of tea and that it wasn't as warming as tea. Nobody packed coffee in the North woods.

Our grub pile was made up of flour, soda, a side of salt pork to season with, dried potatoes and apples, and salt and pepper. That was all. Whatever game we killed was our fresh meat and we never was short of that, and such things as sugar and butter and eggs was sure out of the question. But somehow I never missed them last things much. . . . That's how, with watching Bopy, I learned to cook for myself and make things that was pretty fit to eat without much in the line of tools and grub to spread out with. There was no fancy dishes, but what there was sure filled an empty space, and when the one tin plate was pushed away I felt just as satisfied as if I'd got around one of them seven course dinners which I got acquainted with many years later.

I'd feel pretty tickled when I'd manage to cook up something that turned out real good, specially on the evenings of every third day, and when Bopy would come in about all froze up and with icicles a hanging all the way down from his fur cap to his waist. . . . And when he'd rush near the fire to warm up and smell at the pan of food that was on the coals all ready for him and then grin at me and slap me on the shoulder, why, I felt that what little I'd done had sure turned out big.

Most every day, while Bopy was gone, and during the

daylight hours, I'd strap my snowshoes on my mocassins, take my long rifle and go a hunting, not that I liked to hunt so much but I wanted to have some reason to be out and I'd be wanting a change from moose meat. Big white snowshoe rabbits is about all that was out in small game during winters and I'd once in a while get one. I'd most always have to get out of my territory to get one but I didn't feel like I had to stay inside of my line no more. Besides, the north of that line was buried under many feet of snow and I had the excuse that I didn't know where it was. I couldn't get lost very well because there was always my snowshoe tracks to come back on. Then the bears had all hibernated. I hadn't seen no sign of any, *only once*. . . . It was after a long warm spell, a spell that'd broke that one bear's sleep, and he'd went out a hunting. There was a snowbank alongside the lean-to where we kept the meat and he'd climbed up on that snowbank on top of the cabin. I heard him sniff and paw up there for a long spell. He was sure heavy because even thru that thick roof I could tell exactly where he planted a paw. Then he must of got a whiff of the meat that was in the lean-to because he kept a hanging around there, a climbing up and down and clawing. He'd circle around and sniff, and I got to thinking of the window. I hadn't closed the shutter on it and all he'd have to do would be to stick his nose to the paper and it'd fall apart. I knowed he'd come in then, so as to get to that meat, and I waited for him. I reached for my rifle, not at all realizing that the bird-shot it was loaded with would only aggravate if I did hit him at long distance. Anyway, I waited a spell a hoping he would stick his nose thru that window. But he didn't. Instead, he'd quit his circling and went to tearing at the lean-to like as if he sure enough meant to get to that meat. He made plenty of noise and I got to thinking he wasn't doing the house any good, so I ups and slips on my mocassins, I was all dressed but that, and I opened the door and went out. But I couldn't see him nowheres and all I could get of his where-abouts was sniffs and grunts. The snow was pretty deep and I couldn't get around very fast, but when I got around the lean-to I met him. He looked like a mountain.

I don't think the barrel of my rifle was over a foot from his nose when I pulled the trigger. Bopy had often told me to always stick the barrel away ahead and be ready for work when I really wanted to use it. It was ahead that night, and I pulled the trigger at just a good time. . . .

When Bopy came back two days later and I told him about the bear he grinned at me sort of proud-like and said words that made me feel good, on how I held down the camp and saved the grub. He said that "they was awful pests." But if Bopy was surprised and pleased at me getting up in the middle of the night and chasing the bear away, he was more than surprised when he begin to track him the next day. He hadn't gone over half a mile from camp when he found him stretched out and froze stiff. That little bird-shot at close range had near punctured his head thru.

Bopy had never expected that I killed him and neither did I, but there he was, and when I came up to the answer of Bopy's holler and seen that haired elephant stretched out on the snow I didn't know what to think or say. Bopy said something about a mighty lucky shot and advised me to never try that again with one of them big fellers. He didn't say why right then. But there's one thing Bopy didn't know and that is that I'd got to savvy the old rifle pretty well and I was using twice the amount of bird-shot I'd started out with, and three times the amount of powder. The powder alone would have burned a hole thru him at that close a range.

That bear hide would of covered the whole floor of our cabin. It sure was a nice color too. Bopy cut down some poles to make a stretcher for it. They was long poles.

It wasn't so many days afterwards that I found out things about grizzlies which made me think back of the "lucky shot" on that one night. Bopy and me was going along the trap line when a big dead tree stopped us. Bopy looked it up and down and pawed snow away from the trunk. Then he built a smudge and pretty soon I heard a grunt. It sounded a little like human but what came out in time, pawing his way thru the smoke and snow, sure was all animal and with unholy strength to back it. It didn't stand up only half ways, the front paws was up a bit and sort of dragging along and wanting to reach for something to tear up, something that had disturbed a deserved sleep. Bopy brought up the long barrel of his rifle and, as things happen in life when a feller wants to be most useful, a pile of snow slid down of a tree and landed on the gun. The result was that Bopy just creased the bear and made him mad.

I've read and heard stories of fellers using the stock of their rifle against a full grown grizzly, and the same about using a knife on them, but I've laughed at them stories. . . . It would be sad to see any man use a rifle for a club against a mad thousand pounds of grizzly and worse to see him chest-up against one and try to use a knife, for any man's chest against one of them would amount to about the same as a pill against a bomb the knife would never hurt the bear till too late.

The bear Bopy stirred up out of the dead tree wasn't at all pleased to be smoked out and singed and creased, and when he came out reaching for something to tear up Bopy and me was behind a tree and we was both mighty thankful that the light on the snow blinded him at that time. He tore out thru the timber and then he circled back. By that time Bopy had reloaded, and when he shot again with a heavy ball I seen what chances I'd took that night at trying to get me a bear with light bird-shot. The heavy ball didn't seem to've touched him and Mr. Grizzly was sure looking for the spot where it'd come from, but the snow blinding him kept him from getting straight to us. Instead, he'd bump up against trees and I sure wouldn't liked to had my hide in the place of the bark of them trees no time. Bopy reloaded once more and planted another shot. There was crashes of timber and after a spell all was quiet.

I seen many a Kodiak grizzly during my time in different parts of the North. I see as many as six in a bunch and they'd run away at the sight of me and Bopy, but even tho they would run in the open, I knowed it wouldn't of been so good to bump up in the middle of their trail sudden, and I found out at different times later that sometimes they don't scare well.

Bopy didn't go after bear much, only them that was around camp. A bear hide didn't bring no more money than a marten hide and the bear hide was at least fifty times heavier on a pack than the marten's. Marten, mink, weasel, beaver and fox was Bopy's main catches. Once that winter he brought in a live black fox, just to show him to me. He was pretty pleased with that catch and said he'd get at least two hundred dollars for the fur. After I got thru looking at the fox Bopy tapped him on the bridge of the nose with a stick and then hung him. I don't think the fox ever knowed what happened because he'd never got conscious again. Killing a trapped animal that way keeps the skin from getting bloody, or tore like it would with a shot or blows on the animal's head.

The fur bales kept a piling up in the lean-to. Short winter

days started to get longer and then I begin to notice that
when Bopy came in off his three day's round he brought
traps with him along with his furs. There was remarks about
"hair beginning to slip soon."

I kept on a drawing, writing, reading, cooking, dragging
wood and hunting for changes of meat. Come a time when
Bopy's three day run was cut down to two. That gave me a
hint of spring and I got to thinking of my ponies some
more, wondering now how soon I'd see them. I asked Bopy
about that one day, and I sort of held my breath till he
answered. He finally answered something like this, "Well,
Billee, you can put your pencil away pretty quick because
you'll soon be riding them instead of drawing them." Old
Bopy always had great ways of making me feel good. When
he said them words I just went straight up and hollered and
came down a tackling one of his legs. After I tamed down
some I sat on the floor by that leg and couldn't say a word.

Grub was getting low, mighty low. The potatoes was all
gone and there was nothing much to make a meal out of excepting meat and salt. Bopy had brought in all his traps, his
skins was all baled and ready to ship, and when come one day
of rest and all was ready to go, I got to wondering why we
wasn't starting out. I found out that evening. Four squatty
pig-eyed Indians drifted in on us, about cleaned up on what
grub we had left and stretched out on the floor for that
night.

The next morning, Bopy grunted at 'em, boiled some
tea, fried some moose in bear grease and fed the Indians.
Then he stirred 'em up some more and gave them each
a load the likes of which I'd sure wonder about a good horse
packing. The baled furs was made into packs for two, another got under the traps, and the fourth got under more
traps and other things. Bopy packed the blankets for him

and me. And me, I had nothing to pack but myself and my long rifle.

The whole trip on the way South was like what Christmas is to most kids. I hadn't had no Christmas that winter nor no New Year's present, but knowing that I was to see my ponies and maybe get back amongst folks that's bowlegged from the saddle instead of from walking too young, sure made me as happy on every day of that trip as any kid could be with all Santa Claus might of brought.

The Indians took care of our packs, on water and land. They brought out some dugout and bark canoes which they used often, and all me and Bopy had to do was to see that the Indians kept moving them. I think I was a lot of help there because the long rifle I was holding didn't mean much to me as compared to my rope that was waiting. I was hungry for the strands of that rope, the feel of saddle leather, my boots and spurs, and most of all my ponies.

CHAPTER SEVEN

I WAS at least a mile in the lead when we hit the settlement and Bopy sure knowed where I was headed. He caught up with me at the stable. In one hand I had my rope, in the other my saddle, and at the end of my rope was a horse.

I'd borrowed the horse from the stable man so I could run out to get my own and Bopy's. I was sure aching to see them horses. It was more than great for me to be setting in a saddle again. I rode out of the stable and I wished the old pony I was riding would bogg his head and go to bucking with me, I felt that way.

I'd shed off my mocassins and cap. My boots and spurs and man-hat had took the place of them mighty quick and now, on a horse I was myself again. I loped the old pony out, found the bunch my little black and sorrel was running with, and if I could of been happier at any sight I think I'd of died.

With looking at them, realizing that there'd be a horse under me again, and feeling of the breeze that went past my ears, I think I wasted a lot of time. It was getting dark when I finally hazed the bunch of horses into the corral by the stable. I roped my two ponies and brought 'em in. I forked some hay down and talked to 'em a whole lot while I

filled the mangers. Then I got Bopy's horses in and fed them
the same. I didn't know what Bopy's plans was, but I'd took
it for granted we was going to move, move South and towards the cow country again. I couldn't think of anything
else.

When Bopy asked me where I left my rifle I told him I
didn't know. I had my rope in my hand and I was by my
little black horse. I didn't care about the rifle no more.

We hit out of the settlement the next morning and in a
different way than we'd come into it the fall before. Bopy
had bought a wagon and traded his two pack horses off for
a wagon team. The reason for that was that he'd brought
his traps down and they'd be mean things to pack on horses.
The light wagon took good care of our outfit and with the
big supply of grub Bopy had bought, there was a lot of
work saved from the morning and evening packing on
horses' backs.

Of course Bopy drove the wagon. Me riding in there was
out of the question, and even tho Bopy would laugh at me
while he took it easy on four wheels, his laugh didn't get
by very well because I didn't envy him any, and I sure
wouldn't of traded places with him. On my little black or
sorrel I could run out on the side of the road any time I
wanted, or I could run ahead or stay back. I was free, could
do as I pleased and go as slow or fast as I pleased. I'd laugh
back at Bopy sometimes when I'd ride ahead of the wagon
and look for a good camping place, for he had to stick to a
road a lot where I didn't.

From the settlement we went south a ways, then the trail
was pretty well straight west. We camped at many places,
and for many days at the time at some places, if the water
and grass was good and plenty. It usually was. Bopy didn't
go very far South that summer, he stayed pretty well above

the line of where he'd be apt to be recognized. We struck a
few cow and horse outfits, and at them spreads Bopy would
stick around for a spell. I think that was all for my benefit.
Anyway, I sure made use of them places, and my rope arm
got sort of limbered up with rope and rein instead of with a
long rifle.

I was sure happy to mix in with riders again, getting
kicked around and bucked off, and wether the work was
corral or outside work, I sure done my best to make a hand.
There never was no glad feeling when Bopy would decide to
pull out from any of them outfits, none that I remember of,
and from neither side. But what was ahead and over every
next ridge or mountain would soon make me forget.

I wore out quite a few ropes that summer and near had
the riggin' tore out from my saddle a couple of times. I was
getting wild with that rope. . . . While Bopy set up camp
and went to cooking, it was now my job to unharness the
team, feed 'em grain, and put one of 'em out on the picket
rope. Either horse would stay if the other one was picketed.
It was the same with my two horses, and far as Bopy's saddle horse was concerned he got so used to following our
wagon that he didn't have to be picketed nor hobbled no
time. He never was far away from that wagon when morning come.

That summer's drifting struck me as getting nowheres in
perticular and I sure didn't mind because I was in cow
country most of the time. But Bopy had some place in mind
because even if we did ricoshay around a considerable and
took our time, I noticed that the morning sun was at our
back when we'd start out.

We traveled thru rolling country, sand hills, timber and
prairie, and then more timber. When fall of that year come
we'd left the cow country behind again. There was no pros-

pect lands for Bopy to pick at that summer and I think time
dragged with him some. That's why maybe we got into timber and trapping country a little early the fall of that year.
I hated to see the timber and them big mountains ahead of
us because I knowed what that meant, that I'd soon have to
part with my horses again, and when at the sight of the big
mountains Bopy headed the team North why that sure took
a lot of play out of me.

From the time Bopy turned North I didn't see a cowboy.
We was once more with squatty people that walked, and
packed things on their own backs. I seen more little folks
and got the chance to mix in with them some while going
thru settlements. My horses and outfit sure drawed a heap
of attention from them and the way some followed me
around, a person would of thought I was a whole parade. I
did parade some and showed off as much as any kid could,
specially with my rope. And many a kid took down many a
string and made a loop on one end after I passed.

We came to the last settlement on our trail and there
Bopy drove up to another stable and begin talking back of
old times with another old-timer he knowed. I wasn't listening, and I wasn't trying to cater to no little people about
then. If anything, I think I was looking South and wondering if I could make my getaway. We'd come to the end of
the horse trail and I sure hated to part with my ponies and
what all they meant. I wouldn't minded hoofing it if I could
of seen one of them once in a while, but to be without them
for a whole four or five months sure wasn't what I called
anything pleasant to look forward to.

But it had to be done, and the way I stood up while I
took off my boots and spurs and put on mocassins in the
place of 'em, I don't think Bopy had any hint of how I felt.
I shoved my ponies out to the feed-rack in the corral like

they wasn't anything to me, and I throwed my saddle and
rope in a corner of the store-room of the stable like I was
glad to be done with 'em. I was peeved and hurt, and the
reason I acted up is because I wanted no sympathy. Sympathy at that time would of made me mad. I come near
to a breaking point when Bopy handed me my long rifle.
That meant the end with my rope, my saddle, my horses and
fast breezes.

We mushed on North. I say "mushed on" because from
that settlement we used a dog team. A light snow had fell and
made sledding just right. I pegged along behind the musher
and Bopy, and dragged my long rifle like as if it was a dry
stick. I wasn't interested in it and I'd just as soon throwed
it away. Bopy finally took the rifle away from me and stuck
it in the sled.

Good old Bopy never knowed I wasn't happy because
whenever he'd glance back at me while on the trail I'd grin.
He'd light his pipe and keep on going all peaceful and contented.

But there was one good thing about that one trip North,
there wasn't no pushing of any canoes or rafts and the dog
team took everything we had up to within fifty miles of our
camp for that winter. I don't know how many camps Bopy
had, but, as I remember now, it seems to me like he had a
camp of his own everywhere he went. I wouldn't of been surprised if he'd took a claim on the king's throne and said he'd
built it.

Bopy had camps scattered from the Yellowstone to the
McKenzie. They was all of his own making too. Of course
there was nothing fancy about them, and none of the camps
would take him much over a couple of weeks to build, but
they was *all there* and when we got inside of one, the outside breezes and snows never did hit us. There'd be a few

things in them camps too, things to eat and a few traps and other belongings. I'd look thru them and was always disappointed to never find a spur or an old bit. Broke up snowshoes is about all I'd find in that line.

I wish now I could gather all the traps and things that was in them camps of Bopy's. He must of had at least five hundred traps scattered over three thousand miles of territory. I don't remember of no camp he went to when he didn't have a whole lot of something to start out with, from kindling to grub and traps.

The camp we struck that winter, after only fifty miles of packing, was quite a camp. It had two rooms and was furnished with things that sure wasn't made out of hewed timber. There was a lot of knicknacks sticking around too, and pictures of people, and some books and things. I got to wondering about that gathering a whole lot, and then I found out that this was Bopy's *one* main camp. It was his home and only about a hundred miles south of where he was born and raised. I don't know if his folks was alive at the time, and, outside of him pointing north one day and saying that *there* was the country he drifted from, I got no more inkling as to them.

Bopy's *one* main camp with all that was in it had a whole lot to do with keeping me contented that winter. There was books and blank paper galore. I could read and draw all I pleased and then, to make things nicer, I had a couple of pets to keep me company while Bopy was out on his trap line. Like the winter before, he had a three day circle to make there too.

My two pets was wolves. The musher who'd brought up our stuff had got 'em out of a den that spring and tried to work 'em in with the dog team, but they didn't turn out good as sled dogs and he was going to kill 'em soon as their fur got good. Bopy dickered for 'em and here I was, with two big gray fellers following me around. They was well trained and minded me good because that musher sure knowed wolves. His dog team was at least half wolf, all of 'em. I didn't take to my pets very much at first, but they sure took to me and would have hardly anything to do with Bopy. If they done anything I didn't like I'd kick 'em in the ribs, and all they'd do was whine and lay down and beg for me to quit. It strikes me funny when I think of that, because either one of them wolves would just had to snap at me once and I'd never been able to touch 'em no more. Them gray wolves have powerful jaws and when they stood up on each side of me their withers wasn't so far below my shoulders.

I know of one time when Bopy got peeved at something them wolves had done. He'd hunted 'em up and begin to work on 'em. I came along just about when Bopy would soon been getting the worst of it. He'd got himself a limb off a tree, but it was breaking. Little me ran in and busted up the fight. I kicked each wolf in the jaw and they hunted for a hole like as if a ghost was after 'em. Bopy looked at me sort of funny and then he grinned. I had all the handling of them wolves after that.

But kicks wasn't all that them wolves got from me. The three of us had a lot of fun together. We'd go a hunting, me with my long rifle and them with their speed and killing power. Sometimes they'd leave me and be gone for hours. They'd be chasing something and come back all ganted up. In that time I'd killed some meat for 'em, and lots of times they'd catch up with me while I was skinning whatever I killed. They'd crowd around me, their long red tongues a hanging, but they never tried to reach for what I had because they knowed that all they'd get from me then would be a smack on their long nose. So they waited till I got ready and sort of back up against me while waiting. That was their way of hurrying me. A wolf never shows no affection,—he never licks at a person's face and hands like a dog would and he never wags his tail. The most he does in

Them wolves was a lot of company to me that winter.

that way is lay his ears back and show a grin and somehow try to look pleasant in that way, like a wolf.

Them wolves was a lot of company to me that winter. They'd lay by me while I drawed and read and I'd never make a move but what they did too. If I jumped up sudden, they'd jump up too, and bristle up and look at the door of the cabin, and growl. They'd sure look mean at them times and it wouldn't been so good for anybody to open that door unless they was ready to shoot right quick. Bopy realized that, and he never came in from his trap lines like he used to. He'd whistle a bit first and after he thought I got thru talking to them wolves he'd ease in, and the tone of his voice as he spoke to me had all to do with his welcome. They never got used to him because he'd be gone too long at the time.

Of course Bopy could of made away with them wolves mighty quick, but seeing how they was so much company to me, how they followed me around and partnered with me so well, he figgered they was sure worth having around, even if he did have to whistle a bit before drifting into camp and watch his step after he got inside. . . . Them wolves was mighty ferocious but Bopy knowed that I was the last person they'd ever show a fang to.

Between drawing spells and after I was done with my cooking and dragging in wood, I'd go out and hunt for them gray fellers. I'd fill 'em up sometimes till they looked like they was poisoned. Then they'd be satisfied for a day or two. Bopy would laugh when he'd see me and the two wolves all stretched out in front of the fireplace. I'd be drawing while one wolf's head was resting on my leg and the other on my neck. They'd growl at Bopy but was too contented to get up, sometimes.

I didn't care so much for them wolves, maybe that's why they liked me. I'd kick 'em off and they'd come right back. I'd be drawing horses about then, as usual, and wolf skin wasn't what horse hide meant to me.

Sometimes I'd play that them wolves *was* horses. I'd ride 'em, put hackamores on 'em, and even tried to make pack horses out of 'em. I'd tail one to the other but they never worked well, they'd slip their packs or else pull out of the hackamore. I'd braided me a four strand rope out of moose

hide and I'd throw a loop at 'em once in a while. They soon
got wise to that loop and made themselves hard to catch
when they'd see me spread out one.

With that kind of play to hold me I don't think I missed
my horses as much that winter as I did the winter before.
The wolves had a lot to do with that. They kept me hunting to feed 'em, and another thing, I wasn't held down to no
perticular territory. Bopy knowed that the wolves would
scare out most any other varmint that was apt to hang
around and so I was free to go anywhere I pleased with
'em. But, with all them privileges and company I often
thought of my little black and sorrel when I throwed my
moose-hide rope, and I'd have to draw them once in a while
to keep from being too lonely for 'em.

I seen a couple of herds of caribou that winter. They was
drifting South. I also seen plenty of moose and a few deer,
but I never shot at any of 'em because I'd got to know that
bird-shot didn't carry far enough. I seen one big bear that
winter too, a big Kodiak. My wolves made him back up
against a rocky bank and I took a lot of interest in watching and wondering what would happen. Nothing happened
because after the bear made his stand and sized up what was
likely, he just got down on all fours again and went on
about his business. He'd just look back once in a while and
sort of snort at my wolves, but I noticed he kept on a going
just the same and that might of saved me from doing the
foolish thing of taking a shot at him.

The winter wore on and about February time came along,
time for shipping furs. Bopy was beginning to pick up his
traps once more. Moose and caribou was drifting North,
and one night a pack of wolves went by on their trail. My
two wolves was full size by then. They stood up at the
drawed out howl of one of their kind and begin to talk back

in the same language. They was restless and was figgering on a way out, but I held 'em down that night. . . . It wasn't many nights later, I was sound asleep when I heard something tear. It was the paper on the window. My two wolves had jumped up on my bed and went out.

I listened and a few seconds later I heard the mournful holler of a wolf pack. I knowed then what had happened. . . . I jumped up, slipped on my long coat and mocassins and went out the same way my wolves went. I had my rifle with me and a good stock of powder and ball. I wasn't using bird-shot that time because I finally got to find where Bopy had his heavy lead and I'd sure took on a load. I was going to get my wolves back.

God helps the children and the ignorant. I followed the snarling pack of wolves till I couldn't hear 'em no more. Then, by the night sun, I tracked 'em. I snowshoed and cried and snowshoed and cried some more. I cried because I was peeved to think that Gros and Otay could have left me. I was so peeved at that thought that I'd most likely took a shot at 'em. But, lucky for me the pack didn't turn. . . . I didn't see my wolves. They had gone with the wild bunch.

It was well along towards sun-up when I dragged my long rifle back into camp, tears was froze all along my parka and plum down to my mocassins. Bopy, all eyes and worried, opened the door. He knowed what had happened and he spoke soft as he pulled off my cap, unbuttoned my coat and brought me near the fire. "Tout est bien, mon enfant," he'd said (all is well, my child). He slapped me on the shoulder and looked down at me and grinned. "Tu vas avoir tes chevaux bien vite maintenant" (you're going to have your horses pretty soon now.)

Them words made me perk up a considerable, and it wasn't long when I begin to ask Bopy questions as to when and how quick that would be. Bopy said "bien vite" (pretty soon) and I was put to bed on that. But I was still hurt, Gros and Otay shouldn't of left me the way they did. I went to sleep on that.

I woke up in bad humor the next morning. I was kicking things around from the time I got up and when Bopy sort of called me on my actions I went out with my long rifle. I tracked my wolves some more, but there was no use, and by the time I doubled back I think I'd shot them on sight for running off the way they had. . . . I never seen 'em no more.

True to Bopy's word, we soon drifted South again, and that was good. A squatty musher came to our camp, loaded the furs and bedding and turned his dog team down country. The sight of them dogs, half wolf, made me mad but I soon forgot them in thinking I'd be having my ponies now.

On account of the snows still covering the ground at that time of the year, Bopy and me had no packing to do, none at all. The dogs took all the pelts and bedding with the sled and I didn't even pack my long rifle.

Bopy didn't take no traps with him when he left camp that time. From that I got the hint that we'd be back there along about fall again. Well, that suited me as much as it could. There was no way around that, and I got a heap of consolation in thinking of what a good summer was ahead.

We struck no cow country to speak of that summer, nothing but swampy meadows and high mountains, but I didn't mind so much. It was sure pretty country and I didn't have to walk. My ponies was with me and I'd took off my moccasins and slipped my boots on again.

I wonder sometimes, when I think back, if I ever could of had any interest in anything if there hadn't been no

horses, no boots and no spurs. . . . I seen buffalo that summer, a good size herd of 'em, and they wasn't in no park
either. But I hardly glanced at 'em, for, to me, they was just
more big game. I seen Indians too when we got further
South. They was the "bloods," plains Indians, tall fellers
and riding ponies. At least five hundred in one band of the
blanketed breed passed under my nose on their way to
summer ranges. Scouts, hunters and fighters in the lead,
squaws following behind and astraddle little ponies. On any
one of them little ponies was at least a hundred and fifty
pounds of squaw-flesh, fifty pounds of young Indian on her
back, and a hundred pounds of more young Indian a setting
in the "travois," that bore down on that same little pony's
withers.

The whole conglomeration was something that many an
artist would of given half of his life to've seen. I'd seen the
Crows and the Sioux and Blackfeet on the move before that,
whole tribes of 'em, and bead and quill work and riggings
that went with 'em was sure the same as it all had been
many years before. Sometimes I wish I'd paid a little attention to them "children of nature" as they was then. They
was sure enough what's no more to-day, but they never interested me. Whole parades would go by under my nose and
all I had eyes for was little horses that had to do all the
work. The Indians themselves drawed no more attention
from me than a flock of magpies would.

Bopy struck another one of his camps that summer and
we stayed there for a couple of months. I couldn't see why
we didn't stay there thru trapping season too, because trapping would of been good, I thought, but I thought of myself only, and of keeping my ponies. . . . Bopy said he
didn't have enough traps there to carry him.

When fall come I had to quit my ponies once more, put on

WJ
'30

1930 Crow Indian

my mocassins, get a hold of my long rifle and hit North again. It seems like "North" is all I can tie up with Bopy. That's one thing I can well remember of him. North, North, North.

Once we struck North we never came no further South than where the mounted police was mounted, not till one spring a couple of years later and when I was about thirteen years old. We'd come back to the prairie and cow country again. Bopy had hazed his wagon down and took his traps along. I'd cheered up at that because that gave me the hint we might stay South and I would be able to keep my horses longer than usual, maybe thru a whole winter.

A big river stopped our travels. It was high from spring thaws and, not only that, there was big hunks of ice a floating down it. Any one of them hunks would of knocked a horse over if we'd tried to cross. But we was in no hurry, I had my ponies again and Bopy had shipped his furs a long time before and got his check. He'd filled the wagon with a big supply of grub, bought me new boots and things, for himself too, and he showed me where he hid quite a few hundred dollars after the expense. The money was hid in the wagon seat and under some blankets.

All we had to do was to wait till the river went down and the ice thawed out some. In the meantime I was stretching my rope again, on snags or anything that'd give me a pull. I knowed better than to rope any of the loose stock that was on the range because they hung people about then for doing little things like that. Bopy used to tell me that "my rope was better on my saddle than around my neck."

We had a nice spell of weather during the first few days we was camped along the river, warm spring weather with the smell of green grass in the air. It was during one of them fine spring mornings when the heat of the sun a bearing down on me woke me up to face a new day. It was a day I'll never forget.

The sun being so high made me wonder why Bopy hadn't stirred me. I sat up in bed on the ground. I counted the horses that was picketed and hobbled out a ways. They was all there. Then I looked at the fire, it was down to smudging coals. I wondered why Bopy hadn't cooked the morning bait for he always had that done by sun-up,—the sun was away high now.

I jumped up, feeling that something was wrong. I hollered for Bopy but got no answer, only echoes. I hollered all the louder then, and slipping on my boots, I run out to the river and hollered some more. No answer, and nothing of Bopy was in sight. But glancing a ways down the river I noticed a bucket he used to get water with. It was along the bank and a big hunk of ice manipulated by a swift whirling current, was sure doing a good job of battering and flattening it.

I stared at that bucket. It hinted to something. I didn't want to think of what it hinted. I kept a saying to myself as I turned away, "He's out hunting." . . . But as I walked thru the cottonwoods along the river, a hollering and listening, the sight I'd got of the bucket followed me, and the further I went and the more I hollered and listened, the more I thought of the bucket and of the story it told.

I tried to forget that and, to help me that way, I went back to camp, throwed more wood on the fire and started throwing grub together, *for two*. "Bopy ought to be back any minute now."

But Bopy didn't come back. He never did come back and I never seen him no more. . . . The bucket had made things plain. Bopy had been drowned.

Nothing else could of happened to him because I knowed that if he'd left sudden for some reason, or even got shot or hung, he'd found some way of getting some word to me. But never a word did I get, nothing but the tearing sound of water a churning down river.

CHAPTER EIGHT

I CAN'T begin to tell of how I really felt during the first few days of Bopy's disappearing. Bopy had left me alone for many a day at the time before and it never worried me, but this time, and with the river's steady roar in my ears, my mind sort of run wild.

I tore up and down along the river bank the first morning and hollered for Bopy till I couldn't holler no more. Then I cussed the river and the big hunks of ice that floated down it. I knowed that that river had took Bopy and I figgered that one of them hunks of ice might of been the cause of him losing his balance and slipping in while he was getting the water.

I didn't want to think or believe that. I kept a telling myself that he was out a hunting and that he'd be back soon. But I couldn't wait at camp for him. I made a bluff at having nothing to worry about, but the bluff didn't go far and,

after I choked down on a little something to eat, I caught
one of my ponies and hit down along the river. I didn't spare
the horse, and kept a hitting him down the hind leg and hollering. I got nothing for answer but echoes and the rushing
of water. I loped on some more and covered about thirty
miles by the time I got back to camp. I was in a rush both
ways because I thought I might find Bopy down stream;
then, on my way back, I thought he might be in camp by
now and waiting for me.

But he wasn't in camp waiting for me. He was nowheres
around. I didn't eat no noon bait, I saddled my other horse
and rode up-river a hollering the whole way up and all the
way back. It was dark when I got back to camp again and
I'd covered at least seventy miles of country that day. Being
tired helped me out some for that night. I heated up the
stew, took a lot of it in hunks and rolled up in the soogans.
Bopy didn't show up at camp that night either, of course.
. . . But I still didn't want to believe he was gone. He'd
never leave me without some word, and I couldn't listen to
what the river waters had to say.

I never liked waters from then on.

I had three saddle horses, Bopy's one and my two. On
them I rode north and south and east and west and all
directions between. I rode acrost the river, cussed the swift
waters some more and glared at the hunks of ice as I made it
to the other shore, and come a time when, with all my riding,
three horses wasn't enough for me. They was getting all
ganted up and leg-weary.

I picked on the wagon team then, I wanted fresh horses.
The wagon team'd had a big rest and I wasn't at a time
where I was perticular as to any way of getting to places. I
stepped up on one of the team horses—he'd never been rode
before—and, with the big rest he'd had, he was feeling fool-

ish. He tried to buck me off but I wasn't in no humor for such stuff right then and after I bent my old rusty spurs on him he lined out a stampeding. That suited me fine, I wanted speed. The other horse of the team acted the same way, only worse. He bucked me off fair and proper from the start but afterwards he turned out to be the best.

Sizing up my string, and after I got the team lined out, I had five horses to go on with. . . . I sure made use of 'em.

For a couple of weeks I kept a riding around and everywhere. I didn't care where I was going as long as I went fast. I was just hunting and I think I covered every foot of the country for forty miles each way from camp. I'd meet riders and come acrost ranches along the river and it strikes me queer, *now*, that I never asked any of the riders if they'd seen any man like Bopy. I never stopped at the ranches either as I rode by them.

The lady of a ranch house would wonder at what a kid like me was doing running around loose in that country. I'd keep quiet and ride on. The chink at some of the bigger outfits' cook house would wonder too, but I'd just snicker at him and go on some more.

I had a secret. It wasn't so much of a secret but Bopy had brought me up to never ask any questions and to never let out anything, especially about him. So I went along a riding and looking and hollering, kept everything to myself, and asked for no help.

I don't know how many days or weeks I rode and hunted and hollered. It was quite a spell, then there come a time when my riding for Bopy seemed more and more useless. I begin to quit hollering and finally I got so I rode just to be riding. I'd near lost all hope.

But I held camp where it was for a long time after that.

I couldn't think of taking the outfit and leaving, not without Bopy.

The country Bopy had stopped to make his last camp in was a big country. It was wide open and stretched out in long distances of level and grass covered prairie. The only trees for many miles was them that skirted along the river. I'd noticed that country as being mighty big when me and Bopy first drifted down it, and I was happy then, we'd struck cow country again. But after Bopy disappeared the long stretches of flat range land got to look a heap wider and bigger. That and the river kept a reminding and wearing on me. I got restless and camp got mighty lonesome.

I rode down the river further than usual one day and I come to a shallow wide place in it with a good rocky bottom. The river had went down by then, the ice was all gone, and the water at that place didn't go any higher than to my horse's knees. I thought that'd sure be a fine place to get the wagon and outfit acrost, if I wanted to cross.

I kept a thinking of that crossing often from that day on and, while on a horse, I kept a looking beyond the river and south. The more I looked that way the more I got to dread getting back to camp. Finally, after many days' figgering, I decided to get the outfit together and pull out. I knowed I wouldn't feel so bad after once I begin drifting again. I often thought of Bopy before deciding on that move, what if he came back and so on, me leaving with the outfit and all.

I stuck around a few more days because I sort of felt that me leaving would bust up all that had been with me and Bopy. This had been his last camp.

Finally, one day, I tore a piece of canvas, wrote on it as to the general direction of where I would be headed, and with some loose nails which I pulled out of the wagon box, I nailed the canvas on a big tree near where the camp was.

Then I gathered up the whole outfit, hooked up the team, tied the saddle horses behind the wagon, climbed up on the seat and, taking a last long look around where the camp had been, I started the team.

Going by what I wrote on the canvas before leaving camp, I hit for the river crossing and from there as straight south as I could for the border of good old United States again. My idea was to find that last big cow outfit where Bopy had trapped that winter before going North. I'd also wrote the name of that outfit on the canvas and that I would stop there.

The few hundred miles of that trip was a lot of help in making me forget my lonesomeness for Bopy. Being altogether dependant on myself and having all the responsibilities of taking care of my outfit, making camp, cooking my meals and getting the wagon acrost bad places, all had me watching out and kept me busy. If it hadn't been for missing Bopy at times, I know I'd had a lot of fun. I was used to having to take care of myself and of the outfit, and there was nothing along with that that I didn't know how to do, from setting up camp, cooking, picketing or hobbling the horses and picking out the trail when starting out of camp in the morning. Old Bopy had given me plenty of education that way.

The proof of that is that I didn't have one accident on the way down to the cow outfit. I didn't lose a horse nor cripple any. I didn't burn a pot, didn't get my bedding wet and, outside of the wear, the whole outfit was just the same when I got to the end of that trail as it was when I started. I manipulated my team and wagon acrost creeks and rivers and, further south, when I got into rougher country, I manipulated it some more on steep and sidling roads. I don't take no credit for making that trip without getting lost nor having anything out of the ordinary happen. If any credit is due it goes to Bopy's teaching.

I didn't stop inside a building nor went to a ranch on the whole way down because I knowed the folks there would wonder at me traveling around loose and would begin to ask me questions and want to play guardian to me. I didn't want to answer no questions, I didn't want to talk of Bopy to nobody nor tell why I was drifting alone, or where I was headed.

Sometimes, at long times between, I'd meet riders or wagons from some ranches, and they'd all stop and want me to hit for whatever ranch they belonged to and stay there a spell. I'd laugh and say no, and I'd have a hard time, being I'd about forgot my American, to explain that I'd be meeting my people down country pretty quick. That was my story all along, and when I'd turn down the good hospitality that way, there'd be grins, waving of hands and wishes of good luck on the way.

I said I had no accidents on the trip but there was one experience which I remember. It was in a stretch of rough country where I had to follow a road, and I'd run into an outfit that didn't strike me so good. I felt that, the minute I seen the horses picketed around, they was just skeletons, and I knowed that my horses sure looked good as I drove in. There was about three or four wagons in the outfit, half a dozen men, a woman and lots of kids, and all together it was a crummy looking layout.

They was camped on both sides of the road and I had to go thru their camp. And, as I seen a couple of fellers coming my way as to stop me like they wanted to talk, I sure didn't show where I had any such intentions. I had the stocks of my two rifles showing where they was handy and I know they got a glimpse of them as I put my team into a lope. I hollered hello at 'em as I went by, like as to let on I wasn't suspicious nor scared, but I sure enough was, and if it hadn't been for my horses tied to the back of the wagon I think one of them fellers would of tried to climb on. He'd started to run up like as to do that, but he was leary of my ponies' heels.

I loped my outfit by, slick and clean, and I knowed I was safe then because there wasn't a horse in their camp that was alive enough to go faster than a trot.

Maybe I was wrong to get suspicious of that outfit and do what I did, but I don't think so. The looks of 'em and the shape their horses was in sure didn't give me no confidence. Anyway, they was strange looking people, dark skinned and black hair, and they was dressed queer, the men had rags around their heads. The whole outfit was rags and looked worse than any gathering of hoboes I ever seen since. I can't guess where they'd come from and what they was doing, but I sure do know that they didn't belong to the cow country.

I traveled till late that night and made camp a good thirty miles from them. When I did make camp, it was away off the road and well hid. I never seen 'em no more.

It was a few days later when I stood up in my wagon and glimpsed the scattered buildings that was the home ranch of the big cow outfit. That was sure a great sight to me and I was more than glad to see the old spread again, for during my time in the North I'd so often hankered to be there. I'd so often thought of the boys, and pictured 'em amongst the long log houses, working in the big corrals or loping out for fresh horses, herds of cattle bellering and all, everything that I wanted to be in the thick of.

And now I would be there again, that was all I could wish for. I didn't stop to think that I might not be welcome, or that I wouldn't be able to stay for long, because I somehow felt like I belonged there, or on any other such a spread.

A couple of the boys was cutting out horses in a corral when I pulled up my team. I recognized one of 'em, but he didn't recognize me and I had to talk to him a bit before he could think of who I was.

"No wonder I didn't recognize you, Pistol," he said as he jumped over the corral and started helping me unhook the team. "You sure growed up some. . . . But where is Pap?"

I wished he hadn't asked that last question. But it had to come sooner or later and, that night, after the other boys got in that I knowed, I told the whole of what I'd kept to my chest. It sort of done me good to let it out, like as if the load I'd packed was shared around. The boys thought I sure had tough luck. It took me quite a spell to tell my story because I hadn't spoke nothing but French in the last four or five years and my mother tongue was pretty well forgot.

All the men on that outfit sure treated me fine. Most likely it was because they felt sorry and wanted to make it easy for me. The foremens, cowboys, ranch hands, and even the chink cook, catered to me like I was a long lost brother. Then to make things more pleasant, the next day the range boss asks me if I wanted a job. My clothes was a little ragged and he figgered I must of needed some money. But I was well fixed for money. I had the four or five hundred dollars that Bopy had left on the wagon seat and which I'd later rolled up in my bed. Anyway, when I found out that the job was to wrangle horses on one of the round-up wagons I sure was tickled to take it. Besides I wanted to stay on that spread because of that note I'd left on the tree at Bopy's last camp. If he ever seen that note he'd knowed where to find me and his outfit. I still wanted to hope that he would some day.

I left the wagon and outfit and horses at the ranch and went to riding on the round-up. It was my first job on a big cow outfit and I felt mighty proud and sure enough cowboy.

I finished wearing out my saddle there, the stirrup leathers was wore down till they was as thin as paper and the riggin' too, and both of them important pieces was so all patched up that they'd keep breaking, and most always at a bad time. The saddle tree was too small for me now too, I'd outgrowed it and lucky it was that I shot up more in length and very little in thickness because I'd never been able to get in it. I was tall enough now that I'd come near to most any of the boys' shoulders.

I worked pretty hard on that first job, but I had a great time doing that work. The only part I didn't like was to have to cut wood and carry water for the cook and not being able to go with the boys on the circle. But the rest was fine. I had five good saddle horses in my string and I had a "Remuda" of two hundred saddle horses for company the whole day long. Then I'd get to see the boys three and four times a day, whenever they changed horses, and when the "Nighthawk" (night-wrangler) took my place in herding the horses for the night, I'd see the boys again and get in on the talks and songs that went around the fire at camp.

I'd been riding with the outfit for quite a few weeks when a big herd of beef steers was gathered and headed for the shipping point. I brought along the horses, as usual, and after four or five days on the trail we hit the stock yards. Town wasn't over half a mile away and, after the herd was loaded, the boys and me headed right on that half mile stretch to it. They'd been many days talking about "seeing the sights."

But I didn't get to see much of the sights the boys was talking about. We no more than tied the horses at the hitching rack when they filed into a saloon. A couple of the boys stopped me at the door and told me I couldn't go in that place. That it was "no place for little boys" and if I'd stay out and watch the horses, they'd bring me out something good. I stayed by the horses and pretty soon one of the boys comes out with two bottles of soda pop, one pocketful of pretsels, and a lot of sandwiches.

That all tasted mighty good and held me for quite a while. Pretty soon another rider came out with more soda pop and a lot of different crackers and pickles. Every once in a while over the swinging doors of the saloon, I'd hear one of the boys remark that "The Kid" (meaning me) was being neglected, and in a minute another cowboy would come out with something else. I think they daggone near foundered me that day. After the third helping I had to sit down by the hitching rack.

A feller came out while I was setting there. He was using bull-whacker language but he was no bull-whacker, he had on a regular suit of clothes and a white collar around his neck. I thought he was sick the way he staggered and there was a funny look in his eye. It was the first drunken man I'd ever seen.

He spotted me setting there by the horses and he came over. He was still cussing but I don't think he was peeved at anything. Anyway when he got near me I stood up, and he offered me a bottle. I thought it was some more soda pop and I was going to take a swallow of it to sort of be polite to the stranger. Just about then the bottle was knocked away from me and I looked up to see one of the boys from my outfit a glaring at the stranger. He didn't glare at him long, and there was no words said, but there was no time for words because that cowboy started booting the stranger and kept on a booting him plum acrost the street and up along it quite a ways. The other boys come out by then, they was a pretty mad bunch.

"This ain't no place for you to be anyway, Kid," said

one of 'em grabbing me by the arm. "Come along with me and I'll show you a real place." He took me up the street a ways and walked into a place that made me think this must be what the boys had meant when they'd spoke of "seeing the sights," for, to me, it sure was sights. It was a saddle shop.

I didn't know there was such a place on earth. My eyes popped at the rows and rows of brand new saddles, all kinds, and hundreds of silver mounted spurs and bits. There was ropes and quirts and hackamores and, *everything*.

The cowboy was speaking to the saddle maker. I didn't hear what he said, and I only half-heard him when he spoke to me and said something about fixing it up so I could stick around for a spell and make myself to home anywhere in the saddle shop. He said for me to stay there till he come back. . . . There was no use of him saying that last because I sure had no intentions to go away, not for a long spell, because this was just the place I was wanting to see, and if I'd dreamed there was such a place, and so near, I'd sure been to it long before. . . . I was in need of a new outfit mighty bad.

I tried every saddle in the place, fingered the different stampings on 'em, looked at the riggin' and stood back to look at the general shape and appearance of each saddle. I had a hard time to tell which one I wanted. Finally I decided on one and I called the saddle-maker to find out how much it was. He was pretty surprised when I handed him the money for it because he thought I was just there to wait.

But I surprised him some more, and when I got thru looking around I had gathered me a good pair of spurs, bit and headstall and a pair of chaparejos. I'd never had a pair of chaps' before. I was all fixed now but for a pair of boots and a hat. It was hard to fit me on them two things but, after rummaging around a lot I finally made good there too.

Now I was thru. I went out and got my horse, I was sure anxious to try out my new outfit. My old outfit was pulled off and left in the saddle shop. It was wore out and the change from the old to the new, on both horse and me, and taking in the time of adjusting all straps and latigoes, only took me about five minutes. In another minute I'd told the saddle-maker to tell the boys I'd gone back to camp, got on my horse, and was starting out of town.

The ride back to camp was just right for me to try out my new outfit. The wagon had made camp by a river just a few miles from town and while making that distance I kept a looking on one side of me and then the other. It was sure pretty on both sides but everything was stiff and didn't hang right. It would take a month or two of real wear and weather before everything would set to fit and begin to look as it should.

Some people wonder at the clothes and riggin's of the cowboy, why the silver on spurs and bit, or anything a little fancy. It seems to them that some things are useless and only for show. But the range riding cowboy has nobody around him to show off to and everything he wears is altogether for use. At the same time he can have a little style too, and an outfit to be proud of, specially when he makes his living in it and uses it three hundred and sixty days in the year. . . . There's nothing the cowboy wears that could be near as useless as an imported necktie or a stiff collar.

I had me a pretty good outfit—It was an outfit that had the looks and sure would stand the gaff. All it needed was limbering up. I had the chance to do that soon as I got to camp. The cook wanted some wood drug in, and as I drug that in by a rope around the saddle horn, I had some nice rope marks on it by the time I got thru. Then, being the "nighthawk" took my place in holding the horses during that day, I let him sleep and took his place and herded the horses that night.

But the next morning there was still no sign that I'd used the new outfit at all. The boys all thought I'd sure picked

The cook wanted some wood drug in.

out a good rig all the way thru, but most of 'em was too sleepy or feeling too good to look at it very well. They'd just strung in to camp at daybreak and wanted coffee awful bad.

The first chance I got I soaked the stirrup leathers in water for a few hours and let 'em dry while I was riding. That sure helped a whole lot in the breaking in of the saddle, and as I kept on a riding every day the rains and sun and horse sweat gradually took the squeak out of it. Everything was getting to hang just right and to pretty near as good a style as with most of the cowboys on the outfit. The slushy soaking snow-storms of that fall put the finishing touches in taking all the stiffness out of the leather and, by the time the

foreman was thru with the round-up wagon, turned the remuda loose and let most of the cowboys go for the winter,
my outfit sure didn't look new no more.

The only thing that kept a bothering me about my outfit
was that I'd used some of Bopy's money to get it with. That
sort of went against the religion he'd teached me, but I had
to have a new outfit. . . . I got to thinking of the money
my dad had left Bopy to take care of me with. My dad must
of had quite a little to plan on starting out in the cow business for himself, then there was his horses and wagon and
things.

I figure Bopy must of had a considerable more money
than what had been under the wagon seat too because, as I
see it now, I know he made near four times more money than
it took for our feed and clothes. Maybe he sent some of the
money somewheres but I don't remember of him getting any
letters or writing any, and as many times as I looked thru
the wagon before leaving the North, I never found a piece
of any kind of paper that told of him or of any relative.

When I got back to the home ranch Bopy's wagon was
still where I'd left it. Nobody had seen or heard of him there,
winter was setting in, and *then* I knowed for sure that I'd
never see him again. I was all alone. . . . Whatever I done
now was all up to me. I'd have to find my own trail and learn
to pack and take care of my own belongings. I couldn't follow at Bopy's heels no more.

I kind of wandered around for a spell, and then one day
I begin sizing up Bopy's wagon, staring at the many traps
and other things inside of it. I was wondering what to do,
but I knowed there wouldn't be no trapping for me, nor going North. I'd had enough of that for a spell. So, figuring
that way, I had no more use for Bopy's trapping outfit and
wagon and team.

I stayed on at the ranch. There was no work there now till spring, but the foreman told me to stay all winter and putter around all I wanted to, that he'd put me on the round-up again for the whole next summer. That sounded good, and I puttered around as he told me, but there wasn't many of the boys left at the ranch and while puttering around drawing or riding I got to thinking of many things. It took me quite a spell but, while thinking, it finally came to me of the freedom that was mine.

I was so free that I felt lonesome. I could go anywheres I pleased, do anything I pleased and there wasn't a soul in the whole world for me to answer to. When the full meaning of that begin to hit me good, I didn't know which way to jump for a while, or whether to stand still. There was nobody to care what I done.

But I didn't stand still. I was going to make use of that freedom and see what it was like. If I got lost that'd be all right. I was lost anyway, and it was getting kind of lonesome at the ranch. So, one fine day I runs in my horses, hooks the team to the wagon, ties the three saddle horses behind, and starts out.

I didn't feel so bad to say good-by to the foreman and the ranch this time because I felt free to do as I pleased. I didn't have to go, and I could come back any time I wanted to.

The trail South from the ranch wasn't much like the trail South from the river and Bopy's last camping place. When I left the river I couldn't realize somehow that Bopy had gone for sure, I sort of expected him to meet me at the ranch and we'd be together again. But now there was no more such feeling. I'd left Bopy behind for good and there was nothing ahead for me but great scopes of country and a freedom to match it.

CHAPTER NINE

THERE was no camping out from the ranch on the way South. Quite a few inches of snow covered the ground and a cold wind blowed. I stayed at one of the cow camps of the outfit the first night and there I met a couple of cowboys I'd rode with the fall before. They got a lot of fun watching me start out early the next morning and being I was headed on the road to town they kidded me some on how I'd soon be "seeing the sights."

I passed the line of the outfit's range that noon and, following the road, I came acrost a little ranch where I stayed that night. They told me there that the town was thirty-five miles away. I pulled in there the next day, after dark.

I don't know why I went to town only maybe because it was on the road I was following to where I was going, wherever that was. But I found a livery stable and fed and rested my horses there that night and all the next day. That town was bigger than all the towns I'd ever seen, put together. There was a lot of things in it for me to see that was strange, and there was a fine saddle shop. I stuck around the saddle shop for quite a spell off and on during the day, and all I bought was a fur-lined coat. I was well fixed with everything else for riding use. I wanted some underwear and shirts and socks, cartridges for my six-shooter (my dad's six-shooter which had been left under the wagon seat) and things like that, but the saddle maker told me they didn't carry such like in their shop, that I'd have to go to some other store. He pointed one out to me.

I had a room in the hotel but after I got thru buying what I wanted I took my packages to the livery stable. I never thought of leaving them in my room. It was a nice hotel, there was lots of folks around, cowmen who looked at me like a old broke down cow horse would look at a yearling colt. There was a bar adjoining the lobby. I seen the swinging door and I walked in one time, figgering to get me a drink of soda pop, but I no more than got in and started to speak when the bartender pointed up to a sign and said:

"Do you see that, young feller?"

"Yes," I says in my broken talk, "but I can't read it."

Then he explained it to me. It said "No Minors Allowed" . . . and that was my first time to learn the difference between minors and miners. I didn't get no soda pop there and I went out on the street again. I went around and pretty well all over town and when I seen all I thought there was to see, I got to feeling a little lonesome. It struck me queer that I should get lonesome when there was so many people around. Finally and natural-like I headed towards the stables. There was two cowboys there just come in. They was strangers to me but it wasn't long when the three of us begin to talk. When they found out what outfit I was from they had a lot of questions to ask as to how things was up there and so on.

We was just stringing along good when the stable man came up and asked if the wagon and outfit I drove in was mine. I said, "Yessir."

"Do you want to sell it?"

". . . I would," I says, "all but two saddle horses and my bed."

"Well," he went on, "the reason I ask is that there was an old trapper sticking around this morning and asking about if it could be bought."

The first thing I thought of when the stable man mentioned an old trapper was Bopy, but I soon reasoned that

Bopy would sure recognize the outfit and would never ask about buying it. He'd be asking about me.

The cowboys took off their chaps and spurs and started for the main part of town. I stuck around the stables for quite a spell and was looking over a bunch of unbroke horses when the stable man came to me with the trapper. He was a big rough looking old feller and didn't look at all like Bopy, but he had the same squint in his eyes.

"Kind of late in the season for me to start out laying traps," he says after we'd talked a spell, "but with this outfit of yours all ready to go, I'd sure save a lot of time. How much would you want for it, Son?"

We didn't dicker long on the deal. He wanted the outfit bad and I wanted to get rid of it bad. I showed him the team and Bopy's saddle horse and all that was to go, and a price was soon set and agreed on. He handed me the money right on the spot. There was no bill of sale made.

"Where did you get this outfit, Boy?" he asks as I was getting my bed-roll in the store room.

I turned and faced him as he asked that, wondering if I should tell, but after sizing him up I got to thinking that I could never tell to a better man, and I also figgered that now, being I was rid of the outfit, I wouldn't have to repeat that story no more.

"Did you know Trapper Jean?" I asks.

"Sure, sure I did," he says, all set to hear more, "and where is the old son of a moose?"

"He's dead . . . the outfit you got was his."

"Well, I'll be durned. . . ." The old trapper seemed set back quite a bit at them news. After a while I went on with the story of what happened at the river and, when I got all thru, the old trapper said,

"There aint no doubt but what he drowned." He kept

quiet a bit like he was sort of thinking things over, then he turned to me. "And you," he says, "you ain't the little codger I heard tell he 'dopted some years ago, are you?"

"Yessir," I says.

I went back to town, and early the next morning I was at the stable again and slipping my saddle and bed on my two horses when the old trapper slipped up behind me and slapped me on the back.

"Well, how's the boy this morning?" he asks pleasant. "Better take that bed of yours off that horse and throw it in my wagon and come along with me, I've got a fine cabin *North* of here a ways."

"No, sir," I says, grinning, "I thought I'd drift *South*."

And South I drifted. I wasn't out of town very far when I seen how much freer I was to drift now. I wasn't hindered by no wagon, I didn't have to follow no road and, to get the most of that, I quit the road soon as I got out of the town lanes. I was pretty well lost by the time noon come, lost in the shelter of a grove of willows and where the sun had bared a patch of good grass for my horses. I let my horses feed there for a long spell while I was busy trying to do something I sometimes wish I'd never learned to do. I'd got me a sack of tobacco while in town and some cigarette papers and now I was trying to roll my first smoke.

After trying over and over again I finally got it made. It sure wasn't a neat looking cigarette, mighty fat on the middle and mighty poor at the ends, but it made a smoke and I reared back a trying to see if I could get as much enjoyment out of it as the cowboys seemed to. I did get some enjoyment but it wasn't for long. I done a lot of spitting and my mouth got full of tobacco, but I didn't get sick, just sort of dizzy and I thought I'd stand up and shake myself a bit.

That was my start in smoking. I put in a lot of time prac-
ticing rolling cigarettes over and over and finally when I
got a pretty good one made I got on my horse and started
out, a smoking as I went. It tasted better that way. If I'd
had something to eat it would of tasted still better, but be-

That was my start in my smoking.

ing I figgered on making some ranch by night I wasn't going to bother with taking anything along for noon.

But I begin to wish I had of took something along before
I did strike a ranch. I covered a heap of territory that
afternoon and I moseyed around plum careless as to where
I went. The country was rough and it always had me a wondering as to what it looked like around every point. I didn't
think of shelter and feed for me and my horses till the sun
went down, and it wasn't till it got dark that I got right
serious on that subject. I got to thinking of hot potatoes

and beef and a warm place to eat that in, and from then on and around every knoll I begin to looking for the light of some ranch house instead of at the lay of the country.

I rode on and on. I seen plenty more country but no light nowheres in all that country. I thought of hot potatoes more and more and my ponies was getting tired. Then I happened to think of something, of what the cowboys had said when they got good and hungry while on some long ride, "well I rolled me another smoke." . . . But I couldn't do that while riding, not yet, and besides my fingers was too numb. So I got off, built me a fire and after I got warmed up some I managed to roll me some kind of a cigarette. It tasted pretty good.

I thought I felt a little better after that and I got on my horse and rode on some more. Finally I came to a big creek and I remembered Bopy telling me that in cow country a creek, if you go down it, always leads to some ranch sooner or later. But there was no "sooner" with me when I followed along that creek that night, it was all "later," much later. I rode so late that I knowed all ranch folks would be to bed and there wouldn't be no more light to see. I thought I seen the light of a ranch once. I kept a watching it but it was just a star in the sky, a star on the skyline. It had gone up.

Finally I got tired of riding and looking for lights. I wasn't so hungry no more anyway, so I begin looking for a spot bare of snow and where there was grass for my horses. I had to leave the creek to do that and get up on a ridge. I found a good place there not far from the creek and made camp, or I mean I unsaddled my horse and took my bed off the other. I had a lot of blankets inside of a good canvas tarpaulin and all I had to do, after I'd hobbled my horses and pulled my boots and coat off, was to crawl in at the head of the bed, like with a sleeping-bag. I'd no more than got in amongst the blankets than I went sound asleep, with the cayotes' howl for a late lullaby.

There was no bright sun to wake me up the next morning, it was snowing. But it had turned warmer and there was no wind with that snow. I got up, put on my coat and boots and chaps and rolled me a smoke. Then I looked at the country all around me, there wasn't a ranch building in sight and now I was hungry again. A cigarette didn't satisfy me that morning.

But I soon had my horses packed and saddled and was on my way. I wasn't looking at country much no more only to find some house in it somewhere where there was smoke coming out of the chimney. I followed down along the creek and every once in a while, amongst the willows, I'd see little cottontail rabbits a scampering along and then set up and watch me go by. But there was a couple of 'em that didn't watch me go by. I'd drawed up my long six-shooter, rested it on my left elbow and beared down on 'em, figgering on just shooting their heads off and keeping the other parts. But it seems like I always shot too far behind their ears and when I'd get to where they'd been, there was nothing to show of 'em excepting scattered tufts of fur. The 45' slug was too heavy.

I wish I'd had a light rifle, I was kind of scared of the heavy six-shooter so close to my nose and my aim wasn't so good. I'd let Bopy's rifle and mine go because they was too long and awkward to pack on a saddle and, right then, I decided I would get me a saddle-gun the first chance I got because I'd sure liked to've got me one of them little rabbits. I was mighty hungry and one of 'em would of made me a nice meal.

But I wasn't due to suffer long. I'd no more than gone a few miles when the country seemed to drop all at once, and

there below me was a long wide river bottom with big cottonwoods all along it, and what looked the most good to me was
ranch buildings down there, and corrals with stock around
'em. A tall smoke was coming out of the chimney of the main
building.

It wasn't over half an hour later when I had my feet under a table inside of one of them buildings. A fine old lady
had got sight of me as I rode in, hollered at one of her boys
to take my horses and then liked to busted herself getting
me in the house and getting me something hot to eat. She
knowed right away that on account of dropping in at that
hour of the morning I sure must of slept out and of course
had nothing to eat since the day before.

I had a hard time getting away from that ranch. The old
lady, widowed, had two boys but she seemed to figger like
she ought to have one more. One of the boys was not many
years older than me and the two of us had a lot of fun together. To begin with he liked my saddle and outfit a whole
lot and when he learned that I'd rode for that big spread to
the north he sure hung on to everything I said. Neither of
these boys had ever been away from home only to do their
fall shipments. They'd had to take care of their mother and
the ranch and, like all boys of their age, they sort of hankered to drift a bit. My talk of the prairie country to the
north and what all I'd been doing sure interested 'em, and
before I got thru telling 'em and showing 'em different
things in ways of knots and general cow work, they made me
feel as if I was many years older than they was.

The mother said she had a plenty to keep me on if I would
only stay, but I felt I had a plenty too, plenty to learn, and
I was aching to see what was ahead. Experiencing my freedom kept me going.

I left a few drawings of bucking horses which I'd made of

evenings. The old lady kissed me good-bye, I shook hands with the boys and I rode on.

I don't know which way I went from there, all I know is that I followed a river. I passed one or two ranches every day and I passed 'em because they struck me as small outfits, maybe running a thousand head or so. But come one evening when I begin to look for a ranch-house light again. The snow was deep, it was getting cold and I was beginning to get hungry. Any "one-horse" outfit would do now if I could only find one. It was way after dark when I did. I seen a light and rode towards it. I rode and rode and rode. Finally I got to a fence and I followed that on in the corrals and buildings, and light.

Another good table was spread out for little me, another good lady kept a filling my cup and plate, and many questions was asked me that I didn't answer. I'd come in out of the cold, I was hungry and, after I got my fill, the heat of the stove sort of made me want to do nothing but crawl into my gatherings and go to sleep, anywheres.

But I didn't sleep "anywheres" that night. I was escorted to a room, and a bed that was off the floor. The whole room and bed was for me and I don't think anybody could of ever made any better use of that than me right then. It was the first bed I ever "sunk" into and I never worried about my ponies or where I was at till morning come.

My ponies had done fine. They'd been chewing away on good bluejoint hay all night and now, when I come to the breakfast table, I seen where I was with a family. One boy a little younger than me was behind the stove and a warming up after doing his chores. He grinned at me as I opened the door and found me a chair near it, but I don't think I answered his grin because about that time I noticed the three girls that was helping their mother putting the break-

fast on the table. The biggest one was about the same size
as the boy and the other two sort of tapered down a bit.
Their hair was braided close to the head and at first glance
it looked to me like their eyes was about ready to pop out on
account of the pull in the braiding. They was pretty shy
but I didn't have any the best of 'em because I sure wasn't
bold meself.

Nobody talked during breakfast excepting "Ma" and
"Pa" and with all the young glances headed my way I got
to feeling sort of uncomfortable. We was half way thru eating when a young lady came in and sat down at the table
with us. She was a teacher for the kids, and then is when I
think I first got conscious of table manners. Not that my
manners wasn't so good at the time, but I was sort of nervous
about things, like tipping my plate to run the syrup where
I could get it, by putting my fork under one side of the
plate, or using my fingers to get my biscuit out of the gravy.

I was down at the stable and was saddling to drift on
when the father of the outfit came along and asked me if I
wanted to take a job and ride for him that winter. That
offer made me feel proud and big, and even tho the job only
paid ten dollars a month and I was to ride my own horses,
I took it on for all I was worth.

I rode hard there and helped bring in many cattle that
would need feeding. I got friendly with the boy and the
girls and my evenings was all took up with me drawing pictures for 'em. I especially got to like drawing pictures for
the girls. All was going fine, I was doing my work well and
hardly ever missed a poor cow. I liked the evenings at the
ranch, and all would of kept a going fine that way if it
hadn't been for the boy there. He was the family pet and
sort of spoiled. He didn't have to do anything but get into
mischief. One day I caught him a riding one of them poor
little leppy calves, one of them that could hardly stand up.

I got pretty peeved at that and took it onto myself to educate him some. Besides, being the girls was around, I thought I'd show off a little too. I caught a good big stout weaner calf, snubbed him up close and bucked him out acrost the corral with just a rope around his middle for me to hang on to. That was a lot of fun, I said, and I dared the boy to try him once.

He was kind of scared, but he didn't want his sisters to laugh at him, so he climbed on. He lasted two jumps and, thru his own awkwardness, piled up with his face against the corral. The girls was laughing and so was I, but when the boy got up, with blood streaming down his face, and a bellering like a thousand yearlings, the old man came out of the house and inquired of the goings on. The boy pointed at me and bellered some more.

The father loved his family a whole lot, specially the boy, and that last action of mine didn't go so well. I'd been a little wild with that boy a few times before and now it was seen that something would have to be done so as to save his neck. I didn't see where that boy needed any protection from me because he was every bit my size, but I think the teacher stuck her nose in the last happening, because that boy was her pet pupil and as she'd say, "most remarkable." He should of been, because he sure was no good outside.

Anyway, I found myself drifting again the next morning with all my wages in one pocket, a five-dollar bill.

I drifted on for quite a few days, stopping at whatever place I could find when dark come. I stopped with old "sourdoughs," (bachelors), with families, at cow camps and any place I could find where I'd get a roof over my head, some heat and something to eat. I was welcome at every place and I done all I could wherever I was at to make up for the good hospitality.

I was drifting along as usual one day when a heavy snow

storm which wound up into a blizzard begin to hit me on the
left ear. I went to hunting for shelter, but on account of the
snow stinging and flying so thick I couldn't see only a few
yards ahead. Finally my horse come up against a fence and
stopped. I wondered if it was a drift fence. If it was there'd
be no use me following it because it would take me a long
ways and wouldn't get me nowhere. But it was while I was
wondering, that I thought I heard a small beller, like the
kind a small young calf would make. But as I listened, I
found out it was no beller, it was blatting, the blatting of
sheep.

I knowed there'd be a camp close to where them sheep was,
and some herders around. I kept close to the fence and rode
towards the sound. Pretty soon I come to a gate and a few
minutes later I rode into the shelter of a full size sheep
ranch. The first one I'd ever come near.

The storm howled on day after day, and in that time I
got well acquainted with the general lay of a sheep outfit.
There was lots of log buildings scattered around there the
same as on any cow outfit, but the atmosphere sure wasn't
the same, neither was the smell around. There seemed to be
raw sheep-hides scattered everywhere, from every room of
every house to the stables and sheds. There was sheep even
in the bunk house and hunks of wool a hanging on everything.

There was hardly any corrals fit to run horses in in the
whole big place, nothing but low paneled pens that any little
calf could jump over. But they had good hay back of the
stable and there was plenty of good grub in the house. The
three men that worked there was fine to me, and I didn't
mind it if they did look a little dirty, for any one of 'em
could sure put on a stew and mix up a bait that was good
and which would stick to a feller's ribs.

I made a hand of myself at washing dishes during that storm, and them dishes sure did need washing, specially the pots and pans. That was more than agreeable with the herders because I seen that was one job they sure didn't like. I wasn't so crazy about that job myself, but it was better than trying to help around them stinking wet-nosed sheep.

I was glad when the storm broke so I could move on. I moved on for a couple of days and then one evening I come to where I got sight of a great big tall house against the cottonwoods and along the river. It was a three-story frame house, well built, but pretty old. I thought sure there must of been quite a family living there. The size of the house sort of set me back and I think I'd of rode on only it was getting dark and I wondered if I'd find another place for that night.

That place was sure some ranch. The stables was all frame and painted white with red bordering, the corrals and sheds was all heavy lumber and painted white too, there was a long string of 'em. Sure some difference, I thought, as compared to the sheep outfit where I'd stayed during the storm.

I didn't see nobody as I rode up. I sat on my horse, waited and looked around for a spell and then I rode towards the stable. Nobody was there either, so I put my horses into one of the fine big stalls, gave 'em some hay and proceeded to wait there.

It was near dark when a lanky rider on a fine big horse rode into the stable. He sure looked surprised in seeing such as little me setting inside there and waiting, and he just set on his horse, looked me over and grinned.

"Well, well, Cowboy?" he finally asks, "been waiting here long?"

After my horses was unpacked and unsaddled and fed we

went to the house, and there I found that this rider was all alone in the big place. The boss owner and family had gone to some warm climate for the winter, and left the cowboy to batch there and hold down the place.

That was more than all right with me. I took off my coat, warmed my hands, rolled me a smoke and started in to help cooking the meal. I'd had no noon bait that day and I was hungry again.

That cowboy got a lot of fun out of watching me do things, like peeling potatoes and smoking at the same time and helping along with the cooking like as if I'd been at it a hundred years. He'd keep a watching me and laughing. I'd grin back a wondering what he was laughing at. I got to figuring he was just a happy cuss.

Him and me got along pretty fine and we was well acquainted by the time we hit the soogans. I stayed at that ranch the next day, and the morning after. As I was getting ready to move on, he come along and headed me off and talked me into staying some more.

"It's a big country from here on," he'd said. "The ranches are mighty scattering and so are the jobs during winter like this. Better stay with me, it's kind of lonesome all alone in that big house and soon as spring opens up I'll see that you get a good job right here."

"What doing," I asks, "farming?"

He laughed. "No," he says, "riding."

I was glad I stayed at that place because I soon found a lot there to interest me. In some big box-stalls in the stable was five fine stallions. Not the running kind, they was trim built hackney and French coach horses. The cowboy would ride one of 'em out every day and that way give them good exercise while tending to his work. His work, besides holding down the big place and taking care of the stallions, was to sort of superintend a feeding place that was a couple of miles away. A ranch-hand was there to do the feeding of about fifty head of brood mares and colts and a couple hundred head of thoroughbred cattle.

I'd ride along with the cowboy while he made his circle of the feeding place or on the range where there was loose bands of horses which he had to keep his eye on. He let me have two of the studs to ride and change off on, and as he said, that sure helped him in giving them the exercise they needed.

The big house sure had me guessing and one time the cowboy took me thru it. It was *some* place, must of been at least twenty rooms, all fixed up with hardwood floors, rugs, tapestries and paintings, and all kinds of fancy decorations. In one of the kids' rooms I spotted some drawing paper and colored pencils, and I took on a little of that to use.

I was sure all set, after the first few days there. The first few days had been well used by me in doing nothing much only washing and boiling my clothes over and over again. That was on account of a queer itching feeling which begin on me the first day. It'd kept a getting worse, and one day the cowboy caught me while I was trying to scratch myself fifteen places at once. He asked me what was the matter and I told him I didn't know. Then he opened my shirt and looked down my neck along my underwear. He reached down, pecked at something, then he whistled and laughed.

"Why, you little son of a sea-cook," he says, "you're lousy as a pet coon."

And sure enough, I had a herd of animals on me that was of the same breed as the great forefathers of what got to be well known later as "cooties" during the World War. I'd never knowed of such things before and I couldn't figger out how I got 'em, but after the cowboy asked me where I'd been stopping the few days before I got to the ranch, he had no trouble guessing. The sheep ranch was where I'd collected them pets.

The cowboy laughed some more at that. "Well," he says, "they're still on their own range anyway."

The sheep ranch was where I'd collected them pets.

And that was true, because the man who owned this fine place where I was staying also owned the sheep ranch. But, as I was told, that was just one of his side investments, far to one side.

It was quite a few days before I got rid of them pests, and in them few days I took more baths and washed and boiled more clothes and blankets than I had ever done before in my whole life. I stayed right by the stove and had two tubs working steady, one for me and one for the clothes, and with the cowboy's coaching I finally won out.

I stayed at the ranch all winter, and a couple of times when the cowboy had to be gone for a few days, I held it down alone. I done a lot of drawing there and in stormy days I'd got to visiting the big library in the living-room. Then was when, with my getting back to the American language, I started in to understand what was wrote in them books. When spring come I could make out all the easy words, and I could write them too.

When spring did come I'd decided I didn't want the job the cowboy had promised me for that time. I was rearing to be on the go again and experiencing some more of my freedom. So far, my experiences that way sure hadn't cured me from wanting more. It'd done just the opposite, and wondering always what was on the trail ahead never let me stay in one place for very long.

It'd been a year now since I started drifting alone. I didn't miss Bopy so much no more and I think that my roaming around, seeing all that was new, strange people, in a country to my liking, had a lot to do in making me forget him pretty well, and when I hit out that spring, asetting on top of a good feeling pony, the morning sun ashining on fresh green sod, trees abudding and millions of birds asinging everywhere, there was no room in my chest for anything excepting what was all around, under, above, and ahead of me.

CHAPTER TEN

I'VE often wondered what power keeps drawing a human or animal back to the place where daylight was first blinked at. Many a time a man will go back to the country of his childhood when there's not near as much for him at that home spot as where he just left. I've seen horses leave good grassy range and cross half a state to get to a home range where feed and water was scarce and the country rocky.

That same power must of drawed me, but I was hitting for better country instead of worse when I, so natural like and without thought, drifted to where I first stood up and talked. . . . After I left the ranch and crossed the river, it wasn't but a few days that I begin to notice something mighty familiar about the country. The further South I went the more familiar it got and I begin to feel mighty contented, like as if I was at home and amongst my own folks. There was no people and no landmarks that I recognized to let me know I was in my home grounds, nothing but the general lay of the country itself. I'd ride acrost coulees, crossed creeks, and rode over ridges, passes and hogbacks which made me feel as if Bopy was near and just ahead of me a ways.

I kept a watching out for the camp where I passed my first winter with Bopy, and I also scouted some for the big cow outfit where I got my little sorrel horse. But I had no luck finding any of the camps nor the outfit and I didn't meet a soul that'd ever heard of Trapper Jean. All I really could go by to know that I was in my home country was the name of a little range of mountains which I skirted.

I expect I crossed many a place that I'd crossed while I was with Bopy, and, when I finally left the mountains, I know I must of rode down many a draw and over many a bench where my dad's horses had left a hoofprint. I tried to find out just where in that country I was born, but nobody seemed to know and nobody could tell me of my dad. A few had heard of him, but the ten years that'd passed since his death didn't leave much to remember.

It was pretty late spring when one day, down country a ways, I sees a herd a skirting along swale after swale. Scattered out a bit and grazing the way they was, it looked like the whole country was moving. There was only about half a dozen men with that big herd when I first spotted it, but as I rode up on a knoll to get a better look I could see more riders on both sides of me drifting down from all directions and passing the main herd, each rider was bringing along more cattle and was careful not to let 'em mix with the main herd because in the new bunches that was being brought in was many calves that had to be branded. When that was done the new bunches would be throwed in the big herd too, making it still bigger.

I'd seen quite a few big herds of cattle before, but this was the biggest I'd ever seen up till that time. There must of been at least eight thousand head of cattle in the main herd alone. I wondered why they was moving so many cattle at that time of the year. Then I got to thinking that it was

on account of wanting to save that part of the range so as
the beef herd could be throwed onto it to mature later on.
As I found out later, I'd guessed right, and the cattle I seen
that day was only a good sized herd as compared to what
that one outfit owned.

Further on, down country and past the big herd, I could
see the Remuda and on a little flat in the creek bottom was
the round-up wagon and camp of the outfit.

Leading my pack horse, I fell in with a couple of the
riders that was coming in off circle and I helped 'em shove
their bunch in to the cutting grounds not far from camp.
While riding along with them there was hints dropped that
the outfit was short handed. I didn't pay much attention to
that because I knowed, even then, that all riders like to see
many more come in and hit the foreman for a job, and get
it. The more riders there is, the shorter the nightguard shift
is cut, and the further apart comes the dayherd shift. Them
is two things the cowboy hates to do most, specially dayherding, too slow and monotonous.

Dayherding means grazing and holding a herd in daytime, a herd that's to be shipped or moved to some other part
of the range. On a well-run and full-handed cow outfit the
dayherd shift comes every two or three days for half a day
at the time. Range cattle are not herded only, as I've just
said, when a bunch is held to be shipped or moved. There's
three shifts in dayherding, morning, afternoon and evening
shift. The evening shift is called "cocktail." Two to four
men go on them shifts at a time, all depends on the size of
the herd that's being held. After the evening shift the nightguard begins, from eight o'clock till daybreak, when each
rider takes a shift of from one to two hours (sometimes half
the night and more). The last guard is "relieved" by the first
dayherd shift.

Many riders like to take a "rep" job (representing a neighboring outfit) because with that job there's no day herding. The reason for that is that the "rep" has to be on the cutting grounds so as to look thru every fresh herd that comes in off every day's "circle" (round-up), cut out and brand the cattle that belongs to his outfit, and throw them in the main herd.

I helped the two riders bring their bunch to the cutting grounds, and being I had a pack horse to contend with, I rode on into camp. I unpacked and unsaddled, but I didn't turn my horses loose because I figgered the wrangler would be bringing in the remuda for a change of horses pretty quick. It's a bad point to turn a horse loose at that time because, being the wrangler has to get *all* the loose horses in, that would only give him the extra work of getting mine, besides the unnecessary corralling of 'em.

I was just unsaddling when a rider which I figgered was the foreman rode into camp. He didn't turn his horse loose either, not till the wrangler run the remuda in the rope corral. Then he unsaddled and turned him in with the others. Then all the cowboys rode in, all but a few that was left to hold the cattle that'd been gathered that morning, also the few others that was with the main herd. There must of been at least twenty cowboys with that round-up camp.

The boys got to the chuck box and made the rounds from there to the skillets and ovens for all that was needed to make a meal. After they all was set I started in and done the same. . . . I was still eating when most of the boys was thru, had caught their fresh horses and gone. The "relief" men was the first to go. They rode to take the place of the riders that was with the main herd and the others that was holding the morning's drive. There's fast riding during them reliefs because the men that's relieved still have to eat and change horses and be on the job for the afternoon's work. A "drag" is sure not thought much of in a round-up camp.

There was some mighty good men with that outfit and they was riding some mighty tough horses, tough as a Northern range horse can get, and I got to wondering a bit if I'd better try and get a job there after seeing how some of them ponies acted. One of the riders had told me that each rider had three bronks (unbroke horses) in his string, also a couple of spoiled horses. The rest of the string was made up of the gentler ones.

I was by the corral as the last men was catching their horses. The foreman was coiling up his rope when I walked up to him and asked.

"Are you taking on any more riders?" . . . Just like that.

He looked at me and grinned. "Why yes, Son," he says, "when I can find any. . . ."

I didn't say anything to that, then after a while he asks. "Looking for a job?"

"Yessir," I says.

The foreman shook out two coils of his rope and made a loop.

"I don't know how I'm going to fit you up with a string of horses," he says, as he looked the remuda over, "but maybe I can rake up enough gentle ones out of the two strings that's left. . . . The next rider that comes along and wants a job will have to be some powerful rider."

On many outfits I've rode for, a string was never split. Each string was made up of ten or twelve head of horses for each rider. There was unbroke horses for the short circles (rides), spoiled horses for long circles, good all around horses for any work, cow horses for dayherd and cutting out, and then there was the night horses. About two of each of them horses went to make up a string and ten to twenty of them strings went to make a remuda. As I said before, them strings was never split. If a rider quit or was fired the horses in his string was not used till he come back, or till another rider took his place.

On a few outfits, instead of scattering unbroke or spoiled horses amongst the cowboys, they have a couple of riders who take on and ride nothing but them worst ones. Their string is called the "rough string."

The foreman, being short of riders and having a big herd on his hands, split two strings that day and turned eight head of the gentlest over to me. What was left of the two strings could easy been called "rough" by the best of riders.

I knowed that by the fact that two of my "gentle" ones bucked me off regular and most every time I rode 'em. Two others was bronks, full grown but little fellers. They was mean to handle while on the ground but I got along all right once I got in the middle of 'em. They couldn't buck very hard. My other four horses was pretty good, if the mornings wasn't too cold or wet. One of 'em was hard to get on to.

At that outfit was where I first got initiated with rough ponies. The others I'd tried to ride before had been just for fun and that makes a big difference. I was handed gentle old horses while "wrangling" for the big outfit to the North, but now I wasn't wrangling no more, I was on circle, day-herd, nightguard and being a regular hand.

I felt mighty proud of that, but I found out right there that there was grief and sweat on the way to any ambition. My string furnished me with plenty of that. Thinking of what horse I had to ride was the cause of me eating mighty light breakfasts and other meals. The thought of what they might do to me sort of made me lose my appetite. I wasn't exactly what you'd call scared, I was just nervous, very nervous.

Then again, the boys kidding me about what this and that horse of mine did to this man and that man, sure didn't help things any, and even tho I knowed they was kidding, the laughs I'd hand back at 'em wasn't what you might call right hearty.

It might be wondered at why I took on a job that was too much for me when there was so many other jobs that I could of started in at easy. But I didn't wonder. I never wondered and I never thought of any other work than what I'd started with at the outfit. There was nothing else in the world mattered to me but what went with a horse, saddle and rope, and when I took on that job I done it unthinking, like as if there was nothing else. There was nothing else, for me.

Of course I could of rode on to some other outfit where I wouldn't have to ride horses that was so rough on me from the start. But, there again, the start would of been slower, and I might of had to take on the wrangling job too. As it was now, I was started as a regular hand, and, outside of the wrangler and the nighthawk, I had the gentlest horses in the outfit to start in with. Of course that outfit had a great reputation of having tough horses, but mine wasn't really tough, only too tough for me that's all. I was too new yet, and too young, and they just played with me. Any grown cowboy could of handled and rode 'em blindfolded and with both arms tied behind his back.

I stayed on with the outfit. I kept a piling on my ponies and they kept a piling me off. Finally and gradual my piling off got to happen less and less often. I was getting to know my horses. After ten years of riding I was learning how to ride, and come a time, as the boys kept a slapping my hands with a quirt so I'd leave go of the saddle horn, that I begin to straighten up in my saddle and to stay.

It wasn't long after that that most of my *nervousness* begin to leave me. I was getting so used to handling and riding my ponies in whatever they done or whichever way they jumped, that I got to fit in natural with the work, like a six-month old pair of boots. I got so I never thought ahead of time what horse I was to ride next no more and, being so used to things that way and hardened in, my appetite wasn't hindered by any thoughts of any bad horse. The boys begin to quit kidding me about them horses too, because now I was coming back at 'em with laughs that was sure enough hearty.

It took me about a month or so to get the hang of how to set my ponies when I couldn't see their heads. There was two good reasons why it took me so short a time. One was that I'd been amongst the cowboys and riding pretty steady from the time I could walk and riding had got to be a lot more natural to me than walking. The second reason was that them ponies wasn't very hard buckers. Then again, all around me was the best of teachers, the cowboys themselves. They didn't coach me as to how to set, but they done better, they'd laugh at me when I'd buck off and they'd pass remarks.

"You can ride him, Kid," I'd hear one holler just about the time I'd be hitting the ground. . . . What used to make me sore was to have one of the boys come along and pick me up and brush the dirt off my back with a sagebrush and say something like, "You'll ride him next time sure, but you got to stick closer to your riggin'."

Sometimes, when I'd get pretty high up in my saddle, the boys would ride beside me, reach up in the air and set me back in it. "Now, set there and *ride*," they'd holler.

I finally did get to *ride*, specially when the foreman had a talk with me a week or so after I'd started with the outfit.

It was during the "cocktail" shift and he was riding along as me and a few of the boys was grazing the herd towards the "bed grounds." He rode by the side of me and begin saying,

"I think you better catch your private ponies in the morning, Son, and hit back home where you belong. Your dad ought to have plenty enough riding for you, and horses you can ride, too. This string I handed you is a little too tough for a kid like you."

That talk from the foreman layed me out pretty flat for a spell. Finally I came to enough to say, "I haven't got no dad, and no home to go to."

The foreman had figgered that I'd just got wild and run away from the home ranch. . . . Here was another time I had to tell the story of my life. I told it short and quick and there was a funny look in the foreman's eyes when I got thru. As a wind up I added on,

"And if you'll give me a little more time I'll be able to ride 'em, I think."

"But you're all skinned up now," he says.

"Sure," I comes back at him, "anybody is liable to get skinned up."

I know I won out when I seen him grin, and I sure begin to snap out of it from then on. If I ever meant to ride I started in from there and if I got throwed off I sure left marks on my saddle as to how come.

But the foreman had got to watch me pretty close after that talk I'd had with him. Learning that I had no home sort of worried him, and I think he felt like he ought to be some sort of a guardian over me. I caught him trying to swap my best bucker off to the wrangler for a gentler one one day, and I made such a holler that the trade didn't go.

"I rode him easy the last time he bucked," I says, "and, besides, he's in *my* string."

Well, I kept on riding and also kept my string as it was first handed me, and came a time when it was hard for any of them ponies to loosen me. It wasn't so long after that when they couldn't loosen me at all, and then is when I got to thinking I was *some* rider.

But riding wasn't all I was learning while with that outfit, and, even tho I'd growed up with handling stock pretty well, I learned a lot more there. I wasn't playing now, and I had to be something else besides somebody setting on a horse. I had to know how to find and "shove" cattle while on circle, I had to know where to be at the cutting grounds, what to head off and how. Then I took on calf wrassling while branding was on. Of course I took only little fellers there.

A writer said one time that on account of doing nothing else but riding a cowboy's muscles are not developed, only from the waist down. I never seen a cowboy yet who looked that way, and I'm thinking that if anybody swings a rope for hours at the time, like is done during branding, or wrassles big husky calves for as long, there'll be some exercise found that takes in the whole body, and exercise of the kind where hide-bound muscles would never do, because there's something else besides strength needed in that work.

It's ticklish work at times, such as saddling or handling a mean horse while on the ground, and our horses are not as small as most people think. Few are smaller than the average polo horse, and many size up with the *hunter* of the East. *Wild* horses of that size can jerk a man around pretty well if he don't know how to handle himself. Then while that horse is quivering and about ready to blow up, if anybody is doubtful of the cowboy's shoulder muscles, try and slip

forty pounds of our saddle on such a horse's back with one
hand. The cowboy does it because he has to hold the horse's
head with the other.

With the big herds that was handled on that outfit I had
to keep my eyes and ears well opened if I was to do my
work right. There was brands to read and tally up on. That,
along with making out the earmarks, wartles and vents, was
my grammar while I was riding. There was many other
things, too, that had to be noticed and which, while only
shifting a herd, would take quite a size book to explain.

There was my shift on nightguard where I was bawled
out on for getting off my horse too close to the herd. I was
bawled out for many things I done now and again but never
more than once for any one thing. I always remembered.

I also remember once when I started to sing while on
nightguard. I'd started sudden and on a pretty high note
and come daggone near causing a good stampede. There's
writers who say that cowboys sort of sing cattle to sleep and
sing on nightherd only for that reason. That strikes me
funny, specially when I think of how I near caused a stampede by doing just that. If a cowboy sings on nightherd it's
only because he wants to, and not at all to sing any cattle
to sleep. Sometimes, on real dark and spooky nights, a rider
will hum or sing or whistle while going around the herd, but
that's only so they'll know of his coming and won't scare as
they might if they didn't see him till he got near.

The cattle we was handling on that outfit was pretty wild.
Over half of 'em was Old Mexico longhorn and the other
half was of the same breed only crossed some with Durham
and White Face. Them last two breeds hadn't made much
of a showing the herds as yet. Myself, I liked the old longhorn best and always will, even tho they don't bring as much
money. And, regardless of what all's been said about the

longhorn being of the past, . . . popular talk, I'm saying
now that I've rode for many outfits that owned many a thousand longhorn; and I don't have to go any further back to
tell of the time than 1914, only sixteen years ago.

I know where I can produce many herd of longhorn cattle, thousands of miles of wide open country, thousands of
wild horses right in this time of fast airplanes and 1930.
. . . And, for the past forty years, it's been handed out by
desk-hounds that the West and the cowboy is gone. That's
good small-town boosting, but, like all boosting, very far
from the truth.

Well. . . . Getting back to the outfit, the herds was
shifted, the cattle was graded and throwed on the range they
belonged. I done my little best to be of some help and, outside of wanting to "push" the cattle too hard and dragging
a rope, which I got bawled out for some more, I think I made
a pretty fair hand of myself. Anyway, I'd got so I could
ride my horses. But "that's nothing," said the cowboys,
"you've only been riding *pets*."

CHAPTER ELEVEN

LATE summer come, three round-up wagons was cut down to two. Thirty of the sixty riders (taking in all three "wagons") was thru and handed a "company check." The herds was all pretty well divided and now two wagons could take care of 'em. One wagon was to round up likely beef to deliver to the other, which would "cull out" and do the shipping.

I was one of the riders that was let go when the outfit cut down. "But," says the foreman of the wagon I'd been with, "you better stick on, o' course I cain't [he was a Tejano] pay you wages, but rest up a spell and I'll put you on again soon as I can."

That was fine, but I wasn't wanting to rest up, I was wanting to go. My private ponies was fat and fresh. They'd had nothing to do but cut down grass for the last two months, and there'd been plenty of that grass. The North was never stingy that way.

But I felt kind of lost when I started out on my ponies. They was fat and feeling good, but they, all of a sudden, struck me mighty small and, for the first time, I noticed that they wasn't handling their front feet exactly as they should, specially with the black horse. I never rushed 'em no time after I lined out from the outfit, but one morning, when they was run in from a pasture of a little ranch where I'd stayed over night, I noticed that the little black was pushing his front legs ahead of him, like as if they was made of wood. The sorrel was near as bad. Then it came to me sudden; them ponies wasn't young no more. I'd had 'em for ten years or so, and I couldn't tell how old they was when I did get 'em.

I rode pretty slow out of that little ranch, and I was thinking a whole lot. First, I thought of my two ponies. They couldn't go but a few years more and I wanted to make it easy for 'em during them few years, not that they'd had a tough time with me but they'd been *with me* and I just wanted them to have it easy, and with nothing but green grass and good hay staring 'em in the face for the rest of their lives.

Another thing I thought of was, that no cowboy I ever knowed was astraddle a *"pony."* He was always riding a good chunk of a horse, a horse weighing at least a thousand pounds and standing from fifteen to seventeen hands high, as they say in some places.

Them ponies (I always call horses "ponies." Maybe that comes from handling many a bunch of 'em, all sizes. I've called horses "ponies" when they'd tip the scale at fifteen hundred pounds, work horses, and when they'd have a stand of seventeen and eighteen hands. There's many horses that big on the range, but they're not like the wild horse, they can be turned and corralled) . . .

Anyway, them ponies the boys was riding made my little sorrel and black look like ants. . . . Here I was, setting on two undersized and stove-up "pets" while, I thought, I

should be riding any full-grown tough bronk, like the rest
of the boys was doing. When I'd come to a ranch I'd sort of
sneak in so I wouldn't be seen on what I was riding. . . .

I was glad when one day I finally sees a rider fogging
down a ridge, a trying to put two bunches of wild stuff together. My ponies was sort of warmed up at the time and
lost their stiffness and I fell in on one bunch while the rider
was turning the other. Both bunches mixed down in a draw
and the rider grinned a "howdy" to me. An hour or so later
another camp of a big "spread" come to sight.

It strikes me funny now when I hear tell that the cow
country was all shot in 1890. . . . This was sometime no
earlier than 1907.

It was some outfit too and running along about a hundred thousand head of cattle which was scattered from
Canada to Mexico. (For the benefit of the old cowboy, I'm
not talking of the Miller & Lux, this was a different outfit, and if the old cowboys will remember, this same outfit
had more cowboys one year than they had cattle. The hard
winter before had cleaned the range of all herds. . . . I
broke horses for them when they had no cattle in *one* State.
The horses I broke was for polo. That's all the outfit had
left, horses.)

Anyway, and before that outfit lost out, I met that cowboy hazing two bunches for the same. An hour after I hit
camp I was hired, hired to nighthawk. Of course that was
against my ambition, being I thought I was such a rider, but
I took on that job because I was asked to mighty well and
I thought that maybe I'd be put on as a "hand" soon.

But the jinx seemed to've camped on that outfit's tail, far
as nighthawks was concerned. One had been busted up pretty
bad while riding acrost country which he thought was all
level. It wasn't. Another had been killed by lightning, and
that's the one I took the place of. . . . I was third.

I took on that dead nighthawk's string, rode 'em for a couple of weeks and then something happened that went to show that the third happening is not always a charm.

I was riding along on a good gentle horse, a heap gentler than the night had been; two knot-headed bronks started lining out of a sudden for their home range and I went to head 'em off. The grass was dry and the ground was slick with an early frost. When I got 'em headed off and turned, my horse turned too, and too quick. His four feet went out from under him like as if he'd been shod with soap and running on glass. Him and me went up in the air and came down together. Then he landed with all his weight and a heavy thump on my right foot and slid on that foot of mine for at least ten feet.

I didn't feel no pain much at the time, but my ankle was sure busted, for when I stood up my toes pointed another direction from where I was facing.

Lucky it was my right ankle that got busted, because I could still use my left foot to stick in the stirrup and get up on my horse with. Another lucky thing, I was only about half a mile from camp. It was just daybreak and the riders was all there.

I was made to take a good swig of whisky (my first taste of the stuff) which the cook had hid, while the boys cut my boot off, reset my ankle as best they could, and bandaged it up tight. In a few minutes I was put in the bed wagon, two runaway horses hooked onto it, and headed acrost country to the nearest doctor, about twenty miles away.

There's no use saying that it was a painful ride to the doctor's place, and painful some more when the doctor had to reset my ankle over again. I was handed another swig of whisky before that, but it didn't seem to help much.

I stayed right at the doctor's place for a month, or more, most of the time in bed. Towards the last of that time I could set out in the front window and sort of enjoy seeing the town from there, what there was of it. A little store was acrost the street and handled everything from liniment to flour and meat and ladies' dresses. The owner was postmaster, justice of the peace, stock inspector and horse dealer. There was a couple of saloons, a livery stable, a hotel and about fifteen other houses to make up that town. Close as I remember, I think it was about fifty miles from the railroad.

After it was seen that the plaster cast on my ankle was all right, I was hauled back to one of the ranches of the outfit I'd been working for. An old couple and a rider was there. The lady cooked, her husband kept things in shape on the ranch and the rider was breaking horses. It was a fine place to stay, but being I wasn't to move around but very little and only on crutches, made me feel sort of restless once in a while. I drawed and read a lot and then, if the weather was bad, I'd hop to the kitchen and talk to the lady and watch her mix things.

I was glad it was winter because it'd sure been hard on me to be layed up while grass was in sight and the country open. In good days I'd hop over to the corral and watch the cowboy snap out his bronks. He was a mighty good hand, good rider, and he'd never get peeved at anything a green horse ever tried to do to him. I seen many an ornery bronk strike or kick at him and barely miss him. If he was whistling at the time he kept right on whistling, like as if nothing happened. The only time he'd take it out of a horse is when he was sitting in the middle of him. The minute a horse started to bucking he'd unlimber a long quirt made out of a stub latigo and go to pounding till that horse raised his head and behaved himself. He scared many a horse out of bucking that winter and there was no welts showing on their hide either, because the quirt he used was flat and wide and the smack of it hitting, which sometimes sounded like a shot out of a gun, done a heap more to make a horse line out than any cutting quirt could of done.

I learned a lot about handling bronks from that cowboy that winter, and there wasn't a good day come along that I didn't hop to the corral and watch him.

I'd been at the ranch a month or so. My ankle had been itching and itching and the cast got to feeling big. So, one day, against all advice, I takes a hammer and chisel to the cast and breaks it off. It sure felt fine for a spell, but being so used to the cast, I'd sort of forgot it was off and I begin bumping my big toe on things. That sure didn't feel so good, and then one day I give my ankle a pretty hard bump against the table leg while I was trying to set in at a good meal. . . . I didn't eat any of that meal, and a couple of hours later I had another cast on the ankle. That was made out of red clay mixed with horse-tail and I sat in front of the fireplace and baked it the best I could. It made a good cast too, and was just as hard as the first one. I kept that second one on for a whole month and more, itch or no itch.

By the time spring come, my bum ankle was in pretty good shape. The second cast had been off for about a month or six weeks and in that time I got it pretty well limbered up and strong again. I'd slip on my boots and give it exercise, but I was sure careful of bumps and not to stub my toe.

I guess it was about the middle of the following summer before I really forgot that I'd had that ankle busted. By that time I'd been riding for more than a month and for the same outfit. I'd been with that outfit about eight months and, up till then, that was the longest I ever stayed at one place, but it was a case there where I just had to.

Maybe I'd stayed there even longer if the wagon boss had

let me ride "on circle" (drives) as a regular hand, but he'd said "no" to that and that I'd have to stick to nighthawking or wrangling. I didn't want no more of them kinds of jobs, besides I was aching to be drifting again, anyway. So one fine morning I dabs my rope on my little sorrel and saddles him. Then I dabs and makes another throw for my little black, and I ties my bed on him. Them two ponies hadn't been rode all the time I was with the outfit and they was fat as seals. I felt mighty well mounted and independent as I hit out for new territory, even if they was stiff.

I drifted on down the country, South, always South. I passed and stopped at many places. No jobs was offered me and I didn't ask for none. The outfits struck me as too small. After me riding for a few big outfits like I had, I couldn't think of riding for the small ones. To me, that struck me as bad as going back to wrangling, and I felt that I was above that.

Like most kids of fifteen or sixteen, I had a pretty high opinion of myself about then. I hadn't been knocked down yet and I was like any yearling in any herd, kind of holding my head high. That all was brought on I think by the fact that people sort of quit looking at me as a kid and want to take me in and take care of me. When I rode up to a place now I was treated pretty well like as if I was a grown-up. I was grown up pretty well as far as height was concerned, even tho I sure wasn't very big around. I felt all the bigger when I'd come to some little ranch and begin talking to a kid of my age and size. And after I'd get thru telling of all the big outfits I'd rode for and so on, I'd sometimes swell up quite a bit. Then to put on the finishing touches, I'd roll up a neat cigarette.

But, with my drifting, I often bumped into happenings that'd make me be my own age for a spell. Like one day, I'd rode into a fine little ranch, stayed there over night and was asked the next morning if I wanted a job. I said "No, Sir," that I was headed for a big outfit and would most likely "get on" there. Then the cowman takes me off my pins and cools me down right quick by asking me, "Can you ride?"

I come pretty near snorting at that. What did he mean, could I ride? . . . Hadn't he seen me when I come in, didn't I set my horses good?

But what the cowman meant was, could I ride a bronk, a good tough one, and when I says, "Sure I can ride," is when I soon found out.

"Well," he says, grinning, "if you can ride and read brands as good as you can roll a cigarette I've got a job for you, and I'd be sending you to join the biggest outfit you ever seen and 'rep' for me there."

"All right," I says, "I'll try." I was tamed down a bit.

But I got tamed down some more when he run a little bunch of horses in the corral a while later. The cowman rode to where I'd been waiting.

"Now," he says, "there's a couple of colts I'd want you to take along in your string and ride. If you can't set 'em, I'll just have to get somebody that can, because I want 'em well broke." He looked at me. "Do you want to try one?"

I *tried* one. I tried that one three times, and after he throwed me off the third time I got to thinking I wasn't such a rider as I'd figgered I was. I don't know if the horse bucked very hard. I studied a spell, quite a spell, while I got my breath, and then I happened to think of something, something I'd seen many an old-time rider do and which I'd never thought of doing before.

I'd been riding a slick tree, a hard tree to keep track of, and of the kind that's not in use no more. That was before the swell-fork came in much. . . . I remember well how me and the old-timers made fun of the first swell-fork we seen, and how we wouldn't be caught riding such saddles. Well, the old-timers and me was no better, because when the horses got sort of tough for us, we tied our slickers up in front and that's as good as any swell-fork.

Well, I'd been packing my slicker behind my cantle. Now I brought it up and tied it on the front and let it slap. I lost my head on that horse but I kept my balance and, when I was hollered at "to stick," I stuck.

"Pretty good," says the old man. "Now, let me see you read earmarks and irons."

He took me in the house, drawed a long line and made earmarks "facing me" on both sides, then he gave me his tally book and asked me to read it. I read it all right and I surprised him some when I even read some of his "Character" brands.

"I think you'll do all right," he says. Then he asked "How old are you, Son?"

"About sixteen, I guess."

I turned my old private ponies loose on tall grass and took on ten head of the old cowman's horses for my string.

"Keep your slicker in front, Son," he says, as he opened the corral gate, "and don't be too perticular about them Character brands of mine."

I winked at him and rode on.

In a couple of days I struck the "wagon" I was to ride with. The boys grinned as they seen me running my string in, and I grinned back at 'em while I heard remarks that "Old" what's-his-name sure must of hard-wintered some when he has to hire "kids."

Anyway, *I got out of dayherd,* and when I cut my last bunch out of the main herd, there was quite a few head of cattle amongst 'em with Character brands that couldn't be read very well. I throwed 'em in with mine and called 'em "markers." I let on I knowed the earmarks, and being nobody knowed me, they might of figgured I could show proof and couldn't be tampered with, much.

My *riding* wasn't so bad about then. I'd got to be noticed some for that. I kept my slicker in front and my rope handy, and by the time I got thru with that outfit they sure enough begin to wonder if "old what's-his-name" had hired a kid after all.

Me being looked at as a kid must a had a lot to do with my getting by. Where I worked it some was how I could draw out an "iron" and make different figgures out of it. I was working for *my* outfit, even if I was "repping" with another good outfit.

I was smiling when the wagon pulled in under the home sheds and I lined out with what cattle I'd gathered. This was the last bunch, about a hundred head, and with them I was hazing my ponies back.

I'd sure earned my wages, says the cowman as I rode in one evening. "Maybe," he says, sort of quiet, "*we* can get a few more 'out of the brush.'"

I think I'd drifted on, my work was done, my private ponies was well rested and "blue ridges" was calling me again, but the old man talked me out of that when he pointed down to the pasture where, on a knoll, my two old ponies was nose to rump and swishing flies.

"Why, Son," he says, "you're afoot. You got nothing to ride but fat without legs."

That was true, my ponies was very fat but their age and legs was getting sort of past. But I figgured I'd go on some more with 'em, I was wanting to see new range as usual. About that time the old man had me follow him over to the corral, where I'd run in the last gathering I'd got from the round-up, and pointed me out a few yearlings.

"Now," he says, "them *was* 'sleepers' " (a sleeper is a critter that's earmarked and not branded), "and how you got
away with them I don't know. Some of them are my cattle
and most of 'em are not, but I see you sure drawed the 'character mark' on 'em. Looks like that was done in a hurry, but
it's fine drawing. . . . Being you're so good at that," he
says, "I've got good wages for you if you'll . . ."

About that time a screen door opened by the house, a
freckle-faced brown head stuck out and said it was time to
eat.

I seen that freckle-faced brown head at the table that evening and, like any yearling that's been running with a dry
herd, I forgot I had any other range to see.

When the meal was over and me and the old man went to
the corrals and squatted there with only "the dippers" and
other stars for witnesses, I'd got to be agreeable for anything he wanted me to do, from eating raw bear heart, picking wild flowers, or climbing the chain on the lightning.

"If you'll stay and work for me," he says, "your wages
will be raised half, and not only that. You savvy 'sleeping,'
'mavericking' or 'long roping,' you'd kill 'slow elk' before
you would 'company beef' . . . that's fine."

He kept quiet for a spell, and then he went on.

"And, excepting one, I'll give you the pick of any two
head of my horses. You can turn your little fellers loose with
me and nobody will ever touch 'em. They'll be getting good
grass in the summer and all the good hay they want for the
winter, for as long as they live. All you've got to do is take
them two ponies I want to give you and keep them as your
'privates.' I'll furnish you a good string on the side and
we'll work *together*."

I didn't know just what that "together" meant but it gave
me hints of something that wasn't right according to law.
The old man kept a talking and explained some of what was

pinching in on his chest. There was, as he told me, the death
of his only son just a few months before. That son had layed
and suffered in a hospital. The mother went in too and died
just a couple of months before the boy did.

"While I was in town trying to do all I could for 'em," he
says, "my range was grazed down to dust by tramp sheepmen." On account of the feed being all gone, most of my cattle died during the winter and, on top of that, here comes
mortgage papers slapping me in the face.

"I'm all alone now." I looked towards the house as he said
that. He caught my look. "The girl in there is my niece and
only comes here to say 'hello' to her old uncle and sort of
tidy things up once in a while. . . . Yep," he went on, "I'm
all alone, and I ain't got nothing to do now but try to forget
the weight on my chest and do a little 'squaring up.'

"There's a sheep outfit neighboring me here where I'm
going to do my starting in on that squaring up. They
claimed I sneaked up on 'em by me getting a hold of this
little place I've got. They thought they had it, but when I
got a surveyor on the job they found that their line was two
miles due east of here. They never got over that, and they
been raising samhill with me and my cattle ever since.
They've been happy at everything bad that's happened to
me and now I'm all coiled up, but I won't be no snake.

"They're running about a thousand head of cattle along
with their sheep and feeding their sheep well and letting
their cattle starve." He stopped talking and laughed. "What
tickled me," he went on, "is that the 'sleepers' you brought
in was from them and that goes to show that they shouldn't
have any cattle to begin with, to be so careless with 'em.

"Now, I'm getting a little mean, Son," he says to me, "but
I think I need to be. I'm in a pinch and with your help I'm
going to work this sheep outfit till they're clean of any loose
cattle. There's a couple other outfits I want to work on, too.

Your wages are up to fighting gage from the time you started, . . . are you with me?"

I didn't know how to answer. I knowed what he was talking about, but hiring out that way was something new to me. But I soon was made to feel that there was no wrong in doing what he wanted me to, not unless I got caught, and the only thought I got was that I'd be helping the old man and having a lot of fun getting away with it. Then there was the horses he would give me, and finally I says, "I'll keep on working for you just the same way I have, pick up 'loose slicks' and 'sleepers' when I know I can get away with 'em, but I won't tackle no big bunch at a time . . . and about them horses," I asks, "will you let me have them two bronks I rode out to the wagon?"

"Sure," he says, "and a home for your old ponies and you, for as long as you want it."

We shook hands on that and I felt like I was much of a man when there was no more words said. I felt if my young cannon was handy, thought of my rigging and where I left it last, where the closest horse was and, to cap things, just as I was rolling me a smoke the screen door opened again and a voice was heard that went with me as to say "all is well."

CHAPTER TWELVE

I DON'T know what Bopy would of thought if he'd knowed of me hiring out as a "long rope" artist. Maybe he'd felt the same way I did at the time, because then in that country it seemed like the only big wrong in appropriating cattle was getting caught doing it. It was still less wrong to steal cattle from a sheep outfit. Anyway, that's how I was made to feel, and it wasn't long when I was as much against the sheepman as any cowman could of been.

What turned the cowman against the sheepman from the first is that the sheepman came in the country after the cowman had found it, claimed his part and made the range safe against the Indian. The cowman had fought for it for all he was worth and soon as he had the Indian tamed down and raids was getting far apart, why here comes the sheepman to tramp down the grass the cowman had fought for. The blatting woollies and the herders had no respect for the cowman's territory and not only tramped down his grass, but brought in a lot of loco and other poison weeds.

There's many a part of the range country right to-day where the cowman still mixes it with the sheepman, and that'll always be, I guess, as long as there's open country and cattle and sheep.

The old cowman I was riding for was pretty sore at all

sheepmen and he kept a stirring me up about 'em till I got
to thinking it was sure fine to sort of get even with 'em for
him. It was a lot of fun getting by with it too, and being I
liked the old cowman so much made me try to please him all
the more. While pleasing him I was getting in good with that
brown-headed niece of his too. Far as she knowed, I wasn't
doing anything out of the way, but just the usual riding for
her uncle, and what her uncle had to say that was good about
me sure smoothed things.

All around, I got to thinking I was pretty smart. The old
man would ride with me once in a while and sort of coach me
as to the tricks of the rustling game. He knowed many tricks
and I don't think I could ever got a better teacher in that
line. His work wasn't coarse in nothing he done, wether it
was picking out the cattle or making over an iron. In picking out cattle, he warned me never to take a "marker" (an
animal that could easy be recognized by odd markings).
When he changed a brand he didn't use no knife, no hot iron,
nor wet blanket. He had a little bottle of some acid, which
parts he'd get at different stores and mix. By dipping a
twig in that acid he could work over the old brand and
spread out with the new one. In a few hours the new brand
would show up in a scaly ridge and look as old as the first
one it blended with. There'd even be gray hairs showing and
that brand would stand inspection from the outside of the
hide as well as from the inside, in case trouble come and the
animal would have to be killed and skinned to show evidence.
It takes a burned brand a few months before it shows a ridge
inside a hide.

But the old man didn't do much brand altering. He would
had to have too many registered brands and that would
throw suspicion, with as little a herd as he had. He done most
of his work on young stock, "sleepering."

"Sleepering" is taking an unbranded calf and earmarking him with the same earmark the mother has and turning him loose *unbranded*. The earmark is that of the outfit he belongs to and draws no attention, and if a rider is not on the watch he'll take it for granted, on account of the earmark, that the calf *is* branded. If that goes over well and it's not noticed that the calf is unbranded, the rustler will then get the calf when he's about six months and wean it away from its mammy and slap on his iron. The earmark can be changed then to go with his own cattle.

Sleepering is where I came in at. I was of an age that nobody suspicioned much and, being a stranger, none of the closest outfits ever got to know that I was any more than just a rider drifting thru, and they didn't connect me with the old man. Even my string of horses was strange to that country. I was very careful to dodge meeting riders, and when I took my rope down to catch a calf to earmark, it was always well out on a big flat. The earmarking was done mighty quick and the calf was soon let go to his mother again.

I got a big thrill out of doing that, something like what, I guess, most kids would get when stealing watermelons when there's danger of getting a shot of coarse salt while making a get-away. My work was more dangerous than that because there'd be something a heap more penetrating than coarse salt coming my way if I was caught with my rope on somebody else's animal. It'd been bullets.

Realizing that, only seemed to make me work all the more interesting and, besides, I got to thinking I wasn't really doing any wrong. I wasn't stealing, I was just making it easy for the other feller to do that. Another thing was that some of them sleeper calves would be noticed and branded in time by the right owner while the other feller was waiting for 'em to grow to maverick size so he could get away with 'em.

Everything was coming along fine. Besides my wages, I was getting extra money for every fresh piece of right ear I brought in. I was riding good fast horses and the few scares I'd had from riders bumping onto me didn't amount to much, not excepting once, and that time sure made up for the others. I was just bending over a calf and earmarking late one evening, when my horse turns and looks up. I looked up too and, not over twenty feet from me, was a rider.

At the sight I fell flat behind the tied calf. It was too late for me to try to get away, so, seeing it was too dark for the rider to see what I looked like, I was going to run a bluff. I shot, not with intentions to hit but close enough by him so he'd know I wasn't shooting blank cartridges. That shot seemed to work well and in the next minute the rider had turned his horse and disappeared. . . . That rider had been mighty foolish coming up on a feller like he had me. He'd showed lack of experience with rustlers.

But, with that rider coming up on me and turning tail, it seemed like it wasn't many days later when that country got full of riders. I'd see one or two at a distance pretty near every day and I got to thinking that that one I scared sure must of spread the news of what he'd seen. Another thing was that the far scattered cattle, which I worked the most on, was brought closer and where the riders could keep a better eye on 'em.

"That's sure tough on us," says the old man. "Watching the cattle the way they are now, we better lay off a spell on account they'll notice the fresh earmarks if we keep on, and get onto the fact that somebody's sleepering. As it is now, I figger they just think you was fixing to work over a brand when that rider spotted you."

Anyway, as the old man said, our play was over for a

while. There was nothing to do now but wait and hope that all the sleepers wasn't found out so there'd be a few to run out when they was big enough. In the meantime, with a little acid, we would work on the few grown stuff that was missed, or the furthest ones out, and change brands to suit so there'd also be cows to tally up some when the sleepers had growed to mavericks and the appropriating brand was put on 'em. . . . Too many big calves and not enough cows to go with 'em brings suspicion to any outfit.

But I didn't stay to help the old man do any brand changing. I'd been with him quite a while now and I'd got a hankering to see new country again. I told the old man I might be back again later and help him brand the big calves, but I never did get to come back.

What made me decide to go, some, was that the girl had gone back to her folks. Not that that should of mattered maybe, because I hadn't got any further than to just talk to her a bit. She was older than me and talked about things I couldn't savvy, but I liked her and when she went I asked the old man if he'd take care of my two little old ponies for me and, with my two new horses, I lined out too.

It seemed that girls was due to come into my life, some, for it wasn't over a month later when, riding along for another outfit one day, and being well on the outside circle, I comes along a tall bench to where I can look down and see quite a sized ranch below me. But the ranch didn't draw my attention long, I seen a bunch of horses in a pasture and breaking away from that bunch was two horses at full speed. What struck me queer was that the horse behind was chasing a horse with a rider on him. The rider looked small, like a kid. It was a kid. Another glance and I knowed what was going on, the kid on the horse was being chased by a mad stallion, and such an animal is mighty dangerous to be caught up with, for the power of their jaws would make a lion ashamed of himself.

I more than rushed my horse down off the bench and into the pasture. By the time I got there, the stallion had run the kid's horse straight thru a barb wire fence. The kid had somehow stuck on. The stallion had stopped at the wire and was turning back to his mare bunch when he seen me and come along to chase me out, too. But I didn't chase very well. I planted a bullet in him that layed him flat, and I rode on full speed to see what'd happened to the kid.

I found the kid, a girl about my age but smaller, laying in a thicket of plum bushes. Her horse had brushed her off and left her there in a heap. She was unconscious, and when I straightened her so she'd get air I seen that one shoulder sure wasn't right. While she was unconscious that way I tried to find the trouble. I was in a hurry too, and maybe a little rough, but now was the time to set things to rights. I finally heard something snap like it was going back in place, and I must of hit it right because she looked all right after that.

Then, being I couldn't see no water near and that the ranch houses was only a few hundred yards away, I packed her there. The big lady cook was the first one to spot me and I thought for a while I'd have to hold her up too. Then a younger lady which I figgured to be the girl's mother, came along at the cook's shriek.

"Get a little water," I says. "She's all right."

I packed the girl in the house while they was doing that, and layed her on a couch.

There was no chance of me getting away from the ranch and finishing my circle that day. I was told that her dad had gone to town with some horses and wouldn't be back till the next day. The only two riders on the place had gone with him and there was no one around now but the old chore man. They wanted me to stay, in case the girl should be took to town.

Of course I would be glad to stay, and I was more glad I did when a little later the girl, all propped up on the couch and looking pretty nice and comfortable, asked for me to come in. She wanted to know just what had happened and how, so I repeated to her the same story as I'd already told her mother. Of course I took a little longer to tell it that second time.

But I wasn't thru when I got done with the story. That'd only brought more to tell and, somehow, I found myself talking quite a bit, and pretty easy. I spent the rest of the afternoon and most of the evening doing nothing else much but just that. Sometimes her mother would come along and chip in a few words, see that her daughter was resting all right, and go on again.

Me and the girl got acquainted pretty well the next day. I was sitting on a big screened porch when her mother brought her out, and there they found me with a tablet in my hand and drawing pictures. I hadn't got a chance to draw for a long time, and when I seen a tablet laying on a desk I couldn't help but make use of it.

My drawing went pretty big with the girl and her mother, specially the girl, and I had to make many for her that day. It sure didn't go bad to be drawing, with that girl for company. She was sure pretty and mighty smart too, and by the time evening come and her dad rode in at the ranch, I think she liked my company pretty well, too. We was getting along fine and already beginning to joke with one another.

Her dad was a great big rough-looking feller and, at the sight of him, I got to wishing I hadn't shot that stud. But after he heard from his wife as to what happened to "his little girl" while he was gone, I knowed it would of been all right if I'd shot a few more of his studs.

"I've often warned her never to go in the same pasture where that stud was," he said . . . "but I should of took no chances and shot him myself long ago."

But, as it turned out, the stud wasn't dead. My bullet had just plowed a furrow along his forehead to his knowledge bump, and only stunned him. The girl's father was riding along with me the next day when the stud, not at all scary, came out of his bunch to meet us.

"Well, I'll be durned," says the big man. He drawed out his gun, figguring to make a surer shot of him this time, when another thought come to him. He turned his horse and motioned for me to race back to the ranch with him, and that we sure did because the stud wasn't far from us when we turned.

"I hate to shoot him," he says, as we reached the stables. "He's one of my highest priced studs, and, besides, I think I know how to take the fight out of him for good."

"Here, catch that rangy bay horse there in the corral and I'll mount one that's just as fast."

When we had both our fast horses saddled he handed me a long shot-loaded blacksnake whip. He took one for himself, and we started out again. . . .

So the stud could only pick on one of us at the time, me and the boss was about forty feet apart when he came out to meet us. He was sure a big powerful feller, of the draft breed, gray percheron and near twice the size of the horse I was riding. But his size and weight sure didn't seem to hinder him in action and speed, and for a ways he could easy catch up with an average saddle horse. That's why we wasn't riding average saddle horses that day. He looked us both over as he came and, of a sudden, made a rush for the boss.

The boss turned his horse like a flash and started running, the stud right after him. Then's when the whips came in. The boss was reaching back with his long blacksnake and the lash popped like a shot every time it reached the stud's head. There was fur flying, and hide too.

While that was going on I was doing my part in working on the stud behind. I camped right on his tail and, with my blacksnake, I was burning that end of him. That horse was sure getting it at both ends and we done our best to take all the hide we could off of him.

He chased the boss for a while and when things begin to get hot for him, he turned on me. I turned too, took the lead and worked on his head the same as the boss had been doing. The boss had took my place at his other end.

We kept a changing ends on him that way for a good half hour. Sometimes, when he'd turn right quick he'd come near getting a hold of one of us or our horses. We sure had to watch out for that. But finally his turns got to be slower and slower, his speed too. He was dripping with sweat and his head and neck was pretty well skinned up, so was his other end. Come a time when he wanted to quit us and hit back for his bunch, but we wouldn't let him. We was going to give him plenty of medicine and some teaching he'd never forget.

Sometimes he'd get away from us and break for his bunch and we'd both burn his tail all the way in there. We'd let him rest for a spell and after a while we'd cut him out and take him around some more. He'd quit chasing us by then, he'd had plenty. But *we* wasn't thru. We cut him out again and again and chased him all over that pasture. By the time we did get thru we could ride alongside of him, touch him on the neck and he'd never put back an ear.

"I guess that'll do him," says the boss, finally . . . "and

if I ever see him chase a rider again, it'll be powder and lead for him."

It was after noon when I changed back to my outfit's horse and started back for camp. With me went thoughts of words that was said as to how welcome I would be any time I came back to the ranch. The little girl had said the prettiest words that way. I rode slow while thinking of some of the things she'd said and it's a wonder, in the trance I was in and riding in a strange country, that I ever found my way back to camp, or where the camp *had* been.

The camp had moved, and all there was to show of it ever being at that spot was the stirred-up earth where the rope corral had been, and ashes from the dead fire. It was getting dark too, and then I begin to come to my senses. I got to figguring that it'd been two days and a half since the wagon had moved. It had been moving twice a day before I left it, making from eight to ten miles at each move and, if it'd kept that up since I seen it last, the round-up camp would be over forty miles from where I was, and it would move fifteen or twenty miles more while I'd be riding to catch up with it. There was tall grass and plenty of loose stock covering up the remuda's trail and now I'd be lucky if I could see even the wagon tracks.

Being it was getting too dark to be able to see the old wagon track, and fearing to stray away from it, I stayed at the camp site where I'd seen the wagon last, for that night. I picketed my horse on good grass with my pet catch rope, and me, I curled up by my saddle, with a heap more food for my thoughts than for my belly. I was thinking of the little girl.

I was saddling by daybreak the next morning and being I had no breakfast to waste time on, I was soon on my way. But I lost quite a bit of time finding out just which way the wagon had headed. Finally I rode on as I thought the "pilot" would, and I was lucky enough to find a place at a creek where the wagon had crossed. I hit out on pretty good gait from there and soon the trail acrost the country got fresher and plainer. The round-up wagon seldom followed a road in that country. By noon I'd found the outfit. They were circling back a bit. I'd also rode by three places where I seen they'd made camp, and being my appetite was coming back on me by then and getting stronger than my thoughts of the evening before, I begin scouting around that third camping place in the hope of finding part of some biscuit that'd been throwed away or some bone or something. But the chipmunks and birds had beat me to cleaning up on that and I couldn't find a thing.

I come to another camp site a while later and there I found some remains of boiled rice and raisins. That mixture must of run out of water while the cook had it on the fire because it was sure black and brown, but, right then I liked it that way. At the next camp I found a hunk of salt pork. Nothing had bothered that, and after I et it I was glad that the wagon trail kept along a creek pretty well.

It was getting dark again. My horse was pretty tired but I kept on a going away after I couldn't see the wagon tracks, thinking I'd sure find camp now either by the fire or by the bellering of a herd. The night was cloudy, but it was still, and any sound carried far, but it was at that time of the night when every range animal dozes for an hour or two. I was riding along half asleep myself when my horse near jumped out from under me. Something white had raised up sudden right in front of us, and if I'd ever heard of ghosts before, I'd of thought sure I'd run onto one. But it was just a white horse that'd been laying down and sleeping. My horse had pretty near stepped on him.

The white horse had got just as scared as mine did, at our so close and sudden appearance, and snorting at every jump he'd hightailed it down a draw. Pretty soon I hear a commotion and the sound of more snorts and running hoofs, and then I heard bells. It was the remuda I'd run into.

I helped the nighthawk hold the spooked-up horses together, and after we'd stopped 'em I asked him where camp was. I found it about half a mile away. The fire had died down. I unsaddled and picketed my horse, found me some cold meat and biscuits to chew on, and washed it all down with cold black coffee. In another two minutes I'd located my bed roll, unrolled it and crawled in, and right then I wasn't thinking no more of no little girl from anywhere.

CHAPTER THIRTEEN

IT was a month or so later when the round-up wagon of that outfit pulled in, and I was glad. It had been a cold mean fall and so wet that my wooden stirrups stretched down an inch, from water being splashed on 'em while riding. Everything was wet, the cook was cranky, the herd was hard to work and hold, and the horses was full of snorts and kinky and taking it out on us riders to warm up.

We had a big herd with us on the way back to the home ranch, cows with big "weaner" calves (calves old enough to wean), bulls and old stuff. We had to stand guard every night till one night, about one day's drive from the home ranch, when we struck big corrals. We "weaned" (separating big calves from their mothers) at them corrals the next day, and kept the calves in the corral, figguring on taking 'em to the home ranch the day after. We was taking a well deserved sleep that night, with no guard to disturb it, when along about midnight the beller of one calf was heard going by our camp, then another, and another, till there was hundreds of others. The weaners had somehow broke out of the corral and was running around looking for their mammies.

The first few bellers was no more than heard when all of us had jumped in our boots and pulled up our britches. Our night horses had been picketed as usual, and away most of us went, a trying to round up all calves and grown cattle we could find before they scattered too far, while the others rode for the corral to try and hold what few might still be there. But there was no few there, not a one. Well, we cussed some, and then some more, and rode most of the night. Here, we'd been just one day from being thru with our work when three or four more stared us in the face. . . . A cowboy is just as glad to pull in off round-up in the fall as he is to pull out with it again when spring comes, and every day is sure counted at them times.

It took us two days to make a good gathering of the cattle. During that time it snowed steady, but we kept right on gathering till we got the original count, separated the calves from their mammies again, and finally made it into the ranch, right in the thick of a nice blizzard. But there was smiles on all faces when we filed the calves thru the big gate leading into the corrals of the ranch that day.

And we all was a happy bunch when, after a good bait at the long table at the cook house and under a roof, we gathered at the bunk house. Everybody was joking and full of song. Even the foreman lost his responsible look and begin to turn loose, and the couple of crippled riders that'd rode the bed wagon in, felt like throwing away their crutches.

At the end of the long bunk house was a little office. While we was telling our stories and singing, the superintendent come in, grinned and said "Howdy, Boys," and then walked on to that little office with the foreman. Pretty soon our names begin to be called, one by one. A cowboy would go in and come out with a company check. Only a few didn't come out with the said check and it was found by that that not

enough riders was willing to stay on for the winter. . . .
After six and eight months without no other floor than
prairie sod and no other roof than the sky, seeing only leath-
er-covered humans and none at all with skirts nor long hair,
it was about time for a little change and some fun.

But the cowboy soon tires of town, and if the outfit was
going to be left short-handed it wouldn't be for long. A few
would soon start drifting back, and others would follow till,
by the time middle-winter come, there'd be more riders than
the outfit would need, and some wouldn't be on payroll, just
waiting for spring to come and the round-up wagon to pull
out again. Wages in that country was mighty low in winter
and work was scarce, but the outfit owners liked to have
extra riders stay on during the hard months because when
the spring works opened up they could then line out on time
and full-handed.

I was one of the boys that accepted the company check.
It was my intentions to go visiting, visiting that little girl
down country quite a ways. But them intentions of mine
didn't come to a head for quite a few days. About a dozen of
the boys was headed for some town sixty miles or so away
and they made it pretty strong that I should come along
with 'em. The whole bunch was feeling their oats. They was
good fellers and I hated to part with 'em, so, after I was told
how I needed some new clothes anyway, I decided I'd go
along, as a good wind-up for the long rides and tough shifts
we'd put in together.

We was all riding our private stock, all fresh from many
months of nothing to do, and I was as well mounted as any
man ever was, for I was riding none other than Smoky, the
horse that led me to write the story by that name only a
few years ago. He was all the horse I wrote of in the story.
The happenings was none less as was in it, but they was a

hardly opening his eyes stuck his toes in his boots, pulled up his britches, put on his coat and hat and started for his night horse.

On the range, a cowboy dresses in bed, and none of us really woke up till our boot-heels hit the floor. We'd been pretty sleepy and nobody had noticed where we was at till the thump of boot-heels on wood was heard. About then the old cowboy turned on the light, sized us all up and broke into a laughing fit. We was up, all ready to go, then we looked at the walls and ceiling and we gradually begin to come to.

In the meantime the old cowboy had stopped laughing long enough to say, "Where you all going, boys, there's no guard to night."

I wouldn't begin to tell of the language that was heard for a few minutes following that remark, but when them few minutes of storm was over and we looked at one another, we soon begin to laugh with the man that'd pulled the joke on us. We'd so all fell for it that each man was more than comical to the other.

After many long months of steady nightguard shifts, a rider gets used to waking up at any time of the night by just the touch of a finger and a whisper. He's more than half asleep while he dresses, and does everything thru long habit. He never really wakes up till he gets on his night horse and hits the breeze for the herd to relieve the other men that's on shift before him.

The touch and whisper of the old cowboy in the hotel room that night worked on us the same way as if we'd been at the round-up camp, and sure brought out results that more than pleased him.

"You leppies didn't come to town to sleep, did you?" he asks, still laughing and looking us over. "It's going to be a long time before spring and you'll all get plenty of chance to sleep by then. Besides," he went on, "it's daybreak, look out the window and see."

"Well, anyway," says one of the boys, "being I'm up I'm going to dab a little dew on my face, comb the burrs out of my foretop and run down to the saloon and see if I can talk the swamper into letting me in for an eye opener."

"Now you're talking," says the old cowboy. "If you'll wait till I can get to that wash-basin I'll be right with you."

All the other boys was for the same motion, and me I didn't say nothing but I trailed along. There was no need to talk to any swamper to get in, because the saloon was wide open and the bartender was already working at the bar when we came in. I walked right in with the rest of the boys but stayed hid all I could from the bartender. I hadn't forgot the last time, when I was asked to read a sign and get out. But that bartender's sharp eye finally spotted me and, pointing a finger my way, he asked,

"How old are you, Kid?"

I was just going to answer my guess when one of the boys speaks up.

"Don't worry about him," he says. "Ask his dad, he's right here." He turned, looked at the old cowboy who'd played the nightguard trick on us, gave him a jab in the ribs and asked,

"How old is he, Grandpap?"

"Born in ninety, figger it out for yourself," says the old rider mighty serious-like and looking the bartender square in the eye. Then he turned and looked at me, still mighty serious, and added on,

"And he don't drink yet, either."

I couldn't miss the meaning of them last words and, to the bartender, they must of seemed very fatherly-like. The

other boys acted their part too, and finally the bartender
went on a wiping the bar.

"What will you have, gents?"

Three rounds was spread out one after the other and
spilled down the same route where, for many months, nothing stronger than black coffee had been. Me, I had some
bubbling colored water, and after the third round was down
we went out on the sidewalk a trying to make plans for the
day. A couple of us was to go to the stable and see that all
our horses was well took care of and, outside of that, there
was nothing to do but visit around with the other boys from
the other outfits. There must of been at least a hundred and
fifty riders in town that day.

You'd find 'em in barber shops getting a bath, haircuts
and all the trimmings. Some would be in stores getting outfitted up in working and town clothes, and the rest would be
scattered out between the saloons, saddle shops and the
stables. I outfitted myself in a pair of "oregon pants," a
heavy coat, a dozen plain white shirts, new hat, ties, a caddy
of tobacco and cigarette papers, and other things, which all
took a good hundred dollars from my wages.

"In this daggone country," says a cowboy that was also
buying, "a feller's got to work all summer so's he can buy
enough clothes to keep hisself warm in winters."

Well, I was all fixed and had everything I wanted but a
razor. I didn't need that yet. And now there was nothing to
do that would be much fun till evening come. Some of the
boys had a little fun at the card tables and some didn't. I
went down to the stables and at the sight of my horses I
wanted to go, but the stableman talked me out of it. He figgured I'd better stay overnight and take in the fun and
shows at the Honkatonk. I'd never seen a show of any kind
so I decided I would stick around and make use of the
chance, now that I had it.

It was along in the evening when, according to plans made, a few of us gathered in the saloon. Every cowboy was slick and shining, some even had regular town suits on and, being all set, we lined out for places af amusement. We come to a big Honkatonk, there was enough floor space there to hold a thousand head of cattle. On all that space was tables with chairs around 'em and lanes which run from a long bar at the back to a big stage at the front. Skirting along the walls, in two-story style, was booths where customers could be private while contesting as to which could get away with most of the fire-water that was served.

Us boys didn't take no booths. We scattered out at whatever tables we could get, four and six at each table. Drinks was served all around again and again and the old cowboy, who was still playing father to me, seen to it that I got nothing but colored water.

"Daggone shame to treat you this way, Kid," he would say every time a fresh round was ordered, "but this stuff is no good for a young feller like you. You should never touch red likker till you begin to get 'smooth mouth' or about thirty-five years old."

I was studying the big picture on the curtain when I noticed how it begin to raise. There was fine settings on the stage and a big piano and chairs. A feller wearing a black suit and stiff shirt-front came in and begin to play the piano and sing. He sure could sing good but I lost all hearing and sight of him when a girl pranced in and begin singing too. I thought she was sure pretty, but what struck me the most is that I'd never seen arms and chest so bare, and I know I felt a little warm around the ears when I noticed that she had no skirts on. It was the first woman I'd seen without skirts and it'd never come to my mind that they had legs.

But I hung on to my chair and rode for all I was worth. I don't think I heard a word of what was sung, but I was soon to get another blow. She hadn't got thru with her first song when here comes about twenty more girls without skirts. They all wore "tights" with frilly stuff around their hips. So many all at once was a big enough shock to make me feel sort of vacant for a spell, and I wondered if I ought to be caught looking. But, with the sudden amount of lady legs I seen, I got another blow which broke me right quick as to all seeings and happenings.

The old cowboy had spoke and said to the few of us at our table, "The leader of that little herd is quite some leader, ain't she?" He was speaking of the one that'd first come in, the prettiest one.

"And," he'd went on, "watch me frontfoot her."

"Listen, Old-timer," says a town boy from a next table, "I think you will be a little late getting her. She's been 'gotten' long ago."

The old cowboy looked at him and grinned kind of queer. "Being you're one of the buzzards that seems to belong around here," he says, "it ain't speaking very well for you to let her get away like that."

No more was heard from the other table. We kept on watching the show and after a while the old cowboy got up, saying he'd be back right soon, and left us. When he got back there was a grin on his face a mile long.

"I done got her," was all he said.

I couldn't figger out how a man could have the nerve to go up to a fairy-looking girl as that leading lady was and speak to her, but that's what the old cowboy had done. With me, I'd been scared to death. I'd looked at her the same way as I'd been brought up to look at all women, and being I was mighty careful and not much at ease when any was around, I'd of sure stampeded if that doll without the skirts had made a move my way. That's what I thought anyway.

The show came to an end. There was half an hour or so between the short shows, during which time the girls sort of mingled around some. They had skirts on then and I got a chance to look at 'em at pretty close range. I was at my busiest in sizing up one lady after another when I heard a familiar voice and, looking up in a balcony booth, I spots the old cowboy up there and a motioning for me to come on up. The other boys at our table had left and gone to the bar and dance hall adjoining, and so I runs up to the balcony.

I never thought but what the old cowboy was alone up there, but I sure got the surprise of my life, as he pulled back the curtain for me, to see, a setting right by him and with one arm over his withers, the girl that'd led all the others on the stage. There was another one a setting there too. That other one looked awful cute, and when she grabbed me by the arm and pulled me down right close by her I know that my heart lost many a beat. She took my arm and put it around her waist. It sure was a small waist, not much bigger around than my knee, but it was sure hard like as if it was surrounded with tin.

Drinks was brought in and both me and the old cowboy had ladies' arms around our necks as we took it down. I don't know what my drink was but I know I was drunk, drunk with smells of perfume and a girl being so close to me. That girl was sure a mothering me too, and saying all kinds of nice words. I sure thought she was fine, and then she kissed me. . . .

Me and the old cowboy kept a buying drinks and pretty soon him and his girl left, saying they'd be back soon. I was warned not to drink anything stronger than lemonade. But I think something a heap stronger was slipped up on me a couple of times because things got to looking queer and I begin to get wild. By that time the girl got to calling me by mighty sweet sounding names which I'd never heard before. She'd found that I had my big old six-shooter in my waist-band and she begin calling me her "Iron-clad boy," whatever that meant. As I got to feeling the strong drinks, I begin to try and return them sweet names but I was mighty short on that kind of language and she'd always laugh at me. I thought that was a lot of fun anyway. We ordered another drink and then she begin wrassling with me. That suited me too.

All was going along fine till, during the wrassling, a roll of bills fell on the floor. I recognized it as mine by the buckskin string around it and I wondered how it could of come out, it never had before. I was just going to reach for it when the girl beat me to it, laughed and stuck it down her waist.

"I'll buy the next drink," she says.

That was all right with me, but I didn't want any more to drink. We played a little more, and then she got up to leave.

"I've got to go now, honey boy," she says, giving me another kiss. "I'll be back again right after the show."

"Good," I says, "but you better let me have my money before you leave."

She seemed surprised and hurt at me asking for it and as she started talking so sweet I begin to feel sorry that I did.

"Why, lambie," she says, patting me on the cheek, "aren't we pals?" She pouted sort of baby-like. "You trust me, don't you? . . . I only want to keep it so bad mans won't steal it from you."

I was just about going to let her get away slick and clean with my hard-earned roll when, for no reason that I could of told of, I decided sudden that I wouldn't.

I laughed. "You better hand me my money back," I says. "I'm a 'bad mans' too and I'll take care of it all right."

As we talked on and the talk begin to get serious I noticed that her sweet ways was sure leaving her fast. She got less and less cute and when she stood up full height I seen that she was near a head taller than me. When finally she got mad at me keeping on wanting my money, she looked a foot taller. She reached down her waist for my roll of bills, took the buckskin string off around it and held the roll under my nose.

"Who can tell this is yours now?" she says.

"I can," I says.

She stuck the roll back down her waist, snapped her fingers at me and says, "You try and get it, and if you get funny with me I'll have you put in jail."

I was sure set back a considerable, not by her threats of having me put in jail but by the fast change in her. The few women I'd seen in my life had struck me as all to the good, away above anything on earth, and I wouldn't been surprised to've seen wings sprout on 'em. Now I runs up against one which all of a sudden had changed from what I thought was an angel to something which I knowed should of wore horns.

Being it was my first experience with a female and at such close quarters, I didn't miss a thing, and that sudden change from an adoring lady to a screeching wildcat sure knocked me. But it wasn't for long. I begin to get peeved, and jail or no jail, I was going to get my money back now.

She went to go by me, and the wrassling that went on from then on sure wasn't at all mixed with any petting. It was during that mixup that I heard language which would make a cowboy take a back seat and blush. I'd never heard a woman say a cuss-word before, none of any kind, but what this one had to say sure more than made up for all I hadn' heard.

Pretty soon she started falling apart. Big tufts of hair was begin to come down. I'd never seen "rats" and that scared me, but I was at the point where I'd get my money if I had to scatter her over the whole town. The few strong drinks that she'd slipped over on me made me all the worse, and I was just as ornery now as I'd been pleasant before. Finally, when she seen herself loser she begin to scream. I stuck my elbow on her gizzard, held her against the wall and told her something. When I got thru, she reached down what was left of her blouse and handed me my money.

She was just patching herself up and trying to pat her hair into place some when the old cowboy and his girl came in the booth.

"What's been going on here?" they both asked at once.

I grinned and said, "Nothing, we was just playing," but the girl with the old cowboy had seen me putting my money back in my pocket, then she looked at the other girl.

"What do you mean," she says, "trying to steal money from a kid?"

"Ah-h-h," snorted the other girl, "he's not as much of a kid as you think. . . ."

The old cowboy was beginning to laugh at the sight of both of us, and pretty soon he was laughing good. I begin to laugh too, because I knowed I was some sight. I found that out later when, after all the fun was over, we got back to the hotel and I looked at myself in the glass. My face looked like I'd stuck it in a den of wild cats, one eye was a little darker than the other and my new shirt had seen all its use.

It was from that happening that, like all cowboys then, I got to figguring there was only two kinds of women, the bad ones of the Red Light which wasn't to be respected much, and the others out of such a place which was to be *all* respected. But I found since that a feller is wrong in making a general opinion on things, and amongst the women in them bad places there's some that's good too.

I said good-bye to the boys the next morning, remarked how I hoped we'd all gather again by spring and then hit out of town. I'd seen the sights, sights that had nothing to do with a saddle shop, and now I was satisfied. I was hitting down country and happy with thoughts of seeing the little girl, a girl of the kind which to me was altogether different from the painted ladies I'd seen the evening before. Such as her was to be mentioned a long time ahead of the others and then forget to mention them others.

It was a few days later when I rode acrost the pasture and into the ranch where I'd met the girl. Her dad was just closing the corral gate when I rode up. He spotted me, grinned a "Hello there," opened the corral gate again and told me to put my horses in the stable. Everybody was fine, he said as he filled the mangers with good hay, and will be mighty glad to see you.

"And that stud," he went on to say, "we sure broke him from chasing riders last summer. All you got to do now is put up a hand at him and he sure hits back for the bunch. . . . Well, let's go in the house where it's warm."

I sure got a great welcome when I walked in there, from all, even the cook, and it sure didn't take me long to get back to where I left off with the girl, just about a minute or two, or as long as it took us to swap a couple of glances.

That evening, during the good meal and afterwards, was a mighty pleasant one for me. The father and mother talked to me a spell and then left me and the girl to play the phonograph, look thru the album and at some picture cards. She told me the names and all about the folks in the album, explained the scenes in the picture cards, and when I said good-night to her and her folks and started out for the bunk house, my head was pretty well up amongst the stars. It was a nice world, I thought, but there was nothing in it that was half as nice as a nice girl.

WILL JAMES '30

CHAPTER FOURTEEN

IT struck me as if I'd sure won me a home at that ranch,
the best I'd ever knowed, because I had "company"
there and the old folks took me in as one of the family. The
next day after I'd landed there I was offered a winter's job
breaking horses. I was started out with low wages and the
easiest horses, with promises that if I could break them few
and do a good job teaching 'em something, I would get higher
wages and better horses to work on. That sure suited me
fine. I'd long been wanting to take a job breaking horses but
the right job had never come along, and now, with such folks
to work for and be around with, I went to my first job of
horse-breaking with something more than intentions to make
good.

I took on the "easiest" ones that was pointed out to me and called on for all I'd learned in ways of teaching a horse something. That was quite a job for me all alone. Them horses had just been run in off the range and they'd never had a rope on 'em from the time they was branded, when colts. There's no use saying they was wild, for the range-bred horse is just as wild as any wild horse. He's just as different from the Dobbin of the city or farms as a wolf is from a poodle dog, or an antelope from a pet goat. I had a good snubbing horse to start 'em with, a good snubbing post to hold 'em and, as I was told, plenty of time to work on 'em and do that right.

First, I broke 'em to lead, then "sacked" 'em out and proceeded with the saddling and taking the buck out of 'em. I was easy on 'em, all excepting when they bucked with me, and then was the only time when I'd do my best to make 'em lose all ambition that way. But some of them "easiest" horses wasn't so easy for me to set, and I wondered for a while if they wasn't getting better at bucking than I was at riding. I was tossed around pretty well for a while and couldn't do much but try to stick on. A couple of times I come near bucking off fair and proper but luck was with me at both times and the old rigging slapped back under me.

Finally, with all the jolts and coming from five and six horses every day, there was a variety put together that was sure to soon make me quit or make a real rider out of me.

I didn't quit, and soon it was seen that I was doing a good job breaking them few easy ones, so good that after I had them first few going well I was handed two of the "better" horses. Them better horses, if broke right, would bring a better price, but they could buck better too, and when I climbed on one of 'em is when I figgured sudden that I was now really starting to ride. Them two "better" horses mauled me around a considerable and liked to wiped the corral clean with me, but I'd gone too far to quit now, and even tho they was near too much for me, I figgured on growing so I'd be able to at least set up on 'em.

I got plenty of practice right there and in a short while. These bronks was good stout fellers and half thoroughbreds, and I was inclined to be a little leary of 'em, but if I was leary of them there was something else which I had to watch out for while climbing one that had me plum scared. That was having the girl or her dad catching me trying to set up in my saddle while a big pony was taking me around the corral in hard hitting and crooked leaps.

The girl would sometimes come to the corral, talk to me and watch me ride. I liked the talking fine and I liked to have her watch me ride if I was saddling a horse that I could put up a good ride on, but I was sure scared to death that she'd come along when I was climbing on one of the big ones. She did catch me starting to put my saddle on one of the big ones one day and soon as I heard her coming I dropped that saddle like it was red hot, and letting on like I'd just got thru riding the horse, I turned him loose and caught another one, an easier one.

"Pretty tough pony, isn't he?" she says, after I'd got thru with that one.

"Not so bad," I says, "there's a couple here that's tougher than him."

"Oh, will you call me when you ride one of them?"

Now I'd put my foot in it and all I could say was "sure." But, thinking to myself, I'd sure have to set up better than I did. I wouldn't have her witness the whippings them big horses gave me for anything in the world. But, wether it was from fear of having her catch me putting up a bum ride or if the bronks was letting up some, there come a time soon after that when I could set up pretty well on the big ones and even put in a lick with my latigo quirt once in a while. I sure was meaning business.

I was getting along pretty fine when I was handed three more good bronks. My wages was raised with them, and I was told I was doing well, but nobody knowed how much I was earning them wages, and if it hadn't been for having such a good home there and the girl for company once in a while, I think I might of caught my private ponies and rode on. But I was lucky with the last three horses that was turned over to me. Two of them bucked only a few times with me and the third one didn't buck at all.

Everything was going good. After a while I had a few took away from me that went as broke enough for the time being. I was handed more big horses in the place of them and there was some that I called *tough*. But by the time I'd got so I could set up well on most any of 'em, I had to because I wouldn't been able to last much longer at the job. The girl could come to the corral now most any time and I wasn't scared to have her see me no more, and so I'd have an excuse to call her, I'd often ride the toughest ones before their turn.

Me and the girl had got pretty friendly. Sometimes, as I'd be riding a bronk out of the corral, she'd saddle up and come along and haze my horse for me when he lost his head. She was mighty good at that and could set her horse mighty well at any place and speed, specially her dad's horses which she was bound to ride while he was away. She claimed her own horses was too small and only for kids.

Sometimes when we'd be riding along and my horse was behaving, I'd make a stab at talking about other things than what just good friends talk about, something that had to do with just her and me. I'd gathered up some words which I was going to use in expressing myself that way and which would somehow tell of my love for her. For that was it, I was dead in love with that girl.

And one day, after I'd got to learn all the words I was to use well, and while we was riding along sort of quiet, I figgured now was the time to spring them words and let her know how I felt. I'd thought it all out as to how I was going to start in.

Her gloved hand was resting on her saddle rope. I glanced at it often, and after a while I stirred up enough nerve to lay my hand on top of hers. I was to start speaking soon after that but somehow, when I touched her hand, every one of the daggone words I'd picked out to use had all went into thin air, and not only that, but I couldn't think of any other words. I didn't dare look at her, and I got sort of uncomfortable and to wishing I could draw my hand away, but I felt I couldn't do that without saying *something*.

It was my skittish bronk that finally broke the spell. He wasn't used to seeing my hand stick out like that and he snorted and jumped to one side. After I got him cooled down some, I looked at her and laughed. She *smiled*. I could tell by that smile that she savvied, and understood as well as if I'd spoke.

Far as that goes, she must of knowed how I felt towards her long before, because I've heard since that women can read them symptoms on a man mighty quick. . . . She had a way about her that showed how I sure wasn't the first boy she'd ever seen to talk to. She'd gone to school every winter and now, as she told me, she'd soon be going to college.

But, as I was to understand, her leaving wouldn't make any difference, she'd think of me often and write me. I was *some* happy and proud kid.

The day before she was to leave came, and too soon for me. There was a big feed and dance given that evening. Folks from all around, and even from town, begin to drop in and I hit for the bunk house to dig up my very best so as to appear looking like something alongside of my girl. She was *my girl* now, there was no doubt about that because she'd told me so.

I was set at the table by her and all went fine during the meal. All went fine for a spell after that, and then, just as the fiddlers was tuning up, the door opens and here enters two young fellers fresh from some place and all elegant in well creased suits and flashy neckties. There was a little squeal of pleasant surprise from the girl and she rushed up to 'em. I'd never seen her, or any girl, look so pretty and lively as she was then.

The first dance was announced and, with my back to the wall, I stood there by myself. I couldn't dance and this was my first glimpse of such gatherings. It would of been some fun watching and I might of tried some of the funny steps if the girl had been with me on the start, but now, far as she was concerned, I didn't seem to be around. She wouldn't even look my way when once in a while she'd dance by.

Her mother came along and talked to me for a spell and asked me why I didn't dance and so on, but I wasn't very talkative right then and I finally told her I wasn't feeling well.

I stuck it out to witness three or four dances, a hoping the girl, my girl, would see me. But she'd seemed to've plum forgot I ever lived and all she had eyes for was one or the other of the fellers she'd started out with, and feeling badly hurt, I edged around the dancing couples and went out. I was a pretty sick calf.

I didn't sleep much that night. I layed on my bed with all my clothes on and tossed, and thought sure I was going to die. At daybreak I went to the kitchen, got me a cup of coffee, saddled one of my meanest bronks and hit out acrost country. I just wanted some air, and I didn't want to be anywheres around when the girl left for town on her way to college.

By the time I'd got back to the ranch I'd decided to get my own horses and hit out. I didn't think I could stand to be around where everything was to remind me of her, but I had to stay on for a couple of days, till the girl's father got back so I could get my wages, and in that time something happened which sure made me forget my "calf love" mighty quick. One of the big bronks I was riding went to bucking with me as I rode him out of the corral, bucked into a pile of timber, fell down there and broke my leg.

"That's a fine howdedo," says the girl's father as he pulled in to the ranch that evening. He took on a quick bait while the chore man harnessed and hooked up a fresh team. I was layed in the bottom of the rig and both the mother and the cook piled blankets and soogans over and around me, and soon I was traveling on the same stretch of country the girl had took just the day before.

We reached town before sun-up. There was a regular hospital there and sometime later I was all "set." All I had to do now, for a second time, was to lay there and wait for bones to mend.

I layed there plenty long, all that winter, another spell when I got plenty of time to draw many pictures, and soon as I was put in a wheel-chair, I was made acquainted with my first drawing board. There was many bucking horses drawed on that board and I'd get a lot of satisfaction when I got the feel of a saddle and bronk under me while I drawed. My reading and writing came second and I spent many a long hour at doing just them three things that winter. When I wasn't doing that I kept a looking out the window, seen storms come and go, thaws and freezeups, sunshiny days and cloudy days, and long nights. A tree was by the window and

I was still a patient when I begin to notice little buds coming on it, then one bird, two birds and later, more birds. Some was packing dry grass and moss and things in their beaks.

The grass was tall and spring was well along when I got back to the ranch. I wasn't supposed to ride for a while yet, and I didn't, but one day I got a letter from the girl. It was a nice letter and she asked why I didn't write. Towards the end she said she'd be home soon now, in another week or so.

But I only stayed one day after I received that letter. The next day I bid the folks good-bye, mounted Smoky, and leading my pack horse, I hit out. . . . I'd got over my calf love and now I didn't want to be around when she came back because I felt I'd made a fool of myself by such as me falling in love with her.

My ramblings from the ranch was pretty aimless for a spell. On account of my leg not being so strong yet I couldn't very well take on an average string with any outfit, so I just sort of drifted, and for no reason that I can tell I was drifting North. I crossed a river and the first thing I knowed I'd come up to the post that marked the border of the U. S. A. and Canada. I went on north a little ways further and then found a job riding line for a cow outfit. The line rider's job is to take a stretch of country, about fifteen miles long, and see that none of his outfit's cattle stray out of it, also see that the neighbor's cattle don't get in. It's a monotonous, two-meal-a-day job, breakfast and supper, and you had to cook them meals yourself. A *cowboy* never packs lunch nor canteen on a day's ride.

But I fell in pretty lucky on that line job. A scattering of home-steaders had begin to get in the country, and there was one and his wife had settled on a long bench not far from where I rode every day. They was just young people and being they asked me to eat with 'em when I come to visit one day, I got to repeat my visits. I was allowed to kill beef at my camp and I couldn't begin to eat what I killed before it spoiled, so I more than furnished 'em with meat and that paid well for my noon meal.

The young couple had come fresh from some eastern city just that spring. The husband had been a clerk in a store and she'd been a stenographer. They'd read a lot of boosting stuff about the free farm in the West and, after they got married, they'd come out to live happy ever after on a place of their own. They was happy, they was still on their honeymoon and full of hope. . . . They'd tell me of what all they was going to do year after year and so on, and I'd say, "that's sure fine," to all them *dreams* of theirs.

They liked to see me ride in on 'em. I was used to the country and I helped 'em a whole lot in things they wondered about. I coached 'em on how to supply up with grub and wood for the coming winter, how to take care of their one team of horses, and even how to cook. Neither one of 'em had ever touched a skillet or boiled a potato till they come West. Along with that, they got a lot of fun out of my company and I got the same out of theirs.

But, if I coached 'em in their start on the homestead, them two happy people also stirred something in me which I'd never thought of before. I got to wanting a place of my own, too.

This country I was riding in was a great cow country, and one day, after making a good check-up on my line, I hit out on the best horse the outfit had and found me a place on the bend of a big creek that would sure be fine to start out with. I located that spot on a plat, and when the round-up wagon came near my camp, I told the foreman to put another rider in my place and, riding Smoky, I hit for town many miles to the north and filed on a homestead and pre-emtion.

I had the land now, if I stayed on it, and plenty of range around to run the cattle which I didn't have. But I wasn't going to be no farmer and tear up no earth, and being there was a slump in cattle that year, I had no trouble getting fifty head of fine cows and calves throwed in, making altogether a hundred head, for a piece of paper I signed. I was to pay ten percent on the amount the cattle came to, and there was no set date as to when I should pay the main amount.

With my cattle all cut out and brought *home*, I started in to make a cowman out of myself. First I built me a round willow corral and then I went to work putting up a mud house. I dug in the side of a bank next to the creek and I put up a framework of posts with willows nailed on both sides about an inch apart. In the space between the posts I throwed some mud which I'd mixed with dry grass and as the mud oozed thru the willows I smoothed it with my shovel. It took me about a month to make that house. The floor in it was dirt, the walls was dirt and so was the roof, but it sure looked good to me. It looked like it would sure stay, anyway, and the walls had got as hard as cement. I went to the cowman who'd staked me to my cattle and got me a few boards and a window. Out of them boards I made a door and stuck the window in the center of it. Then I made some shelves and a table, and I was all set but getting a supply of grub.

I went to town, got a pack-horse load of that, and now all I had to do was to winter my little herd. Luck was with me that winter, it stayed open and grass was everywhere. My herd was no trouble and to use up my time I gathered a few traps from neighboring outfits and went to trapping cayotes and wolves. Along with that, I managed to take on a few shindigs, whenever I heard of any being pulled off, and I got to learn a few steps in the art of dancing.

I was setting pretty when spring come, my cayote furs alone had brought me more than summer wages and plenty to keep me in grub for a year. Besides my little herd was beginning to increase, and when I got thru tallying up, I was thirty some odd head to the good. Another thing was that the price of cattle was going up, and with all them things put together, my cattle, my horses and my own place, I felt mighty contented and at peace. I was tired of drifting and now I was started fine in making me a place where nobody had any say but me.

I took on a string of bronks that spring at five dollars a head for just taking the rough off of 'em. I was making money at that and it seemed like for every one horse I'd turn in there'd be ten head more to take his place. With them bronks I could do all the riding I wanted and watch over my cattle while breaking 'em. Smoky and the gray packhorse had nothing to do but eat and stay fat.

While astraddle one of them stout bronks I'd go visiting, some times one place and then another, and I'd be gone two or three days at a time. When I'd get back, my cattle wouldn't be over a mile from where I'd seen 'em when I left. That was a grass country and sure paradise for range stock. They never drifted in summers and stayed in one bunch well.

I was needing fresh meat one day and killed a yearling. It wasn't mine but nobody could tell it wasn't, because it wasn't branded, and having quite a bit of meat to spare, I thought I'd take one quarter of it and pay a visit to the homesteaders I'd met while riding line the summer before. They was only twenty miles from me.

I got sight of their shack, it was still the same and with none of the improvements they'd talked of the summer before. Out a ways from the shack was the husband setting on a sulky plow and holding the lines on a skinny team. Behind him and walking along the furrow was the wife stooping often and throwing things to one side. She was picking rocks, and as I rode closer I seen she was in rags and barefooted.

The shadow of my horse made her look up and I started to grin, but the grin faded away at the face of her. She was all eyes and hollow cheeked and looked ten years older than when I'd seen her last. I hardly recognized her and she didn't seem to recognize me at all.

I looked towards the husband and formed an opinion of him right then that I don't want to put into words. Making a woman work in the field was past me or any man of my country and I was pretty peeved at that stooped figgure setting on the plow and riding, while his wife was dragging along behind and picking rocks.

The woman hadn't said a word when I rode up and now, as I was looking at her husband, I heard her say, "Sh-h-h-h," and I looked down at her to see her finger to her lips. "Don't stay here," she says, in a queer voice. "My husband is awful jealous and he will shoot you. He's crazy."

I could see the whole story as she spoke. A dry summer, all their money in a crop that failed, starvation staring 'em in the face during the long winter, and being into the thick of all that was strange to 'em. I could see she was near crazy too.

I never said a word as I turned my horse and rode towards the shack that was about bare of anything to eat. The inside looked like as if wild cats had denned in there. I layed the quarter of beef I'd brought over on a dirty table and I rode away. I never seen 'em no more.

Summer was on and I kept busy. If I wasn't fanning out a fresh bronk, I'd be putting the finishing touches on another, and with all the horses I had on hand to break, I had to do considerable riding. My riding wasn't all wasted in visiting either, nor in taking care of my cattle, and sometimes I'd make quite a bit of money while I was also getting paid for riding the bronk I was edducating. There'd be horses or cattle stray acrost the border. Sometimes they was supposed to, and sometimes they wasn't, but I'd keep track of all stock along there and sometimes I'd be the cause of some stock straying acrost that was wanted there without the owner having to pay the duty. I was getting so much a head for crossing and delivering the stock, and that sure didn't go so bad. If everything kept a going good that way, I thought, I'd soon be able to pay up on half of what I owed on my cattle. I was setting pretty.

But I didn't set pretty for very long. I'd heard of some doings being pulled off in town to the north. There was to be horse races and a bucking contest and, figgering I was due for a little fun, besides needing some more grub, I got on my best horse, Smoky, took a pack horse along and headed for that town. I was going to enter in that bucking contest there and win me the purse that was offered. I was at my best in bronk riding about then.

I got in town, entered in the contest, rode my horse well and qualified as a contestant for the purse. The contest was for two days and I'd be riding my "final" horses on the next day. That night the riders who'd come to town to contest went a carousing around some. I went along with 'em and stayed till all decided to scatter for bedground.

I was all by myself when I come to the hotel where I was staying and thought as I passed the bar room door that I'd go in and have just one more beer. I was leaning on the bar and enjoying that when I felt a jolt on my left elbow. I looked that direction to see a bewhiskered crazy looking face a sneering at me.

"I expect you think you're a cowboy and want all the room," he says, as loud as he could. "Well," he went on, leaning close, "I'm a sheepherder and I'll bet I can whip you."

That hombre didn't seem to be drunk, but he sure must of been "run" out of the cow country, I thought, to pick it out on me. I seen he was looking for trouble.

The bartender tried to quiet him down but that only seemed to make him worse, and when I begin to edge away is when things happened. In half a wink he'd pulled out a blade. I seen just a flash of it and then felt it skimming along my skull above the left ear, over the bridge of my nose and down to my cheek, where the point went thru and grated against my teeth. Jumping away sudden and to one side was all that saved me from total slaughter, and when I seen that that crazy galoot was going to come some more, I pulled out my dad's old "Hawg's leg" from my belt and let him have it. One forty-five slug out of it spun him around and layed him down.

Things got kind of dark for me after that on account of loss of blood and I slumped down in a corner of the bar room. Then I felt somebody working on me, and when I come to some, and put a hand to my head, I felt bandages there and stitches pulling. I was soon able to stand after that and I went to my room, but I'd no more than pulled my boots off when I heard a knock on my door. Thinking it was the same crazy galoot or some of his friends hunting me up, I didn't answer. Then I heard a voice telling me to "open that door in the name of so and so." I slipped on my boots again and I jerked the door open. When I did, my old six-shooter was pointing straight towards two big red-coated men of the Royal Northwest Mounted Police.

I had the laverage on them and could of used that to walk out, if I'd tried, but I was talked to sort of friendly, and

It was about eight by eight, with straw on the floor.

told that all would be "all right" and I handed my gun over.

I was escorted to The Post in a queer looking wagon. There, a mighty gruffy officer asked me questions and, as I answered, I looked to my escort and I seen there was nothing friendly about 'em no more, either. I was put in a cell at The Post that night. The whole Post was made of heavy hewed logs and my cell was of the same. It was about eight by eight, with straw on the floor, a little hole under the heavy wooden door where grub was shoved in, and the only light was a little barred hole at the top, twenty feet and more above.

It was a cell for the condemned, and even tho I didn't know it then, I thought, at a glance of it, that it'd be a good place to go crazy in. It was well patroled and there was no chance of escape, but I wasn't worrying about that right then. I was weak and only wanted a place where I wouldn't have to stand. I stretched out on the straw as if it was a feather bed.

The next morning I was told in a very official way that the man I had trouble with had died. . . .

CHAPTER FIFTEEN

IT took me many days to realize that I was in a cell, a small space where I had to stay whether I wanted to or not and that, no matter what I done, hollered or went crazy, there was no way out of that space. That was mighty plain to understand but I couldn't make myself believe it. I'd never knowed anything but wide spreads of country around me and a freedom that was just as big. I'd always come and went as I pleased and with never a thought that anybody could ever have any say about it. Now I was in a cage that was just as small as the country around me had been big.

Every morning and for weeks I'd wake up and with my natural free feeling. I'd even think of what horse I'd be riding first, and it wouldn't be till I bumped my head on the wall that I realized how I wouldn't see no sun-ups and I wouldn't be riding at all, nor get outside of the little coop that day, nor the next day, nor maybe never while alive.

But there was more a bearing down on me, that was the thought of the penalty coming to me for killing a man. In my ramblings I'd often heard that men was hung for that, and I had no doubt but what a loop would settle around my neck one day or the next. I wasn't wise to laws, that I would have a trial or a chance, or that I could get advice. The stiff necked officials would never talk to me and wouldn't even answer the few questions I asked.

Taking in the feel of the pulling stitches on my face and along the side of my head, long days and nights in the small coop, and the thoughts of me swinging from a loop around my neck sure didn't leave any room for cheerful thoughts, and when that all was capped by gruffy words I'd sort of feel something click inside of me and I'd see red. My disposition was fast running short of being sweet.

Sometimes, when I'd get tired of pacing up and down, I'd lay flat on the straw and stare up the little square hole

I wasn't wise to laws.

at the top of my cell. There'd be a little sky to see up there and many thoughts came to my mind as I kept a staring. I'd think of Smoky and my other horse, wondering if they was still in the livery stable or if they'd been turned out on the range. I'd think of my little cabin and country, my cattle

and the good little start I'd had there and which I'd have
to give up now. I thought of many other things and lived
over and over every hour of my life. I'd imagine I was with
Bopy and went over the same trails that him and me had
covered together and up till the time he disappeared. Many
a time the bandages around my head was wet with tears
from the thoughts that I'd never see such days again. I
often thought that if Bopy was alive I wouldn't be where I
was. I had that confidence in him that he could of got me
out easy. But I was all alone now, very much alone, and
being so lonesome for all which I was took away from, made
me give up at times and I'd cry like a baby, but after them
spells I'd usually get mad and get up and pace around. I'd
get mad at the man who'd started the trouble that was the
cause of me being in such a fix. I hadn't wanted no trouble,
and if I could of got away from him I'd of sure done it,
but I didn't have the chance and I only shot to keep myself
from being cut to ribbons by the crazy galoot. I tried my
best to explain that when I was first brought in at the Post,
but I was pretty weak then and they didn't give me much
time to talk. Maybe the sight of my bandaged head and
face told enough story. There was a few questions asked me
and then I was asked for my name, which I gave wrong,
and where I was born and so on. I gave that all wrong too.

Things looked mighty dark and more than hopeless as
long days and nights drug along by. If I'd had something
to read, or something to draw on, or somebody to talk to, it
wouldn't been so bad, but there was nothing like that, not
even a good light, and sometimes I'd get sort of desperate
and want to tear up things. Other times I'd get scared. Life
had been too good for me to want to leave it.

Weeks wore along like that. I don't know how many because I had no way of keeping track, nor anything to make

a mark with; besides, there was no use of me counting the days because I didn't know just when my last one would be.

Then one day, while I was feeling as bad as any human possibly can, I hear the heavy key in the lock of my cell door and when it was opened a "Mountie" tells me to put on my coat and get ready to go. My heart lost many beats at that order because, getting ready "to go" could mean many things. It could mean to go to another jail or, far as I knowed, it could mean to go to the rope.

I was scared stiff as I walked along the row of cells in to the office where my name had been took down so long before, and being so scared that way, I know I sure didn't come to fast enough to appreciate what went on in that office during the next few minutes. In a hazy way I seen some of my belongings on the desk, some money, my pocket knife and a few other belongings that had been took away from me when I was first brought in. I don't think there was two words said as I was handed my belongings back, not a word as to what had been done while I was cooped up and not a word as to what was to be done with me now. Of course I had a hunch as to what was going to be done with me as my stuff was handed back, but I couldn't believe that anything as good as being turned loose and free could come true, and I didn't realize that as being a fact till I walked out of the office, all alone.

I didn't linger on the way out of the Post to ask if I was dreaming. If I was dreaming, I didn't want to wake up. My sudden freedom into so much sunlight and air made me weak, but I was sure happy to be in the thick of that and keep on going. Every once in a while I'd look back to see if there was a Police following me. I thought maybe they'd made a mistake in letting me go and that they would find it out before I got away.

I can't begin to tell of the good feeling I had when I got to town and started talking to people again and laughing. My own voice and laugh sounded strange to me, and when I looked at myself in the big mirror at the bar, I had to make faces to make sure it was me I was looking at. My hair was long and the scars on my face was still red and swollen, I'd lost some tallow too, and all that had changed my appearance a considerable.

I'd come to the saloon to see the bartender who'd witnessed the trouble I had with the lunatic, but they told me he wasn't there no more, that he was in jail for shooting somebody. . . . Shooting sure must be popular around here I thought, and, investigating around, I found out something, plenty of something.

I found out from two or three different people, who told the same story, that, "one night, quite some time back, a crazy feller comes in the saloon, starts a row with a kid, and goes to cutting up on him. The kid backs away and shoots at him and the heavy bullet grazes him alongside of the head and knocks him flat for a spell. He'd went out then and came back later to finish up on the kid, but the kid was gone and he begins picking it out on the bartender. The bartender didn't take no chances with this crazy feller and his knife, so he takes a shot at him too. It was a good shot, and the bartender, thinking he'd killed him, hits out and hides. The crazy man was took to the hospital and they thought he was dead the next morning. He was just about like dead for a long time after that but he finally come to, and then later, blood poison set in and he come near dying again. But you can't kill such scrubs and now he's up and pacing around a cell at the jail.

"Well, the kid had got the blame for shooting him because nobody knowed that he'd come back a second time and that the bartender was the one who'd put in the shot that counted. The kid was held in jail till it was seen the crazy man would live. I guess he's in jail yet, and in that time the bartender kept clear away to be on the safe side, but he found out somehow that he hadn't killed the man and thought that he would go clear now if he came back and gave himself up. So that's what he did, and I think he'll be turned loose now, specially with what the kid has to tell about what that crazy feller tried to do."

Well, I was mighty glad to find out I hadn't killed the crazy feller and, after I made sure of the story, I took a couple of tall beers to sort of celebrate, and then went to a restaurant and got me two orders of ham and eggs and coffee. I felt like a man by then and full of life once more. I rolled me a smoke and headed for the stable, figguring on getting my horses and hitting out of town as soon as I could, get home to my little place and stay there till my whiskers, which now was only fuzz, got coarse and gray.

But another snag got in the way of my peaceful intentions. I got to the stable, the stable man had gone someplace for a day or so and the kid that was there told me that the two horses I inquired about was being "watched."

"Y-e-a-h . . . ," I says, "watched for what?"

I tried not to show any interest as I asked, I was just being plain curious.

"Well," says the kid, "one of them horses is a stolen horse, the gray one, and they're watching for the feller to come back to claim him and the other. They say there was a big bunch stolen about the same time the gray one was, and they want to get the feller that done it."

That was a fine howdedo, I thought, and as I kept on thinking I got visions of the cell I'd just got out of. That was mighty fresh in my mind, and now it looked mighty likely that I'd be in that small place again, because, as I figgured on the subject, I seen where I'd have a hard time to prove that it wasn't me who stole that bunch of horses the gray was with. The old cowman to the South who gave me the gray horse might of had his finger in that deal and he could well say that he never seen the horse before. I didn't have no bill of sale for him, and there was plenty of people in the country who could say that they seen me riding him. The right owner's brand was still on the horse too, and none other to hide it.

Of course there might of been some way where I could of cleared myself, but that way was a thing I knowed the least about. I was plum ignorant of the laws in the books, and besides, the fear of being locked back in a cell and waiting there till all was straightened out, and maybe getting the blame after that in case I couldn't prove I was innocent, was a plenty to make me hanker to move, move fast and get far away.

It made me pretty peeved to think that I'd got out of one trouble just to get into another one, but there was nothing I could do about that but think fast and get into action. So as to throw off suspicion, I begin grinning and joking with the kid as I asked him where the two horses was kept at, and after he told me, I kept on a grinning and joking some more. The kid told me they was in a little pasture a ways back of the stable. I was sure lucky the old stableman wasn't around because he'd sure recognized me when I first come in. As it was now, I had a good chance to get away.

It was getting dark when I asked the boy if I could rent a saddle horse for a few hours, and while he was feeding

some stock in the corral, I found my own saddle and shaps
in the saddle room, saddled up the livery plug and rode out
for the little pasture. I had no trouble finding it and my
two horses. They was pretty spooky as I rode up on 'em, but
I manouvered around slow and soon got 'em quieted down.
Then I cornered 'em, and that good horse Smoky let me
walk up to him. I took my saddle off the livery plug and
slipped it on him and half an hour later I'd got past the
fences that was around the town and I was hitting out
acrost good old open country. I left the gray horse where
he was, with the livery horses.

It sure felt good to be on Smoky again, hitting the breeze
on good prairie sod and stirring up the night birds, and,
for the time, I forgot about the second mess I got into. But
I'd already decided this, nothing was ever going to take my
freedom away from me again.

I rode fast that night, for a long ways, and covered a distance that would take two good days of riding to make. The
sun had just been up a short while when I rode in at the
ranch of the cowman I'd bought my cattle from, and he
was mighty surprised when I walked in the house while he
was eating his breakfast.

"Well, well, well," he says, "where did you drop from?
Did you have anything to eat yet this morning?" he asks,
and when I grinned and shook my head he says, "Go put
your horse up and I'll fix you something in a jiffy."

It wasn't long after I got back from the stable and set
down to eat, that I found out I'd been hunted for down that
country, hunted for horse stealing. And after I told my
story to the cowman, he agreed with me that it might be hard
to prove where I got the gray horse, also to prove that I
didn't have nothing to do with the rest of the bunch.

It was lucky for me, I thought, that I wasn't connected

with the stealing of them horses while I was at the Post. That's where changing my name as I had, might of saved me, and now that I was free I wasn't going to take any chance of trying to prove my innocence. The cowman had been watching over my cattle while I was gone and now I offered 'em back to him at any price he would give me for the increase. He was glad to take 'em back because cattle had gone up. I took some cash. I was well heeled for money now. I bought from him one of the best saddle horses he had, and then made him promise to take good care of Smoky for me, that I'd be back for him sometime.

After packing up a few things like dried meat, rice and salt and a box of cartridges, I mounted my new horse and started out.

I was sure keeping my weather eye open for riders as I went. I was riding a mighty powerful and fast horse, but I didn't want to take any chances of having anything interfere with my getting to the border and the freedom that was past it. Every once in a while as I rode, I thought of the cell I'd got out of only a day and a night past. I'd get the shivers at that thought, touched my pony's neck to make sure I was free and on a good horse, and looked around at the skyline to see that all was clear.

I crossed the border sometime that night and kept on riding and, by the time daybreak come I seen I was in a country I'd been into before. By that I knowed I was about a hundred miles from the cowman's place, and close to two hundred miles from my eight-by-eight cell. But I wasn't safe yet. The cowman told me that they get horse thieves back when they was as far as five hundred miles from the line. I was going to put a thousand miles between me and that line, and I was going to do that as quick as I could.

When daylight come I was riding on a long bench, a creek

was to my left, and making sure there was no ranches along
it for as far as I could see, I rode down to the creek and
picketed my horse on tall grass amongst the willows that
was there. Me and my horse was well hid for that day, and
that's what I wanted. I didn't want any riders to see me that
might give my description and tell of the direction I was
headed, in case somebody inquired. They would inquire all
right. I was going to travel at night and keep hid in daytime, and I was going to keep that up till I thought I'd be
well past of where I would be in any danger of being caught
up with.

I knowed the cowman would never tell that he'd seen me,
or give any hint as to the direction I took. So I felt pretty
safe that first day in the thick of the willows. I cooked me
a bait of rice and jerky, chewed on a couple of soda crackers,
and as the fall sun begin to throw a good heat I got to feeling sleepy. I was mighty tired too, and soon I went to sleep
at the peaceful sound of my horse chewing away on good
grass.

I hadn't had no sleep for forty-eight hours. Fear of losing
my freedom had kept me wide awake and on the jump, and
when sleep caught up to me amongst the willows, I sure
went under and made up for lost time. The sun was just
tipping the western ridges when I woke up and blinked at
it. My day's sleep had went by so fast that, if it hadn't been
for the sun being on the wrong side of me, I'd of thought it
was the morning sun I'd just went to sleep by.

I went to the creek, sprinkled a lot of cold water on my
face, cooked me another bait of the same I had that morning, and was ready to go again. My horse was ganted up
pretty bad from the long ride he'd had, but he was strong
and he lined out good. It was dark when I come to some
fences, then into lanes, and pretty soon I seen the flickering

lights of a little town. I crossed a bridge and rode slower. When I got to the town it was late and the streets was deserted. I circled around thru the outskirts of it, and past it into some more lanes that led out, and after a while I was in open country again.

I covered a lot of territory again that night and when daybreak come I found me a place against a rimrock by another creek, and I hid out in some more willows where there was tall grass.

While I was cooking my meal there, I noticed that there was a lot of little cottontail rabbits a scampering around thru the willows and along the rimrock. I'd sure liked to've had one of them, but I didn't dare shoot on account that a shot would draw attention maybe if somebody happened to be riding close by. I thought of a snare and something to make one with. After sizing up my whole outfit for something that would do, I finally looked down at my shaps. These I had now was the leather batwing, a straight piece of leather that went around the leg and snapped. There was a flap I could cut a long thin string off of and I could take one of the rings from the snap to make and tie that to one end of the string to make the loop slip good.

That was no more thought of than it was done, and soon I found a well used rabbit-run and bent a green willow twig to a catch so it would jerk up as a rabbit got in the loop, and hang him that way. I set my snare and went to sleep. When I woke up that evening I had me a rabbit to mix in with my handful of rice. That sure went well and I kept my snare for more use later.

I didn't ride so far nor so fast that night, but that wasn't because I didn't want to. It was because my horse was getting leg-weary, and sore-footed. Horses are seldom shod in the grass country of the North. He was beginning to stumble, and by the time morning come and I turned him on the grass, he didn't seem to take much heart even in eating. I sure felt sorry for him and I wished I could of let him rest up for a couple of days, but I couldn't take any chance on that, I had to keep a going and as fast as I could.

It was while I was snoozing along that afternoon that I was woke up sudden by the sound of horses' hoofs on the rocky trail into the creek. Thinking it was riders, I jumped up mighty sudden and peeked thru the willows. It was only a bunch of loose range horses coming to water. I drawed a long breath and watched 'em for a spell. I wasn't sleepy no more, the scare had knocked that out of me and I started in to cook me something to eat.

In the meantime the loose horses was making a lot of noise down the creek from me. They was pawing at the water and playing, and at the sound I wished I had one of them playful horses. . . . With that wish a sudden thought came to me and something like a little voice which said, "Why not get one?"

I straightened up at that and figgured and sort of answered, "Yes, why not get one? You're on the dodge anyway, and have to make speed."

I looked at my ganted-up horse and that decided me. But how to get one was the next question. My horse was too tired to run fast enough so I could rope one. The only thing I could do was to find a corral somewhere away from a ranch, or a place where I could corner the bunch so I could get a close throw with my rope.

I saddled my tired horse and rode up on a bank by the creek to look around. There was no corral nor no place to corner nowheres in sight. The only thing to do then was to keep track of the bunch, wait till dark so I wouldn't be seen, and then drive the bunch along till I did find a place where I could catch one without having to make a run.

I hid back in the creek bottom and from there I seen the

horses file out one behind the other. They was fine big fat horses and I was tickled to spot two in the bunch with saddle marks. At a glance I seen that one of 'em was an old stove-up horse but the other one was all a feller in a hurry could wish for. He was sure some horse.

I went up the bank of the creek afoot, layed flat there and kept sight of the horses. They just grazed along slow. When it was dark enough and I figgured it was about time folks would have their feet under a good table at home, I came back to my horse and rode out on the trail of the bunch.

They spooked when I rode up on 'em, but they cooled down after the first mile or so and I didn't have much trouble hazing 'em the direction I wanted to go. As the night wore on and mile after mile was covered, they cooled down some more. I sure wished I could find a corral somewhere because I was wanting that fresh horse bad. That one kept in the lead, and I knowed I couldn't ride up close enough so I could reach him with my loop, but there was one great satisfaction as I rode, that was the sight of that fresh horse. I'd get him sooner or later.

I must of been at least twenty miles from where I started the bunch and it was getting past midnight when, crossing a little creek, I sees what looks like a corral to one side. I left the horses to graze and rode towards that. It was a corral sure enough, but some poles would have to be put in place before I could expect to hold any horses in it. That took me about an hour's work and then I was ready to run the bunch in and get me the fresh horse.

I was just riding back to the bunch, and going under a limb of a cottonwood, when I felt something like a bird's wing touching my face. I stopped my horse and looked up the limb, and there I could see three short pieces of rope dangling from it. That couldn't be where beef was hung, I thought, not with three short pieces of rope. Then my horse stepped on something that sounded like bone. I got down on

I felt something like a bird's wing.

the ground and seen that that's what it was, and I seen some more. Under the three ropes was three skeletons with a patch of tall grass growing thru the bones of each. The skulls of them skeletons was round, and of humans.

I held one of the skulls in my hand for a spell while I thought some. I looked at the corral and at the tree and from that I figgured out the story. There'd been a "hanging bee" at that spot a year or two before. Cattle rustlers or horse thieves had had their horses led out from under 'em while a rope held 'em by the neck to the tree's big limb.

I dropped the skull I'd be holding like it was red hot. Here I was with a bunch of stolen horses too, and under the same tree. Of course I was only going to take one horse, and I was going to leave another in the place of that one which was as good and maybe better. The other horses would go back to their range too, but that wouldn't of mattered if I got caught, for that part of the country seemed kind of hard on fellers that was too free with other people's stock.

That spot wasn't what I called right encouraging for me to change horses at. I dickered some with myself. I brought up the true point that my horse was all in, and that I'd maybe get caught if I didn't cover a lot of distance right quick, and then I brought up the good point that here was a fresh horse ready for me to take and do some traveling with. . . . I finally decided to take him.

I run the bunch in the corral, tied my rope hard and fast to the saddle-horn and spread my loop over the fresh horse's ears. The loop had no more than drawed up around his neck when I begin to wonder if he wasn't *too fresh*. He pawed the air and bellered, then went past me and tore a hole thru the corral and out of it, but my horse held good and so did the rope.

By the saddle marks on his back I figgured that horse to be broke and I didn't expect him to act up that way, but maybe he hadn't been rode for a long time and got kind of

wild again. I soon seen that he'd been handled and broke to
ride all right, because he didn't choke himself down like a
green horse would. He'd tried to make a get away, but as he
found out that he couldn't, he quit his fighting and waited,
quivering. When I walked up to him is when I got to know
quick what kind of a horse he was. He reared back on the
rope and struck at me and from his general actions I seen
that that horse was a sure enough outlaw. He knowed how
to fight, and when, and that was why he was running loose
with nothing to do but pack a big fat.

There's many kinds of outlaws. Some will fight and buck
till they're wore out and won't go a lick, and there's others
that's hard to saddle, hard to ride, but will travel a long
ways afterwards. I was hoping this one was like the second
kind. I took my cotton rope off my hackamore and hobbled him with that. Then I tore a piece off my shirt-tail and
made a blind. I could see that he'd had a rope on him many
times before and been blindfolded as often, for he knowed
better than to fight the hobbles, specially with a blind over
his eyes.

But the fun wasn't over yet. It hadn't started, and pre-
paring for what I knowed would come, I doubled my slicker
and tied it good and solid in front of my saddle and where
I'd get the most grip from it.

If I'd had daylight to work by, things would of been
easier, but I was managing all right and, being so used to
the dark, I didn't fumble around so much. What I was leary
of was that horse's hind hoof. I couldn't of seen it coming.
But I got along lucky, got him well snubbed and switched
my outfit from my tired horse onto him easy enough. All I
had to do now was to take the hobbles off of him, stir him
out of his tracks a bit and then mount him and take the
blind off.

I mounted him where he was, outside the corral. He stood plum still while I did, and waited nice till I felt my saddle good and got the right holt on my reins. I figgured he was too nice, and I seen quick that I'd figgured right as I pulled off the blind. About then he set on his tail, sort of pivoted there a while and, getting his legs under him, went straight up like a kangaroo that's stepped on a fire-cracker. I went up too, and I thought my chin made a hole in my chest as he hit the ground again, but my legs was hugging my old slicker and I don't think, right then, that any horse could of loosened me.

The first long hard jumps was followed by short, fast and rough ones, and I was taking 'em all for everything I was worth. I was more than riding to be riding, because my get-away depended on this ride, my freedom. And no purse ever offered at any rodeo was ever more rode for than on that night, handicapped by darkness, on somebody else's outlaw horse, I rode just to be free.

I wished that horse would quit bucking. There was a long ride ahead and I wanted to save him for that instead of bucking foolishness. But finally I felt his head beginning to give and soon it came up. He was breathing heavy and while he was getting his second wind I got off of him, opened the corral gate so the horses would go back to their range, and then mounted him again. I done that so quick, and he was so busy getting his wind, that he didn't seem to notice that I'd got off and got back on him. He didn't start any more foolishness again till I begin stirring him out of his trance, but that second round wasn't so bad and his jumps gradually got longer and longer, till finally he lined out in a nice stampeding run. I was in a strange and rough country and I was scared he'd fall in the dark and leave me afoot, but I didn't think too much on that subject and, besides, I was busy trying to head him the direction I wanted to go.

When I finally got him turned, he begin to slow down and then he went to bucking again. Then he'd stampede some more, slow down and buck again. It was no wonder, I thought, that nobody rode him. He was sure no good to do any work with, not unless somebody rode the tar out of him steady and every day.

Well, I figgured, if he didn't buck me off, that now would be one time when he'd see plenty of use and lose plenty of meanness. . . . But by the time I got thru with that horse, I also got to figguring that I should of received a gold medal and a big cash prize for just riding him out of the country.

But I will say for him that when he behaved and lined out, he could sure cover the ground, and keep it up. There was no killing him.

On account of wanting to give him some work so as to tame him down a bit, I rode him quite a ways the rest of that night and till pretty late the next morning, too late to be safe. The sun was a couple of hours high when I begin to look for a hideout place for the day. I seen a big clump of willows ahead. I rode towards that, but I couldn't find no water there, so I rode along to where I figgured would be a spring. There *was* a spring. Also, by the spring and not over thirty feet from me, was a rider looking square at me. He was mounted on a fine big dun horse, there was a rifle under his stirrup leather and a six-shooter at his belt.

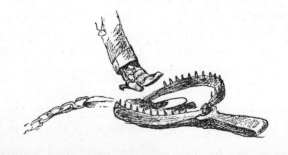

CHAPTER SIXTEEN

I'VE read stories where it said people froze in their tracks at the sight of this or that, but with me, and at the sight of the rider, I didn't freeze, I petrified. It was as if a bear trap had sprung on my foot, for there was no turning tail nor backing out. I was too close to him, he was well mounted and had a good rifle. There was nothing for me to do but ride up, try to grin, and say something.

But my horse, like horses have done for me before and since, saved me from the mighty bad fix I was in. He was pretty spooky of riders and at the sudden sight of that one, he just squatted on all fours and quivered for half a second, then he let out a whistling snort, threw his tail over his back and scooted out of there like as if he'd run onto a stack of grizzlies.

At first I tried to turn him, but every time I'd try, he'd go to bucking and I'd have to give him his head again so he wouldn't fall. The actions of my horse more than excused me to the rider. He could see it sure wasn't my fault that I couldn't stop to say "howdy" and palavey a spell. And that way, with my horse stampeding like as if the devil was after him, I figgured would throw off all suspicion that I *did not want* to turn him and come back. When I got further away I was letting on that I was sure trying to do that and my efforts that way was all play-acting. Instead, I was doing my best so that horse would keep on stampeding.

But he didn't need no encouraging. I was half a mile from the spring and going over a ridge when I glanced back and seen the rider about halfways from it and following me. Maybe he was just following to see if my horse would quit running and see that I wouldn't be getting hurt in case he jumped off a bad place. I was sure hoping that was all. I would soon find out.

I rode on over the ridge and out of his sight, and a quarter of a mile from there I circled my horse around some and stopped him. The rider was on top of the ridge and watching. I waved my hand at him as to say everything was all right and then rode on. I glanced back after a spell to see if he was following and I was mighty glad when I couldn't see him nowheres. I was going east when he seen me last, just to throw him off the general direction I was headed, but now I turned my horse south again and at a good speed towards some mighty rough looking hills not far away. I was going to hide, and hide well, till the sun went down again. I didn't want to see no more riders.

But it was high noon before I decided to stop, and then I was mighty careful to cover my tracks before I did. I was riding along a wide shallow creek. It was over three hundred yards wide at some places and the water just sort of skimmed along in four or five different places in the same creek bed. There was very few trees along the creek and very few places to hide, but that creek was a mighty fine place for me to lose my tracks into. I rode down alongside of it quite a ways till I found a little stream which run into it. The stream come out of a deep coulee and there was plenty of willows there. I rode past that and down the creek some more and then I put my horse into the water and back-tracked up it till I come to the little creek again. Then I rode in the water of the little creek till I was well in the willows, and there I stopped. I felt a little safer after cover-ing my trail, for most any rider following it would go past where I was stopped, to where my horse tracks went into the water, and naturally think I went on down the creek in-stead of coming back up it.

But it more than had me guessing to make it back up in the creek bed for so far. It was sure boggy and full of quick-sand, and many a time I wondered if I was going to keep my horse or not. But that was sure worth going thru to feel safe. That rider I'd seen wasn't packing a rifle and six-shooter for nothing. I figgured that him, riding in plain daylight the way he was, couldn't been a horse thief. Not unless he wasn't "working" in that territory and had no fear to be seen. Maybe he could of been looking for a place to hole up too, like I was. But I don't think so. He struck me more as a stock detective, a rider in the profession of get-ting the drop on anybody that's in the habit of appropri-ating other people's stock.

I was mighty glad he didn't have the chance to ask me any questions. I'd had a hard time to answer, and I was mighty thankful to learn that, if he *was* a stock detective or a sher-iff, he wasn't after me. That's what had scared me so when I near bumped into him at the spring. I thought sure he'd rode out to cut my trail, and even tho my horse had stam-peded away, he could of caught up with me if he'd been out to get me. But now that he wasn't on my trail, there was something else to worry me and which would keep me on the run for considerable further, and longer than I first figgured. He had that description of me which he could give if any-body asked him. He'd also been close enough to my horse to read the brand on him, and being he was headed the direction I'd just left, there'd be some talk about seeing me on that stampeder. The rider would of thought at first that I was one of the boys of the outfit where the horse belonged, and I was just hitting for town or going visiting, but with the talk it would soon be found that I wasn't one of the outfit's riders, and now I was running a fine chance to be hunted down as a horse thief. So, with that fresh happening and with being seen, the three hundred miles or more that I'd put between me and likely trouble had sudden dwindled down to about sixty miles. My next stop now, to feel safe, could be no closer than the Mexican border.

I wish I could of rode on that afternoon but I didn't dare take any chances of being seen by any more riders. I twisted my horse's ears, got off of him and hobbled him in tall grass. To make sure of keeping him, I also side-lined him. Side-lining is hobbling one front foot to the hind one, leaving about three feet of rope between, that keeps the horse from loping away as he could with just the front hobbles.

I didn't sleep much that day. Instead, after eating some, I walked up a little knoll, layed down on top there and watched the backtrail for any riders that might come along it. If any come, I would have at least a couple of miles the advantage of 'em, and with my trail lost in the creek, I could branch out and cover a heap of territory before my fresh trail could be found, if it was found.

I was glad when dark come. And it *was* dark too. It had started to rain and I was glad for that some more. Even tho I knowed I would get wet, the rain would wash off my tracks. I didn't dare as yet take my slicker off the front of my saddle because my horse sure wasn't thru going the rounds with me, and I was needing it a heap more where it was than I did on my back. But my horse didn't stampede or buck with me much that night, the country was too rough and dangerous, and now the rain was making it mighty slippery. He was pretty careful of not skinning his own hide and that was sure all right with me, I didn't want to get skinned up either nor have him fall and have him get away from me and set me afoot. I stuck mighty close to my rigging.

I covered a heap of territory that night, slid my horse down steep places that I couldn't see the bottom of, and up other steep places that I couldn't see the top of. It was so dark that I couldn't hardly see any further than my horse's ears. He fell down with me a couple of times but they was sliding falls and I stayed in my saddle. I kept him going right along and for two good reasons, one was to make distance, and the other was to take the kinks and meanness out of him.

Being it was so dark, it was hard to tell what kind of country I was getting into, and all I had to go by as to which way I was going was the breeze and rain which kept hitting me on the back and right shoulder. If that breeze switched I'd be going the wrong direction. Before morning come, the rain turned to a wet snow and after that begin to stick some, it helped me a considerable in lighting up for a few yards around me, and that done a fine job covering up my tracks. But it was turning cold and I was wet thru, and as I rode I was glad that I was headed south and for warmer climate.

I don't know how I got any idea of climate or the lay of the country that was ahead. I'd never seen a geography and still, on my run South and when I'd come to a river or a range of mountains, I knowed the name of it and I knowed pretty well how the country would stretch on the other side. I expect that all come from hearing different riders from all western states talk of their own country and how each bor-

dered. I had as good an idea of the country ahead as if I'd
been studying the geography, and more too, because the
boys that rode in them different states would tell things
about them that wouldn't be in a geography. That's why
in the dark of night I was making my way near as well as
if I'd been on that trail before.

I put my outlaw horse over three hundred miles of mighty
rough and heavy traveling. It'd snowed and the wind had
howled most every day and night during that whole distance, and the days' rest wasn't so restful. It was cold and
I'd have to have a fire. Sometimes it was hard to find anything to burn when day found me, and half of my time
would be spent pulling sagebrush.

It was snowing good when early one morning I rides into
a hollow and comes acrost a sheep wagon. A sheep wagon is a
canvas-covered home on wheels for the herder. There's a
stove in there, a bunk and grub and everything necessary
to make life comfortable, specially on a day like that day
was when I seen it. But I got pretty leary at the sight right
then, I didn't want nobody to see me. . . . Figguring the
herder would be in there at that time of the morning, I
started circling around and getting out of sight, but something about that sheep wagon struck me as deserted. There
was no dogs around and no sheep, and there was no smoke
coming out of the stove pipe sticking up out of the canvas.

That would be fine if it was deserted, I thought, specially
if there was some grub inside. I was beginning to need some.
I stopped my horse a spell and watched the wagon. My horse
was willing to stop by that time. The more I watched the
wagon the more I felt it was deserted. Then being it was
snowing so good and how my tracks would soon be covered
in case there was somebody in, I thought I would take the
chance and investigate. But I wasn't going to take too much

chance. I stayed on my horse and hollered "Hello." I didn't get no answer. I got off my horse then, stepped on the wagon tongue, opened the door and looked in. It was deserted all right, and had been for quite a few days, I could see that. But there was a lot of grub in that wagon and soon I had me a new supply of the most necessary, and enough to last me for ten days or so. By that time I'd be far enough away so I could show myself and get more.

I was all set, and a few miles further I hunted up a hole where there was a lot of good timber and water, cooked me up a big feed and took on my day's rest.

The storm was still howling when I got on my horse that evening for another long night's ride. I must of rode on about ten or twelve miles when, like ghosts, two dogs shot up from the white landscape and begin to bark. Then my horse snorted at the bundled figure of a man who stood up and right close. The thick falling snow had kept me from seeing 'em before, but I couldn't afford to be sociable and I was going to scatter out of there and ride on when the man, in a weak voice, hollered at me to hold on a bit. Then I heard the blatting of sheep.

I found he was the sheepherder whose camp I had been to that morning. He was an old feller with long white whiskers and he told me that his sheep had started drifting, and that he hadn't been able to get them back to his camp for two days, that he hadn't had anything to eat for that long, and on account of the sheep drifting he hadn't been able to stop and build a fire. Now, he said, his hands was too numb to strike a match. I pointed out the direction of his wagon for him, but he didn't think he could find it again.

There was nothing for me to do but see that the old feller was took care of. There was timber around and where the sheep had finally found shelter, so I built a big fire and warmed the old feller up. Then I made a canful of coffee and by the time he took that down, and the other courses of rice and some of his own salt pork which I'd took a piece of, he felt pretty good and, as he says, "As good as new."

It was fine to talk to somebody again, and as sleepy and tired as the old feller was, he seemed mighty tickled to talk to somebody too. He was sorry to see me get up to go. I drug in plenty of wood for him, and with a note which he'd scribbled on an old letter he had with him and which I was to leave at the headquarters of the outfit he was working for, about thirty miles away, I left him, also left enough grub with him to last for a couple of days or more.

As a parting word I asked him to forget he'd ever seen me in case anybody asked. The old feller had looked at me sort of queer when I asked him that but his face soon was all good smiles and he'd said.

"Don't you worry, Son."

I knowed at the looks of him that I didn't have to worry and he sure appreciated my taking the chances of delivering his message. The headquarters of the ranch was west and out of my way a considerable, but the only thing that worried me about then was to get there and leave my message before anybody was up. The snow kept a falling steady and now I was facing the storm pretty well. My horse was getting pretty tired too, and I was feeling sorry for him and forgetting all about the meanness that'd been in him.

I figgured it must of been a couple of hours before daybreak when I got to the ranch and there, with snow blinding me, I begin to look for a place to leave the message where it'd be noticed first thing in the morning. The stable would be the place. I rode into a corral, opened the stable door, found a piece of rope and stretched it acrost there, and with one of the strands tied the message in the center of it, then I closed the door again. I figgured that even a blind man could find it then.

I was just getting ready to leave when, thru the storm, I heard some horses under a shed in one of the corrals. Then I noticed that the wind had just about blowed a gate of that corral open. What would be the matter, I thought, with opening the gate just a little more, just as if the wind had done it, and me taking a horse out from under that shed? . . . The folks would maybe think that the horses went out on their own accord and come back and that one of 'em just hit out for his range.

But taking a horse from the shelter of a good shed was a mighty risky thing to do because horses seldom leave shelter during a bad storm, specially when there's mangers full of good hay, as there was there. Another risky and foolish thing for me to do was to leave my horse there in the place of the one I took. He sure was an evidence that somebody had come along and traded horses. I knowed that too, but I couldn't think of turning him loose in a snowstorm after me riding the life out of him. I wanted to leave him under the shelter and by them mangers full of hay. Besides, he'd make a good horse in trade for the one I took, if he was put to use before he got rested up too much.

Anyway, not thinking of the risks on account of the storm which was howling and which would cover up my tracks, I took the likeliest looking horse out from under the shed, put my saddle on him and rode on. This horse was gentle and being fresh and in fine shape he felt mighty good under me.

I lined out of the ranch in a good long lope and when I got well away I brought my horse down to a trot. I was going to save him all I could because I figgured on making a lot of distance with him and didn't want to tire him from the start. But after I got away from the ranch ten miles or so the country begin to get pretty rough. There was long ridges that I had to go over, and them ridges kept a getting taller and the canyons deeper. The snow kept a getting deeper too and I seen by that that I was getting into the foothills of some high mountains. I begin to cut down country then, and as I got to the point of all ridges, I come to a road. I didn't want to follow no road, might meet somebody on 'em, but as I got off of it to my left, I run into some more ridges. I was getting into the mountains and that road was leading to a pass. The road was the only place for me to be on if I wanted to make speed. In the ridges on the side I'd only wear my horse out and get nowhere.

Mountain passes are bad places to ride a stolen horse thru, because them is the places that's watched, but I had to cross them mountains, and, with the help of the storm to keep people inside and to cover my trail the while, I rode on, a hoping to get thru the mountains and be out in open country again before the storm passed. The storm held on all right, but there didn't seem to be no end to them mountains.

I covered a good hundred and fifty miles of them before they dwindled down to hills. Then I got out of the storm, and by that time I felt pretty safe again. But my horse was wearing out on me and needing rest pretty bad. I'd be needing another fresh one right quick.

But I'd got down out of the mountains and snows and I had to ride a couple of nights more before a chance come for another change of horses. And here was one time when I didn't have no horse to leave in the place of the one I took, for the one I had had broke his hobbles and got away somehow while I was snoozing and I couldn't find a track of him nowheres. I'd stopped by a corral that morning and with the idea of finding a bunch of horses close when evening come and run 'em in there. The corral was more of a trap, like. There was a spring inside of it and horses would have to get in the corral to get water. I often thought how lucky I was to be by such a place when I lost my horse, for all I'd have to do now would be to wait till a bunch of horses come in, and then close the gate on 'em.

But that wait was pretty long for me, part of that day and most all of the night. It was near daybreak when I heard hoofs on the trail that led into the trap. I held my breath and hid while they went in the gate and after the last one got inside the corral, I pounced on that gate and closed it. I had about twenty head to pick from in that corral and I felt pretty lucky, but it turned out that I wasn't so lucky after all. Daylight was coming good about then and when I got inside the corral with my rope I seen that I'd caught nothing but mares and mule colts, a big jack was in the bunch with 'em.

Well, that was my first time to ride a mare, but, I thought, even a mare was better than being afoot. I caught the biggest and speediest looking one and she put up so much fight from the start that I didn't think she'd last over ten miles of country. She'd go to bucking, and then sulk, and then stand in her tracks. I'd sit in the middle of her till she was ready to move, and roll me a smoke. Sometimes when I lit a match she'd spook up and travel pretty well for a ways. But with all the strength she wasted with her fighting, she surprised me some and covered quite a scope of country. The next night she done about the same and by then I was wanting a fresh horse mighty bad again, but I was thru with unbroke horses—they wear themselves out fighting instead of traveling.

But before I got anywheres near the Mexican border

there was a couple of times when I had to ride unbroke horses again, and I sure earned every foot of my way on 'em. An unbroke range or wild horse needs a few days of handling before he can be lined out for a fair ride. I didn't have the time to give them the few days of handling and breaking, and so I had to make the best of the unbroke horses and have them pack me till I got another change.

I got many changes in many different ways and with many different horses. Once I caught me a mule to ride. That mule had collar marks and that went to show he was at least bridle-wise. That helped some but I was worried some too by the fact that it was sure hard to keep my saddle on that long-eared animal's back. It kept crawling up every time he spooked. But I made a lot of distance on that mule after he settled down to traveling.

The last change I made was my luckiest one. There was three horses along a fence, all saddle horses and gentle. The gentlest one was the one I wanted, he was the youngest. I got off my tired horse and I was sure surprised when he let me walk up to him. I'd never seen as gentle a horse as him before. Well, even tho the sun was up and I was taking chances of being seen, I swapped horses right there, and it wasn't long when I found me a hiding-place for that day. While in my hiding-place I done a neat job "picking" a brand on that horse and changing the original so it wouldn't be recognized by looking at it. To pick the new brand I used the end of a broken blade of my knife and just sort of plucked the hair along in the line of the new brand. When that was done, I plastered some mud over the whole thing and I brushed it off again when it got dry. I left just enough on so the brand was hard to read and so it wouldn't look disguised.

The reason I took so much trouble with that horse is be-

cause he was a good one, and being the border was only a
few hundred miles away now, I figgured on him doing me till
I got there. I was getting tired of changing horses the way
I'd been, good ones was hard to find out loose, and after
changing about twenty times like I had, I thought I'd keep
this one for my last change and ride him slower so he would
last me.

He did last, and in fine shape, and when I got away into
Mexico and went to work for an American-owned cow outfit down there, I gave him many a long day's rest.

I'd come to the end of my long days and nights of dodging, riding by night and hiding days, eating rice and jerky
and speaking to nobody. Now I could ride while the sun was
up and sleep after it went down, and as I went to riding with
the vaqueros of that country I figgured that that long
ride from the North, crossing prairies, rivers, mountains,
deserts, running up against wall canyons, always in the
dark nights, thru storms, on all kinds of horses and with a
steady fear of being caught, was more than worth going
thru so as to really appreciate the getting back amongst
men again, any kind, and talk and laugh and feel safe to be
free.

Of course, if I'd knowed, I wouldn't of had to ride away
down to Mexico to feel pretty sure of staying free. Crossing a couple of states would of been enough, but I'd heard
so many of the Southern boys I'd worked with in the North
speak of "crossing the border" when things get to crowding,
that I figgured it was the only place to go.

Well, I was there now, and as I kept a riding for that outfit, I soon begin to forget that I'd been on the dodge at all.
I was even used to the wrong name I'd given when I started
to work. I was also getting used to the queer ways the Mexicans had of handling cattle and horses, but I didn't like

them. About the only thing they done which I admired was
the way they handled their long ropes. They sure had me
beat in throwing any kind of a rope, but I made many a
vaquero jealous with my riding, and the meanest of their
horses was just pets to me. I was used to the big Northern
horse, and any Southerner that's rode them would say that
there's a heap of difference.

There was only a couple of white riders on that outfit.
The rest was all Mexicans, and, as time wore on and I sort of
forgot why I took the long ride South, I begin to look North
again and towards the mountains that was on the American
side of the border.

One day I finally drawed my check and hit for that direction. I was wanting to ride circle and be on herd where there
was plenty of white men to work with. I was homesick for
my own people and my own country.

CHAPTER SEVENTEEN

I OFTEN think, as I write this story, of what a time I'd have if I was to try and follow the same trails I made and which scattered from Canada to Mexico. If I was to mark them down on a map of the Western country it would look as if a centipede had dipped all its legs in ink and then just sort of paraded around on that map for a spell. Some states would be more marked up than others of course, and then there'd be many zigzagging lines going acrost here and there. All them zigzag lines and circles and doubling-backs would look like a puzzle that would be impossible to figger out as to where the start of that line could be.

That line would be zigzagging good about the time I got back to U. S. A. from Mexico. I had me two good horses again by then, a new bed on one and a new saddle on the other. My last saddle had wore out and thru in many places. I was all set now and enjoying my first winter where there was no snow only on high peaks. That was fine. I took on a job, then another, and I stuck pretty close to the border. One time I even went back into Mexico. It was after I'd went into a little town and spotted a feller there who looked like a sheriff and who seemed to want to ask me questions. He didn't get to ask me them because, as another feller came to speak to him for a minute, he'd no more than turned his head when I disappeared into a building, went out the back way and hot-footed it towards the stables. I was acrost the border again and right quick.

Maybe I was all wrong in hitting out the way I did, but, anyway, I liked Mexico better that second time. I got another job there, and this time I was to use a rifle as well as my rope. I was hired to ride line on an outfit and help "smoke out" whatever raiding Yaquis and Mexicans that

I shot at a few but they was too far away.

tried to run off any of the cattle. There was always two men rode together on that line, and that was one outfit where the boss wanted drinking and fighting men. The tougher they was the better he liked 'em because the kind of breeds his men had to "mix it" with once in a while wasn't at all to be turned with kind words.

It struck me kind of funny when the boss of that outfit hired me. The first thing he asked was "Do you drink?"

I says "Some."

I answered the same way when he asked me if I could shoot or rope. He seemed pleased.

"Fine," he says, "I'll furnish the likker, the ammunition, and the ropes."

Few outfits I ever rode for ever liked a man to drink. Some wouldn't hire men that did, and even card playing or shooting dice wasn't allowed on account that them pastimes would start fights. A cow outfit is not a place to fight or drink or gamble, it's a place to work.

But this outfit south of the border was different. They didn't care how wild their men was, so long as they protected the herds, and they preferred straight-shooting outlaws that'd knock a Yaqui over every once in a while. If I knocked any Yaquis over while I was on that job I don't know of it. I shot at a few but they was too far away, and no matter how many there was, they'd always turn tail and hit for thick brush before a feller could get to 'em.

There was a mighty fine bunch of men on that outfit, a little reckless maybe but they was *all white*. None of us ever had an argument and we had a lot of fun to boot. But, as it was with me, never staying at one place very long, I caught my private horses one fine spring day and rode away. I rode north, skirted along the border and crossed back in The States again.

I went to work for one outfit getting wild cattle out of the brushy country. Some was shot, quartered and packed out, others was trapped into stockades. There was many ways of trapping 'em. One way was to build a trap and then leave it alone for about a month and keep blocks of salt inside. The wild cattle, which was just like deer, would in time come in and lick at the salt, and if the trap wasn't bothered by riders, there'd sometimes gather quite a bunch to get at that salt. Sometimes the trap would be around a spring. They'd most always come at night, and when good-sized bunches begin to come in, a couple of riders would hide down in a pit by the heavy gate and swing it closed. That had to be done mighty fast, and even when the gate was closed I've seen some of them heavy stockade corrals go down as if they was toothpicks when the wild bunch spooked and went against it.

After some cattle was caught, there come the big job of getting 'em to open country and where they could be held with gentler cattle till there was enough gathered to ship. That was done in many different ways. After the wild ones was a day or so in the corral, a bunch of gentle cattle could be brought in and mixed with 'em, and then the whole bunch was took out together. That worked all right if the brush wasn't too thick, but a few would most always break out and get away that way, and sometimes the gentle cattle would go too, because even the gentle cattle wasn't at all like them that's on the farm. They was about the same as the wild cattle, only they'd got used to seeing a rider once in a while. When any of the wild cattle broke out of the herd they could seldom be turned back in, it'd be just the same as trying to turn a jack-rabbit, and in that thick brush they had all the advantage over a man on a horse. These cattle was all of the longhorn breed.

Another way of taking 'em out, if it wasn't for too long a distance, was by horse and rope and "lead 'em." That was

These cattle was all of the longhorn breed.

hard work on horse and man and critter, and sure brought on a lot of action right from the start.

I think the best way was to neck 'em to a gentle ox and let him tame the wild one and bring him out to where he wants to go, back to his home range and out of the brush where the cowman has more room to attend to the wild ones.

There was also a lot of action brought on when the wild ones was roped instead of trapped. The country being so rocky, rough and brushy, made it mighty hard for a rider to throw his rope. We had to use little loops and use 'em mighty quick, because the openings where a feller could throw his rope was mighty small and scarce.

Some folks wonder why a cowboy wears shaps, but if them folks would ride a half a mile of that country they'd soon find out, and also find themselves mighty scarce of clothes. Some of the old brush-riders used to cover themselves with heavy leather and rawhide from head to foot, and for the horse there was a sort of apron made of stiff leather which hung from his withers, and around his neck, covered his shoulders and chest and a ways down to his knees. The apron run back to the stirrups over the rider's knees to the saddle, where it layed over the fork. That was for protection against the thorns, daggers, bayonets and claws that country was full of. It seemed like everything that growed in that country had stickers on it, and a horse not raised there would snag and cripple himself before he was rode very far.

I worked for different outfits in the brushy country but not for very long at a time. I knowed of too much good open country to like it there. I got tired pulling out stickers that even went thru my shaps and not to be able to turn my head one second without having a bayonet jab me in the neck. Besides, all I was good for in that country was to chase or lead out. I couldn't get onto the hang of roping the way them boys did. They could catch anything that walked or flew. There was lots of wild burros in some parts. They're mighty fast and few horses can catch up with 'em in their own territory. A feller was lucky to get *one* throw at 'em, but many of them little fellers was caught. Them boys even caught deer, mountain lions and wolves with their short ropes. That's what I call roping, but with me, not being used to the brush, my loop had a failing to hang on snags, and if I did catch something it was only by luck. Then I'd most always get in a mix-up with what I caught, a lot of thorny brush and my horse.

So I finally left that country to good ropers and went on to where the need would be more for good riders. That was in my line, and as I roamed around in the mesa country I had no trouble getting plenty of that. I took on job after job of breaking horses. The wages wasn't so much as they was to the North where I left in such a hurry, but the horses wasn't so hard either, and that sort of evened things up. About all the roping I done in that country was when I caught the horse I was to ride.

Zigzagging around and riding for one outfit and then another, I bumped up against many strange ways of handling cattle and horses, and found that what was right in one country was wrong in another, and the other way around. Sometimes there'd be a big change in the short stretch of one little county. On one side of a mountain I'd see all riders using double-rig "remmy" saddles, short grass ropes, small loops, and the other end of the rope was tied fast to the saddle horn. On the other side of that same mountain the riders, called *buckeroos*, used single-cinch center-fire saddles. They had long rawhide ropes, made great big loops and instead of tying the other end, they take wraps, "dally welta," around the saddle horn. The hats and boots and spurs and shaps and whole outfit the men wore was all different too from one side of the mountain to the other, or from one county or state to the next. There was some outfits that was mixed of both styles and ways, and I figger the reason for that is the lay of the country. Like with some outfits I rode for, they couldn't use no wagons to haul the chuck and beds on round-up. The country being rough and rocky, everything had to be packed on the backs of horses or mules.

Another reason for the difference in styles of riggings and ways of doing things, comes from the first that started in the cow game. Further West and along the coast, the Spaniards was the man who set the styles and ways for the American to follow up where he left off. Further East of there the American set his own style pretty well and started handling his cattle without the help of any other's experience. Them styles and ways of doing things go in strips which start from Mexico and trails, as the cattle and horses did in the early days, away up into Canada. Here and there along them strips they sometimes mix.

Working for different outfits that way, I had to learn and catch on to many things that was new and strange to me. I had to fit in if I wanted to make a hand of myself, and sometimes it was hard, like working for outfits that rode from permanent camps and where I had to go on two meals a day. That was tough on me at first because I could never eat much more than a biscuit for breakfast, and supper seemed a long time coming. But I soon got used to that and going without water too during the day, and I worked quite a few years for outfits of that kind.

A feller wrote a review of my books one time, without being asked, and he said something about my language not being true cowboy language. As I found out afterwards, that feller had been a cowboy all right enough but I also found out that he'd only rode in one state all his life. He'd compared his language with mine and mine had been picked up and mixed from the different languages from different parts of the whole cow country. The languages of the cow country is just as different as the style of the rigs and ways of working.

But even tho my language and my ways of doing things was mixed from being in different cow countries I worked in, I always stuck to my same style of saddle and rest of my outfit. Sometimes, when I'd first ride into some strange cow-camp, that outfit of mine would be wondered at and a few would grin. But there was one thing I was never grinned at no time for and that was my riding, and if I stayed on any outfit of that kind long enough I'd notice before I'd leave that some of the boys would begin copying. They'd maybe get spurs like mine, or shaps, or hat, and a few went as far as getting saddles with the same riggin' as mine.

While knocking around the way I was I got a good chance to keep up on my riding and being, on account of higher wages, I hired out to break horses most of the time, I was handed some mighty tough ones. I found my toughest horses amongst them that some other rider had started to break and didn't finish. It would make me pretty peeved when sometimes I'd hire out to ride only unbroke horses and they'd slip me a few that'd already been handled and turned out-law. It wasn't so bad if they'd tell me and didn't expect too much out of me in breaking 'em. Trying to make a good horse out of an outlaw is just about the same as trying to make butter out of skimmed milk. I got so I could tell an outlaw as soon as I layed eyes on one. They're the kind that's famous for rodeos these days.

I had a couple of them kind of horses kill themselves while I was sitting right in the middle of 'em. One went up in the air and came down on his neck instead of his feet and broke it. Another one run smack bang in the side of a log stable and done the same thing. Others tried such stunts, but managed to keep on living. Some would run blind, and if there'd been a hundred foot drop ahead they wouldn't of turned for it. I've quit a few while they was on a run that way.

There was a few outfits I broke horses for where I was all
alone at some camp. I'd have to cook my own meals and I'd
ride from eight to ten head of bronks every day. Sunday or
the Fourth of July or Christmas could come along and I
wouldn't know anything about it. Every morning as sure as
daylight come I'd cook my breakfast, then go to the corral,
rope a bronk, tie up the left hind foot, slip the saddle on
and off of him till he quit acting up, then cinch the saddle,
take the foot rope off and get on and off of him till he got
used to that and quit bucking, then turn him around the corral a few times one way and then another, and then open the
corral gate and ride him out for half an hour or so, come
back to the corral, unsaddle him and start the same way
over again with another bronk, and another one, till the whole
eight or ten of 'em had their daily lesson.

That daily lesson goes on with each horse for about a
month before he's called fit to do work with. Many horses
are broke while working with cattle, but being a bronk
shouldn't have long rides at the start, I think it's best to
edducate him a bit first or till he's at least bridle-wise. Most
horses are broke when they're four years old. I liked 'em best
at three if I could give 'em short rides, at four a horse sheds
his teeth and he don't feel so good, and at five is a better time
than four because the horse is pretty well developed by then,
and he can stand harder work from the start. I broke horses
that was smooth-mouth and well past twelve years old. Them
was hard to break but they was also hard to hurt, and they'd
most always be good horses when as old as twenty.

I don't know how many horses I broke. I broke quite a
few and rode quite a few others but I never seen two that
could be handled alike. Horses are all as different one from
another as people. Some will learn fast, others not so fast,
and there's some that learn nothing excepting how to buck

better at every saddling. With me, there hasn't been more than three horses out of ten that didn't buck while I was breaking 'em. Some men can break ten horses and seven will never buck. It ain't kind treatment that does that, because an unbroke range horse don't appreciate kind treatment at first, he's too scared of the human and too fighty and all he wants is to get away from him and be let alone. The feel of a hand on his neck strikes him no better than the forked tongue of a rattlesnake would feel to that hand.

No rider that's ever hired out to break horses ever abuses 'em. If he did he wouldn't be breaking 'em, he'd be spoiling 'em and no outfit wants spoiled horses. He wouldn't last long, just long enough for him to ride one horse. I've seen many a bronk stomper talk to a fighting bronk like as if he was talking to a child, and regardless of how many murders that bronk wanted to do right then, he'd just dodge him and talk on or whistle. I had a habit of talking to three-year-old colts and calling 'em "Baby." I'd call them horses "Baby" because they struck me that they had much to learn, and I got so much in that habit that right to-day, nine years since I rode my last bronk, I still once in a while put a hand on some of my horses when they get excited and call 'em "Babe." I was called by that name with a few outfits on that account.

Getting back to where I said that only three bronks out of ten didn't buck with me, I have to add on that I never tried to keep a horse from bucking, specially when I got to thinking I was a pretty fair rider. I was wanting practice for one thing, and another thing was that I always believed a green horse should be let buck if he wanted to. I even encouraged a few jug-heads to buck when they didn't want to, and on the first saddling I'd always ride a bronk with only a loose hackamore, nothing in his mouth. Sometimes I'd ride 'em with nothing on their heads, just a rope around the neck, so they'd have the freedom to buck all they wanted to and get it out of their system. When they did have that out of their system and seen that bucking wouldn't get 'em nothing, the most of 'em took more interest in learning other things. A horse has a lot of brains, as much as any dog, and there's no way to know of them, I don't think, like getting a wild one off the range and watch him do his studying with the first saddlings.

I liked to break horses while alone at some camp. I felt more like they was my own when there was nobody around to watch me and I took more interest in teaching 'em something. The only thing I didn't like about being alone was while I was handling my horses I'd have to break away and do my own cooking. I didn't mind the cooking so much, but I sure didn't care for the dish washing. I don't know of a cowboy that likes to wash dishes, but I don't know of one that ain't a good cook, because there's many times when he's in a camp by himself when he has to cook. And most of the time he's glad of the chance so he can mix up something that's more to his taste than the round-up cook can give him. During winters, specially in the North, there's many a cowboy that goes to batching and takes on a bunch of horses to break on contract, or he might go to trapping and just taking life easy for a spell. There's some great baits cooked during them winter months.

When I was alone at a camp and doing some cooking, I'd go to the cabin between the saddlings of every bronk and stir up the stew and fix up the stove to do till I'd rode another bronk. The cabin would most always be close to the corral and while the bronk I'd just rode was thinking things over, I could rest up a bit in the shade of the cabin and roll me a smoke before saddling another one. The dish washing came once a day, in the evening after all the work was thru.

I liked to break horses while alone at some camp.

After all the tin dishes was washed I liked to be in the cabin, alone, and go to drawing on some little pad. I'd be drawing of what I still felt from where the cantle had been pounding me all day, bucking horses, and sometimes if a horse fell with me that day while bucking around, I'd draw a picture of that, and anything they done or any shape they got into was pretty well put down in drawings when evening come.

I never kept any of the drawings for very long. I wished I had, but a feller can't keep much while knocking around the country with only two horses, one to pack you and the other to pack your gatherings. I scattered them drawings around as I went. I'd either gave 'em to the boys or leave 'em on the walls of the camps, and I never missed 'em nor needed 'em to go by in my drawings now. To prove that, I'd like to say that one of the best bucking horses I ever drawed was done in a hotel in New York City a few years back and while I was there for a spell. Even while I'm at home on my ranch, I never go look up any of the good bucking horses I have when I draw one. I stick in the place where I work and never glance out the big window to see where they're grazing. I feel a good horse under me wether he's bucking, or running, or cutting out a wild cow, and it don't matter where I'm at when I draw or paint 'em because I can always feel 'em and from the tip of my boot-toe to my hat-band. What's inside of that hat-band is not anything I'm bragging about, it's just some place that seems to hold what other parts of me has felt and flinched at while going thru the mill, and that all only runs down my neck and arm where my fingers do the work of putting the happenings down on paper or canvas.

CHAPTER EIGHTEEN

ALL the time, and while working for one outfit a couple of months, and for another the same, I noticed one time that I was gradually getting back North. Of course I was doing a heap of zigzagging around while getting back, but what struck me queer is that I had natural-like worked back towards my home country without me figguring or deciding on it. Sometimes, while edging towards the North, I'd circle a bit and cross my trail to the South again, or I'd drift East or West till my horses got tired, or till I found a job that would hold me for a spell, but always, and steady with my ramblings I found I was making two miles to the North while only one to the South.

But it took me a few years to get back to my home territory, years enough for one change of sheriffs anyway, and after my ramblings to the South and the deserts, the grass-covered brakes of the North looked mighty good to me. I'd worked for different outfits and all the way back, it was seldom that I rode over a hundred miles at a move, most always about fifty miles, and then I'd turn my private horses loose and go to work again for a week or a month or two months.

It was during one snowy winter day, after I'd crossed into Canada again, that I came up to the ranch of the cowman who'd staked me to the little herd of cattle. He hadn't changed a bit in all the time since I seen him, and he was still a bear with the sourdough crock. He'd done fine with his cattle, was running a good-size herd and had three riders working for him. By the time he got thru telling me what all I'd have now if I could only of kept the little place and herd I had to begin with, I felt like hunting up the sheepherder who'd been the start of my causing to leave.

With all the good chuck and comfort that I seen around that ranch the few days I was there, the good horses and the fine cattle, it come to me right there that I should start me a little place again, somewhere on good range where I could build me a little house, good corrals and raise good stock to pack my own brand on ribs or thigh. But I was going to get in my home country to do that, south of the Canadian line and near the mountains where I first remember seeing my dad and good old Bopy. Now, all I had in mind when I come to see the cowman was to get my horse, Smoky. He was out on the range, I was told just where, and I could see soon as I spotted him that he'd sure been well took care of. He was fat as a butter-ball and looked and acted like a three-year-old colt. He didn't know me when I dabbed my rope on him in the corral and he made me sit tight to my rigging when I got in the middle of him, but all that was fine with me and Smoky, and still finer when, after he had his fun over with, he looked back and seemed to recognize me. He seemed happy over that and bowed his neck, and when I lined out of the ranch I figgured more than ever that I wanted to make a home, a place for me and Smoky, a place where we could pass winters in the middle of tall feed, where I could have my own lamplight of evenings, so that when I got tired of heading on my own critters, or lining out a few bronks, I could tickle the fire under my own roof, lean back on my old tarp on the bunk and read something, or else prop up my knees under a pad of white paper and draw pictures.

But fate, or what you may call it, sure cut my cinches so I couldn't ride up to them ambitions of mine. Being I wanted to get more money to start my little spread with, I took another job breaking horses for the rest of that winter. I was furnished any amount I could break and the most of 'em was fine horses, but I climbed up on a scrub one day, a big hammer-headed brown. He wasn't hard to sit but he was rough, and during one of the jumps I took while in the middle of him, I felt something snap inside of me and I fell off in the next jolt. I didn't remember falling off, but some fellers watching me ride told me afterwards that I came down like a rag.

I was like a rag for a couple of weeks after that. I'd take spells and near go blind for an hour or so at a time, and I couldn't get my breath very well at them times. Something had sure been jarred loose, but I stayed at the ranch and sort of rested up there for a month or so. When I did go back to riding again I went on round-up and I was handed a gentle string of horses, and I noticed that I'd lost a certain amount of balance and couldn't sit a horse like I did before. Sometimes I'd feel sort of groggy and I would fall off my horse even while riding a gentle one and poking along with a herd.

Feeling the way I did kind of knocked me from wanting to settle down to building a place of my own for a spell. I didn't think I'd have so far to go at times and I didn't want to start a place with the thought of maybe having to leave it before I got it going or before I could get to enjoy it much.

Then I got to thinking of another thing, something that never had much chance to come to a head before on account of knocking around too much. But now, and from the time when I first got layed up, on till afterwards when I wasn't sure of myself on a horse, it came to me that I could do something else and one fine evening, after falling off a gentle horse once again, I come to decide to become an artist.

I had no doubt but what I could be one and go to making lots of money soon as I got to a big town. I figgured all I had to do was to get there and go to drawing pictures, which would sell as fast as I made 'em, and why couldn't I? . . . There was an artist feller in a big town not far away which the cowboys all knowed or heard of, he was making lots of money at that game. I'd got to hear a plenty of him myself and at every cow camp I'd been to in the Northwest, and for the last few years I'd been packing some post cards which had been printed from his work.

I'd been told many a time before, and at many an outfit, by many a good cowboy, that I was a daggone fool to waste my time and risk my neck at breaking horses when I could draw like I did, but I'd just laughed at that because I didn't care much, and I was very satisfied to be in a breaking pen, handling snuffy bronks, watch my shadow while I rode 'em, and be admired by the best of riders for my riding. I couldn't think of being an artist when there was happenings such as a tough bronk being brought for many miles for me to ride and have the cowboys point a thumb my way and say, "he'll take the rough off of him."

I took great pride in doing that, and the two-and-a-half

or five dollars I'd get for the job meant more to me than any hundreds for any paintings I might make. This I was doing was living, where painting would be working. But, as I've said before, I didn't care as yet as to what a good paint-

Watch my shadow while I rode 'em.

ing could mean. I'd only drawed small pictures with a stub pencil and my fun, after drawing them, was to see the boys grin when they seen 'em, and hear remarks such as "that pony is sure 'romping.'" . . . What I liked the most was to see the pleased look on the face of a "ranny" (top hand) when I'd give the picture to him.

But I begin to change my tune when one time after another I kept a falling off horses that was standing still, and I couldn't stand a jolt. I rode on my nerve, and many a time

I slapped myself in the face so I'd wake up when I begin to feel groggy and slipping.

About that time, and being I couldn't make much of a hand no more, I begin to think back of the many times I was told how I should be an artist, but being sort of thick-headed it took many a fall to make me decide to swap my saddle for a paint-brush. But the last fall I had finally turned the trick. I was "piloting" the round-up wagon acrost country when the leaders of the chuck-wagon team broke loose and run off with the stretchers. I had a new rope and it was stiff: I tied one end of it down in a hurry and made a loop out of the other end. I was riding a big black horse and I caught the team all right but as I went to hold 'em, my rope had come untied at the saddle horn and the team run off with it. I rode along to get my rope again but the team was pretty fast, and they kept turning, so I thought I'd just reach down on the ground and get the dragging rope at a distance from 'em. I reached down and got the rope, but just about that time one of them groggy spells took a hold of me and, to help that along, my black horse kicked me right at the part I used to sit on the cantle-board of my saddle with. I was loosened like a bug on a man's hand, and right then I dug my nose in about sixteen thousand pebbles that covered the knoll of that perticular spot.

My nose was pushed back in my face and scattered there and when I was took to a doctor *again* and had it fixed is when I sure enough decided that I'd took my last fall and would now become an artist.

The doctor done a mighty fine job on my nose. He put two tubes in and shaped it to look pretty near like it had been, long and with a crook in it. There was only one thing he didn't save and that was the sense of smell, but I figger myself lucky sometimes, specially when there's a skunk around; queer part of that tho is that sometimes I imagine I smell a skunk when I'm on the top floor of a twenty-story stone building.

Winter had come on by that time, my nose was fixed and pointed the right direction again and one day, with bandages and clamps still holding it, I pointed that same nose towards another town, a bigger one and where the artist lived that was to tell me how much I would get for every one of my drawings, how many hundred dollars I could make in a day, and so on.

It was mighty cold when I left the little supply town for the bigger one where the railroad run thru. My nose felt it and every bit of air I brought thru it was just like so many icicles, but it felt good to be drifting again, even if it was cold. Smoky seemed to enjoy it too, and he'd snort frost at every step as we rode out. The pack horse wasn't dragging either.

But I didn't get very far out of the little town when my enjoyment to be drifting begin to dwindle down. My nose was hurting and that scope of country was under what's called a "cold snap," and on my way down to be an artist and before I got to the other end, I got to wondering a few times if I would be able to make it to shelter again.

The snow was deep, and one afternoon I come along to a farmer's shack upon a wide divide and asked if I could put up till next morning. I would pay them for my keep, and that was all right, but I found that they had no hay to feed their stock and that I'd have to turn my horses out in the snow and let 'em rustle. I'd been riding my horses too hard to do that and so, as cold as I was and as much as my nose hurt, I thought I'd ride on, even tho, as I was told, the next stopping place was about thirty miles away and near the big town.

The days was short, and I wasn't but a few miles from
the farmer's shack when it begin to get dark and as a cold
wind was shifting the deep snow, I had a hard time keeping
track of the stage road I was on and which led to town. The
stage only run twice a week. The night kept a getting colder
as I rode, and come a time when I had to get off and walk so
I could keep warm and my blood circulating. I'd walk till
I was tired, and then I'd get back on Smoky again. Him
and the other horse was getting tired by then. We'd already
been drifting for fourteen hours, the snow was deep and
there was a crust under the top snow that made traveling
mighty hard. I couldn't stay on my horse for very long at
the time, because me being on my way to town life, I didn't
have any of the real heavy winter clothes. Then to make
things worse, I had a new pair of boots on and they was
pretty tight. I could feel the cold steel of my spur-band at
my heels, and I took them off. I'd ride till I begin to feel
warm and drowsy. Feeling warm and drowsy was a sign of
freezing and it would of been mighty easy to lay down in
the snow and go to sleep, that was hard to fight against doing too. . . . Freezing is an easy death after a feller gets
over his first cold spell. But I'd sort of shake myself and try
to wake up when I begin to feel warm and drowsy and get
down off my horse and rub my face with snow. Then I'd
jump around a bit and go to walking some more. When I'd
begin to feel the cold again as I walked, was when I knowed
I was all right.

That was one of the coldest rides I ever put in. I put in
some rides when it was fifty and more below zero and when
the frost would nip my face good. I used to peel off in the
spring like a lizard, and I remember one winter, me and a
cowboy had gone a long ways to a dance, we'd wrapped up
good and we was all right and when we got inside we un-

wrapped and warmed up. We'd no more than unwrapped when some more folks drove in at the ranch and, being the stable was full up, me and the other cowboy decided to take our horses out to a feeding place about half a mile away, to make room. We just put on our coats and didn't wrap our ears, and taking two extra horses along to ride back with, we hit out on a high lope. We split the cold air and hadn't gone over half ways when I felt a sharp pain in both my ears, like as if I'd stuck a needle thru' 'em. That was all, for the time being, but when we got back to the house, warmed up and started to dancing, my ears got to feeling heavy and like they was bobbing up and down with every step I took. I put my hands to 'em and they'd swelled up two or three times their size. They was pretty sore ears for a while and when spring come the frozen skin peeled off, leaving a brand new pink skin underneath.

It was a wonder I didn't freeze at least some skin on that night while on my way to the big town. It was a good thing my nose was well covered. I got in town away after the middle of the night and I was told it was thirty below zero, and with that wind blowing that made it worse than if it had of been fifty below. I was mighty glad to get in and after I put my tired horses up to plenty of hay in a good stable, took on a feed for myself at a Chink restaurant, and when I got in a room at the hotel I didn't care if I moved on any more for some time to come. At that hotel was where I first got acquainted with steam heat. That sure went well, and being now that I was going to be an artist, I figgured I'd have plenty of comforts like that for when winters did come.

I slept till near noon during my first day in town and after I cleaned up good, got my boots shined and a hair-cut, and took on a good feed, I picked up the little bunch of

drawings I brought with me and begins strutting towards
the artist's place. It was sure a big town and his place was
hard to find, and after I walked for what seemed miles, I got
to wishing I'd rode one of my horses. But I finally found the
place and after making sure of the number on the house, I
knocked at the door. A nice lady met me there and told me
that the artist, her husband, had gone some place in town
but would be back any time now and invited me in to set
down and wait. I walked in the big room. It was sure fine and
big, and after she left me alone in there, I begin glancing
around and at the pictures on the walls. They was paintings
by the artist. I'd never seen paintings before, and all I'd
ever seen of that artist's work had been just little post cards.

My eyes roamed over them paintings and the more I
looked at 'em the more I admired 'em, and then I begin to
lose hope. I could never be an artist half as good as him,
I thought. After a while the artist himself came in, and staring at his good work like I had, I felt mighty insignificant
as I stood up to meet him. He was a bow-legged, light-haired
man of over twice my age and the whole map of the cow
country was right on his face. I could see at a glance that
he'd squinted over many herds of cattle and that he was all
cowboy as well as an artist.

He looked at me pretty well like any old-timer looks at
any kid. He wasn't a man that spoke much, he just grunted
like a Sioux Indian, but there was a look on his face as I
talked to him a bit that went as to say how he wished he
could talk to me more. He was very busy, there was a couple
of town men with him, and after he got rid of 'em, or turned
'em over to his wife, he thumbed me in the ribs and had me
follow him out of the house. Alongside of the big frame
house was a small dirt-roof log house and inside of there is
where I followed him. It was his working place, and as I

walked in, seen a half finished picture on an easel and many others stacked along the walls, also a gathering of many Indian saddles, war bonnets, Indian fighting rigs and a lot of other things like ropes, hats, six-shooters and horns, I felt a whole lot like a bronk might feel in getting out of

He'd went to work on the half finished picture like as if I wasn't around.

a blizzard into a warm stable and white-washed box-stall. I was sure stepping light and careful, held my head low and my hands close to me.

I gawked around the place and then turned to the artist. He'd went to work on the half finished picture like as if I wasn't around, and seeing he was right deep into that work, it was hard for me to begin to say anything to him. I stood on one leg and then the other and watched him work, but I got to thinking that wasn't the right thing to do and finally, wanting to get out of his way, I up and spoke to him on what I'd come to see him about. He kept right on a working and only grunted once more as I got thru talking, and when I told him I'd brought over some drawings, he just kept his eye on the canvas, never layed his brush down, and only held out his free hand for me to pass 'em to. He layed the drawings on his lap for a long time and kept right on working at his picture. Finally he layed his brush down and begin looking thru my little pencil drawings.

It was then I reared back and grinned to myself in expecting a look of surprise, hearing compliments and then being told of a way where I could sudden make a gunnysack full of money before sundown and keep right on just that way. I figgured I'd first buy me a nice cow outfit with that money, big enough so I could use a couple of round-up wagons. I'd also get all the boys I thought a lot of and have 'em come and work for me. Then maybe once in a while I'd ride in one of them coaches that traveled on rails. I'd never been in one of them yet.

I was thinking mighty fast right for a minute or so, and now that I'd come to the end of my trail, met the artist and delivered my drawings in his hand, I figgured I had no more to worry about. . . . Well, hadn't the cowboys told me that I'd make a mint with them drawings of mine, hadn't they told me that I could get at least ten dollars apiece for a drawing? . . . I figgured I could make at least twenty drawings a day, that would be two hundred dollars. That would be easy to get now because I'd figgured that to be only about half of what I'd really get, just to be on the safe side.

I was grinning right along and sort of proud as the artist shuffled my drawings. He was handling 'em as if they was cards, getting ready to play stud poker and deal out a hand, and just as quick as he shuffled 'em, and while I was waiting for surprised remarks, my deck of drawings was handed back to me, and he went to work on his picture again, just as tho I still wasn't around and like he'd never seen them pictures of mine.

He never even gave me a smile or a grunt, and when I finally asked him what he thought of 'em, he just said "good." When I asked him what I should do with 'em, and where I could sell 'em, he explained that in a very few words too.

"Just scatter 'em around in saloons," he says. "Somebody might buy 'em."

He'd kept right on working as he spoke, and when he got thru with them few words there was a sound of grand final about them that gave me to understand he was thru on the subject of my pictures and couldn't say no more.

I said good-bye to him and walked out in the cold air. The trails from there, as I stood out on the sidewalk, seemed very dim and scattering, and thru the fog of my thoughts it came to me that I wouldn't be an artist, not on that day at least.

I didn't go back to my hotel. I only went towards it some. I wasn't wanting to be in my room alone and begin thinking, so I hit for the main part of town and tried to forget I wasn't an artist by looking at different strange things that was in the windows of the main streets. A girl come along as I was looking at a windowful of brass knuckles and second-hand six-shooters and asked me if I knowed where the Tenderloin was. I thought she was talking of a part of a beef and she laughed at me when I told her I'd just passed a butcher shop a ways back. She took my arm then as natural as you please, asked me what was the matter with my nose, and I followed her to a place that we called "honkatonks" in cow camps. She knowed where it was all the time but I never

knowed before that such a place had more than one name,
and as I got there with the girl, kind of in the back of the
place, that was another time when I was called "My iron-
clad boy."

She went well with me, because I was sure needing sympathy and right then I was wanting just her kind of sympathy. It was about time for reliefs to the grave-yard shift
(one o'clock), when I broke loose and went back to the hotel.
My room seemed sort of dreary, and even tho it was warm, I
couldn't appreciate that. I throwed my drawings on the bed
and went out again. I was headed for the stables, and I
wanted to talk to Smoky, but the stable doors was closed when
I got there, and there didn't seem to be anybody around to
open the doors when I kicked at 'em. If I'd got inside I'd
most likely got on Smoky and rode away, but as I was kicking at the doors, without sense enough to get in the back
way and thru the corrals, my nose begin to hurting and on
top of that I felt one of them groggy spells coming on.

I woke up from that spell by hands feeling around me.
They wasn't my hands, and when I stood up right quick, I
come face to face with a feller that handed me back something,—it was my roll of money. He put a hand on my
shoulder in a patting way as he handed that back, and begin
to tell me that he was just watching over me. That went all
right, but I begin to feel if my old cannon was still with me
as he spoke. It was, and then I begin to talking back to him
and getting friendly. He couldn't hurt me.

Me and that feller did get pretty friendly, and it only
took us about ten minutes to do that in. I, myself, got so
friendly with him that I invited him to come along to the
hotel with me and help me make use of the big bed I had
there. That seemed mighty agreeable to him, and now being
I had somebody to talk to again, I was more satisfied. I shed

my troubles good and plenty once more, and this time to a
listening ear, but I didn't mention my main troubles nor
any names. I just brought out some that was crowding them
bigger ones and I seemed, right then, to have quite a few.

I talked on till about time for "fourth guard" and by then
the strange feller begin to talk too. By the time we crawled
in the blankets we'd come to a scheme that sort of made me
forget my disappointment. It was a brand new thing for me
and with an idea that was fine, the way I felt.

The scheme was that we'd ship to South America, Argentine. I'd heard of that country many times before, because
about then it was in most every cowboy's mind to go down
there and start in the cow business for himself. Many cowboys did go and done well, and now, as the stranger told me,
we had a chance to ship down there on contract for three
years at a hundred dollars a month wages. The fare and
expenses would be paid. According to the stranger there was
a big packing house down that country that owned many
cattle and they wanted American riders for foremans over
the natives, the natives was too slow. And where that sort of
interested me was that, for one thing, I'd be seeing new country, another thing I'd be getting about twice the wages I'd
been getting for breaking horses and, as foreman, I would
be riding the pick of the gentle ones. There was many other
things this feller brought up which went to make things look
mighty rosy for me down there. All we'd have to do now, as
he said, would be to wait for this agent who was doing the
contracting and hiring. He ought to be in town any day.

As for the stranger, he told me that he'd be shipping down
there as a high-powered clerk, getting a big salary and
would be in some office where he would see that I'd get the
best of wages and a fine spread to handle. In the meantime,
and while we was waiting for the South American agents to

come in town, he would be needing a little help. He was short of cash for the present, and being we was pardners *now* he didn't feel backward in asking me to carry him along a bit. I didn't mind doing that: he had fine ways of reminding me that he'd sure see I got a big job and what all he'd already done and would do for me. He made me feel that I should apologize for letting him share my bed and room, feed him and give him some expense money so he'd look "presentable" and be able to "impress" the packing house agent when that feller showed up. It would be for the good of both of us, he'd say, and being he already had the job promised, it would be easy to put over a good big contract.

Well, a week went by, and then another and a whole month wore along without me getting one squint at the agent. I didn't go see the artist in all that time, and now I was getting to where I begin to figgure my expenses. I'd been feeding and sheltering myself and supporting a promoter that had nothing but a reputation that sounded good but which I didn't know nothing about. Then my horses at the stable was taking expensive room and eating hay that was just as expensive. My roll of money was getting thin, and I wasn't getting fat, but I noticed one good thing: being I wasn't riding I'd begin to get away from the groggy feelings and now I was going around without any bandage on my nose.

I was walking along a main street of the town one day, just killing time and waiting for the agent which should show up "any hour now," when I come to a saloon adjoining a honkatonk. Me and the day-bartender there had got pretty friendly. With a bar of soap I'd made him some pictures on the big mirrors that was back of him, and any drink I wanted was free to me because them pictures drawed a lot of attention and many people bought a lot of drinks while discussing the drawings. I'd just come in the place to say "hello" when I noticed a feller trying to draw a picture on a big sheet of paper, the biggest sheet I ever seen. He was trying to draw a Indian's head and he was doing a poor job. When the bartender spotted me he had me try and do that for him, and that other feller was so tickled when I got thru with my drawing of what an Indian should look like that he reached down in his pocket and gave me a whole half of a silver dollar, fifty cents.

With all my figgering and hopes, that was as far as I got with my first attempt at the art game. Of course, and as the artist had told me, I left a few drawings scattered out in different saloons, but while I was in that town there wasn't any sold and I'd reduced my price from twenty dollars to ten, and finally on down to four bits each. Even then they didn't sell, and far as I know they might still be in them places right to day. I left 'em there.

With no agent showing up hour after hour, day after day, and week after week, I finally begin to think that he most likely wouldn't show up at all, and, one day as I was keeping wearing out my boots on the sidewalks instead of in the stirrup, I come acrost two cowboys that looked as lonesome as I did. I'd seen plenty of fellers with big hats and riding-boots in that town, but none that struck me as cowboys. I'd sort of snicker at them and walk on by, but when I seen them two, I knowed at a glance that they was of my breed. They seen the same thing about me, and it wasn't over five minutes from the time we'd spotted one another that there was three of a kind running together and like as if we'd just lost the remuda.

Them two fellers had got into town and now was looking for a way to get out without walking. They was afoot, but, as they told me, they had plenty of good horses somewhere if they could only get to 'em. One of the boys had a brother who had a good string of saddle horses, and that one boy's idea was to get down there, borrow them horses from that brother of his, and us three go to work running and catching wild horses, mustangs. As I was told, there was a lot of money in that.

They'd take me in as a partner and furnish me with fresh horses if I would only give 'em enough money so they could eat while on the way down. They would "beat" their way on a freight and I could catch up with 'em by the time they had the saddle horses gathered and the wild horse traps built. That would give me about a month, and I figgured I could make the six or seven hundred miles down there a horseback, and taking my time, in less than two weeks.

I gave 'em each a five-dollar gold piece, that's about all I had about then. And that evening I told my promoter to South America that I had changed my mind and would stay in the U. S. for a spell yet and go to running wild horses. That didn't seem to fluster him any, he just shook his head and remarked as to how it was too bad the agent hadn't showed up. But, he'd went on, that agent was bound to show up right quick now, and he didn't slow down on that till finally I told him I was broke and had just enough to pay my last bills. That seemed to take him down a considerable and he shook his head some more for a spell, but, all at once he begin to perk up. He'd come to a new idea where *we* could make a heap of money and without having to go to South America.

According to his new idea, I could go ahead and chase all the wild horses I wanted to and make all the money I could off that for my own self.

"But," he went on, "what would be the matter with you making a lot more money on the side?"

"How?" I asks.

He leaned closer to me and begin pointing one finger to other fingers.

"It's just like this," he says. "While you're out there running a lot of wild horses you'll be riding by many a bunch of good range horses that's worth ten times more than any mustangs you'll catch. Now, I know how to ship, and where to ship so there won't be no inspection, and once in a while if you'd bring me a carload or two of good range horses where I tell you to bring 'em, I'll take care of the shipping and getting 'em the rest of the way to market where I'd get top prices."

I sort of reared back at him as he spoke and told me how much money could be made. I didn't want to steal no horses, and that's what I told him. He called me a daggone fool for overlooking such a good bet, specially with him handling things so it all would be a cinch, and finally, to sort of break up with him, I told him that I'd think it over. He was sorry that right then he couldn't pay me back the money he'd borrowed from me but that I could figgure on the first shipment of stolen stock to be all clear to me. He would pay me back by not keeping his share in handling that first bunch.

He gave me a card and address where I could write to him as soon as I located a few good bunches, but I grinned to myself as I left him and headed for the stable to get my horses, and thought this way: I wouldn't be stealing no horses, and as far as the money he owed me was concerned, I would figgure that as a price I paid for my edducation in taking up with strangers.

CHAPTER NINETEEN

I WAS happy to be at the stable, snapping on my old shaps once more, buckling on my spurs and lifting my saddle up on good old Smoky's back. I was going to drift, and as I rode out of town I begin to feel relieved. I was shedding out from under the many things that'd been bearing down on me while there, things like supporting a tramp crook. The trip to Argentine might of been just a play with him, but with me it was different. Then there was my failing to be an artist, it hurt me not to've made a go of that because I'd thought I was pretty good.

Well, I figgured, as I rode out, I sure wasn't afoot anyway, and by the time I got out of sight of town and around a bend, I begin pointing my peeled nose towards another country and where there'd be wild horses to run. Wild horses was in my line and I knowed right then that I was cut out to be nothing else but a man with a horse under him.

That sure brought no grief to me, and as I was headed South, towards the wild-horse country, the breeze by my ears sort of combed out all the webs I might of accumulated from the disappointments, steam heat and sidewalks of the town. I was living again, and what pleased me some more was that I could sit in my saddle now and in the way I used to. None of the groggy spells was coming on me, and now I only wished I could straddle that hammer-headed bronk that'd been the cause of me wanting to be an artist. I could of took both ears off of him with my spurs while he brought out his best in giving me a rough ride.

My stops on the way South was kind of far apart. I didn't

ride fast, but I rode a long time, and I wouldn't stop at many places. I'd only stop at some ranch and where I knowed I wouldn't be charged anything for the stopping. I had no money, I didn't feel good about that, and even tho I knowed I was welcome on any cow outfit, I always had a fear of being asked for some now and again. That was my first time to be without the crackling or ringing pieces that buys things.

But I got down in the wild horse country without any argument. I rode in a little town that was right in the heart of it, and where I was to get word of the whereabouts of the two boys I was to run with. The place was at a saloon in that little town and as I walked in there one evening, after putting my horses in a good stable, I come up to them two boys and they was right at the bar taking down some drinks. They asked me if I wanted one, I says "sure," and after I took down three or four more of the same, I begin to get the whole story of a story I never figgured on.

The boys was feeling bad about telling me that story. It seemed like, as one went on to tell it, that that brother of his who had all the saddle horses, had got into trouble in some way. The trouble had been too many horses not his own, and one woman too many. He'd got a little wild, and now I learns that all his horses and belongings are took away from him and that he's having a hard time getting bail.

Well, me being broke and wanting to make a little money right bad, them news didn't strike me as cheerful. I'd traveled a long ways. Us fellers bunked in one room that night, it was the bartender's room and which he said we could have. We all made good use of it and by the time morning come we'd all decided that we split and do the best we could and forget about running wild horses.

It was many years later when I met them same fellers. They'd both done well and I still get to see them every once in a while. But that morning, after we'd decided to split, I wasn't feeling too good about it. I offered to sell my pack horse and bed to help out. (I would never sell Smoky.) But it was decided that we split and each feller keep what he had. Nobody had anything. I had two horses, but three men can't run wild ones with only two horses. . . . A feller needs many horses when he's running wild ones.

They finally talked me into hitting out. They would hit out too, and then we would gather again, when we could all be mounted. I shook hands, and being I seen none of us would be of any help to one another, I scattered on my way.

I went to the stable to get my two ponies. The stableman was there to greet me, with a little news. He said he couldn't water my horses and that the mouse-colored horse (Smoky) kicked him. He was limping around to prove it, and when I laughed, it made him sore. The sorer he got the more he hollered and finally we hear a voice coming down off a high stairway of the house telling him not to use such language and for him not to bother with these "cowboy horses." That made him all the madder, and me not saying anything, just laughing, finally made him a little reckless. He offered to bet me that he could pack my bed on my gray horse and ride that mouse-colored son-of-a-gun of mine without anything on his head. I'm not much on betting, so I just laughed again and that made him sore some more. He was bound to prove to me that he could handle any horse, from Pike's on down. He was big enough to do that, and I wished I hadn't laughed so long, because when he went to fool with my gray pack horse that pony took all the buttons off his shirt and layed him out flat. About that time I heard the same squeaky voice from upstairs and I had to quit laughing long enough so I could tally up on what had happened.

It seemed like everything had happened. My bed was scattered all over the stable corral, the man was down, and

now my gray horse was burning himself up with the pack
rope. I thought I'd let him buck out of that, and I run over
to pick up the big boy so the horse wouldn't step on him. I
was laughing some more when I tried to raise the heavy
weight. He wasn't giving me no help in raising him, but, at

That pony took all the buttons off his shirt and layed him out flat.

another sound from the squeaky voice, he begin to come to
life and I sort of carried and pushed him out of the corral
towards the steps leading up to the house.

"I told you," said the squeaky voice, "that you shouldn't
fool with them cowboy horses."

The lady looked at me and she was going to give me some
blame too. I didn't say anything against that, just held up
a hand to let her know that no words was wanted and
brought him in the attic above the storehouse, where they
lived. I layed him down on a couch. I'd quit laughing by
then, and went to get a doctor. I saddled Smoky to get that
doctor and when he followed in his buggy and climbed the
steps to the attic, he said some words about a "busted hip."

I remember I was pretty sore, hearing of that. I hadn't
asked that big boy to handle my horses but he'd wanted to,

maybe just to let on he could, and now I blamed him for trying to handle 'em and then him getting hurt.

But my bristles smoothed down a considerable when I
heard the lady's squeaky voice begin to change tunes. It'd
lost its squeak and now was sounding soft, and real worried.
She sure seemed to feel bad, and now her big husband had
calmed down a whole lot too. I tried to do something while
the doctor was working on him, but there was nothing I
could do. I'd liked to tried to cheer up the lady and there
again I felt I should keep quiet, that somehow she was blam-
ing me for what had happened. There was nothing I could
do that would be better than just gather up my bed and my
horses and move out. I was glad for one thing as I finally
lined thru the gate, and that was that the big boy didn't get
to ride Smoky.

Of course it wasn't my intentions to let him get on Smoky,
but he might of made me sore and then I'd left it to that
horse to edducate him. As it was now I was glad he didn't
try that because I didn't feel so good about what had already happened.

I rode in the thick of town and tied my horses back of the
saloon where I'd met the boys. (They'd just left town.) I was
going to try somehow to raise some money to pay my stable
bill and any amount more that I could, and leave it with the
livery stableman's wife, to sort of make up for me being so
foolish as to let a stranger handle my horses. The bartender
I'd met just the night before was on shift again. He passed
me a drink, with his compliments, and after I took that down
I told him of what'd happened at the stable and asked him
where I could sell a powerful good horse and bed so I could
raise the money I wanted.

"You don't have to sell anything to get that," he says.
"There's a cow-boss just dropped in town, he was here to
see me and asked if I knowed of any riders around that

might be wanting a job. If you can land a job with him he'll most likely advance you a month's wages."

That was fine, just what I wanted, and as the bartender went on to tell me that this feller was in a hotel acrost the street, I wasn't long in getting over there. In a few minutes I did have me a job. But I couldn't get that advance of a month's wages. The cow-boss told me he wasn't allowed to do that, and now I was stumped. I had my job, but I couldn't move out of town without at least paying my stable bill. I went back to see the bartender again, talked to him a spell, and without me asking him, he reached in his pocket, spread some bills on the bar and told me to help myself.

"You can pay me back whenever you can," was all he said.

I've met many a real white man amongst the old bartenders.

I took the money I needed (paid him back within a month) and hit out for the stable, where I met the missus and handed her what I'd gathered. She seemed mighty pleased and grateful as I handed her the money and made me feel, as I left, that it sure hadn't been my fault. As she said, she'd often warned her husband and how she hoped now that this would be a lesson to him. He would only have to lay quiet for a few months.

I rode up town, seen the cow-boss and told him I was pulling out to fill in my job. That suited him fine, and it suited me fine too, because I hadn't had no job now for some months, and I wasn't only broke, but I was in debt, my first time to be that way.

But, even with being in debt, I sure wasn't afoot yet. The thing that dug a sore spot in me was how the cow-boss had turned on the little advance of a month's wages. Any cow-foreman I'd knowed before would of been glad to've done that for a cowboy, and as I rode along to where I'd been told the spread was located, I didn't feel like I should bust myself a trying to make a hand there. I was just going to stick long enough so I could pay up my debt to the bartender and have enough left to go on a ways with.

And that's just the way it happened too. I'd struck a kind of a queer outfit, a placeful of "home-guards" (fellers that'd never been out of that county, pets), and any stranger that drifted in was bound to get it in the neck while there. I sure was no exception as to being treated like all strangers. I was handed a pick of the worst horses, after me making it strong that I was hiring out as a cowhand and not a bronk fighter. There was nothing for me to do but take the string of horses I was handed or else quit.

I didn't quit, but I've wished afterwards that I had because being with that outfit and having to put up with what I did, is what turned me to doing something which I paid a heavy penalty for. I went to pulling the fool stunt of wanting to get even and handing back wrong for wrong.

That all started when one day I was handed a horse that was supposed to be unbroke and instead, as I found out later, was one of the crookedest outlaws in that country. I never got to riding him out of the corral. He kept throwing himself and trying to get me under. He finally did get part of me under, my bum ankle, but when he did, he lit on his head and broke his neck. That was one of the two horses which I've already told of that killed themselves while I was in the middle of 'em.

Killing that horse sure didn't go good with the big boss. He figgured for sure that I'd done it a purpose, and there was even one low remark passed by one home-guard that I done it because I couldn't ride him. I called that feller about that remark, but that didn't do any good, and now that my bum ankle was barking again I couldn't do any riding only with a gentle string. I was mighty thankful that my ankle wasn't busted, only twisted some, because with that outfit I wouldn't of enjoyed being layed up any. Now that I couldn't very well handle the rough horses, they still found ways of handing me raw stuff, and when I told the boss that I could ride a bit yet, he picked me a string of ponies that was just as dead as the ones I'd had before was alive. They was old ponies that should of been pensioned long ago and of the kind that would make a cowboy hang his head while riding 'em. But there was nothing for me to do but stay there and ride the poor old devils, and till I at least had enough money to pay my debt.

I was dealt a lot of misery on that outfit, and for no reason that I could see only that I was a stranger. But I stuck till I got my month's wages and a little more, and then I rode in town to pay my debt. For interest I drawed the bartender a picture and on the biggest piece of paper I could find in town. That sure tickled him.

My ankle had quit barking by then, and now the bartender tells me that there's a bucking contest to be pulled off in town right soon and that I'd better stick around to see it. I seen it all right, and that same bartender paid my entrance fee in bronk riding. I won second money and I was scared stiff all the time because of them groggy spells that used to come on me. But they didn't come, and to cap things off right, after paying back the bartender again and having plenty enough money left, I runs acrost this home-guard who'd passed the remark that I'd killed a horse because I couldn't ride him. He'd been contesting too and got disqualified in the semi-finals.

"Now," I told him, after I had my "second money" in my pocket, "I've sure outrode you, and I'll lay a bet right here," I slapped my hand on the bar, "that I can knock you over, send you home afoot and a-bawling."

I never got to know if I could of done that or not. I got a few licks in and was just getting good when some fellers got behind me and pinned my arms down. The worst part for me was that nobody had got a holt of the home-guard and he took advantage of that to do some pounding. I guess I'd got pretty well the worst of it if my old friend the bartender hadn't jumped up on the bar with a bottle in each hand and went to work.

I looked for the home-guard for the rest of that day and all the day after, and, not seeing him, I got to figguring then that he must of hit the breeze, he couldn't of stayed away from home any longer. But I wasn't thru with him yet, and now I decided to raise perticular samhill with him and the whole outfit he was working for.

I guess maybe I'd never thought of getting even in any certain way, but while I was in town I got a letter, addressed to the bartender for me, and that letter was from that feller who'd promised to get me that big job in South America. He was doing well, he said. He'd seen the South American agent but he'd refused to contract with him on account something else that would bring more money and quicker. He said as to how I'd understand, and he put some figgures down as to what I could expect if I got what he wanted. Them figgures looked mighty good, but they didn't attract me for a while, not till I got to thinking of what was most on my mind, the home-guard and the outfit. I read the letter over and over again, and the more I got to reading it, the more I thought of what a fine scheme it would be for me to get even with that outfit. I would most likely cross trails with the home-guard while doing that too, and that's what I wanted.

It was mighty early in the morning when I rode out of town. About that same time, a day and a night later, I come

to a spring that was on the outfit's range. I knowed that
spring well, it was where the stock horses ranged and came
in to water, and as I picketed my horses on salt grass that
day and went to sleep in the reeds, I had it all figgured out
that at least a carload of the stock horses would be located
by me before the sun went down again. There was fine horses
there, good size and of the kind that'd bring a big price,
and sixty head or so of them would be a lot of fun to run off
with. That would give the outfit something to worry about,
I would be getting even, and then I would be making enough
money to take me quite a ways.

But with all of that which I kept a studying to do, there
was something reminding me that I wasn't doing just right,
and that spoiled my fun quite a bit. I got to thinking of
Bopy pretty often the evening before I took out, more often
than I'd thought of him for a long time, and now it seemed
that I pictured him the same way as I did when I run out of
my reservation that time in the North, like as if he had a
finger up and wanting to tell me something.

But I begin to think of more pleasant things, like getting
even, for instance. A few hundred head of mighty fine horses
came into water that day while I hid in the reeds. They'd
come fifteen and twenty in a bunch, and with all the bunches
I seen, I begin to spot the few I would fog into and take
away. I watched 'em graze back after they'd watered, and
kept track of 'em as they hit for the white-sage flats so I
could easy find 'em again after the sun went down.

I wished the home-guard would of rode along about then
so I could quit seeing Bopy, but there was no home-guard
showed up and I tried to forget Bopy as I saddled Smoky
and packed my gray and lined out after the few bunches I
was going to take out of the country.

I fogged in on the horses and got four bunches together.

Two studs was left behind to fight it out and the other two I took along, they seemed to be peaceable. I kept the bunches down country, where they'd naturally run, because even tho I was trying to get even with the outfit, I wasn't so bold as to let 'em know I was getting away with any of their horses. I would only get caught that way and the laugh would be on me.

Me and Smoky worked pretty hard that night, we was both wet with sweat. The horses was hard to hold together and they wouldn't drift like I wanted 'em to. They was home-guards too, and at that thought I took my rope down, let twenty feet of it drag and brought the end to pop along many a flank. I had 'em on the way about twenty miles before they begin to drift good. I still only had about two hundred miles to go to be at the "certain point" where I was to deliver them to my Argentine promoter who was to take charge of the shipping on the rest of the way to market. All was going along pretty fine and I was even enjoying the dark scenery, when I come to a big wide-open landscape in front of me. That would be good too, I thought, and I could make good time with my horses acrost that big stretch. I shoved 'em along on the start acrost there, and I figgured that by the way I was going I would cover a good forty miles that night, too far away for them home-guards to catch up with me.

I was patting myself on the back as I noticed what a fine bunch of horses I had, and what a good start I had to make a slick and clean get away with 'em, when I begin to notice that the ground was getting soft under my horse's feet. I kept a shoving the horses and the ground got softer and softer with every mile. Queer too, I thought, because that country had always looked so hard and dry. I'd rode along the edge of it many a time before while working for the outfit and often thought, as I looked at the big stretch, what a fine place it would be for riders to pull off a contest and wild-horse race. There wasn't even a blade of grass for a horse to stumble on. It was a lake bed of hardpan and about a hundred and fifty miles long. I'd figgured I could get my horses acrost there, and getting on the other side, before the home-guard outfit woke up to the fact that they'd been stolen.

But I figgured wrong, for the ground kept a getting softer, and in some places the horses come near bogging down. I couldn't put 'em in a trot or run no more. I done well if I just kept 'em in a walk, and every time each horse pulled a leg out of six inches of the hardpan there was a popping noise like a shot out of a gun. But I kept a shoving 'em on, hoping that the ground would get hard again and hold a hoof. In the meantime, as I looked back I seen I was leaving a trail that could be seen for a mile, *at night*. I wasn't making no speed either, and besides, the horses was getting tired. But I kept a shoving 'em, and till I seen they wouldn't shove no more. I wasn't going to quit till I had to. But I had to. I seen where I'd made a big mistake in trying to cross that dry-looking lake bed, and I also seen that I was in a fine fix to be cornered in that stretch if I didn't get out of it by sun-up, because the tracks I'd left with the horses was more than plain to see without anybody trying to look for 'em. My horse was more than tired, so was all the other horses. I couldn't shove them no further and now I wasn't far from being afoot.

I sure hated to quit, but I finally decided that it would be a whole lot the best for me if I did, and hit back for the shore of that lake bed. I caught my pack horse, and knowing that the range horses would work back better by themselves, I rode away with just no more than I had when I started, Smoky and my pack horse.

But I had a lot more experience, and now I would line out my trail before I started to get away with stolen stock. I'd find a sure way of getting 'em out and delivered.

I got back out of the lake bed by sun-up and hit for a range of hills by the edge where I could find water, and hide, and still be able to look down a big stretch and see if the horses I'd tried to get away with would pull themselves out. They did, and better than if I'd tried to shove 'em out. They came to water right at the spring where I was camped, and I counted 'em to make sure that none was missing. The count came right up to what I had, and after they got their fill of water they went to grazing on the shoulder of the hill and on the good feed that was all the way to their home range. They'd be back there that day and there'd be nothing about 'em to show that they'd been away excepting they was ganted up and signs of hardpan mud that run from their fetlocks on up.

I let them horses drift back, but I wasn't thru with 'em yet. I was going to locate me a trail where I'd be sure nothing would interfere with me getting to the other end, and then I'd be back after 'em.

It took me two weeks or more of hard riding to find a likely way out, so I could be sure to get to the other end with the stolen stock. I even rode up to the railroad and sent a letter to my helper and shipper in the deal, that I'd have two carloads of something good for him to ship soon, and for him to be ready and waiting.

I got the two carloads all right but these carloads was made up of cattle this time and not horses. I'd got to thinking that cattle was worth more money, and another thing that made me decide on cattle was that they went to the slaughter house for beef and didn't last long, where horses lived to be traded and are always packing a brand that identifies 'em and also lead to indentify the man that brought 'em.

I got my trail located, over two hundred miles of it, to the shipping point, and as I went along it, I also picked out where I'd hold my cattle and hide myself during the day. It took a lot of riding to do that, and I took my time too, because I wanted to do a good job and my ambition was, as I layed out my get-away, to worry that home-guard outfit a considerable and to also meet one special home-guard where it would be just him and me.

I got back to this perticular outfit's range, found me a nice high spring where I could look down many a valley, and then proceeded to rest up. Good old Smoky was needing a rest too and he was getting sore-footed. I'd found many horseshoes along the trails, this was a rocky country and where all saddle horses was shod. Many shoes was lost and I also found many that was pointed the right way, spelled and held good luck, and them is the kind I picked up to fit Smoky and my gray horse's feet. I'd picked some shingle nails off a roof of a deserted shack, and that's what I used for horseshoe nails. A horseshoer would say that they can't be used to shoe horses with, but I did and I didn't have no hammer to pound 'em with, just a hard rock, and every one of them nails that was pounded in came out with a hold and to where I could clinch 'em, not "too close to the hair" either.

Well, I got Smoky and my gray horse's feet fixed up so they'd be good to go over at least five hundred miles of rocky country. I rested for a couple of days at the high spring and in that time I had quite a bit to do. My main job was to look down the valleys and see how the cattle was ranging between day and night. Other things I had to do was to feed myself up and prepare for a long hungry ride. Then I had to see that my horses was on good strong feed, too, all

the time, and when I had that all caught up and tended to
I'd sort of relax and sleep, or once in a while dig into my
war-bag and pull out some frazzled-edge letters that I kept
a reading over and over again. One was from my shipper
that had failed to have me shipped to Argentine and was
now wanting to ship anything I could get away with. I

The big night come.

knowed that letter by heart, and then some. But the other
letters, two of 'em, brought me a lot of pleasure to read.
They was from the last girl I'd met at the honkatonk. She'd
been a nice girl and had told me a lot of things that sounded
fine and made me like her a whole lot.

The big night come. My ponies was well rested and shod.
I'd fed myself so I could go a long ways too. I watched
bunches of cattle drifting in to a big water hole that evening, and as I seen that the bunches made enough of a herd
for me to pick a couple of carloads of beef cattle out of, I

begin to grin towards the lights that shined thru the windows of the scattered buildings of what the home-guard outfit called "the headquarters."

I got on Smoky, reached for my pack horse's lead rope, and as I rode down the edge of the timber towards the white-sage flats and cattle, I looked at the lights of the headquarters once and said,

"I'll give you 'punkin-rollers' *something to ride for now.*"

CHAPTER TWENTY

I DID give 'em something to ride for. They rode around
like hornets in a bonnet and didn't get nowheres. Before
they found out what'd happened, I had picked two carloads of their prime stuff, trailed 'em the distance of the
trail I'd mapped out, got 'em in the yards where they was
no inspection, and got back to home guard the country in
time to get up to the high spring and where I could watch
'em tally up. I got a lot of fun and consolation out of that,
and now I thought I'd make 'em ride some more, as soon
as they got over their first stirring up and settled down to
thinking such a happening would never happen again.

I had a lot of time to rest my horses while waiting for
that, but while waiting I had ambitions to settle something,
and I was watching for one certain home-guard to show his
shadow anywheres near close of me. I waited and watched
but with no luck as to any sight of him, and then, when I
got to thinking that all was peaceful and I could get away
with two or three more carloads of cattle from that same outfit, I edged down along the timber once again to the white-

sage flats and went to gathering and cutting out what I would take.

It was pretty dark when I rode down to the flats, and a heap darker by the time I started gathering another bunch of cattle. And then, when I did get a bunch together, I sure got disappointed. All the beef stock seemed to be missing. The home-guards had most likely "rodeered," cut out the beef and shipped 'em, and now that left me with only the "culls" and mixed stock. . . . That went bad against my pride to doing a good job of getting even.

But I'd make up even with the culls. I'd take three car-loads instead of two.

I gathered up many bunches, looked 'em over. I savvied cattle enough so I could do that in the dark. The size and the line of the back would tell me all I wanted to know. I cut out about forty head of dry she stuff. That was all I could get out of the herd that would bring any price on a market.

I had a tough time on that second trip. The weather had turned cold and I was sure feeling it. The only thing good was that the cattle was traveling nice and headed for the railroad like they sure enough wanted to be shipped. But they got sore-footed by the time I got 'em halfways to the railroad and I had to take 'em pretty easy on the rest of the way in. I traveled by night all the time. Cold winds was blowing, flurries of snow come and I shivered thru that whole two-hundred-mile drive. It took me about ten nights to make it.

During the days, I'd water my cattle and shove 'em up some draw, where there'd be good feed and where they could rest. They'd seldom move over half a mile from where I'd leave 'em. They was glad to stop and graze and then lay down, and sometimes, as I'd watch 'em, I'd begin to wish again that I had a little place of my own to take 'em and keep 'em and start in again to making a little spread and behave myself and forget my grudges. This last bunch I had was all she-stock and they'd made me a little start, enough to keep me and Smoky.

But I had no little place of my own to take 'em to, and besides, it would be best to ship the cattle, get what money I would have coming from these and the first bunch, and then maybe get me the little place and *buy* me a few head and settle down. I was getting to want my own cabin again, my own corrals, cattle and horses, because now I'd got to feeling good. I wasn't getting no more groggy spells and my bum ankle didn't hurt in a stirrup. I felt now like there'd be plenty of time ahead for me to enjoy what I gathered.

I'd hanker for a place of my own when some nights I'd be shoving my stolen stock by within a few miles of a ranch house. I'd be seeing the lights of it and I'd sort of picture the family there, the bunk house and the boys by the stove a joking with one another or leaning back on their bunks, reading by good lamplight while the old box stove hummed and throwed sparks from cedar wood. I'd be shivering about that time, shoving sore-footed cattle, riding tired horses and looking back often for riders that might come up on me. Sometimes I'd ride thru groves of joshuas and, at night, some of them would take the shape of a rider with a rifle.

The country I was taking the cattle thru was all desert range country. Ranches was far apart and there was a few prospectors' cabins and tents scattered out thru the hills. I come to a deserted prospector's tent one night, it was flapping on a frame, and right there I thought I'd stop for a while. It was the closest I'd seen to shelter for more than two months. I turned the cattle up a draw, hobbled my horses and came to the tent. I could see it hadn't been used for at least a couple of years, and being it was snowing and the wind was cold, I went in there and built me a fire in the tin stove.

I wished I could of let the cattle go, and stayed in that tent. I was tired, had hardly any sleep, was cold, and hungry for many things. I stayed in the tent for about twelve hours, slept and cooked up what I had left of the grub I'd took along, that was about two cupfuls of flour and nothing else. I mixed that with snow-water and made me three hard flapjacks. I still had three days to go to get to the railroad, and I figgured I could use no more than one flapjack in twenty-four hours. That had to do me while I rode all night and watched the back trail during the biggest part of the day. I was getting just as short on sleep as I was on food.

The tent got to be of some help to me. With my pocket knife I cut up one side of it and made me a sort of a coat, something that would cut the wind, and then made me a pair of mittens. The whole thing was mighty awkward and I guess I must of looked like a ghost while riding thru the night, but that outfit cut the wind pretty good and it helped spook the cattle to better speed.

I'd et my last flapjack and still had a day and a night to go to get to the railroad, when one morning a feller with a four-horse team drives along not far to where my cattle was hid. He'd spotted 'em, and being he seemed sort of inquisitive, he anchored his team and started towards my cattle to look 'em over. I didn't want him to look at the cattle because he'd be a bad witness against me in case something went wrong and somebody was needed to identify the brands. So, I had to show myself and head him off, saying that them was pretty wild cattle, they was resting and I didn't want 'em to start running by the sight of a man afoot.

I had to do quite a bit of persuading before I could turn that inquisitive cuss, but I finally got him turned, talked to

him about different things and I don't think he had any
suspicions when he went back to his team.

I had quite a few scares on that last trip that way. It
seemed like I was bumping up with everybody in the country. The biggest scare I had was when one time I seen three
riders coming my way on a high lope and like as if they
was following my trail of the night before. My cattle was up
on the side of a mountain, well hid, and at the sight of the
riders which I seen coming three or four miles off, I left the
cattle and rode back on my trail about a mile. I got off my
horse then and begin to disguise myself. I wasn't going to
run unless I had to, and I was wanting to see if them riders
was after the cattle and me or not.

I'd bought me a pair of shoes and a cap while I was in the
big town, just to sort of dress up with. I'd took them along
with me and now I seen good use for 'em. I slipped off and
hid my boots and hat and slipped on the shoes and cap.
Now, I thought, nobody would ever think of connecting
me up with stolen cattle.

The riders came right along the trail and up the mountain. I hollered as if I was looking for help, or wanting to
talk, and they came up to me. My idea was to turn 'em away
from where I hid the cattle. I begin to get scareder as the
riders came nearer. They acted like they was on a trail and
mighty anxious to catch up to something, and they was. But
they wasn't after me nor any cattle. They was mustang runners and on their way to meet other fellers and start a big
drive. That relieved me a considerable and I wished I could
of rode along with 'em. But I had the cattle to deliver and
now, to keep the riders from seeing 'em, I lied and told the
riders that I'd seen a bunch of wild horses, about ten head,
and I pointed to a draw the opposite direction from where the
cattle was. They rode on that way.

Another good scare I had was during a pitch-dark night. I'd come to a river, the water was still and it looked more like a long shallow pool. The cattle was hard to get started to cross it, but finally some lead in, and the water didn't seem to be above their knees. I brought along the other cattle and I fell in behind 'em plum careless and thinking it was as it looked like, a shallow pool. All at once the leaders and them following went out of sight, and me too. We'd all dropped into deep water and there seemed to be a strong under-current that drawed all animals towards a place what looked like a big whirlpool. Smoky managed to swim to a bank but it was too steep for him to climb. I just managed to reach up and grab a bush and I pulled myself out that way. I hung on to the bridle reins then, kept Smoky's head up, and pulled him along the shore till finally I got him to a place where he could crawl out. The pack horse crawled out behind him and so did a few head of cattle.

I had to stay where I was for the rest of that night, ride along the bank, rope cattle and pull 'em out. When I couldn't see nor hear no more cattle in the water, I took the pack off my gray horse and scattered it out to dry. I was wet thru myself, and the cold wind turned my clothes to ice. So I went to work and pulled out a lot of grease-wood and started a fire to warm up by. I went to sleep by it a few minutes. The wind blowed my hat off and towards the fire while I was sleeping and the whole crown of it got burned. I had to wear my cap from then on.

It was a long cold night, and I was glad when morning come so I could see how many cattle I had left. Half of 'em had turned back while in the water and was acrost the river. I counted all I could see. The count showed that there was three head missing. Daggone lucky, I thought, after I sized up where we'd crossed. The river, as I found out, was an un-

derground river. I'd crossed over it before but on solid
ground. This time I'd crossed it where it'd broke to the top.
Some places was shallow but the most of it was deeper than a
rock hanging down at the end of my forty-foot rope, and
the whirlpools in there where the river sunk underground
again made it mighty dangerous.

I gathered what cattle I had left. I still had at least a
good carload, and I was glad for that. I'd also know where
to cross that river the next time I got to it again.

But as I rode away from it with the cattle, and on towards the railroad, I didn't think I'd ever have any reason
to cross that river again. I'd decided I was even with the
outfit now, and I didn't want to run off with no more cattle from them nor nobody else, and no horses either. I'd
turn this carload over and wait for my money from the two
shipments and then hit out for new country where I could
dicker for a little place and settle down with my own little
bunch of cattle and horses. I was tired of looking over my
shoulder and watching the back trails and dodging homey
lights in cold nights.

I finally got the sore-footed cattle to the railroad and
shipping yards. The shipping yards was small there and it
was already full of cattle, all but a little space in the loading
pen and just about big enough to hold my little bunch. But
there was no outside gate to that little pen, and being I
didn't want to mix my cattle with the others, I'd have to tear
a panel of the little pen down to get my cattle in. My cattle
had to be shipped at night because I didn't want anybody to
see them nor me right there in daytime.

I tore down a panel of the loading pen and shoved my cattle in. All that was a heap more ticklish to do than it is to
write about. But, anyway, after I got my cattle in the pen
and put up the panel again, I went and hunted up the feller

that was to handle my shipping. I found him at a small
hotel. He was sound asleep, looked well fed and rested, and
that was just the opposite of what I was. I hadn't had a bite
to eat for twenty-four hours and just a few bites for some
days before that. I'd been riding right along, and freezing,
and as far as sleep was concerned, I felt like I could take on
a whole straight month of that.

The feller jumped right up as he recognized me. "You're
just in time," he says, "the freight is due thru here in another
hour and will pick up our two cars. We'll have 'em loaded
by that time."

"I could only get *one* carload," I says.

He looked at me sort of funny at that, but he soon begin
to seem cheerful again. He patted me on the shoulder and
says,

"Well, we'll make up for it next time."

I grinned at him and says, "You bet." But, to myself, I
grinned some more. There wouldn't be no next time.

Me and the feller loaded the cattle. He wasn't much use
at that. He just took the place of a post, the same as the
time before. After I got the car door clamped down and he
got back with the billing papers, the freight pulled in and
the engine begin to switch for our one carload. While that
was done I asked the feller for my share of the money from
the first shipment, also the money he'd borrowed from me.
He handed me three or four twenty-dollar bills and said he'd
send me a check for the rest as soon as he delivered this second load. He was in a hurry and that struck me all right
right then. I was too wore out to think very good at the
time anyway.

It was daybreak when I seen the tail-light of the freight
train disappear, and I thought as I seen it go that there
was another bunch of cattle that I'd sweated, and froze, and

starved, and took many chances to get. I got on Smoky, said
something to him about us being thru riding between suns,
and hunted up a stable where I could give him and my pack
horse plenty of the best grain and hay, and a good warm
stall to eat that in. And then slipping on my shoes for disguise again—I already had my cap on—I hunted up a
place where I could get a side of beef, half a sack of fried
potatoes, a dozen loaves of bread and a creekful of coffee to
wash that down. I was hungry.

The sun was away high by the time I made away with the
bait I'd ordered, and now, as I looked at myself in the glass
acrost the counter, I figgured that a hair-cut and a bath sure
wouldn't go bad. I hunted up a barber shop, got in the back
of it, shedded off my clothes and crawled in the tin bathtub.
I went to sleep in there. I don't know how long I slept but a
barber came in and woke me up.

I was setting in the barber chair a while later. I got my
hair cut, and being as the barber told me I should have a
shave, he layed the chair down. I told him to go ahead and
went to sleep some. That was the first time a razor ever
went over my face. I didn't get to appreciate that first shave,
and when he woke me up again to setting up, I hear voices.
Some fellers in the barber shop was talking. One said that a
carload of cattle had been shipped "last night" and that
things looked suspicious. A panel of the yards had been tore
loose, one post had been set back *upside down* and that's
what had drawed attention. The sheriff around there was a
good man and he'd sure catch up with the men that done the
shipping. It looked like cattle stealing.

My face was covered with a hot towel as I heard that, and
I begin to thinking how I would look when I stepped off
the barber chair. I had scuffed shoes on, my clothes was *now*
looking like any laborer's clothes, and then I had a cap

to wear. With that combination, I'd never be recognized as anybody that would ever steal a whole carload of cattle.

I walked out of the barber shop, tried to act like a farm hand, and I walked out without any glances throwed my way. I didn't think so, anyway, but as I got out I bumps up against an old cowboy friend of mine. He was out of his territory, and he recognized me even with my disguise.

"What are you doing out here, Old Son?" he says as he slapped me on the shoulder.

I was glad to see him, too, and I slapped him back. We got to talking about things, and as we was talking, I noticed a feller sticking around that was sort of sizing me up.

"Well," I says, to try and put that inquisitive feller off, "I've got to get back home. The woman and the kids will be worried and I'm afraid the sheep will be scattering away."

I dodged away from my friend and hit for the stable. By that time I was scared. When I got to the stable, I noticed that the man there was sizing me up too, and he begin to talk to me in a queer way about the cattle that'd been shipped out "last night." It seemed like the whole town knowed about that.

"What cattle?" I asked, as I was saddling up Smoky and putting my pack on the gray. "I don't know anything about any cattle. I'm farming up here a ways and raising a few sheep."

"Well," says the stableman, "I never seen a farmer or sheepman look like you, and I never seen neither with an outfit like you have."

"Look at this one then," I says, as I started to ride away. "I'm farming and running sheep, both."

I didn't want to stop and argue with the stableman, he was too wise, and right there I seen that my cap and scuffed shoes didn't disguise me so well. I figgured I'd just better be drifting.

I drifted. After I got out of the town lanes I hit out for a range of mountains where I could find water and plenty of grass for my horses. I rode the whole afternoon and all that night to get to them mountains, and I'd got above the foothills of them, where I found a little sheltered meadow with a small stream running by it. The grass was white with frost

Something was pulling against my shoulder.

and there was snow amongst the granite boulders. It all looked like a mighty fine spot for me to stretch out my bed and take on a lot of something I hadn't caught up with for many a day, sleep. I took my bed off the gray horse, spread it out, picketed the gray and turned Smoky loose, and then crawled into that bed. But it didn't seem to me that I'd been laying in it over five minutes when I was stirred. Something was pulling against my shoulder, like a willow that bent but wouldn't break. I was dreaming that I was chasing some wild pony and got caught in a limb. When that limb kept a holding and pulling on me, I stirred up, and I found myself blinking into what looked like the mouth of a volcano. It was the busiest end of a forty-five six-shooter.

Still thinking I was dreaming, I tried to turn over for more sleep, but that limb wouldn't let me turn. I tried to dodge it, but it hung on, and when I went to reach for it I seen it was *a hand*. I woke up at that, and while blinking, I sort of leaned under my war-bag and layed my hand on that long six-shooter of mine. It was a forty-five too.

I guess maybe I'd of drug it out and used it, because I didn't want to be bothered right then. But I didn't have no chance to do that. There was a man on each one of them arms of mine.

I remember grinning as I blinked at the both of 'em, and I remember saying "Well, take the d—— thing [I meant the gun] and let me sleep a bit more."

But they wouldn't let me sleep a bit more. These officers had got word I was headed a certain way; they'd come from another direction to head me off and, as they told me afterwards, it was just pure luck they found me. They'd wanted rest themselves, after being only fifty miles from the comforts of home, and come to the stream where I was camped, and there I was. . . .

"Too bad I didn't have a little bit of sleep and could think a bit," I says to 'em. "I'd been up above the spring then and watched you fellers go by."

But, as it was, I was separated from my dad's gun once again. I was sure disgracing that old gun, having it took away from me so often. I thought of that, and also thought of something else; that gun would of been disgraced a heap more if I'd used it against anybody that was only doing their duty. I couldn't, even if I had the chance, begin to slant a gun at anyone unless it was a case of have to, not even for my freedom. I didn't want to be an outlaw. I've knowed quite a few and their lives was short and fast, or long in a little dark space that's barred. I didn't think much about life being short, in such cases. What I thought most of always was to be friendly and to take my medicine when I done wrong. I could never think of shooting at a man that handed me that medicine, not unless he made me peeved.

Them two officers didn't make me peeved. When I seen I was caught and I grinned at 'em, they grinned right back, and in a friendly way. One of the officers, a little bit of a man, told me he was glad he caught me while I was asleep, and he went to the trouble of showing me where he was going to keep my gun, right alongside of his own.

After that I was told something, like, whatever I'd say from now on would, or might, be used against me, or something to that effect. After the little officer was thru with the ceremonies he dug up a pair of handcuffs and he says,

"Will I have to put these on you, or can I trust you?"

"You can trust me better without 'em," I answers.

We shook hands on that, and even tho there was no words said, there was an understanding as to a promise, that I wouldn't try to escape, and that I wouldn't try to pull anything on him. The other officer, the big feller, had his gun leveled at me all the while. The little officer told him to put it down now, and as much as the big feller hated to, he did it.

It took us two days to get to the town where I'd brought the cattle. In that time I was plum free to handle my horses and ride along. During the one night on the way we all three slept together in my bed. As needing for sleep as I was, I was the first to wake up when morning come. I'd woke up often during the night. I could of got all the guns, took the horses and made my get-away. But I was still mighty tired and, what's more, I'd shook hands and had made it understood that I wouldn't try that.

We got into town late in the afternoon, and it seemed like the whole population for a thousand miles around was there on the main street. The big officer was acting like a general that'd just got back from a big war he'd won. He kept a saying "hello" to many friends and pointing back at me, as much as to say, "I got 'im." But *he* didn't get me, it was the little feller that did. And right at the time, while riding thru the town and while I was supposed to've been disarmed and so on, I had a thirty-eight caliber on a forty-one frame right inside of my boot and next to my leg. . . .

I could of used that to a mighty good advantage, and I come pretty near doing that as the big feller kept a showing off. But the little feller winked at me a few times at the right time, just like to tell me not to mind the hot wind, and I only winked back at him, and kept my promise.

My horses was took away from me a little while after we got in town. I was kept in that town that night, and the next morning I was escorted to the sheriff's office, to another town about forty miles away. That distance was made by stage. That relieved the officers a considerable, specially the big one, and I found when we got there that there was no charges against me, only that I was suspicioned in connection with a shipment of cattle.

"Well," I says, "I guess I'll go then."

"But, if you want to try to leave," I was told, "we can put a charge against you that will hold you, and that is for carrying concealed weapons."

I did have a weapon concealed, but the one they meant was my dad's gun and which had been under my war-bag. . . . I *decided* to stay, and take a chance of clearing the name I was then using. I didn't want to be on the dodge. I'd done what I wanted to do, and now I was quits.

I was turned over to the powerful-great sheriff. He told

me that I'd been identified by a teamster as the feller that
was bringing in some cattle, that the cattle had been shipped,
and evidence being of a panel being tore out of the loading
shute. A post, set back upside down, had called attention to
the fact.

"But I won't put no charges against you if you'll give
me your promise to stay till all is cleared," says the sheriff.
The little deputy had said something about me *keeping* a
promise.

The sheriff squinted at me as I said I would stay, and
he seemed satisfied. I liked that sheriff. His eyes wasn't of
the cold steel gray that good sheriffs are supposed to have,
they was brown and mild, but there was something about 'em
that hinted to plenty of cold and steel, and more. There was
also a light in 'em that made you want to shake hands with
him even if he took you to the gallows.

He was the first to offer a hand. I was glad to shake it,
and then he went to talking to the little deputy about me.
I sat down on a bench, and when the deputy left, the sheriff
said it was about time him and me went to eat. He took me
to his own home that night, after me being under suspicion
of cattle stealing.

But there was no handcuffs nor gruff words about him,
and, as we two walked along a little narrow dirt-walk covered
with branches of many trees, him and me got to talking a bit.
By the time he got me to the house we got to both figguring that I wasn't guilty. . . .

"If I thought you was guilty," he said, pointing to the
house, "I'd never take you in my home and have you eat at
my table."

Wherever he got to thinking I wasn't guilty I don't know.
It might of been because I looked sort of young. But I got to
making up my mind right then that I was *not* guilty, just
for him.

That sheriff held me for over a month. He was in another state from where I'd got the cattle, and he had to wait for some kinds of papers and things that might connect me up with the cattle stealing charge. In the meantime he was going to hold me.

He held me by my promise only, and being that things seemed sort of mixed up as to what cattle had been stole, where from and so on, I felt pretty safe in making that promise. I et at the sheriff's home three times a day. I met his wife at every meal, and her and me and him got to be of liking one another a whole lot. I'd walk along with the sheriff to his office and I'd spend a few hours there, drawing pictures or something. Sometimes he'd spar with me a bit and hit me right where things had been turned upside down by that rough bronk, and when I'd get my breath again and begin to see straight, I'd come back at him, and to his nose. He was sensitive about that spot.

I slept in a shed at the back of the sheriff's home. I was never put in jail, and I could of got away any time. What's more, I still had the .38 in my boot. But I'd given him my promise not to try to get away. Him and his wife made me feel that I wasn't guilty, and all I was trying to do now was to show them that I wasn't. I would lie so they wouldn't be disappointed.

A long-distance telephone call came along one day from the neighboring state. It said to "release" me and a few other words. That went well, and I was mighty pleased when the sheriff and his wife said that they knowed all the time I wasn't guilty. The sheriff told me I could go now, providing I would let him know of my whereabouts and that I would come back if he called for me. I promised him I would.

I got the stage and sat with the driver the whole forty miles back to where my horses was. That drive seemed like a five-minute-merry-go-around. I was mighty happy to get back to Smoky and my gray, and now, even if I didn't get any money from the cattle I'd brought in, I was more than glad to get back to my horses, get in the hills again and go to raising something that was my own, a few head of cattle, where it would be me and my horse and my cabin.

But I was due for a sudden stop in them ambitions. The constable met me as the stage pulled in the little town where my horses was, and told me that he'd just received word for me to get back to the sheriff's office, something had been dug up. That constable, trying to make some kind of a rep for himself, was going to escort me back and see that I got there. I jumped down off the stage, and made it strong that I didn't want his escort, that I would get back to the sheriff by myself if I had to walk. He seemed to see something of my feelings, and the driver grinned and snapped his whip, the four-horse team took to the collar and we left the constable behind.

The sheriff seemed proud of me as he met me at the coach. But I could see that he wasn't happy for what he had to tell me.

"Just got word that you was the man that was wanted for cattle stealing," he said. He seemed worried a whole lot. "I didn't think," he went on, "that you was a thief. I told you I'd just as soon have a rattlesnake in my house as a thief. I kept you there, and now you tell me: Are you a thief or aren't you?"

"Yes, I *was*," I said.

CHAPTER TWENTY–ONE

IF all sheriffs and officers was like that one sheriff, I think there'd be less outlaws. When I told him I had been a thief, he swallowed hard and then said,

"Well, I still don't believe you're a thief, and you can still come and set to my table, any time."

His wife was there with him when he said that. There was tears in her eyes. I'd never seen tears in a woman's eyes, and now, as I got in the neighboring state's sheriff's car I wanted to say that I'd made my last "wild catch." But it wouldn't of done to said that, so I just tried to grin, and the last words from the sheriff was that he'd see me thru and help me, that me being young and not trying to get away after all the chances I had, would go a long ways towards making the sentence smaller.

The two-hundred mile ride back to the neighboring State's sheriff's office was a pretty cold one. It was my first car ride but I didn't enjoy it much. What was ahead for me when I got to the other end didn't strike me as so cheerful, and I got to wondering a few times if I shouldn't use the hole-card I still had in my boot and have them two fellers that was in the car drop me off, or else have 'em take me to some place where I could get a good horse. I was setting alone in the back seat of the car, a State chauffer was driving, and a State official was holding a thirty-thirty rifle right affectionate, and looking back at me every once in a while. I grinned at that. He didn't know I had a gun, and I could of poked the business end of my thirty-eight right in his ear and made him get out and walk. I could of handled the chauffer after that too, and have him drive me around. I'd also grabbed the rifle and would of had plenty of ammunition.

It was while I was thinking right deep that way that I begin to finger the handle of my thirty-eight. . . . I got scared about that time, got scared that I might use it. . . . I throwed it away, seen it land in a thick patch of sage, and I guess it's still there.

I was thinking of the sheriff I'd just left when I done that, and of what he'd believed me to be. I didn't want to spoil that belief.

After many hours' driving thru fine wild-horse country the car finally slowed down at the neighboring State's sheriff's office. His office was adjoining the jail, and there's where I was put.

I was kept there for a few days, and then I was told that I would get leniency if I would plead guilty.

I pleaded guilty (I don't know, right up to to-day, if they got the other feller or not, the feller that done the shipping).

After a few months' time I was sent to the big place, a place where they kept fellers, whether them fellers wanted to be kept or not. In the meantime, and before I got there, I had the chance to see the home-guard again, but it wasn't the chance I wanted to have with him. There was a deputy on each side of me. The home-guard had been brought in as a witness that I'd been seen in the country a short while before the cattle disappeared. That connected me up with the same cattle that had been shipped. But I wasn't worried about connections right then, all the connections I wanted to make was with that home-guard. And there again I was reminded as I was made to sit down, that whatever I would say would be used against me. I kept quiet, and grinned at the deputies. They savvied how I felt.

The judge that sentenced me afterwards must of savvied

how I felt too, because he didn't "throw the whole book at me." He just gave me plenty of time to cool off good. He was a stern old feller but he must of seen a lot of a kid in me.

I got to the big place, where men done time, and I didn't like the looks of the place so well. It was a place that could hold any mountain lion and where even eagles couldn't fly out of. Two fellers tried to get out of it once. I seen 'em try it. They got up the high wall and "somehow" got thru the electric-charged wires that was above, but they only got buried in the prison graveyard for their trying.

I didn't want to try and get away. I wanted to take my punishment, get out as freed and so I wouldn't ever be jumping whenever a dry limb cracked. I was "quits."

I won't try to tell much of my time in the prison. It would be too monotonous, too long. Every day dragged on to another one that dragged some more, and on and on that way. There was the cells for the night, two men to each, the clang of steel doors closing, a few hours when prisoners talked or read, and then the sound of a gong and "lights out," time for sleep or lay awake and think of "outside." There'd be clanging of more steel doors as they was opened in the morning and the men would file down the long lane between the cells and to the mess hall. After that there'd be the big prison yard where all men scattered out to different jobs.

Most men had some job or other to do. Some was detailed to scrub out the cell house and other places around, some would be out in the big yard cutting cord wood or working in the rock quarry that was right there and shaping out building stone. Many of the prisoners had jobs of their own that they was busy at, making shawls that was sent out to different dealers, or making different work from rawhide,

like quirts and bosals, and which was sent to saddle shops for
hundreds of miles around. Some done horse-hair bridles,
belts and many other things. The old prisoners would teach
the new ones the art of the game with rawhide or horse-hair
or wool, and the money that would be gathered from that
would go to the prisoner. He could buy himself things for
the table, have the prison tailor make him a special-cut uniform, or send the money to help take care of kinfolks on the
outside.

The prison system was that every man should be working.
If a man didn't want to line out on some special job for himself, he'd be put to doing something for the State. The prisoners got along pretty well together and there wasn't much
trouble with the guards. There'd be a few of the prisoners
start something once in a while and all they got for that was
"time" in the dungeon on bread and water. I didn't get to
see them places, and I never hankered to.

There was nothing special I wanted to take up while
there. All I knowed was riding, and that outfit sure didn't
care for me to do any riding, so I was put to one job after
another. I'd be a flunky in the mess hall for a while and then
I'd be put on the wood-pile, and back and forth that way.
I was surrounded by tall walls for about a year when, one
day, I was took out and made a trusty. It sure was great to
be on the outside and see country again. But my job as
trusty wasn't to look at the country too much, nor do any
riding. It was to wait on the guards' tables. There was
about twenty guards or more. I stuck to that job till I got
in an argument with a big nigger cook and then I was put
back inside the prison yard again.

I was kept in there for a few months, and in that time
I got to say "howdy" to a cowboy that'd got a little wild and
received a pretty stiff sentence. Him and me was the only

cowboys in that whole herd of prisoners, and it was only natural that we got pretty thick. Wether it was cutting wood now, or being flunkies in the mess hall, him and me was together. We finally managed to get a cell so we could be together there, and the things we talked about sure made us both mighty homesick for the same kind of country and rigging.

I sure thought of my old ponies while we talked, and often between them times too. I'd left Smoky and the gray in charge of a feller who said he'd sure keep his eye on 'em. They was supposed to've been turned out on the range and brought in to be fed if they needed it. I'd given that feller my saddle, bridle and bed to do that for me, and some money too. And now, at nights, or while me and the cowboy talked, I'd get to thinking of Smoky and how I'd like to be alongside of him some place, any place, so long as it was open.

I'd get pretty starved for the feel of his hide once in a while, and sometimes I wished that I'd tried to break away while I had so many good chances, and rode old Smoky acrost the South border again, just to be with him and where there'd be hills around. It was hard for me to be with any crowd. The prisoners made quite a crowd. The most of 'em was fellers from towns, they didn't talk my language. I hated to brush elbows with so many people that was all so strange to me in ways and talk.

It made it mighty hard on me, after being used to all the freedom I'd had, to find myself surrounded with walls and crowded by so many people. The men there was used to people, they liked crowds. They was men that was brought in for crimes that's done amongst crowds: forgery, pickpocketing, murder, and all kinds of crimes that's committed where folks lived close together. They could bear the life of a prison better than I could, I think, because none that I seen there would ever wanted to get outside of any city limits. Their life had been closed in, anyway, and that's why I say they could bear the prison life better than I could.

But many of the men felt the pinching of the prison walls, for, even tho they wasn't craving for wide-open country, there was other things. Some had folks they thought a lot of. Then folks was worrying, and the way I seen some fellers worry too, made me feel lucky that nobody was worrying about me. I had no folks, nothing but a couple of horses for *me* to think of.

I thought about them a plenty, and I also thought, what about the poor feller that had a life sentence to serve and had a mother grieving over him while he was serving it?

I was glad when, a few months after my argument with the nigger cook, I was took out of the prison yard and made a trusty again, and gladder when I seen that my next job now would be to take care of a few saddle horses that was kept there in case of a prison break, when prisoners had to be rode down. The prisoners could be rode down easy around that country because it was wide open sagebrush flats.

These horses I was to take care of was very different than the horses I'd been used to. They was gentle and of the stable kind, but they was horseflesh just the same, and I was more than pleased to be near 'em and taking care of 'em. I'd took care of 'em only about a week when I was told by the guard who had charge of all the animal feeding around the prison, that I'd been feeding the horses twice as much as they was allowed to get, and that if I didn't cut down on feeding the way I did, I'd have to take them out once in a while and exercise 'em. That suited me fine, and when I got permission to ride out, on one horse and then another, I felt more pleased than I'd been for many a day. I was on horseback again, and even tho I was a prisoner, rode horses and saddles that wasn't my kind, I was with horses and on 'em, and that sure went a long ways towards making things agreeable for me.

There was a stable all by itself for them horses, and after I'd get thru taking care of 'em, exercising 'em and sweep-

I was on horseback again.

ing out the place, I found myself a corner in that stable where, in what spare time I had, I could draw a bit. My drawing board was the lid on the grain box, and my páper and pencils was furnished by the captain of the guards. He'd liked a drawing I showed him once. I'd given it to him, and now he wanted some more. I made him quite a few. The other guards got to wanting some too, and the first thing I knowed I was swamped with paper and pencils. I drawed horses mostly, the kind I knowed and in all the shapes they got into. Smoky was often before me as I drawed. To me he was all what a horse should be, and missing him the way I did, I drawed many a horse that looked like him.

I drawed many a picture in that stable. All of 'em went to the guards, and as I'd hand 'em over, I got to thinking of the artist I'd met who said for me to "scatter 'em around." I never thought I'd be scattering pictures around a prison.

But that didn't matter now. I wasn't going to be a artist no more, anyway.

Another place where I could draw was in my cell in the trusties' quarters. The cells in them quarters was good size and there was a pretty good light to work by, till time for "lights out," nine o'clock. I'd work there a setting at the edge of my bunk, and sometimes, when I'd look around the walls, at the rings and chains fastened there, at the big iron ring in the rock floor, and which had held many a bad hombre, I got to drawing pictures of old outlaws that got tangled up with the chains to that ring, and before there was any laws much.

An old guard told me of the names of many an outlaw that he'd helped fasten to them rings. He'd point at the one in the middle of the floor of my cell, and "One time," he'd said, "we had one man that come near taking that ring out. We had to add them chains onto him from the wall there.

"That was a long time before you was born," he'd went on to say, "during the 70's."

This old cell house I was put in during nights and while I was a trusty, was sure enough an old one. The natural stone floor had been wore down by many a step of many a man that hadn't been so good, also from many that hadn't been so bad.

The old guard showed me the place, against a wall of

stone that nature set up, where men had been backed up to be shot, executed. Right alongside of that place was an old stage station. That was made of stone, and of mud, and anything that would turn an arrow or a bullet.

"Well," I said, once, "I'd sure liked to've lived in them days."

"Don't you fool yourself, Son," says the guard. "Them was tough days. . . ."

I wished I could of had a few tough days, off and on, anything excepting putting in time. For, even tho I mixed with horses during the day and pranced 'em around a bit, I was craving often to be free on one, and wanting wide open country, some place where I could do as I pleased, where there'd be no "lights out" and where I wouldn't have to answer to a number, three times a day.

"But," I'd remind myself, during them tough-feeling spells, "you have to square up for the wrong you done. If you want to do some more wrong, go ahead and break away; you've got horses to do that with from the guards' stable. . . . But, remember, you'd be on the dodge again."

I didn't want to be on the dodge. Only there was times when "time" seemed awful long going by, and then was only when I wanted to be a little tough.

But time, as slow as it was, somehow wore along till one day I heard that there was a meeting of judges to hand out paroles. I made out my parole papers, brought out all the excuses I had to show that I wasn't so bad. . . . I was turned down, and that meant six more months for me to wait, with no hopes that the judges would listen to me even at the end of that time. I was brought up the second time, and turned down again. I was told that there might be some hopes for me with the next meeting.

The time for the next meeting finally come. I was brought

up before the board of parole once more and, for the third time, told my story of the crime I'd committed and how I come to commit it. The judge was looking at some records of mine as I talked. I happened to glance down at the papers once, and I noticed a long letter with mighty familiar writing on it. It was from the sheriff who "still didn't believe I was guilty."

I don't know what the letter said, but I seen that the men around the big desk paid more attention to me this third time. I felt some excited after I got thru answering the questions and finally was let out of the office. There was something in the air as I left that made me feel like I would split it pretty quick and for directions away from where I was, out where there was creeks and springs, range galore and cattle and horses, and where men didn't wear numbers.

It was a few days later when I got the good news that it had been decided I was to be let out on parole. The day set for my release was a few weeks later. I sure counted the hours to that day, and when it did come I sure didn't think, right at the time, that any day could tally up with that one. On the morning of that day, I was handed a sackful of the clothes that I'd wore before coming to the prison. Them clothes had all been pounded into the sack. They was all wrinkled, and to the average person they wouldn't of looked like much. But to me they looked like real clothes, even if they had been pounded, layed away and was all wrinkled. I was mighty happy to reach down the bag and get to feel the heel of my boots. My spurs was still on 'em, and by the time I put 'em on again, heard the old spurs ringing, I sure didn't care if the rest of my outfit was wrinkled. I'd take them wrinkles out pretty quick.

I bid some of the fellows good-bye and was took to town that same day. I went to a hotel for the night and it was late that night when I did. I'd stayed outside as long as I could and just breathed. When I finally went to sleep, and morning come, I jumped up, and stared acrost for my cell-mate in the next bed. There was no cell-mate and there was

I sure didn't care if the rest of my outfit was wrinkled.

no next bed. I glanced around then, and it took me quite a few minutes to realize that I was in a hotel room and not in a prison cell no more.

It took me quite a few days to wake up without thinking a barred door was staring me in the face. In that time I et and drank many things I hadn't had for a long time, and soon I begin to look for a way out of the town. I wanted to get back in the hills, amongst riders, range and stock, back to home.

I didn't have much money with me, no saddle, and Smoky and my gray was far away, and now I wanted to get a job so I could get out and earn enough to get back to them ponies of mine. But there didn't seem to be no jobs in that country right then, not for riders. There was no cowmen around just at that time. They was all out on round-up, and all men that wore spurs was in the thick of that.

I stuck around town for a few days. I'd made friends with another bartender, and one morning that bartender tells me that there's a feller in town looking for a man. He pointed that man out to me that afternoon, and I went to talk to him. That man wanted a milker, somebody to milk cows. His milker was wanting to quit and he wanted a man that could take his place. I found out how far he was away from town. He said fifty miles. He pointed me out the direction and when I got to figguring he was running some dairy farm right in the heart of the cow country, I was wanting to go. I was going to try and milk cows and stick with the job till I got my bearings and located outfits that wanted riders instead of milkers.

When this man asked me if I could milk cows I says "sure."

"How many can you milk a day?" he asks.

"As many as you want me to," I says.

"Well, you don't look like a milker to me," he says, "but I'll try you out. You'll only have to milk about twenty-five head of cows twice a day. I'm going away for a few weeks and I want you to hang on to that job till I get back. If you think you can handle it, we'll start out in the morning."

"Sure I can handle it," I says, "easy."

Maybe I wasn't playing square, but I was just wanting

to get out of town the worst way and I didn't care right
then how I done that. I couldn't milk no cows. I'd never
done that in my life. But I thought maybe I could learn,
and stay with the job till I could get a saddle and horse
under me again.

I didn't do very good at the cow-milking job, not near as
good as I expected I could, and I only milked about six
cows out of the twenty-five the first evening. The next morning I couldn't begin to touch any of the cows. My thumbs
was sore and any pressure against 'em felt like as if needles
was run up my wrists and plum to my elbows.

I didn't get much wages out of that cow-milking job.
None. But the Good Lord was around, and in the shape of
a cowboy that came along that morning and passed remarks
about the dairy farm holding some cattle of the outfit which
couldn't be held. . . . It seemed like the dairy farm had
been holding range cattle, expecting to collect damages on
account that they'd broke into some crops or something.

"We're gathering now," says the cowboy to the boss
farmer-and-dairy-man, "and if some of our cattle broke
into your little pasture it was because your lousy little
fences wasn't up. I'm going to take our cattle out now, and
try and stop me. . . ."

"Wait a minute," I says to the cowboy. He came back to
me mighty fast when I hollered them few words.

"Can I," I went on, as I layed my hand on his horse's
shoulder, "go along with you? . . . I need a job pretty
bad, a string of horses and any kind of horses, and I'd only
ask for the loan of a saddle, till I got my own, so I could try
to make a hand of myself."

"What are you doing here?" he asks.

"Trying to milk cows," I says, "but I don't know how."
The cowboy grinned at me, snickered at the boss-farmer

and said he'd be after me right quick, and with a good horse.

He was back right quick, and with a good horse. I thought of the fact that I was breaking my word with the big boss as I climbed on the horse. But somehow that didn't worry me right then. I'd just been hired as a milker. The men around me that worked there was all short in the back and they all wore suspenders.

I went to work for the big cow outfit. Like all cow outfits I'd ever worked for, it was a spread where no man ever drank milk or ever "pumped" a cow. The men handled range cattle and their only job was riding. There was plenty of that.

This last reminds me of a story that's been told often. There was a foreigner who'd come into America. He run acrost an old cowman and asked him how many cattle he owned. The old cowman said, "Twenty thousand. . . ."

"Why, impossible," says the foreigner. "Where would you get all the milkmaids to milk all the cattle?"

I worked for the outfit for two months or more, till they got thru gathering and shifting their cattle. It was pretty hard work for me to put in from twelve to sixteen hours a day in the saddle after I'd been cooped up for so long. I was soft, and it took me a couple of weeks to get back to myself again. I made enough money while working for the outfit to buy me a new saddle and a good stout bronk from an Indian. I broke the bronk while working for the outfit, and hardened him in so he could stand a long ride. I was figguring to get back to my Smoky and gray, and I had a whole State to cross to get to 'em.

I finally rode in the country to where they was one day, or to where I'd left 'em. But they wasn't there no more. The feller I'd left 'em with said they'd disappeared quite a few months back. He said they'd been stole.

I couldn't find out any more than that from him, and, to make sure, I rode around that country for a few days, a hoping that I'll find good old Smoky again. I sure felt bad about him disappearing. . . . I rode thru many bunches of range horses and sneaked up to many a bunch of wild ones, always looking for my mouse-colored horse amongst 'em. I didn't want to think he was stole, I didn't want to think of a stranger on him, because to me he was the only horse I ever had.

CHAPTER TWENTY-TWO

IT was while I was riding along one day, still looking for Smoky, that I seen a rider off on the side of a mountain and fogging after a bunch of fuzz-tails.* I could see as I rode along that he wasn't doing a very good job, fogging. His horse seemed tired and all he could do was lope along and a quarter of a mile behind the wild ones. I could see the rider was trying to turn 'em, I figgured towards a trap somewhere in the mountains. But he couldn't get his horse any faster than a lope and the wild ones was easy getting away from him.

I got off my horse, rolled me a smoke and watched.

I haven't mentioned it before but I'd run and caught many wild horses during my knocking around in different States. Now, as I watched the rider with his wild bunch, I could see at a glance what the trouble was;—that rider had rode too far before he jumped his bunch and now he had a tired horse under him. I could see which direction he was trying to turn the bunch, and I got to thinking there was another rider on a fresh horse acrost the valley and in the other mountain that was waiting for him, to take the wild ones on and give 'em a run all the way into the trap.

*Mustangs.

341

The wild ones skirted down off the side of the mountain and begin to come up the valley. They was wise. They knowed the rider couldn't catch up with 'em to turn 'em, and now they was just loping along towards a clean get-away. They was coming straight towards me too.

I'd got off my horse at first so I wouldn't spoil the run. I knowed that a man *off* his horse leaves just a horse to the wild ones. They can see far, and a rider on a horse is what they want to keep away from. That's why I got down to the ground, and when I seen that the wild ones was headed towards me I led my horse down in a little hollow and I layed down flat. I just wanted to make sure of what direction that rider wanted them horses to go, and help all I could to turn 'em that way.

I thought I'd take a chance, and just as the wild ones run up within a quarter of a mile of me, I raised up quick, and got on my horse. They turned like a flash. The rider had spotted me most as quick as the horses did, and when he waved an arm I knowed that I'd turned 'em the right direction. He slowed his tired horse down to a walk. All he had to do now was to try and make it to camp.

I took the fuzz-tails on for a good stiff run,—tore in alongside of 'em, acrost the valley and towards the other mountains. I was getting pretty well up in the mountains, amongst the juniper and scrub oak, and begin looking for the other rider that I'd figgured was stationed somewheres to relay on the wild bunch and chassay 'em the rest of the way on into the trap.

I'd figgured right, and I'd got well up in the foothills when that rider bobs up sudden, turns the bunch and fogs 'em on up towards a pass in the mountains.

I was thru now. I'd just turned a hand to help the runners along while wanting to see if Smoky was in that wild bunch, and now I turned my horse and started back for the ranch where I'd been staying. I got down at the point of the foothills, when I come to the rider that'd let the wild bunch go to me. He was surprised to see me and see I was a stranger. He'd thought all the time, by the way I'd turned the horses, that I was one of the boys he was running with.

"You seemed to know just where to turn 'em to," he says.

"I could tell that by the way you was riding," I says. "I seen that you couldn't turn 'em. I happened to be at the right place to do that and I just figgured that somewhere in the hills to my right was a rider waiting for the bunch when you brought 'em along."

We talked on for a spell, and then he says to me that I'd better come to camp with him and stay there for the night, that it wasn't long till sundown anyway. I rode along with him. It didn't matter where I stayed and I thought that maybe some of the other boys at the camp might be able to tell me that they'd seen my Smoky horse somewhere while they was running the wild ones.

It was late in the evening when four boys rode in. They'd caught the bunch I turned and they was mighty thankful for me turning 'em. It was a fine bunch, they said, eighteen head, and they'd left 'em up in the trap for the night. When morning come they'd try and catch some more to put in with 'em.

And when morning come I was one of the riders that was to help at that. None of the boys had seen any horse like that Smoky I described, but, as they told me, he might be found any time and being now that I wasn't doing anything in perticular, I'd better throw in with 'em in catching a few of the wild ones. I could run on shares with 'em or on wages. I took wages, because I knowed from past experience that mustang-running wasn't much on profit. I told 'em why I'd

rather have the wages and the boys just grinned at that.
. . . They was boys that'd made a profession of the mustang-running game, they savvied it and they was the only
mustang-runners I ever knowed that made any money at it.

These boys (the youngest one was twenty-five) had run
wild horses on contract to rid the range of 'em and the con-
tracts was signed by superintendents of big cow outfits. The
one contract I read said all the wild and unbranded horses
they caught was theirs, and that a pasture would be furnished by the company to hold what was caught and till
there was a big enough bunch to be worth shipping. Another
thing was that the runners was allowed to kill company beef
for their own use.

A good string of saddle horses was turned over to me, my
wages was agreed on and now I went deep into the game of
wild horse running.

That struck me fine, it was fast, and I was with a good
bunch of fellers. Besides I was right in the country where
any day I might see Smoky's silky hide again. . . . But I
didn't get to see him all the time I was on that range.

The wild horse trap them fellers had built was in the shape
of a heart. At the point of the heart was a small corral and
which would hold about fifty head of horses. Whatever was
caught would be run in there to hold for a couple of days
and till they got fence-broke. At the mouth, or top of the
heart, was an opening about fifty yards wide, and from that
opening there run a wing on both sides and spreading out
for a mile or more. The wing was what we called a "rag wing."
It was a smooth wire that was strung along on pickets or
trees and which was about four or five feet off the ground;
on that smooth wire there was rags that hung down a couple
of feet and them rags was strung from two to six feet apart.
The boys had raided many a cow camp and deserted places

to get them rags, and they sure seemed to do the work while hanging on that long wire. They'd go with the breeze and looked mighty spooky to a wild horse. Them is what made the wings which was on both sides and which kept the horses coming straight for the trap. The trap itself looked like an opening and a way out from the spooky rag wing. It was what we called a "blind trap."

But the trap was a sure enough trap, for just about the time a wild bunch thought they was getting away they found themselves inside of it. The trap itself was built so it could hardly be seen. There was double woven wire, nine feet high, stretched amongst trees and posts, the posts was decorated to look like trees too and they was about six feet apart and four feet in the hard ground. Each one of them posts weighed near half a ton.

I find it mighty hard to describe the wild horse trap, the way we had 'em, with writing, so I'm drawing a sketch of the size of one and what it was shaped like.

Well, my job at the first trap was to fall in alongside of the wild ones as they was run by and see that they didn't "break" by me before they got inside the tip of the left wing. That was a ticklish job. If I rode too fast they would break behind me, and if I rode too slow they would break ahead of me. I had to sort of juggle with 'em, notice how tired they was or how tired they was *not*, keep in mind the lay of the country I had to ride over so they wouldn't get the leverage on me, watch out for the ones that was wise to a trap and which would make a break even thru the spooky rag wing.

What made that job ticklish some more was that I was at the end where it was up to me to run the wild ones on into the trap, after the boys had went to a lot of hard riding, jumping the wild ones and making a big circle to get 'em headed towards the trap. I'd hated like samhill to say when evening come, "that bunch slipped by me."

That happens with the best "wing-men" because right close to the trap is where things are most likely to go wrong and where the wild horse is wisest. There's where if he can't see anything suspicious he seems to smell it, and he might do most anything that's not expected. But right there, where the rag wing pinches in and connects to the solid wire wing that leads to the main entrance of the trap, is where four riders gather sudden, and waving slickers and ropes and hollering behind the wild bunch, stampede 'em into the entrance.

It was a great sight to see a nice big bunch stampede into that entrance. For one thing, they was pretty to look at, and then it meant another bunch caught, another little success. But there was something else that followed right soon as the wild ones got into the trap that I didn't like so well, and that was to hear 'em hit the wire. It was something like hearing a wild bird hit a window-pane after he found himself inside a house, only many times worse. The horses would hardly see the wire. They didn't know what it was and they'd hit it with all their speed and weight. Of course we used smooth woven wire, but that skinned 'em some just the same, and a few hit the panels so hard that they was throwed back like a ball and with broken necks.

In the trap is where the wild horse would get "fence broke." After he got thru hitting the woven wire and was kept in the trap for a day or two, any little string stretched from one post to another would hold or turn him as well as a ten-foot-high picket fence. He was a lot easier to hold inside a pasture than any gentle horse raised there.

Hard work came in after a two days' run, when all horses caught in that time was gathered into the round corral at

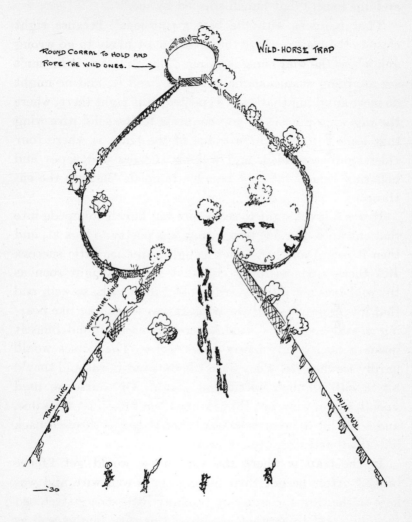

ROUND CORRAL TO HOLD AND
ROPE THE WILD ONES. →

WILD-HORSE TRAP

WOVEN WIRE WING

RAG WING

RAG WING

30

I find it mighty hard to describe the wild horse trap, the way we had 'em, with
writing, so I'm drawing a sketch of the size of one and what it was shaped like.

the point of the trap. Every horse had to be roped, throwed and tied down. One front foot was tied to the tail with a short piece of rope and so he could rest it on the ground but not so he could make a step ahead with it after he was let up. After the whole bunch was fixed that way, the gate was opened and we took 'em out of the trap towards a company pasture ten or twelve miles away. On the way to the pasture was where the wild horse was "herd broke,"—made to turn the way a rider wanted him to and to stay with the bunch. With one front foot tied back, he couldn't make much speed and then he could be handled. . . . After the pasture was reached, every one of the horses was roped and throwed again, the front foot was freed and now they could go on grazing the same as ever, till a big enough bunch was gathered to make a good shipment.

We made quite a few shipments, and built many traps in many different parts of the wild horse country, many different kinds of traps too. But we all liked the blind trap the best. One of them would only last us about a month, till the wild horses was wise to it and we couldn't run 'em in it no more, or till on account of us riders stirring up the dust in that country they would drift to some other range. After our trap location petered out on us we'd take the smooth wire down, coil up the rag wing and go to build another trap in some other place that looked promising and where the wild ones was thick.

I wasn't much of a hand at building traps,—not much at anything which I had to get off my horse to do. So when trap building time come I was left at camp to watch the forty-odd head of saddle horses, feed 'em their grain twice a day, and doctor the ones that had saddle galls so they'd be in shape when the trap was finished and good for many long runs after the wild ones. I had to watch their feet too and keep 'em shod. Every cowboy can shoe a horse. He knows mighty well how a horse's hoof is built and he knows how to make a shoe to fit it. Most of 'em can do fine in shoeing a horse and take pride at doing a good job of it. It took from two to four weeks to build a trap, and during that time the horses would sure rest up and get to feeling good.

With taking care of the horses I also had to do the cooking and sort of keep the camp in shape. There was cutting wood, killing a beef once in a while and other chores. I was kept pretty busy.

Our camp was always a few miles from the trap, out of the way of where we'd be running the wild ones or where any of them would be apt to come. There's nothing like a camp to scare them out of the country. Them wild ones had been chased by many a mustang-runner many times before, they was wise to the human and his tricks and his traps, and there was always a few in every bunch that had been caught once or twice, got away and wised up the others by taking the lead whenever a rider showed up. Some of them that wouldn't come to within a mile of the spooky rag wings when they wasn't being chased, would dive right for it and on thru as soon as a rider got after 'em. They knowed there was a trap at the other end.

They'd get suspicious of everything around 'em as soon as a rider showed up, even if he was a mile away. They'd dodge and turn from anything that'd been disturbed,—the stump of a fresh cut tree, the coals of an old fire. Even a boot track on the trail has sometimes turned 'em. The way to the trap had to be as smooth and natural as a set steel trap would have to be for Mr. Fox to plant a foot into. I've had cawing crows flying overhead turn a few bunches back on me when I'd got 'em to within a few yards from the rag wing, and when a wild bunch turns they *turn*. It takes a lot of running to turn 'em back and very seldom that can be done. We've had bunches turn on us right at the entrance of the trap and when they turned then, nothing could stop 'em. They'd go over us, under us, and right thru us. I'd get a lock of wild mane as they'd brush past that way, sometimes. We seldom tried to rope 'em, that was too slow.

I could go on and tell a lot of things about wild horse running, building different traps, experiences and so on. But it would take a big book to touch that subject right, and I've got other things to talk on, so as to wind up with this one book.

I'd been running the wild ones quite a long spell, this time, when one day while helping tie down a few in the corral I'd got so busy that I wasn't watching around me. A stud reached up, kicked me on the chin, and split and loosened all my teeth.

That blow was the start of me having to quit the wild horse game. Fall was coming on about that time, cold winds was blowing, and after riding in them winds all day I got so I couldn't sleep at night for toothaches. My whole head plum down to my neck was aching from that, and after a hard day's ride I'd have to keep my boots on most of the night and pace up and down thru the sagebrush by my bed with a rag around my face. I couldn't eat anything but cool soft grub, and one day when a snow come and covered the ground I decided I'd draw my wages and go some place where I could get them grinders of mine tended to.

I wanted to go to a good place, to a big town where I could find the best to work on me, and the closest best place, as the boys told me, was a town on the west coast.

I didn't ride to that town on horseback. I was told that I'd get tangled up with too many farm lanes before I got anywhere near it, and get lost. Besides I wanted to get there

in a hurry. So I rode to the closest railroad and to a place
along it where there was a few buildings and a water tank.
I sold my horse there, sacked my saddle and took it along
with me as I hopped on the first train that stopped. I hadn't
bought me no ticket, I'd always thought that a feller paid
for his riding after he got inside and as he went along. I had
to get off at the next station and buy me that ticket.

It was my first time on a train. I sure liked to see the different country roll by, and I'd enjoyed the ride a heap more
if my jaw hadn't kept aching. A few fellers would come
along once in a while and try to talk to me but talking didn't
go well and they didn't stay long. One feller stopped and
asked me if I was a cowboy, and when I said "no" he seemed
mighty disappointed and went on.

I didn't eat a bite while on the way to town. I didn't want
no food much, and anyway I didn't know where to get it.
I finally got to the end of the railroad trail one morning,
and with my saddle still with me, I begin looking around for
the place to go where I could find out about a good dentist.
I seen a cubby hole in the station with letters in front of it
that spelled "Information." I started towards that, but I
was stopped on the way by a feller in uniform who seemed
anxious to take me some place. I told him what I wanted,
and he said he knowed just where to take me. He sure struck
me as obliging, specially when he wanted to pack my saddle
and escorted me to a big car that was waiting outside.

He took me for quite a long ride right thru the town, but
finally he stopped by a nice building not quite outside of it
and he told me just how I would find such a man as I wanted
in that building. Then the driver mentioned a certain sum
for taking me, it was quite a sum and it surprised me, but I
was glad to pay so as to get strung out and know for sure
where I was headed. Now I knowed.

I packed myself and saddle into the building, up stairways, asked around of the doctor's whereabouts from a couple of folks I seen, and finally spotted his name printed on a door. I went inside there, layed my saddle down while folks waiting in that room stared at me. I didn't have to wait long, a girl came to me and, after I told her what I wanted done and everything, she said that the doctor couldn't see me till that afternoon. I told her to be sure and put me down for that time, that I'd be around.

When I got back down on the sidewalk I looked both ways from me for a place where I could drop my saddle and get something to eat. I was getting mighty hungry by then. I don't know why I took my saddle along on that trip, just because it was my working rig I guess and felt like it was part of me. Up the street a ways I seen a hotel sign. I made it towards that place, got me a room, layed my saddle down and came back out of there to throw me a bait. I found a restaurant close, and now I was all set. I'd found me a doctor, a place to sleep and a place to eat.

I'll give credit to the taxi driver for taking me to that doctor. He turned out to be a mighty good one. It also turned out that the job on my grinders would be a long one, they would take a lot of treatment and care and work. I would have to stay in town a few months to get the job done right.

That wasn't very good news for me, and time drug along pretty slow: the next day was always a long time coming, and stayed a long time too. I didn't have so much money, and I got to wondering how I was going to live there all that time, along with paying my dentist. I had just about enough to pay for half of that, and then what would I do? . . . Going to shows or spending money to amuse myself in any way was plum out of the question and, as I said before, time was sure dragging by slow.

But things sometimes happen to break the rough lock on

what's slow coming, and one day, walking along the street with my hands in my pockets and killing time till next day and another appointment come, I'd walked along further than I usually did. I was standing on a street corner looking at nothing in perticular when I hear hoofs a pounding in a side street. I turned, and I spots a half a dozen riders coming along. They looked like sure enough cowboys, but I couldn't believe they was, not there amongst the brick buildings.

I sure kept a watching 'em as they rode towards me, they looked mighty good, anyway. When they got closer I begin to look at their faces, one by one, and when I spotted one face with a long hook nose I couldn't for a spell let out the war-whoop that I wanted to. It was a face I'd knowed anywheres, any time, and even tho it'd been quite a few years since I seen it, the whole time of when I did flashed to my mind.

I finally hollered, and as that face that looked like a hawk's turned my way there was another holler. In another second me and that cowboy, he was a sure enough cowboy, had tangled our mitts. There was questions as to "what are you doing here," from both sides and so on, and after a bit of that was explained he told me to hop behind him on his horse and come along. Them instructions was mighty easy for me to follow.

I learned as I rode along that the hotel I happened to pick on wasn't over half a mile from a gathering of big motion-picture studios. This cowboy I knowed and many other cowboys was working at them places and taking parts in making Western pictures. . . . And here all this time I'd just been feeling sorry for myself for being so lonesome and having nobody to talk to, nobody but the dentist, and the most he'd ever say was "Does that hurt?"

One time he said something else, something about me getting my teeth fixed just in time so I'd pass the examination for the service. War had been declared at about that time and there was talk of men being drafted for the army. The dentist had went on to say that some men instead of getting

"Put his name down, you don't have to worry about his riding."

their teeth fixed now was doing their best to ruin 'em so they wouldn't be accepted.

The war didn't worry me any, and after I run acrost the boys from the picture studios it was the last thing in my mind. Them studios was sure big places, and pretty too, but we rode right by 'em that day while I was setting on the rump of my friend's horse. We rode on till we come to many corrals and stables, there was many horses and longhorn cattle and the sudden sight of all of that so close to where I'd been holing-up was sure away past anything I could ever dream of. A few cowboys was around, some was riding in and out of the corrals, the same as if they'd just got thru or was going out on shift with a herd. They was on shift all right but now it was all in front of a camera.

I was wondering how it would be to work in front of a camera, pose around or make a wild ride, when my friend stopped his horse by the corrals and where a feller in puttees seemed busy counting things on a long sheet of paper.

"I've got a good man for you," says my friend to him.

The other feller never looked up from his sheet. "Can he ride?" he asks.

My friend grinned and turned to me. "Do you want a job with us in the pictures?"

I never thought he'd been talking about me for a job there. Working for picture outfits was the last thing I could think of ever fitting into. I was sure took by surprise.

"Sure," I finally says. "I'll take on a job with you."

"All right," says my friend to the feller in puttees, "put his name down, you don't have to worry about his riding."

The feller wrote my name down on the long sheet. . . . And that's how come I broke into the moving-picture game.

CHAPTER TWENTY-THREE

"GET ready,—Camera. . . . Come on, boys."
It was the director hollering at us thru his mega-
phone, and when he said "come on, boys," we *came*. Six of us
rode down a steep hill for all we was worth. The hill was
more than steep, it was near straight up and down, and
down for a long ways. Two horses turned over before they
got halfways down it and rolled the rest of the way with
their riders rolling after 'em. My horse didn't fall till he got
to the bottom and where he struck sudden level ground. All
riders and horses piled up in a heap there. . . . But, according to the story in the picture, we was chasing some bad
hombres and we didn't linger at the bottom of the hill long.
We untangled ourselves, caught any horse we could get a
hold of, and rode on till we heard the director holler "all
right, boys."

That was my first acquaintance with the moving-picture
game and I got to thinking right there that it was a pretty

tough game, and it was. We was made to ride thru many bad places that day, and one boy was paid extra for falling with his horse over a twenty-foot cliff. By the time that day's work was done I got to wondering if I had any of the fillings left which the dentist had put in my teeth.

No wonder, I thought, why the feller asked if I could ride before my name was put down on the sheet. But the riding wasn't all wild and furious all the time. There was times when it was right peaceful, and then other times when it was right monotonous; times again, when we was off our horses and posing and trying to act in front of some saloon, when it was tiresome and then some. Them scenes often had to be took over and over again. But as tiresome or rough as the work was, I was mighty glad to be there, amongst the boys. I wasn't lonesome no more.

I was put on the payroll from the first day. The pay wasn't so much but it sure beat knocking around as an extra and working two weeks and laying off two as most of 'em had to do. Anyway, now I seen my way clear to be able to stick around the whole time till the dentist got thru with me, and I'd be able to pay him when he got thru too.

I went to see him one day, after it'd come to me what I'd drifted to that country for. I was a few days late on my last appointment with him and he'd wondered what happened to me. I told him I had a job now, and if it was all right with him I'd come twice a week instead of every day or so. That was all right with him, but he said it would take a lot longer to get thru.

But I wasn't in no rush about getting thru right then. Riding for the movies was new to me, lots of things happened and most all was interesting.

It all kept being interesting for me, till one day, when we was called on to play Indian, just plain naked savages, and all we had on was war-paint, jee-string and mocassins. We rode our horses bareback. Playing that part wouldn't of been so bad if the weather had been with us, but it wasn't. There was a cold wind from the ocean and the biggest part of the day was foggy. But the picture had to be took, and we shivered on thru two weeks of that. What I hated the most was putting on the war-paint over my whole body in the morning and taking it off in the evening. Another thing I didn't care for so much was the girls at the wagon-train that was raided. They kept giggling at us as we was shivering while waiting for the director to debate on a new scene, but we sure made them girls scatter when the time come for the big massacree. I liked one part best where I was to grab one by the hair, put her on my horse and run off with her. I grinned at the director after the scene was took and asked him if he didn't think that should be took over again.

There was always lots of girls in most every picture we worked in, some nice ones, too, of all styles, from running to draft types. I'd never seen so many girls together before in my life and it wasn't long till I got used to seeing 'em around. Finally I got up nerve enough to speak to one one day, but I couldn't very well help it. The director had set me by her at a table during an indoor scene of a Western dance hall. I was told to talk to her and drink with her and so on. Well, I did, and her and me got acquainted.

We got pretty friendly before that whole picture was done, and wether it was at the dance hall or at the outside Western set, we'd managed to get together. But she was just an "extra" girl, and when the picture was done I never seen her no more. I never thought of trying to make a date with her. . . . None of us was much on making dates, anyway, nor try to make a mash with any girl. If we talked to 'em it was when they talked first.

I got acquainted with many girls while in the movies and there was a few that I liked pretty well, but it was most always my luck to pick on an "extra" and when she'd leave I'd have to wait till I got acquainted with another one. I met one one time that seemed to have quite a failing for me and I liked her pretty well myself, but she kept a looking at my teeth when I'd laugh, like as if I ought to get 'em fixed or that something ought to be done about 'em. I know they did look like splinters, the outline of 'em was pretty jagged. The next time I went to the dentist I told him to work on my front ones first, from now on. I finally got 'em fixed and to looking good and then I begin shining 'em with cigarette ashes I'd put on a corner of a hankerchief, my finger was my tooth-brush. . . . But by the time I got my teeth to looking good she'd gone and went to work for another outfit.

My love affairs didn't amount to much while around the studios. I wasn't worried enough about that, anyway. I was having too much fun when the bunch of us boys was together, and if there was any wild parties, which there was plenty of, there was no girls around to tame us down. The girls didn't drink then, that is I never seen 'em take any.

I got to know quite a few great actresses and actors. Some of them are still great today and draw a full house whenever they appear on the screen. I also got to know a few that was just "hams" while I was there, who now play the leed in the biggest pictures. The same way with directors, and when I see their names or faces on the screen I'm just one of them fellers that points and says "I knowed him when . . ."

Us boys got along fine with all the stars, directors, camera men and everybody around the lot. There's only one leading man I can remember that stirred us to use our power on him and edducate him. He'd highbrowed us, held his nose kind of high as any of us passed him, and seemed hard of

hearing when one of us would happen to say "hello" to him.
. . . We'd formed a court amongst us and that had always
worked well. There was a judge, a sheriff and about ten
deputies. We always got our man.

One fine morning this leading man come along with his
same ignoring look. The sheriff'd had his eagle eye on him
for quite a spell, and that morning he couldn't stand them
looks of him no longer. He walks up to this leading man,
taps him on the shoulder and tells him he's under arrest.
That feller don't seem to hear, so the sheriff winks at two
deputies; I was one of 'em. I grabs the highbrow by one arm
while the other deputy grabs him by the other. He starts
to struggle and acts very insulted, and just about that time
the sheriff grabs him by both legs and we takes him to court.

We find the judge by the corral, on his horse, and by the
time we get our prisoner to him he was putting up an awful
holler and making some wicked threats. We let him down
in front of the judge and tells him to keep quiet. He did.

"What's the charges?" asks the judge, mighty severe-like.

"Not acting human," says the sheriff; "resisting an officer
and threatening the court, Your Honor."

"H'm," says the judge, "pretty serious."

Just about that time the prisoner begin to act up some
more and hollering.

"And contempt of court," the sheriff adds on.

"That's enough," says the judge. "I sentence him to be
hung by the neck till he's drawed his last breath."

Quite a few of the boys, all deputies, had gathered around
by then, and all faces was mighty serious. One of 'em came
up to the prisoner, put a rope around his neck and throwed
the slack over a sycamore limb. . . . The whole proceedings went on in a very quiet and business-like way, and here
come the funny part for us. The leading man had got quiet

of a sudden, he looked at all faces around him, and then he begin to shiver. Pretty soon he begin to mumble, to try to reason with us, and finally to beg. . . .

We had a hard time keeping a straight face; we never expected him to believe us, and that sure took us by surprise. When we had enough fun out of seeing him beg, and so that our authority wouldn't be doubted afterwards, the sheriff pulls a brand book out of his vest pocket and begins to read here and there. After a while he holds up a hand and says,

"Wait a minute, Gentlemen. We don't want to be hasty. I finds here, by the records and earmarks of the prisoner, that his mammy died when he was pretty young, that he was raised on skimmed milk, and so never had a fair start in life." He looked up at the judge. "I make a motion, Your Honor, that we just break his horns off, rub sand in his eyes, give him a good shapping, and turn him loose for a chance to do better."

Six out of ten of us seconded the motion and we started to inflict the punishment. Of course we had no intentions of doing anything but giving him a good shapping. For a shapping, the prisoner is stretched over the back of a feller that's on all fours, a man is on each arm and leg to hold him there and the punishment comes in on his rump from a pair of leather shaps. The blows from them can be made to pop and sting like a whip, but there's no cuts like a whip would make, just general bruises where the victim sits.

This punishment being decided on, the judge passed a sentence of ten licks. "And romp on 'em," he says. That meant make every lick pop heavy.

Our prisoner sure squirmed during them ten licks, but we handed 'em to him plenty heavy, and when we let him up, told him he was free and that his behavior would be watched close, he didn't have nothing to say. He looked and acted like a child that'd just received a hard spanking as he turned and started to walk back to the studios, where there was *no* cowboys. . . . We hit for the stables so we could get inside and laugh without him seeing us, and there, back of the door, was that leading man's director all doubled up in a laughing fit. He'd seen the whole thing from start to finish.

It took the leading man many days to get over what we'd handed him, and, as the director told us, that shapping sure done him good. We noticed that ourselves. At first he dodged around us, but afterwards he seemed to go out of his way just so he could say "hello" to us. He was sure afraid of another shapping. . . . That leading man is still one today and is now making good in the "talkies."

We shapped another actor that's in the talkies today and who is now a star of stars and one of the biggest favorites. He was just a ham actor when we shapped him, and the reason we did was because we suspicioned him of wearing bustles and padding himself here and there so he'd look like a real man. But he was a real man without them things, and when we did catch him with a bustle on one day we brought him to the judge, took the bustle out for evidence, and he was sentenced to ten licks, without the romping. I don't remember if that cured him or not.

We used to shap a lot of extras that was brought in to play cowboy. Some of 'em thought that they had to run their horses to death so they could look the part. They'd always do that on good level ground, often when there was no camera grinding and when running wasn't necessary. That was plum against our sentiments, and the penalty for that offense was always ten heavy licks of the shaps. We edducated quite a few that way, and no director ever interfered with us in that sport. They seemed to enjoy it as well as we did.

There was lots of times when we wanted to do some shapping and couldn't very well because we'd be working in pictures when we didn't wear no shaps. We only took on the worst cases then and used a board or anything we could get that would sting. . . . Us boys used to work in about every kind of picture that was made. Every kind but where fairies or sheiks was the main subject. That was during the time when there'd be a spell between one Western picture and another. Then we'd be used as background, just to make a crowd and fill in the cracks.

None of the bunch I was with could act, none cared to, and none was a "foreground hog." We left that to the other fellers, and if we was left out of the line of the camera when a scene had to be took over and over again, that pleased us a whole lot. We could then sit down while the scene was being rehearsed and took over and over or else fool around some. Our specialty was riding.

And there was plenty of riding for us, most of it in the natural and with our shaps on. Once in a while we'd ride as jockeys on race tracks and steeple chases. There was a lot of falls in that last that was a purpose and many that wasn't. I remember going thru thick brush while in one of them one time, and my horse and me went down a ten-foot sinkhole that couldn't be seen on account of that brush. The other riders went by and I wasn't missed till all had rode past the camera. When they came back looking for me I'd crawled out of the hole and was trying to get my horse out too. But it took four saddle horses and four ropes to get him out.

There was bucking horses to be rode pretty often while

taking pictures of cow camps or cow towns. Sometimes our
horses bucked when they wasn't at all supposed to and while
we was in white French soldier's uniform with gold braid all
over it, shining helmet with a plume, and packing a long
lance. We played in many soldier pictures. . . . There was
one time when I got on my horse while rigged up in a rattling steel armor, for a picture of them times. There was steel
armor on my horse too and all kinds of draperies. I was riding a high-back and high-front wooden saddle, and I had a
long heavy lance to carry. All went well till the "prop" man
asked me to pack a roll of bunting over to the set which was
about half a mile away. The roll was about as big as a flour
sack, and as I was loping along towards the set, some of it
begin to get in between my horse's hind legs. . . . Well, my
horse had already had a hard time a trying to behave with
all the rattling armor on top of him, and when that bunting
begin to tickle him he spooked up for fair.

He started to running and kicking, and when he seen that
didn't do no good he bogged his head sudden and went to
trying to unload all of the contraption that was on him. He
done a fine job: first I dropped my lance, then I dropped the
bunting. But I dropped the bunting on the wrong side, and
as it was I was in the middle of quite a few hundred yards of
the stuff, it was floating along behind, all around and snapping. My armor was getting pretty well dented up, and then
it begin to coming apart. I'd shed off one part on one side
and another part on the other. The helmet was last to go,
and there I was, with nothing on but my underwear and a
pair of boots.

But I wasn't thru yet. The bunting was still hanging on,
and as my horse kept a bucking I was sure feeling the high
front and back of that saddle. It was more than misery, and
I was going to quit the whole outfit when my horse saved me

the trouble. He bucked and stampeded all the way into the set, where there was about a thousand extras all dressed for the event of the picture. They sure scattered when they seen me coming, and there, in front of tall pillars where Nero or somebody was to make their play, I was spread out and measured my length.

My wooden saddle had turned, and I was sure glad of that, because it would of killed me, I guess. And now that the saddle and draperies had got under the horse's belly, he went on to finish up what he'd started. He kicked that whole rigging apart, and when he was caught he didn't have much less on him than I did, just a piece of bridle. Neither him nor me worked in the picture that day.

There's many things that happens behind the camera that makes it too bad they can't be took. I think some of them happenings would be more interesting than the picture that's being worked on, but there usually ain't no film in the camera at that time, or the camera is too far away or else facing the wrong way. Them happenings wouldn't very well fit in the picture anyway, but if they could be caught on the film that all would sure make a dandy picture by itself. I'd travel a long ways to see it.

Like one time, while working in a Western, a big feller was called on for a little part he had to play. He was a handsome cuss, all dressed fit to kill and shining, his eyebrows was plucked just right and makeup on his face was just right too. But he had no horse for his little part, so he borrowed mine. The director looked at me and grinned as he climbed on. Then the camera begin to grind. All went fine for a spell, he made a handsome ride past the line of the lenses, and then something happened. My horse bogged his head, made two stiff jumps and scattered him down a hillful of dry brush and cactus. The funny part of that was the sudden change in the looks of him as he climbed back up the hill. He'd sure made a good ad for the well dressed man to look at, as "before and after," or "after and before."

There was many things happened when sometimes there'd be "extras" to fill in as cowboys and make a crowd. What some of them fellers would get by with without getting killed was always a mystery to me, but to us the happenings they brought up wasn't very funny, they happened so often that it got monotonous and we'd only have to go back after a ride, past the camera and catch loose horses.

There was always a lot going on, and even if we worked on a picture for a month straight, there was a variety with every day. It would be a change of sets, one day in the studio and the next on one location and then another; then there was mobs of new people come and go all the time, new pictures, new directors and new actors and actresses. Us boys managed to have a lot of fun thru all the changes all the time, and in many ways. One of the funs we had was to get out of pictures we didn't like to play in, like for instance playing in a wintry Far North picture during hot days. There'd be cotton and fake snow scattered around, us boys would be made up as prospectors and have to wear a full beard "full muff" which was something like horse-hair glued on our faces, then we'd have to put on a heavy mackinaw coat and pants of the same stuff, parade around thru the streets with a bundle and picks and shovels on our backs, and act like we was shivering to death while we was roasting to death.

Me and another cowboy figgured many ways of getting out of such pictures, and one of the best we had was to leave some of the longhorn cattle out of the corral at night and take 'em out a long lane to some brushy hills a ways back of the stable. It was always me that was called on to hunt up

any stock that broke away because I'd worked in plenty of
brush country before and I'd already found the stock a few
times when other boys had failed to. I could always take another rider along with me on them hunts for the get-aways.
So, when pictures come along that didn't suit I'd pick on the
rider I wanted and turn out a few head during the night.
The next day I'd be sent out to get 'em, me and the rider I'd
picked on would get a few sandwiches, something to drink,
and hit out, laughing. . . . I'd most always spot the cattle
within an hour or so after leaving the stables. We'd leave
'em there and get up on some high knoll close to where the
set was and watch the other boys sweat in what they was
wearing. We'd laugh some more at that, and when middle
afternoon come, just too late to get back in costume and on
the set, we'd start the cattle for the corrals.

Sometimes if the picture was real unpleasant to work in,
we just *wouldn't* find the cattle for a couple of days. But I
think somebody got to suspicion me. The gate the cattle
kept a breaking out of was fixed one day, but they kept a
breaking out just the same. "And it strikes me queer," says
the feller in puttees to me at one of them times, "that they
always break out when there's a 'full muff' picture coming
on."

The next time they broke out he sent two other fellers
after 'em.

I didn't get very far as a movie actor. For, as the saying
goes, I didn't have my heart in it. That saying run mighty
true with me, I had no interest in acting, and my interest for
the rest of the goings-on begin to dwindle down mighty fast
after the first few months, even if I did have a lot of fun.
. . . I got a few little parts in different pictures but that
didn't stir up any ambition in me and I didn't try to work
to get more. Towards the last I got so I was all after fun

and none after work. I should of quit when I got to being
that way. My grinders was all fixed now and there was nothing to keep me from going. I was going to quit once, but I
was made to feel that I was wanted to stay. I stayed a couple
of days more then I got a little wild and reckless during one
scene and I was saved the trouble of quitting. I was fired.

That's just what I wanted, then there'd be no come-back.
There was a couple of good jobs with other movie outfits
that I could of got but I was thru now, there was no strings
on me and I was happy as a lark. For the past month or two
I'd been hankering to get back on the range, in a cabin, with
just a string of good ponies and lots of cattle around. I'd
got wore out on hearing "camera" and "let's try it over
again, boys," being a Arab one day and Esquimo the next,
and being on horseback one time and afoot another time.
Most all, excepting the cowboys, liked the variety, and as
for me, now I was craving for something else, where there
was no variety and not so much going on every day.

"You'll be back," said one of the boys, as I was stuffing
my saddle in a gunny sack again, "The most of 'em come
back."

It was a great sight for me when just after one night's
ride on the train from the studios, I woke up and looked out
to great scopes of sagebrush flats surrounded by sharp
clear hills. The air and whole country had changed to what
I was used to, and just in one little night's sleep. I wasn't
awake very long when I hit for the back of the train where
I could stick out my nose and take a look at the country
without a pane of glass interfering. On both sides of the
track I could see little bunches of horses and cattle. They
was standing still and the early morning sun was shining on
'em and warming up their hides after the night's chill.

I'd bought me a ticket to a little town that I knowed was surrounded by cow country. I'd never been to that town before but it struck me great when I got off the train into it. I didn't need no taxi driver to take me around there, I had a hunch of where the livery stable would be and as I packed my saddle towards it a couple of boys rode by. They was covered with dust, and it wasn't the kind that's sprinkled out of a paper box either, it was the real old alkali.

I got me a job the next day after I hit town. I'd just got out of the restaurant and was standing on the curb of the sidewalk picking my teeth when an old feller come up to me and begin talking. He talked sort of neutral and just long enough to find out if I "savvied the cow," then he asked me what I was doing. I told him "nothing," and we both came to an agreement on a job and wages right there.

He said he couldn't ride out to the ranch with me, but he'd tell me how to find it. We both set down on the edge of the sidewalk and with a match he begin drawing a map in the dirt street. The main ranch was about thirty-five miles away, there was a road leading to it but he said I'd make better time cutting acrost country. He made a few landmarks in the dirt that I could go by. Once I got to the ranch, I was to go from there to the horse range, run in a bunch of saddle horses, pick me out a string and shoe 'em. I'd find plenty grub in the house. I was to fill two "kiaks" (rawhide covered pack boxes) of what I wanted in the line of grub and hit out with a pack horse and my string of horses to a camp that was on his range and over fifty miles away from the ranch. On the dirt he mapped out where I'd find the horses, they ranged all the way from four to fourteen miles from the ranch. Then he drawed some more lines and told me how I would find the far camp. There was no water on the way to that camp.

What I was to do when I got to the far camp was to get

It was a little place, just a house and corral.

what cattle was out in the valleys and bring 'em up to the spring where the camp was. He said there'd been a rain but that the dirt tanks would be pretty dry by now and the cattle would be drinking mud from the hardpan flats rather than go back up to the spring. A few of 'em had died not long before from drinking the muddy water. There was two or three springs in the same hills and a few miles from where the camp was, and I was to divide the cattle to them springs. While doing that I was also to brand all the calves.

This was a small outfit, the old man only had about a thousand head of cattle and I'd be the only rider on the job. The old man said he'd come and help me whenever he could and that as soon as he was thru with some business in town he'd come and show me all the springs where his cattle grazed from. This was a desert country. Springs was far apart and his little bunch of cattle scattered over a territory of about eighty miles long and fifty wide. In the North, where the grass is thick and the water is plenty, that would of been enough land to carry a hundred thousand head of cattle.

I rode the old man's horse out of town. I got to the main ranch in the afternoon and made myself acquainted with the place. It was a little place, just a house and corral, and not an inch of plowed ground in sight. I had no trouble finding the horses the next day. I read brands, looked at saddle marks, and run in about twenty head. I picked out eight head of the likeliest out of the bunch and turned the rest loose to go back to their range. It took me till about noon the next day to put shoes on them eight head. Some already had shoes on but they needed reshoeing. Some was mean to tack shoes on. I spent the rest the afternoon in making a mulligan-stew and filling up the kiaks and getting the pack outfit ready for an early start the next day. I hobbled the horses up high on a hill and on good feed for that night, there was no hay and no pasture to turn 'em loose in, none in that whole country. And that's what I liked about that country, no fences, and a feller could ride a couple of hundred miles any direction and not have to open no gates, none but the gate of the corral where he caught his horse.

I got an early start the next morning. The sun hadn't been up long when I lined out with my string and pack horse. I had some trouble with the horse I'd picked out to ride but after I drug my quirt off of him a few times he finally held his head up and behaved. I got to the far camp that night and went to it just as tho I'd been there many times before. But I knowed desert country: there was three ranges of hills to cross, two by direction and the last one by a high flat-topped butte that was the landmark I'd been told to hit for.

It sure was all peaceful for me to strike that camp, and as I went to work day after day getting cattle out of the flats, branding and all, it came to me that this was just what I'd been craving for while I was in the picture game. Queer too, I thought, because this would be just as lonely to most fellers as the other was lively, and few would want to hibernate the way I was doing. I remembered the boys telling me when I left the picture outfit that I'd be back. I laughed often at the thought of that. I wouldn't be back. I was happy now, I had my work to do in daytime, where I didn't have to rehearse and where I didn't hear "camera." I had my table and lamplight to read old magazines or draw by when evening come. There was great scopes of range country around me, my horses was up on the side of the hill, and it was fine to hear far away bellering of cattle mixing in with the nighthawk's cry and the cayote's cheerful howl. I wasn't lonely.

CHAPTER TWENTY-FOUR

I STAYED and rode for the desert outfit for quite a few months. The old man was mighty pleased with me and my work, and he'd often tell me that he never worried a bit when he'd go away and leave the whole outfit in my charge. I brought in ways of handling cattle in the desert that was new and which went mighty well with him. It was savings in riding and cattle. The old man would be gone for weeks at a time and I'd go along shifting cattle back to one spring and then another after each shower, and brand as I went. There was many cattle from neighboring outfits in the country, and it was quite a job, for a man alone, to cut out the old man's cattle and start 'em for the hills. Then I'd often shove the other outfits' cattle away too. My meals was mighty far apart at times and I sure wasn't picking up no fat. Sometimes, when work piled up on me too fast, I'd get an Indian to come along and help me, some of 'em was pretty good hands in that country.

While riding for that outfit, it would of been mighty easy for me to've got away with a few carloads of cattle, shipped 'em and got back without the old man knowing anything about it. Being the cattle was scattered over so much country, he wouldn't of missed 'em for a year. He'd just figgured they strayed a bit. . . . I thought of the subject once in a while, but I'd just sort of snicker at that thought. Not that I was afraid of getting caught if I tried, and not that the prison had scared me out of doing any more such tricks. It was just that I wasn't interested that way no more. I'd done passed the stage of when I was a fool kid.

As much as I liked my job and the old man liked me, a same old failing of mine begin to get a holt on me again. That was to drift. New country was calling and finally one day, after I'd given the old man time to get another rider to put in my place, I catched up two bronks that I'd bought and broke while on the job, and hits out for beyond a range of hills to the north and west. As usual, I wanted to see what was on the other side of them.

I drifted along for a hundred miles and more, and I come acrost a railroad. On the north side of that railroad a ways I struck a big cow outfit that I went to work for. I worked there just a little while when I begin to listen to rumors that there was a war going on somewhere, and that the government was making a *second* round-up on the men that had registered. I wondered if *I* had been called. There'd been no way for me to know while I was in the desert, I wasn't getting no mail. . . . But I remembered now, while there, how one time I found a feller wandering acrost the big flats afoot, lost and about dead for thirst. His tongue had swelled out of his head. When I told him where to find my camp and came back there that night he was delirious. I pulled his shoes off and the skin of his heels came off with 'em. He tried to talk, in some foreign language; once in a while he'd say a few words in American and from that I got the drift that he'd left the mines where he'd been working and had run away so he wouldn't get in the war. He kept a repeating that he didn't want to go to war.

The old man came long with a wagon-load of grub one day and started towards town with that feller the next day. I heard afterwards that blood poison set in his heels and he died from that.

From the ravings of that feller while he was with me was when I got the first hint that there was a war. But I didn't pay much attention to that then, I wasn't worried about no war nor what it was about. Not till I got further North and where all the riders was talking about it, where some had already enlisted and where others was expecting a call any day. I was advised that I'd better find out if I'd been called.

I had registered while I was with the movie outfit. I wrote down to find out, and I found out plenty quick. A rider from the home ranch brought me a telegram which said that I'd been called a month before and for me to report *immediately* to a certain town for examination.

I sold my horses and outfit, all but my saddle and boots and spurs, I always took that with me, and within twenty-four hours from that time I received the telegram I was in the town where I'd be run thru the chute and inspected.

That inspection struck me funny. The old Doc could hardly see nor hear, and he seemed to have a grouch on to boot. For some reason he held me for a few days.

By that time I'd got to know what the war was about and where the big fight was being pulled off, and thinking I'd be sent acrost right away to most likely never come back, I used them few days I had to have one last great ole time. I went down to the joints where the painted ladies was, picked me out the best looking one, and me and two other cowboys that also had girls and was waiting for orders, done our best to keep the town lit up all night. Our main sport was to wreck Chinese joints and dance halls. We got in a few fights, and when I got word to report I went to the train with one eye well closed and a cut lip. But I'd had a fine time. My girl came with me to the train, so did the two boys and their girls, and we sang "Somewhere a Voice is Calling" till the wheels of the train begin to turn.

My fun was over now, and I was glad I had it when a day or so later I begin to jam in long lines of men, many of 'em looking mighty pale and feeling mighty blue. There was where I was glad once again that I wasn't leaving a mother or a wife behind to grieve over me, not even a sweetheart. . . . When I was asked who I wanted to make my insurance to I couldn't tell. I finally gave the name of a good friend of mine, a cowboy.

It made me laugh when I was asked if I wanted to claim exemption and if I had any dependents. I didn't know of even a far-away relative. . . . But even tho there was no one to grieve over me, there was something that I missed as I got in file after file of men. That was the range I was leaving, the big open country,—and somewhere there was my little horse Smoky. I'd never forgot him. As it was now, I was jammed in crowds again and hearing talk that was strange. I felt about as bad as I did when I was took to prison.

In my life I'd never "punched a clock," I wasn't used to regular hours and time for everything, nor to take orders from anybody. A cowboy, if he knows his work, never gets no orders on the range. He's pretty well his own boss and there's no time set for anything he does. He's also mighty independent.

But there was no such a thing as being independent nor free when I went thru the second examination and, filing along with long strings of men that was handled like a herd, I went from one desk to another a collecting my O D outfit, leggings and shoes. The shoes was sure some contrast to my light riding boots, with every step I took I felt like them shoes covered and crushed a whole acre of gravel.

The place I went to report was on an island on the coast. After a big herd of us got fitted out in our soldier outfit we was hazed away from the buildings, went where the "point men" and "swingmen" wanted us to. And when we reached an open space amongst the eucalyptus we was made to crawl in "pup tents" for the rest of the night. Many a boy caught bad colds there.

But war is war, and I think I can dig up worse names for it than what it's been called. . . . About a thousand head of us rookies was loaded on a train the next day and was took for a long ride. Everybody was at every station we went thru to cheer us along the way and was giving us fruit and cake and things. When the train stopped at the end of the long ride I could see some hills that was in Old Mexico. I was close to the border again.

Our drilling and training begin at a camp a few miles outside of a big town there. But there wasn't much training for the first few weeks. All of us was getting "shots in the arm" every few days and many of the boys would get to feeling pretty sick each time. It struck me kind of funny when the men would get in line to get them shots. There was a little shack where a couple of doctors done the work of injecting the long needle. Some of the boys would watch the shack and get paler with every step they took. One or two would fall by the wayside in a faint, then some feller ahead would look back, see them sprawled out and faint too.

We was at this first camp about a month and then we was marched out quite a few miles to a great big spread of tents and long frame buildings that was all around a big stretch of open level ground. That all was the cantonment and where we was to fall in real drilling. My first drilling was to peeling potatoes. I never seen so many potatoes in my life as I seen them first few days and I thought for a while that that was how I was going to help win the war. But soon enough I was made acquainted with many different steps and then, with the rest, I was handed a rifle. That made me feel a little better, but that rifle was the cause of me getting a day or so of "kitchen police" every now and again. I wasn't interested in keeping it too clean. All I seen was that it was in good shooting order and with a little grease in it all the time. That didn't go so good in inspection and I peeled quite a few stacks of potatoes on that account.

But I took pretty good to the drilling and come a time when I was used for platoon leader, and often I was given a whole platoon to drill. But I didn't like that much and I'd be apt to take my platoon away some place and have 'em "fall out" pretty regular. . . . I was told a few times that I should apply to be an officer. Many boys filled blanks and a few made the grade, but with me I had no army ambition, no more than I'd had movie ambition.

The only ambition I had while I was drilling was somehow to be transferred in some part of the army where I didn't have to walk. I wanted to get in the remount station and go to breaking horses. There was a couple of cowboys I knowed there, but I was told that only enlisted men could get in the remount, and besides I'd have to have good references to prove that I could ride and had broke horses before.

"I can prove that mighty quick," I says. "Just pick me out a bronk and let me straddle him."

There was plenty of tough horses at the remount. Many was outlaws and shipped from all over the Western States. But, as I was told, showing that I could ride one of them wouldn't do. I'd have to get the references, something to show to the Captain or Major.

I took pen in hand that night and wrote to two outfits I'd broke horses for. I received mighty fine letters as me being a No. I rider and horse breaker. I showed the letters, they went the rounds, and I was finally told that the remount had all the riders that was needed, that many of the horses was soon to be shipped acrost the ocean to another remount.

But them two letters done me some good. I took 'em to the Captain of headquarters and after a while I was transferred to that company as a mounted scout. That was fine, and even tho I was informed that mounted scouts was the first to get shot when they got acrost, I didn't worry about that. I'd be a horseback, anyway, and not crawling along the ground like a terrapin. As I was told, the mounted scout is the one that's the first to investigate a place or town where the enemy is supposed to've just left, and as the enemy always leaves a few sharpshooters behind, I would be in a fine way of getting it quick. This company I was with was due to go acrost the pond in another couple of months.

The couple of months went by and we didn't budge from the cantonment. We was told we'd be going in another month, but that time went by, and more time, and when we was finally due to go acrost sure enough and was all prepared we got a last word to hold on a spell longer. There was a few more days and then the armistice was signed.

I was in the army over nine months and I was afoot only

during the first month and a half of that time. I was mounted scout and orderly, taking messages here and there for a while, then I was put on special duty taking the rough off officers' horses, making 'em do what the officers couldn't. Some officers would go to the remount, pick out fine looking horses and then find out afterwards, they couldn't ride 'em. Some of the horses would go to bucking again. There was others that was hard to handle and climb onto and some that the officers couldn't make go any direction except towards the picket lines and stables. Of course any of them horses could be took back to the remount and exchanged for others, but some officers would be too proud to do that or made a brag that they could ride. Like there was a big tall feller who'd claimed to been a cowboy and could ride any horse. Now, anything that makes me sore is for somebody to claim to be what he ain't. Well, he drawed a pretty good horse at the remount, but after this would-be rider handled him a few days the horse got wise and so that this officer couldn't even get on him. Then is when I came in on special duty for that job.

I had no trouble with that horse after I rode him the first time, nor with none of the others that was handed me afterwards, and sometimes I'd be scared that that job would run out. But I didn't have nothing to be scared of because them horses got to know me very well from the other fellers, and they'd soon get back to their old tricks again when an officer would climb 'em. I had a few horses handed me from the scouts too and which they hadn't tried to ride but once. . . . Sometimes I had four or five horses at a time to line out, and there's where my own saddle came in to work again. I was allowed to use it, also my own boots and spurs, and outside of my army hat and breeches, I was dressed and riding the same as I did on the range.

I can say that I was on horseback wherever I went, in the moving-pictures, in the army, and even in prison.

My riding while I was in the army was in a lot of fun. My biggest part of the fun was that all the time I was on special duty I didn't have to drill, I didn't have to stand no inspection and I wouldn't be getting no more K. P.'s. Then again I was free to go anywhere I wanted to while riding the meanness out of the horses. Sometimes I'd lope into town. . . . I was loping out of town one time and getting back to the cantonment when I looks over my shoulder and sees two M. P.'s loping up behind me. Wondering if they was on my trail, I gets off the road and hits for the thick brush. They was after me all right, because I seen 'em turn in the brush right there where I did. I knowed what they was trailing me for. They'd suspicioned I'd come to town to get a little likker. There was lots of places in that town where a soldier could get any amount of the stuff.

Well, when I seen them two M. P.'s trying to catch up with me, I thought I'd have a little fun. I was riding in the brush now, in pretty rough country and I was right at home. I'd ride on ahead and when I'd leave 'em too far behind, I'd get up on a point where they could see me and wait for 'em. I wanted to make that chase interesting. . . . Sometimes I'd branch off in the thick brush, watch 'em go past and then I'd ride up on a high point behind 'em and holler. They'd run back then for all they was worth. I could see they was getting mad, and by the time they got to where I'd been I'd made a little circle and dodged 'em and was heading on for the cantonment again. . . . I played with 'em like that all the way and when I got near the cantonment I left 'em in the brush a wondering as to which way I went. They'd wanted to find out which stable I'd go to and catch me there.

My range experience, riding from the time I was big enough to, in all kinds of country, often at night and hid-

ing, outguessing men, wild cattle and wild horses, along
with the general range work, gave me a big advantage in
the army. . . . There was one time, on that account, that
I can say I had a considerable to do with our side winning
in a big sham battle. There was about ten of us mounted
scouts and our orders was to locate the position of the enemy
and report. I took the smallest horse I had for that job, the
brush was thick, and when the Sergeant took us out and
scattered us each to our part of the country, I leaned on my
little horse's neck and tore thru the brush to do my scouting.

Soon I begin to see fresh tracks in the dirt. I slowed my
horse down, and keeping where the brush was the thickest,
I came to within a few hundred yards of half a dozen tall
eucalyptus. I stopped and squinted at the top of the trees
for a long time, wondering if there was a lookout up there.
If there was I might take him prisoner, and if there wasn't
I'd climb up myself and look around. But I finally spotted
a lookout in the top branches of one of the trees. I left my
horse and started afoot to catch me that feller when I spots
the hat crown of another soldier at the bottom of the tree;
further on there was another, and then I begin to skirt
around and do some real scouting. When I got thru I'd
spotted a lay of about four hundred of our enemies, at ease
and quiet, and waiting for orders. . . . I marked their location down, got my horse and rode on to report, and I
thought as I rode that if there was brush like this on "the
other side" I'd have a lot of fun.

I was very careful of tall trees and high points and kept
my head close to my horse's ears. Once in a while I'd stop
him and stand up in my saddle, a trying to look over the
brush a bit. . . . It was at one of them times that I seen
something move. I watched that something and finally made
it out to be a foot, then I seen a whole soldier crawling

along on all fours. "Gee," I thought, "I must be getting close to the line."

I no more than thought that when I hear brush cracking, and I spots hats bobbing everywhere thru the brush. The soldiers was running towards me, and the whole country seemed alive with 'em. But they hadn't seen me, and even tho I figgured my goose was cooked for sure, I sit down in my saddle and begin to do some riding. I seen I was cut off ahead and that the only possible way out was to go back the way I came. . . . With spotting all these troops and their movements I sure had some report to make now, if I could only get out and get to do that reporting. I rode thru the brush like a streak and as if I was chasing a bunch of wild ones. Every second I expected to hear a rifle shot which would put me out of the game, as a prisoner or a dead one.

But I made it around past the dangerous place, circled back and rode full speed to find my Captain. He was mighty pleased at my report and told me to go to it some more.

I did go to it some more. I rode about fifty miles during that battle and changed horses once with an officer who got lost and which I took prisoner. He didn't like that, but I told him that's what I'd do if it was war, and I needed a fresh horse. He finally grinned and let me have his horse. . . . I located an enemy supply train a while after that, also a company of ours that wasn't where it belonged, and when I made that report the Captain was pleased some more. The Major was there with him to hear my second report. He recognized the horse I was riding and asked me how I got him. He was mighty serious while I told him, but he never said a word. He dismissed me and when I looked back both him and the Captain was having a laughing fit.

That one happening introduced me to the Major pretty well and I think saved me from putting a little time in the guard house once in a while for things I'd done later which wasn't just right.

As you would know, by now, my failing is horses. Not a one ever goes by that I don't see and look over well. My first offense in the army was by watching a horse too much and not seeing the officer on top of him. I was called on by a shave-tail officer for that one day, one of them kind who was tasting authority for the first time in his life. I was down on the ground fixing my saddle or something, when this shave-tail rides up on a fine big sorrel horse. Outside of Smoky that horse had the prettiest legs and build of any horse I'd ever seen. I was in a sort of a trance looking at him, and I didn't hear the officer talking to me the first time. But I sure heard him the second time because he hollered so you could hear him for half a mile. His vanity was hurt and he was mad clear thru.

"You," he says. "Stand up to attention and salute. Don't you recognize an officer when you see one?"

I stood up and saluted and said, "Yes, sir." . . . But the shave-tail was still mad, and he went on to order me to report to the Major.

He was already there when I rode acrost the parade grounds to report, and he spilled his story to the Major, how I didn't want to salute, and so on. The Major recognized me, and he must of seen that I was getting pretty peeved as the officer talked. He asked me what I had to say.

"Sir," I says, standing mighty stiff, "he was riding a mighty fine looking horse, and I forgot for watching the horse that there was an officer setting on him." The Major put his hand to his mouth and coughed a bit. . . . I went on, "I saluted the officer soon as I seen him, and . . . he didn't return my salute."

From the corner of my eye I could see that the officer

squirmed a bit when I passed the last remark. Specially when the Major squinted at him. . . . "You may return his salute now," he says to him.

Me and the shave-tail both faced one another and he saluted, just *him* saluted. The Major then gave me a little talking-to and dismissed the both of us. . . . I could see that the Major was disappointed in that shave-tail as an officer, and as for me, all I hoped for while riding back to the stables was that there'd be another sham battle and have the shave-tail on the enemy side. I'd sure do my best to make him prisoner and take his horse away from him.

But that chance never came. I faced the Major a couple of times more on the same charge, of watching horses too much and officers not enough, by other shave-tails. The Major gave me a good private talking-to on the last time, and from then on I begin to look up a bit when I seen a horse coming.

But, with officers, like with anybody else, there was many good fellers amongst 'em. Sometimes, forgetting I was under army discipline, and during war time, I'd even catch myself talking back to one when he gave me an order. Like one time while on shooting practice an officer caught me aiming my rifle at a target, with a cigarette in my mouth. He ordered me to throw my cigarette away, and then went on to remark that I wouldn't be smoking no cigarette while shooting from the front-line trenches.

I looked back from where I was laying and leaning on my rifle and grinned at him.

"Then is when I would want one," I says, "so I could shoot good."

He only grinned and walked on to the next recruit. . . . When the few days of target shooting was over, my points counted up to well above Marksman and not so far from Sharpshooter, which is the top.

Discipline was the hardest thing for me to bear up under while in the army. I knowed that had to be but that didn't make me like it any better. Another thing that used to make me feel ornery once in a while was to know that I now was with an outfit I couldn't quit, and I often wished that I'd either be sent acrost to fight or else be turned loose. I was again missing the range and wanting to see many cattle instead of the many men I was mixing with every day. My first month was the hardest for me in mixing in with the men. I was talking different than they did and wanted to talk about different things than they talked about. With most of the fellers around, the talk was the girls. They called 'em "broads" and other names and said things I didn't like. Sometimes I'd butt in and ask 'em if there was anything else they could talk about, if they had any respect for women and if they had any mothers or sisters. I'd go on to remark that if they *did* they sure didn't act that way. . . . But I found out that they didn't mean half what they said, it was just their way of talking.

At the mess hall was a place where I'd hate to gather at. Some of the boys acted just as human as full grown hogs and reach past two or three fellers in their hurry to get at something, like they'd never had anything to eat before in their lives. I'd often wonder at some fellers' actions, how long they would last around the fires of a cow camp. They'd been roped and drug out for sure.

It took me quite a spell to get to mingling, and then, whether the army life teaches the boys some things or whether I finally got used to 'em, there come a time when I didn't mind 'em no more. Two or three that I was in the same tent with I'd got to liking a whole lot, and they was boys from big cities too, the kind that was raised in offices and had worked all day by electric lights.

I think being in the army for a time was a great thing
for them kind of boys, and while I felt that I was cooped
up they took it all as if they was in wild open country and
on a camping vacation. They was more in the open than
they'd ever been before in their lives. During a march they
got to learn how to cook a few things for themselves, how to
build safe fires, how to make a camp and do many things
they never had a chance to do before and while they'd been
between brick walls. I noticed that the army teached many
a boy good manners too, and how to take care of his own
clothes and look neat in whatever he wore. There was many
a sloppy careless-acting recruit came in the army who went
out looking neat and packing himself like he had a sure
enough backbone.

The army, with the discipline that was handed out during the war, changed many a boy, and there come a time
when instead of dodging and disliking everyone I seen, I got
to thinking they wasn't bad fellers after all. Before I was
discharged from the service I thought that the whole bunch
was a daggone fine bunch of fellers all around.

I got to have many good friends long before I left the
army. They was fellers from everywhere, from big cities of
the East and North, and some of us would have a lot of
fun together when we'd hit for town on Saturday nights to
stay till Sunday. We'd go down along the beach and visit
one dance pavillion after another. I couldn't dance very well,
and being I didn't want to impose on the good nature of
any girl, I'd get in a corner and watch the boys till they
was ready to leave. Sometimes they'd dig me up a girl that
would be brave enough as to volunteer to teach me to dance
and then *maybe* I would, if the girl was good looking enough.
If she was real good looking and her feet was very small,
I'd ask her to sit the dance out and just talk to me. The

boys brought me girls of all kinds. They knowed how to get 'em, I didn't.

There come the time for the "flu" to start in doing its dirty work. We got to wearing gauze masks over our nose and mouth. I went to eating lots of onions, smoking lots of cigarettes, and riding to town for whiskey off and on. One of my friends took sick one night and I poured half a pint of the stuff down his throat. I kept a pouring some more down him the next day, got all the blankets off my bed and covered him up so he couldn't move, and by that night he got to feeling so good that he wanted to take me to town and give me a treat. He was all right the next day.

But I lost three of my good friends from the flu, all fellers that at one time and another had been in the same tent with me. After the boys had died, some of their folks would come and see me and others would write, and all told of the good things them boys said about me and how welcome I would be to now take their place in the family.

I'll never forget the day when, finally, the war came to a sudden end and the armistice was signed. I was by the stables a trying to get one of the spoiled horses into his stall when I hears a commotion and noise and hollers like I've never heard before or since. Thousands and thousands of soldiers was war-whooping and acting like as if they'd kicked a hornet's nest. I had no idea of what the commotion was about, but it sure looked and sounded exciting, so I saddled the horse I'd been trying to lead in and lined him out towards the parade grounds. I never seen so many crazy-acting fellers in my life as I did when I got there, and when I got the news of what they was acting up about, that the war was over, I went just as crazy-happy as any of 'em did. I layed both spurs on my spoiled horse's neck and drug 'em

back, and while he tore holes in the parade ground with
every jump he made, I whooped and fanned like I never
whooped and fanned before.

The first thing I thought with the news that the war was
over, was my getting back to the range, to home and free to
roam again, and it was no wonder I got wild. It was no
wonder anybody got wild, we was all going to home. . . .

But it took some few weeks after the armistice was signed
before anybody begin to leave for home. There was a lot of
men to handle and things had to be done in a regular way.
It was a week or so after the day of the good news that I
received some bad news. I was told that I was in a depart-
ment where I'd be the last to be let go, on account of
handling the horses and waiting till they was disposed of
and so on, and that I might have to stay in the army for
another three months or so longer. That was sure some bad
news for me. But now that the war was over I made up my
mind to get out and long before three months' time too. I
got to thinking of many ways on how that might be done,
and finally I stumbled onto one way which I figgured would
turn the trick.

I sent a long telegram to the old feller I'd worked for
before coming in the army. I knowed he wanted quite a few
horses broke and that on account of the war taking most of
the riders, he'd had a hard time getting anybody to do that
for him. I told him I'd break his horses and ride for him for
forty dollars a month and for as long as he wanted me to,
if he'd only get me out of the army right quick. He'd been
paying seventy-five a month for that. I knowed I was making quite a promise but it was sure worth it to me to get out
of the army, I was sort of desperate.

I told him to get a petition up of the stockmen of that
country, also the stock Association to make a holler and

say they was needing their riders. That was sure enough the truth.

It was about a week after I sent the telegram when I heard from the old man. His answer sure sounded fine and he said he'd go to work on the petition right away and do

I was heading back for the cow country again.

all he could. . . . . A couple of weeks later I was told to report to the Captain. He asked a few questions which I was mighty glad to answer, and then I was sent out to get an examination, to see if I was as fit as I'd been when I entered the service. I knowed that if I wasn't they might hold me and see what was the matter with me, so, when I went in the building for that last examination, I sure stepped lively and done some graceful prancing around.

The next day I was handed transportation and a honorable discharge.

I folded the papers neat, put 'em in my pocket and then I grinned at the Captain. "I'm sure getting away with something," I says to him.

"What's that?" he asks.

"Six days of Kitchen Police," I says.

I'd been handed them K. P.'s before I went in special duty and I'd never been called on to serve them after that.

"Don't crow too much," says the Captain. "You're under army rules and orders for three days yet."

"That would still leave me three days to the good," I says.

He laughed and put out his hand for me to shake. "Well, I'll let you get away with the whole six of them K. P.'s. . . ."

That same night I got on the train, and with my saddle by my side, I was heading back for the cow country again.

WILLJAMES
—'30

CHAPTER TWENTY–FIVE

I MET the old cowman in the same desert town where he'd hired me near two years before. He didn't recognize me when I went in the lobby of the hotel where he was stopping. I had my uniform on and that made quite a change from the way he'd been used to seeing me. We was both mighty glad to see one another and him and me celebrated quite a bit that night. Just him and me. That was my home-coming reception after the war. There was no sweetheart to greet me, and no wife and mother that most of the boys had to fall into the arms of when they stepped off the train.

But I'd never knowed nor thought of such bliss and, as it was, I felt I was as happy as any man. And something else came up which made that reception all that I could wish it to be. That was along the next morning, when me and the old cowman started for the stables to get the horses and ride out. I walked in there and, as in my habit, I went to looking over all the horses that was in the stalls. The stocking hind feet of a horse caught my eye, so did his color. Some picture away back in my mind was trying to make itself fit in as I went on to sizing up the horse. I went in the stall, looked at his head, and the picture begin to fit more.

394

But, I thought, it couldn't be, not after all this time. I untied the horse, led him out of the stall and looked at the brand on his thigh. It had been worked over, but I could see the original brand there. It was the brand that had been on good old Smoky, and the horse *was* Smoky.

"What's the matter with you there?" hollers the old cowman as he hears me letting out a whoop.

"This is my horse Smoky. Been stole from me four or five years ago."

The stable man came up about then and heard what I'd just said. He asked me, if it was my horse, where did I get him in the first place, where was he stole from, and many other questions, and when I answered 'em all and showed him the original brand that had been made by a stamp iron and how it had been worked over by a running iron, he seemed convinced that that mouse-colored horse was mine sure enough.

"This boy has worked for me long enough so I know he wouldn't lie about that horse," says the old cowman. That settled it.

"Well," says the stable man, "I'm not out anything on that horse. I only paid twenty-five dollars for him and I cleared more than that from renting him for the last six months." He looked at me and asked, "Did he ever buck with you?" I said "Some." . . .

"I thought so," he went on, "because up till about a year and a half ago he was the toughest bucking horse in this country, and that's saying something. He was took to all the big rodeos as a final horse and he throwed many a good rider. Then for no reason that anybody could tell of, he quit bucking. I got him about a year after that and he's never bucked since."

Well, that was sure news for me, to hear of Smoky's bucking record. I was proud of him for that, but it hurt me to learn that after he quit bucking he was rented out as any common livery horse and for anybody to ride. . . . I soon forgot about that, tho. Now I was happy to have him again and I just wanted to go away with him to where both him and me belonged, back to the range.

I didn't ride Smoky out. He was looking old and weary and he wasn't in the good shape I used to keep him. I led him behind the horse the old cowman had brought for me, and when I got him to the main camp I begin shoving hay and crushed barley to him. Hay and grain was expensive because that had to be shipped into the country by rail and then freighted out of town by teams. The old man had got quite a few tons of hay and some grain freighted in for the bronks I was going to break for him. He'd wanted to keep 'em up while I was breaking 'em. I paid for Smoky's feed and I was mighty glad to do that. I floated the old pony's teeth, got him condition-powders and got his hoofs in shape. Poor shoeing had caused 'em to contract pretty bad.

In a month's time I had him looking slick as a whistle. His hide had loosened up and begin to shine like it always had before he'd been stolen from me. I kept him around for a few weeks longer, and every day, after I'd get thru stomping out my string of bronks, I'd go to looking him over and wondering what more I could do for him. The old man used to say that he'd seen plenty of cowboys act like daggone fools over a horse but that he'd never seen such a big daggone fool as I was over that old smoke-color horse.

"You'd think he was a ten-thousand-dollar race horse," he'd say.

"A heap more than that to me," I'd come back at him.

I took a lot of pains putting new shoes on Smoky one day, and when a bunch of mixed horses came at the spring

to water, I turned him loose with 'em. The feed was good
and strong where that bunch ranged, but it was mighty
rocky, and I shod Smoky so he wouldn't get sore-footed
while going back and forth from range to water. A sore-
footed horse never picks up much fat. There was colts and
yearlings in the bunch, and when I turned old Smoky loose
he begin to buck and play, just like them colts and yearlings did. He mixed right in with 'em, and soon the bunch
went to running, over one ridge and another and out of
sight. Smoky stopped and looked back just before going
over the last ridge, and he acted like he would turn back.
But soon he went to playing again and headed for the
bunch and wide open range.

I got to see him every day or two after that, when him
and the bunch would come to water. He'd leave the bunch
then for a time and stick his head over the corral fence
where I was always busy edducating one bronk or another,
and he'd nicker a hello to me. I'd always have crushed barley
in a morral (nose bag) and ready for him when he came,
and while he'd chew away on that, I'd get to feel his slick
hide and talk to him. Often the bunch he was with would
water and leave before he got thru eating his grain, but he
didn't seem worried about that, and when I'd take the morral
off his head and turn him out of the corral he'd sometimes
stick around for an hour or two, just as tho he wanted to
confab with me.

Smoky was a great horse. If any man ever said a word
by mouth, that pony done near as much by the way he'd
cock his little pin-ears. I knowed the language of them ears
mighty well. I'd seen a lot of country over them, and if
ever I was dubious about what was ahead while riding in
dark nights, I could tell by the feel of 'em if I should go
ahead or turn back. My hand on his neck would tell me a

lot of things his horse-sense knowed, and that way him and me talked to one another.

I never rode Smoky after I found him again at the livery stable. He'd done his work, I had more than plenty other horses to ride, and now all I wanted to do was to have that pony around, see him once in a while and see him feeling good. . . . If I'd ever caught anybody riding that horse during that time I think I'd been mighty tempted to sight down on that hombre and pull a trigger.

Sometimes, when old Smoky would come to water with the bunch, then to the corral for his grain, he'd stick around so long afterwards that I couldn't keep him company. I'd go to work on my bronks and sort of forget he was there. Pretty soon I'd hear squeals and poundings on the earth, I'd look out thru the corral to see him playing and bucking all by himself, and then he'd throw up his tail like a wild one and hit out to catch up with the bunch. The bunch might be three or four miles on the way back to the range, but I knowed he always caught up mighty easy, because he was right with the same bunch every time they came to water.

In a couple of months' time I had two fine strings of bronks lined out and ready to be put to work. A young feller had come along one day and he was hired to take the first string I had started and keep 'em going till they was well edducated to the ways of the range cow. I kept the second string for myself, and now, being I'd broke all the horses the old man had wanted me to, I went back to range work, from one spring to another, branding, getting cattle back in the hills after the tanks got to be more mud than water, and driving back cattle that had drifted.

The old cowman's herd was bigger than it had been when I worked for him before, and now he always kept a rider to help me. This rider and me seldom rode together, we could do a better job watching the cattle by being separated. As for the old cowman, he couldn't ride much any more. He'd stopped a couple of bullets once in a fight over some range, and even tho that had happened a long time before and the wounds had healed, there was times when he'd feel pretty stiff in one leg and hip. He could hardly get on a horse and riding was mighty painful to him. As he told me, he was sure glad when the war came to an end because he'd had to do most of his own riding during that time, with just an Indian kid to help him, and he couldn't of rode much longer. He'd been mighty pleased to get my telegram from the army, and he never held me to my offer to ride for forty dollars a month. He paid me ninety dollars and gave me charge of the outfit, and all he'd do himself would be to haul grub to me and the other rider once or twice a month, and stick around and cook for a few days. He spent most of his time in town, in the hotel lobby, smoking cigars and talking to other old-timers like himself.

I took Smoky along with me to whatever camp I'd go to. I'd take him along so I would have his company and so I could take care of him. Another reason was that I was afraid somebody might steal him again. Then being I'd sometimes be away from the main camp for a couple of months at a time, I thought of his shoes wearing off, him getting tenderfooted and me not being around to put new shoes on him.

There was about twenty springs that me and the other rider had to watch and where the cattle came to water. I'd stay at one spring from one to two weeks at a time, and all Smoky had to do was hunt for good grass and shade in the hills around the camp. There was most always plenty of that, and with his little feed of crushed barley twice a day and all the few left-over biscuits which he bummed me for,

he was sure what I called in shape. Maybe not in shape to
jump right out and make a long run or anything like that,
but in shape to dodge all the diseases that catches onto
weak animals. I don't know if anybody has ever seen a horse
chew on a beef bone before but I have seen Smoky do that
many times. Maybe that's what made him so brainy. He'd
pick up an old bone with some meat still on it and roll it
in his mouth like he sure seemed to enjoy it. It wasn't the
lack of salt that made him do that either because there
was plenty of salt blocks at every camp where there wasn't
alkali licks.

I always had from ten to fifteen head of horses in my
string. I liked lots of horses, specially in that rocky country
where, if they was rode steady, they'd get sore-footed even
with shoes on. I'd hobble 'em for night, and sometimes for
the day, and shove 'em up a hill and above where cattle
would generally go. There was always good bunch grass on
top of the hills.

I never hobbled Smoky. He was free to go as he pleased
all the time, and never left a camp where me and my horses
was at. When I'd move from one spring to another I'd leave
him poke along behind and travel to suit himself. If he
wanted to graze a while he'd stop and graze and then catch
up on a high lope. Sometimes I'd pass bunches of horses,
and if they was close enough, Smoky would run to one side
to rub nostrils with 'em. I'd keep on going with my string
of horses till there was many times when I left him a mile
or two behind. But pretty soon, and after he was thru sizing
up the bunch he run acrost, I'd see him stir a dust and
here he'd come a bucking, a playing and a running.

Smoky was like a big spoilt old kid, with nothing to do
but eat and play and stick his nose into whatever I was
doing when I was around camp. He was more company to

me than I can tell, and during the two years I worked for that outfit and while he was around he made this cowboy mighty contented and pleased to stay in that one country. I never stayed so long in one country, not since I was left alone. But now I somehow didn't care to drift no more. It was mostly because I didn't want to take Smoky on any long trips, and I sure didn't want to leave him behind.

Something else held me there. I didn't want to leave the old cowman. A few times he dropped some hints as to how he'd like to turn his whole outfit, cattle, horses, range and all, over to me and have me run it on shares of the calf crop. He'd remark as to how I was young and that I ought to make a start for myself and have an interest in the outfit instead of just plain wages.

"I've got to turn this outfit over sooner or later," he said once, "and I'd just as well make it soon, because all I can do now is hold down a chair in the hotel lobby and talk to old has-beens like myself. That last trip I made out with the grub and while the wet snow was coming down sure didn't help my bum hip and leg any."

I couldn't quite answer to the old cowman's talk. I still had it in mind to have a little spread of my own but I didn't care to have it in the desert so much. I liked the desert, it was sure wide open and a fine country to ride in, while riding for wages, but for a place to make my start and home I couldn't think of any other country than where I was born and raised,—a rolling country covered with a thick carpet of grass, plenty of good running water in every coulee, tall pines, cottonwoods and quakers for shade, where cattle that are not sore-footed graze in big herds instead of little scattering bunches; the old home of the buffalo, and where elk, deer and antelope still roamed.

Till I got to that kind of country, I wasn't thinking much

on making a start. As it was now, I was happy to just be working for wages, handle the outfit for the old cowman that way, and keep Smoky rested and feeling good.

I liked my job there, it was paying me better wages than I ever had before and I had a responsibility that made it mighty interesting for me. This was my third job where I had full charge of an outfit. I liked to have the say as with such jobs. I liked to see pleased looks on the owners' faces when I done something well, like pulling cattle thru drought and disease, bringing in a likely beef herd when shipping time come, and the many other things that a good cowman can appreciate. This old cowman I was working for was one of the best I ever seen and the most appreciative of what I done for him.

Like with most all cow outfits I'd ever rode for, my working hours wasn't very regular. They're less regular with desert outfits on account of water holes being far apart and where riding is mostly done from permanent camps. It's not like riding for prairie outfits and where the round-up wagon follows the works. While riding for the old cowman I'd sometimes be in the saddle twenty out of twenty-four hours, with nothing to eat during that time. That would be when a snow or rain storm would come. Cattle would then drift to fresh range and where there was no spring water. I'd have to see that they didn't drift too far, so they could get back to the springs again when the snow and rain-water was all gone. Cattle that I'd sometimes miss would barely make it in to the springs and when they did, if I wasn't around to watch 'em, they'd near kill themselves with water. A few would, once in a while. Sometimes big thirsty herds would drift in to troughs that could water only fifty head at a time, and many a time, after a long day's ride, I'd have to get up in the middle of the night, get on a night horse that

I always kept up, split the herd and scatter it to other springs. It was hard work to get the thirsty cattle away from the troughs, and sometimes the sun would be high when I'd get back to my camp. I'd heat up some coffee then, swallow a cold biscuit, catch a fresh horse, and go a hunting for more cattle that was holding out on far-away range and feeding till thirst drove 'em in.

With such work that has to be done, a cowboy can't form no union and go by no union hours. If a rider was to quit when a certain hour come and there was work still to be done, he wouldn't be no cowboy, and in some countries there wouldn't be no range cattle. . . . Sunday is no day of rest for the cowboy, and there's no celebrating of holidays. They're just days like all others.

But it wasn't always long hours in the saddle. There was whole weeks at a time when I'd ride out of camp after sun-up and could easy get back in the middle of the afternoon. That was when there was no water in the flats and cattle watered at the springs. Before leaving camp in the morning I'd always wrap a big can of tomatoes with gunny sack and plant it by the spring or slip it under a trough where water would drip on it. When I'd get back from my day's ride the first thing I'd do was to open up the can, sprinkle a little salt on the tomatoes and take the whole canful down. That was sure what I called refreshing. Then I'd ride to where my horses was hobbled, change to a fresh one, ride back to camp and go to cooking me a bait. My day's work was done, unless cattle came to water and there was calves in the bunch that needed branding.

I sure always liked them late afternoons and evenings at the camps. Everything was sure peaceful, and I'd stretch out either on my bunk or under a cedar tree, looking at saddle-makers' catalogs and old magazines or at the distance.

When dark come I'd light a candle and draw a bit by it. I thought I was getting to draw pretty good about that time, but no new ambition of me trying to be an artist came to me.

I don't know how long I'd kept on with the desert outfit. I figgured to stay with the old cowman for as long as he

They're just days like all others.

wanted me. Then come a time when, as the old feller seen I wasn't right anxious to accept his outfit and running it on shares, he begin talking about selling out to a big neighboring outfit. He'd heard of some place where there was hot mineral waters that would keep the stiffness out of his hip and leg and he was wanting to sell out, take the money and go to making himself a permanent camp by them waters.

Finally he did come to a deal with the neighboring outfit and sold out to 'em. The old cowman drove up in a buckboard to tell me about it one day and say how he hated to leave his little outfit go,—also to make me a present by handing me a bill of sale for two of the best saddle horses he had.

Well, after the old man bid me good-bye and as I watched him drive away, I got a sudden hankering to drift. Smoky and the hobbled horses came in to water as I got to thinking on the subject, and I talked things over with him. I decided then that I'd just as well stay where I was, one place was just as good as another, and besides, I didn't want to have Smoky knocking on the rough trails he would find while following me around.

But I found it hard to stay. I wasn't boss of the little outfit no more. The foreman of the big outfit took charge of everything and my wages was cut down to what the company allowed the cowboys, sixty dollars a month. Besides, I was asked to trade three of my broke horses off and take green bronks in their place. . . . That last didn't go so well with me, because after I broke that string of bronks for the old cowman near two years before and got 'em gentled, I hadn't broke any other. I'd been riding only them, and for the past year or more not a one had bucked to speak of.

Any rider that's fighting bronks steady will tell you that he don't want no broke horses in his string. Riding a horse that broke gentle will cause the rider to sometimes be off his guard when he's on a wild one, and he'll maybe get throwed off or struck or kicked. As for me, and now that I'd been riding horses that I'd gentled, I'd drawed the line on bronks. I'd decided that I was thru with the rough ones, and the main reason was that I was getting scared. I'd been hurt and took thru some mighty tight places by many of 'em. I'd lost a considerable of my nerve and now, instead of getting to be a better rider all the time, as most people would think, I'd passed the peak of my good riding and was going downhill.

The rougher and more dangerous a game is, the younger a man is when he quits it. Mighty few bronk fighters that's been at the game steady and hard are still at it when they're thirty years old. I know many that didn't know what it was to be scared of a horse or anything under the sun, but as bones was smashed now and again, skin was peeled and months was spent laying and waiting for that to mend and heal, a rider would gradually begin to get more careful as he went back to riding each time. And when a bronk fighter begins to get careful as he handles his bronk is when he better quit or what he thinks is apt to happen most likely will, and too soon.

I'd had horses fall with me in every way, shape or form, while running, stampeding, or bucking, at night or day, while the sun shined or while the stars was hid by dark clouds and lightning played, in the thick of cloudbursts, hail and blizzards. . . . I'd rode stampeders that swept me off in the thorny brush of the South, run off the side of tall Northern mountains, and bucked in places where a man couldn't walk. My breath had come short many a time. I'd been kicked and struck, rolled over the top of and dragged, and, as happening after happening accumulated and left me with scars, my mind begin to tally back to them many happenings as I'd climb a big snaky bronk, and come a time when my spur rowel rang and sounded like a warning tune as I stuck my foot in the stirrup.

That was the fix I'd got to be in when the company handed me three big husky bronks to snap out and keep in my string. I took 'em, and outside of getting my saddle tore up pretty bad as one fell over backwards and got wedged between some rocks I got along pretty well with 'em. But I didn't care to ride bronks no more. I was thru and all the interest I had in 'em was to see that none got me under and that I missed the hoofs that came my way.

There was one thing I was glad for as I kept a riding for the company and that was that I was left to stay on the same range which had been the old cowman's. I knowed that range and camped at one spring and then another the same as while he owned it, and I was left alone about as much as before.

Everything was going pretty good. I'd got the three bronks so they'd quit bucking and also quit their snorting and spooking at every move I made. They was fast getting gentle and to doing good work, and now things was pretty near the same as they had been.

One evening, after I'd tied up one of the bronks for a night horse, I happened to look up a draw where I'd took the hobbled horses up thru, and sees old Smoky all by himself and poking along down towards camp. I'd never seen him leave the bunch during the evening, before. I laughed as I watched him come and I says to myself, "That old bum wants another biscuit."

But Smoky didn't want no biscuit. He refused the one I held out to him, and for the first time. He didn't seem to want anything, and there was a kind of a far-away look in his eyes. I thought then that he was sick. I felt of his ears but they was warm and I couldn't find any signs of anything being the matter with him. I figgured he just wanted company, and after I talked to him a spell I went to making some cedar kindling to start the morning fire with. I didn't pay no attention to him while doing that and when I got thru I looked to see him laying down by a cedar tree and with his head propped against it. I went to him again then to watch for signs of sickness, but he was breathing easy and regular and he seemed all at peace. He sure didn't look sick, and he was round and fat as a butter ball.

I squatted by him, rolled me a smoke and while taking the burrs out of his foretop I went to talking to him. He seemed to enjoy that a whole lot, he liked me to rub his ears too. I sat by him there thru the whole evening and till dark come, and then after one more pat on his slick neck I left him to go into the cabin and crawl in between my soogans. There was a long ride ahead for me on the next day.

It was sure some surprise when, waking up the next morning, I looked out the opened door to see Smoky still laying where I'd left him the night before, still in the same position and with his head propped against the tree. He looked asleep, but I jumped out of bed into my boots, pulled up the pants they was always left inside of, and hit out to Smoky's side. He didn't move an ear nor open an eye when I came near, and as I layed a hand on his neck it felt cold . . . with the cold of death.

Old Smoky had just went to sleep thru that. I don't think he ever felt a pain or that a muscle even twitched when he drawed his last breath, and far as I know he might of passed away while I was talking to him the evening before.

I didn't go on that long ride that I'd planned on. Instead I dug a deep hole right by where Smoky layed, rolled him in and buried him, and stacked rocks on his grave so the cayotes wouldn't dig him out.

Smoky's going made me feel down-the-mouth quite a bit, and now that I couldn't do no more for him, I wanted to ride and ride, in one straight line and for many miles. It was noon that day when I caught the two horses the old cowman had made me a present of. I put my bed on one, my saddle on the other, and taking the hobbles off the other horses, I started 'em out of the corral and turned 'em towards the headquarters of the company. It was late that night when I got there. I asked for my time check the next morning and rode on again, a looking ahead for new ridges to cross.

CHAPTER TWENTY–SIX

I CROSSED many ridges, valleys, creeks and mountains.
I was again heading North, towards my home grounds
and with my mind made up that when I got there I would
locate a place on some likely creek bottom, build me a cabin
and corrals, get a brand recorded and go to accumulating
a herd and make me a place where I would want to stay.
. . . Many things had kept me from making a go of that
before, but now the sky looked clear that way, and being
that I now was thru with rough horses, I felt like I was also
thru with rambling around and hanging my hat on the
ground. I would make a go of settling down this time, and as
I rode along I went to picturing in my mind as to how the
lay of my cabin and corrals would look.

I'd rode a few hundred miles towards them ambitions and
nothing had interfered much with my going on, nothing excepting that I had bad luck with one of my horses. It was my
bed horse, and I'd just pulled my bed off of him during a
heavy thunder shower when lightning struck and killed him.
I wasn't over ten yards from him at the time and I was
knocked down flat. But that and a shock was all that happened to me. . . . I sure hated to lose that horse, he was a
good one. I rode my other horse to a ranch the next day,

bought me a bronk that had just been broke to lead, tied my
bed on him and went on facing north some more.

It was a couple of days later, and while following a road,
that I found myself in lanes, and then I spotted smoke and
high chimneys of a town away ahead. It turned out to be a
pretty good-sized town, and being I hadn't been in one for
many months, I thought I'd stick around there a day or
two, take in the sights and wet my whistle a bit. I figgured
I was entitled to that.

I'd no more than put my horses in the stable when I found
out that I'd struck that town in good high time. A big
rodeo was going to be pulled off soon, and as the stable
man went to talking to me he asked if I wouldn't like to take
a job helping him gather bucking horses, range steers for
bulldogging, and everything that would be needed to make
that rodeo a good one. That struck me all right, and I figgured I could spare a little time at the job and make some
money while I was seeing the sights and having a little fun.

I met the promoter and manager of the rodeo the next
day. I was hired on good day-wages and expenses paid to
boot, and I went to work a scouting around for bucking
stock. That town was in the heart of a fine stock country and
bucking horses and range steers wasn't hard to locate and
contract for. I had a young feller with me to try out the
bucking stock, he was a good rider but I found many horses
that was too rough for him and which he couldn't sit. Them
was the horses I picked on.

I soon had all the horses and cattle that was needed, had
my fun while locating 'em and was sleeping in a hotel bed
most every night. . . . It sure struck me queer to be in
town that time. For the two years or so that I'd been riding
for the old cowman I'd been in town only a couple of times
and for just a day or two each time, to deliver beef herds.

Being so used to be in open country and on horseback always, it sure was some change to be amongst so many buildings, people, going along sidewalks and afoot. I'd laugh at myself when sometimes a piece of paper would blow in front of me. Being so used to have a horse under me and knowing how the horses I rode would of spooked at the paper, I'd sort of expect a jolt and brace for it. I think I even snorted at a paper myself a few times.

This might sound like just a story, but I think any man that sticks to one work as long and steady as I stuck to mine, and from the time he begins to walk till away after he quits growing, will live that work even if he changes to other works, and till he draws his last breath. It's been about ten years since I quit hard riding, and if I walk the streets of a town today I'm still apt to shy when a piece of paper or anything flies up that would scare a horse. I at least always think about it. Many a time, while home on my ranch and walking from the house to the corrals, I catch myself holding my left hand out a bit and like I had bridle-reins in it. I've reined myself around many a sagebrush without knowing I was doing it. Others with me would sometimes remark about that. Mixing with horses as much as I have and often feeling that I'm still on a horse, while I now might be sitting in a chair or walking, makes me laugh and wonder sometimes if I ain't part horse. And I don't think it would surprise me much to look at myself in a glass some day and see a combination of man and horse together, like a drawing I remember seeing where from the shoulders of a horse there sprouts a man. I think that's called a centaur.

People often ask me how I get to catch horses in action, or how I get my models for my drawings and paintings. I've never sketched from life and never watched any animal with intentions of sketching it. And to the people who ask I say that I get my models thru my tail bone, and from the many connections it got with the cantle-board of my saddle.

It took quite a few days for me to get used to be in town while getting stock for the rodeo. Of course, I'd be out

Like a drawing I remember seeing.

riding to close ranches most every day, but finally, when I'd get back at night, I got so that I wouldn't shy so much while walking from the stable to the rodeo manager's office. Me and the manager got well acquainted. I'd be in his office pretty often, and while I was waiting for things to be decided on as to what I should do next, I'd help myself to blank pads and pencils that was scattered around and which kept inviting for me to use. I'd draw sketch after sketch on 'em and leave 'em in the office as I'd go out to do some job that'd been decided on—like hunting up old stage-coaches for use in the parade, and many other things that's needed for every rodeo.

I came in the office one day as the manager was sizing up one of my sketches, and after finding out it was me that done it he asked if I could draw him a picture that would do for a poster in advertising the rodeo. I says "sure." . . . I made three pictures, he took the third one, and I'll never forget the thrill I got when he handed me a fifty-dollar check for it. That was sure a powerful price, I thought, and I felt like I was cheating him when I took the check. . . . It came to my mind again about being an artist.

And it stayed in my mind. The manager had been mighty surprised at my drawings and took quite an interest in me on that account, and one day he told me that as soon as the rodeo was over and all was settled he'd show me a way to make a lot of money out of my drawings. That one picture I made for the rodeo poster had drawed quite a bit of attention and a newspaper wrote a nice piece about it that made me feel mighty proud. It was the second time to see my name in print, the first time had been when I was sentenced for cattle rustling.

With all the encouragement I was getting as to my drawings, my ambition to ride on North and build my own cow camp sort of vanished. I'd forgot all about that, and now I was anxious for the rodeo to be over so I could get to work on my drawing and make a lot of money.

The first day of the rodeo finally came. I had entered for a few events, the wild-horse race was one. I didn't try to tackle bronk riding because I was thru with that. But I didn't get a chance to compete in any of the events I'd entered in. I was kept busy helping the manager and riding around tending to different things and I hardly got to see any of the contest.

There was four days of that contest, and when it was over and the cowboys had all gone it took me a few more days to return the stock. Everything was done, finally, and then the manager told me of his scheme for me and my drawing. I was to make about twenty good drawings on range life and he would take them to a publisher friend of his who was on the Coast, have them printed and put into a book, and sell the book.

I kept my room at the hotel and quit riding. Every day I was drawing instead, till I got all the drawings made. I thought they was pretty fine drawings and so did the manager, but in the time I took to make them he gradually seemed to've lost some interest in doing what he told me he would. He was a busy man and he didn't have the time right then to see about putting the drawings into a book.

I waited a long time for him to tend to that, and while waiting I went to mixing with a couple of cowboys that was in town for a spell. One of 'em was the cowboy I'd made my insurance to when I went in the army during the war. I'd knowed him quite a few years. I'd knowed the other cowboy quite a spell too, he's now foreman on my ranch. . . . The three of us fellers had a lot of fun together, we was ready for anything that came up and we was always stirring something to bring a laugh.

And I was needing a laugh about then too, because it was beginning to look like my second try at being an artist was going to amount to no more than the first. Time wore on, nothing was done. I was spending my money and feeling disappointed, and then one day I finally decided to give up being an artist as a bad job and ride on North as I'd first figgured. I'd go to work again up there and some time get me the little spread I wanted and *stay there*. I'd fell back on that hankering again.

I told the boys that I'd decided to ride on, but they talked me out of rushing off and said I could find plenty of work with them on some outfit and make up for the money I'd spent while in town. That struck me all right, I liked them boys' company and being I had to go to work again, I thought one place was just as good as another. So, I stayed with 'em. We would stick in town for a few more days, celebrate a bit and then hit out. . . . Being all was settled now, I begin to cheer up some, and a day or two later, while thinking up of something exciting to do, the three of us thought of putting on a little bucking-horse exhibition. We borrowed three good bucking horses that'd been used in the rodeo and we all took one apiece. I was the first to ride, and being it was all for fun, I thought I would ride *just one more* bronk. I would even do that with my slick roping saddle.

I was laughing when I jerked the blind off the horse's eyes and he made his first jump. It was a wicked jump and so was the many others that followed, but I kept on a laughing till I thought he was thru, and then I prepared to jump off of him before he started stampeding with me. There was only a halter on his head and I was riding him in the open, by a railroad track. I didn't see the railroad track, not till I was loosened and about to quit the horse. About that time he started to bucking again and I never could get back in the saddle. He throwed me against the railroad track and stepped on me as he went.

The boys told me afterwards how they thought I was killed sure. I was in a twisted heap and half my scalp was tore off my head and layed over one ear, and the way I felt inside wasn't so good. An old internal injury which I'd received from a hammer-headed bronk years before had been renewed, I'd lost the same sense of balance, and once in a while I felt like I was going blind. A doctor's examination, two years ago, showed that there's a part inside of me that works up and down instead of down and up.

Well, I was layed up, my head was bandaged till I looked like a Turk, and felt pretty much out of luck. There was twenty-two stitches took in my scalp and the whole side of my face was skinned. . . . When I got to thinking straight again my art career came to the front once more, more than ever now, because it was necessary. I wouldn't be able to ride again for some time and now the doctor bills and other expenses had took the rest of my money. I had to sell my two horses.

That last bronk I'd rode had sure fixed me so I'd have to be an artist. It seemed like he'd brought back all the old injuries I'd received and piled 'em up on me. But how to be an artist was what had me stumped. Soon as I was able to navigate again I went to see the manager. He hadn't been able to do anything as yet and I took my drawings away from him. Things looked pretty dark, and it was while things looked darkest one day that a sudden break come and everything brightened up.

I was talking to a clerk in a hotel, showing him my drawings and asking him if I could stick a few around the lobby, I thought maybe I would sell some that way. . . . I was talking along with the clerk when a big well dressed man edged in to the desk and put his name on the register. When that was done he happened to glance over my drawings. That one glance made him take a good look, and as the bellhop hopped to get his baggage he asked me to come up to his room with him.

Once in the room, and when we got to talking, I found that the big man was also a big man in the mining business. He was sure interested in my drawings, and even tho he didn't seem to want to buy any right at the time, he done something else which meant a heap more to me. He said he had a good friend who was Editor of a magazine in a big city of the west Coast, and that he was sure I could sell him some drawings to use in the magazine. He would give me a letter of introduction to him, and that all I'd have to do would be to catch a train and go see him.

As weak and unsteady as I was, I didn't lose my balance nor miss a step as I came down to the lobby of the hotel and out again. I run acrost the two boys a ways along the street. They'd stuck around town all the while I'd been layed up, to make sure that I'd be all right, and when they seen me ambling along towards 'em with a grin a mile long they wondered if something good had happened or if I'd gone crazy.

It didn't take me long to tell 'em the good news and show 'em the letter the mining man had given me, and they was just as happy as I was when I got thru. The next thing now was to rake up some money for railroad fare and to eat on for a few days after I got to the big town. We was all about broke, but the boys reached down their pockets, and without counting it, gave me all the money they had, saying they didn't need any money now,—they still had their horses and they'd be hitting out for the range soon as I left. But the money that was raked up wasn't near enough. Then I thought of my saddle. I had the boys bring it to the hock shop. It was the first time any saddle of mine ever seen a hock shop, and the first time I ever separated from one. But I didn't need a saddle no more now, and the money I borrowed on that one set me up so I could buy a ticket and have a little left when I got to the other end.

The boys seen me to the train that evening. Under one arm I had the bunch of drawings I'd made and under the other I had my war-bag with my clothes and other gatherings in it.

I was mighty happy and full of hopes as the train pulled away and went to chugging along at good speed. It couldn't go too fast for me, and if I did feel a pain once in a while when the train stopped or started too sudden at stations, I'd just grin, and paid no attention to it.

It was a great event to me when I finally located the building where the magazine was published and where the Editor was that I was to see. The sight of it struck me as a landmark where I'd be starting on an entirely different trail. I opened the big door, walked in and eased around to a desk where I told a girl that I wanted to see the Editor and that I had a letter of introduction to him. The girl asked my name, talked to somebody over a phone and then asked me to sit down and wait, the Editor would see me "in a few minutes."

I sat down and waited. The few minutes went by, many more minutes went by and till a whole hour had gone. I was getting mighty nervous by that time and wondering if the Editor hadn't forgot about me, but finally the phone buzzed once more, the girl called my name, said the Editor would now see me and told me how to find him. It was another great event when I come face to face with that feller and I handed him my letter of introduction, but the greatness of that event dwindled down a considerable after I'd unwrapped and showed him the drawings I'd brought. He seemed sort of fidgitive and like he didn't have much time to waste, and while he glanced at the drawings he didn't act like he was seeing 'em. His mind was a whole lot on something else. He didn't say a word while he shuffled the draw-

ings. When he got thru he had to blink a couple of times so
he could get back on the subject of 'em. Then he spoke.

"We couldn't use such drawings as these," he says. "They
would have to be a lot better . . . come around again some
other time."

"When?" I asks.

"Oh, in a few months or so, when you have something
else to show me. . . . Good-bye."

Well, there's no use of saying that I was disappointed
with my visit to the Editor. I was more than that, I was
peeved. He'd treated me as if I'd just come from acrost the
street to see him and like as if I had nothing else to worry
about but get back there, better my work and show up
again, as he'd said, in a few months or so. That sure was a
long ways from the reception I'd expected.

I had no way of knowing then that editors are more than
pestered by many beginners with writings and drawings,
some good ones and many that just think they're good ones,
and if the Editor was to waste time on all beginners he
would never get his magazine out.

Everything is up to the beginner, and I sure was one. It
would of been easier for me if I'd been used to the city because then I'd been more apt to know something about
magazines and editors, but I'd just come out of the brush
and all I knowed was horses and cow foremen. I would of
got to know some more horses and cow foremen too, after the
Editor said "good-bye," but I wasn't in no shape to ride no
more, not for a long spell.

I went to a little hotel close by, was given a gloomy room,
and there I stretched out on the bed and begin to do some
tall thinking. The first thought was that I didn't have much
money, enough to last me just a few days, then what would

I do? . . . A little voice at the back of me said, "Work, of course." "Work at what?" I asks. I didn't know nothing but cows and horses and range. Now I was in the heart of a big city and about as hard a work as I could do would be to sell ribbons behind a counter or some such like job where I wouldn't be wanted. The future sure didn't look so good.

But as I think back to that dark spell of time, feeling bad both in mind and body, I don't remember of being discouraged nor giving up in wanting to be an artist. I had to make up my mind to that because there was nothing else I could do.

I was walking along the streets a day or two after I'd seen the Editor, when I come to a place where many men was gathered and looking up at blackboards stuck up on buildings. There was chalk writing on them boards that read "Men Wanted" and for many kinds of jobs. There was one job listed where it said "Helpers Wanted," and I thought maybe I could fill that, helping a bit would be about all I could do. The helpers wanted was for the Ship Yards. I went in the office, applied for the job and was given a slip to sign my name on. The next morning I was herded over to the Yards with about a dozen other men and there I was put down as a riveter's helper, turned over to the riveter himself, and told to "come along."

I followed him by piles of sheet steel, timbers and every daggone thing that goes to building a ship. Most everything was covered over with soot and rust. I never liked steel and soot, I liked flesh and dust. . . . There was many big ships all around and propped up on dry docks. They looked as tall as mountains to me, and by one of the biggest ones the man I was to be helper for stopped, and pointing at a box of tools, told me to take it. He started up a ladder then, and as I followed him up it it looked like an awful long ways, and when I looked down, after I got up there, it looked a heap further down. There was scaffolds up there and planks to walk on that looked awful narrow, and along them boards is where my work begin. Red hot rivets was tossed, caught in a bucket, and, with pincers, was put in one after another of the many holes that was on the side of the tall ship. The rivets was supplied by a feller from the inside of the ship. Me and the feller I was helping was on the outside, and every time the red-hot tip of a rivet would show thru a hole we'd go to work on it with the electric rivetting machine. There was two long handles on that machine, one for each of us and to press against while it pounded on the rivet.

The pounding of that machine didn't go very good with me from the first. I had to hold the handle sort of against my ribs and I felt the jab of every pounding right thru me and all the way up and down my backbone. I got groggy a few times before that first day's work came to an end, and once in a while I had to grab a timber so I wouldn't fall. A fall from where I was would of been a last one.

But I thought I would get used to that machine, and the next day I went to the yards again and at my same job. I lasted till noon and I had a mighty hard time doing that. When I filed out amongst hundreds of men at the noon whistle, I stepped to one side, to the office, and drawed my time. I went to the hotel. I felt some queer pains and layed down and I went to sleep a bit. When I woke up I was surprised to see how dark it was, I didn't think I'd slept very long. I fumbled for the light button and turned it. I couldn't see no light, and I turned the button again and again. I looked out the window, no light, and then I knowed. *I was blind.*

The steady jar of the rivetting had somehow aggravated a nerve, or something that'd been loosened during my last rough ride, and now, along with the pains I felt inside, I wasn't only blind but my eyes was hurting. They felt as if somebody had throwed sand in 'em and rubbed it in and made tears stream down both sides of my face as I layed on the bed. I thought of calling a doctor, but knowing I didn't have enough money to pay one, I didn't. So there I was, in the thick of a big city, amongst thousands of people, in a bad fix and not a one to call to. . . . The first thought that came to me and which hurt me most as I realized my blindness was that now I couldn't even be an artist.

A long night and day went by, then another night. I didn't go out of my room in that time. I had the chambermaid bring me a little something to eat. . . . It was in early morning of the second day when I woke up and opened my eyes. The pain was gone out of 'em. I jumped up as fast as I could, turned on the light button, and I blinked in glad surprise. . . . I could see the light, I could see a little bit around me, and by noon that day I could see as well as ever again.

I've been near death many times and in many ways, while riding a bad horse, while swimming rivers on one, or while drifting thru blizzards with a herd, but I'd go thru every one of them experiences again rather than go thru the thirty-six hours I did while I was blind.

With my sight back to me I was as happy now as I'd been sad a while before. I went out in the street and sunshine that day, to appreciate seeing. It didn't matter what I seen. And walking along that way I again came by them places where the blackboards was stuck to the wall. I seen the same Ship Yard sign still there and shivered at the thought of that place. I wouldn't go back to that sooty, clattering and noisy place again for anything in the world. It seemed to me like I could still hear the hammering roar from the many rivetting and other kinds of machines.

I looked along the lines of chalk writing, and then I come

to a place where it said "Teamsters Wanted." Why didn't I
see that before, I wondered. I couldn't ride a horse but I
could drive one. I applied for that job and got it. The next
morning I was on a train and headed out of town towards a
farm of a big fruit-packing outfit. They raised nothing but
beets on that one farm, and there I was handed a four-horse
team and wagon and went to hauling beets from the farm to
a station. A wagon was always filled and ready for me when
I got back form every trip. I'd switch my team to the full
wagon, and at that job I had nothing else to do but drive my
four horses and take care of 'em.

The jar of the wagon didn't hurt me much, the road was
pretty smooth and I'd fixed me a seat with springs over and
under that eased most every jolt. . . . While sitting on
that seat, going back and forth on my trips and holding the
lines over my four horses, there was many things came to
my mind which was given plenty of time to be figgured out.
The reader will most likely suspect what them many things
was. It was ways in how I could break into the art game and
be a sure enough artist. I done a heap of thinking while sitting on that wagon seat and letting my team poke along.
I'd do more thinking when I'd get back to my room after the
day's work was done, till way late in the night and again
first thing in the morning.

There was a few magazines in the room where I was put
and I begin studying 'em, studying 'em for an idea of what
I could do that would fit in the pages. It was then I got to
figguring on some subjects in my line of work which would
interest the Editor, something of the life I knowed and
which would also interest the folks in general. I got to working for ideas where I could draw pictures of happenings on
the range, pictures that would tell a story by themselves and
which would bring a laugh or a tear, and explain things in

range life that folks never heard tell of. . . . Sometimes I'd get an idea for a drawing which I thought would be good, and I sketched it down on a pad so I wouldn't forget.

As I was studying on such subjects, and near wore out the magazines in wondering how my stuff would work in this and that page, I run acrost a few Western stories and illustrations of them that made me pretty sore. They was all out of whack and showed where neither the writer nor the artist knowed a thing of what they was doing. They was misrepresenting the cowboy,—and me being one, I felt that pretty deep. They knowed as much about the cowboy as I did about Wall Street and what went on there.

One day, after I'd been hauling beets for a few weeks, I run onto a brand new magazine which had been put out by none other than the Editor I'd been to see. His name was on one of the front pages, and I camped on that magazine from evening till late in the night, studying what was in it, what it all meant, and where I could maybe edge in. It was while I was thumbing the pages of that magazine that I run acrost some Western drawings I figgured I could sure improve on. They was illustrations for a would-be Western story, and the sight of them started me to boiling. I noticed many things in the drawings that was worse than wrong, the cowboy, horse and rope was all wrong-side-out and looked like something that'd been starched and then went out in a heavy rain.

I had quite a few sketches made. I stuck 'em in that latest issue of the magazine and went to get my time check. I was back to the big town in a few hours, there was another hour of waiting to see the Editor, and then I came face to face with him again.

He sort of grinned as he listened to what I had to say, but I noticed that this time he was listening. I was peeved, and went on to remark that if he wanted to have real Western work in his magazine I'd make up for how little I could draw by what I knowed. While I was talking I begin shuffling him the sketches of the ideas I'd thought of. He looked at the sketches in the same way as I would look at a bunch of scrub ponies and he took in my jabbering like I would take in their nickering.

As he glanced at the drawings, I thought sure he'd say "good-bye" to me again, run off and tell me to come back in a few more months. I think he was just about to do that, when one sketch seemed to catch his knowing eye. He looked at it once, twice, and a third time, then he begins to studying it and the idea there. He was fumbling it like I'd fumble a rope while wondering if I should make a throw or not. Finally he says,

"If you can make a good drawing of this sketch I'll pay you twenty-five dollars for it. Good-bye."

That "good-bye" sounded like a million dollars to me. I went out of the building, hunted me up something to draw on and with, got me a room in the gloomy little hotel, and went to work on the drawing of the sketch. The sketch which the Editor had hung back on was from what the thoughts of Smoky had inspired me to do. I'd missed him, often thought of him and of the range country he reminded me of. . . . Out of imagination I'd made a sketch of that horse standing over me after I'd been shot by a sheriff. It showed Smoky on the fight, on guard, and where he wouldn't let the sheriff come near me. It was something I'd figgured Smoky would of done if I'd got in a fix where he thought he could help. The idea might of been a little sentimental, but it would happen with men and horses if they was as me and Smoky had been. . . . Some day I'm going to model a monument to that horse.

I made the drawing with a common pencil and on a cardboard I didn't know nothing about. I worked hard, maybe too hard, because I wanted to do a good job, and all I thought of in that time was Smoky, getting him down on paper, and of the new game I was trying to break into.

I more than held my breath when I took the finished drawing to the Editor, and I hoped I wouldn't get sore if he refused to take it. I'd put everything I had in that drawing.

I finally got to see the Editor again. He looked at the drawing, grunted and smiled. I liked him when I seen that smile,—I hadn't ever pictured him smiling. He looked the drawing over good, and after a long while he says, "We'll take this one."

That sure went fine with me. . . . But I wasn't thru yet. I showed him another sketch I'd thought of after drawing the picture of Smoky standing guard over me. He squinted at that one a spell, and then he says, "Yes, make a finished drawing of this, too."

I was started in the art game.

The second picture I sold to the Editor was of where a cow with her calf had turned the point of a granite boulder while on the summer range and came face to face with a mother grizzly and two cubs. There was a kind of a tense feeling in that picture, a wondering as to what the mother cow and grizzly would do. Anybody knowing them animals would easy guess. The calf would get scared of the big grizzly and cubs and run away; the cow, after shaking her horns at the mother grizzly, would follow. The mother grizzly would get her cubs close to her and watch the cow that every once in a while would look back while following her calf. Neither was cowards. . . . I called that picture "Mothers."

I sold many pictures to that Editor. The price of 'em kept crawling up a bit after I sold him the first twenty-five, and in the meantime him and me got to calling one another by our first names. He begin to suggest that I should go to school and learn to draw real well. I didn't want to go to school, but after he made me acquainted with a great artist, the both of 'em doubled up on me and made me feel that I should. They got me a free scholarship in a Fine Arts university, and I went, more to please them than to please myself. . . . Far as they know, I went regular, but I seldom went, and when I did I'd be drawing a steer, a horse or a cowboy instead of the clay and life models I was supposed to copy. I could never copy. I went to that art school about ten times.

I stayed in the big Coast town all one winter and till away along in the following summer. I was getting pretty daggone homesick for range country by then, and there was more than that to make me hanker to get back, it was a girl, the girl I married. She's the sister of one of the cowboys I was running around with when I got busted up, and I first met her thru him. We'd corresponded all winter, and when I got back to the country I met her again. I'd recuperated pretty well by that time and I could now ride a gentle horse easy enough. I done my courting on horseback, dressed in a plain white shirt and "Mexican serges." She didn't see me in a regular suit of clothes till the day before we was married, a couple of months after I got back.

Pickings was pretty slim for a time. I'd furnished the Editor of the magazine with enough of my drawings to last him three or four years, and now he didn't want to take any more till the most of 'em was used. They was all drawings telling their own story. Once in a while the Editor would send me a story to illustrate but there was long spells between them. Then I begin to try and connect up with some Eastern magazines which I thought might use my work. I painted some covers for 'em, drawed 'em some pictures, and the most of the work was returned.

Being married now, I rented a house on the outskirts of a little town, and come a time when the rent was due I couldn't pay it. We hit out, and I took a job on a ranch where I had a pretty fair place to stay and watch over some stock and do a little branding once in a while. I had plenty of time to keep on drawing and painting and now I didn't have to worry about rent and food; that was furnished.

But I wanted to do a heap better than just that, and I kept a figguring for ways to break into the art game right. But that took time and plenty of hard work.

Then one day I thought a good chance come. It was while up the high mountains of a great cow country, another place I went to where I didn't have to pay no rent, that I met the Dean of a big Eastern university. He liked mountains and open country and come out as a guest of the company I was with. Him and me got to talking and it was decided that I should go East. He helped me get there and fixed things up at his university so I could go to Art school. I sure appreciated that, but somehow I couldn't take any interest in that school either. I went there three times, to draw more steers, horses and cowboys instead of the models that was before me and which I was supposed to work from. I never liked to draw anything that was standing still and posing.

At the university and the others was where I got my only teaching in art, a few hours a day for, altogether, two weeks' time. I don't figgure I got any teaching, because I wasn't interested. Always I was thinking of open country. I'd been cooped up in cities a bit by then and I drawed pictures of the range so I could live that life again as much as I could.

After leaving the second university I went to the Big

City and there I begin making the rounds and seeing art editors of many magazines. I thought of getting acquainted with 'em, come back West and do work for 'em from here. I landed a few little jobs, but most of the time as I made my regular rounds it was a case of where they'd just put my name down and forget about it. When I came back West I got less of the little jobs than ever. Most of the editors liked my work pretty well but they said I was too far away.

I kept a pegging along, doing the best I could and drawing to suit myself. Me and my wife somehow managed to live and I could once in a while buy a few clothes and boots for me and slippers for her. I drawed till sometimes I couldn't see any of the drawings I made, and I got to thinking that I'd never get no further in the art game than where I was. My drawings all told of things, things that I knowed, but of things that not many folks are familiar with.

Then, after about three years of fishing around for a good start, I got to thinking of writing,—writing of things I wanted to tell of and which no picture could be made of, only with words. But thinking is as far as I got to writing for a long while. I'd never been to school and I figgured that whatever I would write would only bring a return slip and a laugh. Then one day, after I'd told my wife for the hundredth time how I intended to write, she talked that idea over with me well, so well that just to prove to her that I couldn't write and what I sent in would be returned right quick I buckled down and wrote a mixed-up thing on a few sheets of yellow paper, in long hand, made a half a dozen pen-and-ink drawings to illustrate the writing and sent the whole outfit in to a high-class magazine. It was sent to the best.

The writing was about something I knowed well. It was about bucking horses and bucking-horse riders. It was accepted, and when I got word of that I went pretty wild with joy. My wife was close second in keeping up with me. When the check come I bought her a new saddle and I took mine out of hock, where it had been for quite a spell.

I was told, afterwards, how that story had barely made the grade, that the drawings I'd sent with it was all that carried it over. The Art Editor had liked 'em, and he'd worked to get the story thru so he could get the drawings in the magazine. . . . I'll sure be always mighty thankful to the Art Editor for that, because, without him, I don't think my first story would ever have been accepted. And if it'd been returned I'd never wrote another. . . . (My wife don't agree with me on that last. She says that I was headed towards writing anyway and I'd tried my hand again at it, even if I'd failed at my first, or tenth try.)

I sold five stories straight-hand running and to three of the best magazines. I got to thinking that none would ever be returned, and when the sixth one came back to me I couldn't quite figgure out why. There was more returned off and on after that, but I've been lucky and managed to sell 'em sooner or later, and as it is now, I've only got two that didn't sell.

What I write is built around facts, from things I've seen happen or experienced myself. I don't hunt up material nor local color, and I'm glad I've found a way to put down the life I know, proud to tell of it in my writings and drawings. I don't claim to know anything about writing, but if folks keep on going to the trouble of reading my work that's all I'll ever need to make me very happy in doing it.

WILL JAMES
'30

The Sheddings Of A Long Tale

Now — I've finally gathered me a little scope of range like I've always hankered for — A place away from lanes, and in the heart of a wide-open cow and horse country — only a hundred miles from where I was born — I have my ponies, cattle, corrals and all to my taste — There's hundreds of wild horses around, thousands of cattle from neighboring outfits — timber — big creeks with trout in 'em — plenty of grass on both sides, and on the ridges where riders fog down off of to drop in and say hello or rest and feed up while on their way from one cow camp to another ——— I'm at home ≡

WILL JAMES
'30